THE LAST STAND
OF
DARK HORSE

THE LAST STAND OF DARK HORSE

OF

DARK HORSE

BUCK RAMSEY

Buck Ramsey

Copyright 2012; Revised 2015

ISBN: 978-0-9964538-8-2

To all Marines, past and present- "Honor, Courage and Commitment" *Those are not simply words that guide Marines. In my opinion, it's what they truly live by and what sets them apart from others.*

To all Navy Corpsmen, past and present- "Semper Fortis" Always Courageous- *They stand with Marines and care for them through thick and thin.* On my webpage, "buckramsey.com" under "The Heroes Among Us" View - US Navy Corpsman

To my father, George Klindt Ramsey (1921-1996) Great father and patriot. *By your example, I discovered the joy of reading books.* R.I.P. Arlington National Cemetery Former Captain, USAAC B/N B-24, Shot down on 25th mission 14 months POW, Stalag Luft III

ACKNOWLEDGEMENTS

THE LAST STAND of Dark Horse is a work of fiction. My use of "Dark Horse" in the title of this book refers to the nickname given to a fictional character by an Arapahoe chief.

Some of the characters and actions in this story were inspired by the many Marines and Navy Corpsmen that I met in San Diego while serving meals to wounded warriors on Thursday nights at Balboa Hospital's Liberty Center and the Combat and Poly Trauma Care Unit (5th floor, West) from 2009-2013. During this time, I was a volunteer with the charity "Marineparents.com" and their local subsidiary, "Purple Heart Hero Support."

The 3rd Battalion, 5th Regiment (referred to as the "3/5" Darkhorse Marines), of the 1st Marine Division, stationed at Camp Pendleton, California, was deployed to Afghanistan during the 2010-2011 time frame and was heavily involved in the deadly and vicious campaign known as the Battle of Sangin (2010). I, along with a number of my fellow volunteers, served meals weekly to a great many injured 3/5 Marines and their Navy corpsmen when they returned to Balboa Hospital for medical treatment. The 3/5, however, was only one of the countless Marine Corps units who served with distinction in Afghanistan and passed through our complimentary chow lines (*see list below).

To Marines and Navy corpsmen, past and present, I hold all of you in the highest regard. Your courage, selflessness and sacrifice are what makes our country great.

In addition, to Marines and Navy corpsmen, we served meals to wounded Army, Navy and Air Force personnel who also bravely served our country.

I would also like to thank those who helped me along the way to create this story.

- Amanda Gibson for her insightful and experienced editing advice.
- Joyce and Curtis Orrell for including me in the "Purple Heart Hero Support" volunteer family.
- David Harper for related marketing and photography matters.
- Murph Hayes for his fine editing and encouragement.
- Those who allowed me to use their names in this fictional story. (Please see my disclaimer for the rules pertaining to my use of their names)

Last, but not least, my daughter, Kelly Meilstrup who encouraged me to finish and publish this book. And, my wife, Lynne who kept my storyline credible, moderately influenced my conservative writing voice and greatly assisted in the editing of this book.

* United Sates Marine Corps units- 3/7, 3/5, 3/25, 2/8, 2/9, 1/5, 1/7, 2/7, 1st Tanks, 1st/2nd/3rd Reconnaissance Battalion, 7th ESB, 1st CEB, 3rd CEB. Plus Marines serving with MARSOC/USASOC/NAVSOC (SOTF).

Details obtained from Wikipedia.

PROLOGUE

Monday June 16, 2008
7:38 PM Eastern Daylight Time (EDT)... 5:38 PM
Mountain Daylight Time (MDT)
Washington D.C.

PLATES OF FOOD sat untouched on the large conference table. All, but two, of the conference chairs were empty and still perfectly placed around the conference table. A steady stream of senior presidential advisors moved smartly in and out of the Situation Room. No one lingered to sip coffee or lounge in a chair. The tension in the air was palpable.

At the end of the table, two men were hunched intently over a speakerphone. Behind them a three-foot by four-foot aerial map was taped to the wall. The map depicted a high definition section of Route 20, five miles west of the East Entrance of Yellowstone National Park. Colored stickers and pins filled much of the map.

Five small, digitally prepared block labels were at the center of the map's markings. At closer inspection, one could see that the yellow labels weren't block shaped, but bus shaped. To one side of the labels was a large, light blue post-it note. The note read:

- **Ambush of 5 school buses & 5 personal vehicles- 3:45 PM (EDT)**
- **Received confirmation from Commandant USMC 3:57 PM (EDT)**
- **305- 6th graders; 27 civilians; 3 Marines(lightly armed) Total 335**
- **60 al-Qaeda terrorists (approximate)…heavily armed**
- **Terrorist Primary Mission: Kill all children; plus others caught in ambush**

"What was that? What did he say? Can't he hold the satellite phone closer to his mouth?" asked President Jed Adams to General Randy Rexman, U.SA.F., Chairman of the Joint Chiefs of Staff.

"I missed it too. There is a lot of static. We're simply connected to an open channel on a satellite phone that is lying next to Bobby Ridger. Remember, he's nearly a quadriplegic. He does have some movement in his hands and arms, but we're talking inches," said the general.

"Bobby, what is your situation? Are you holding or have they broken through?" asked the president nervously.

No answer.

Urgency and anguish was obvious in his plea, "Bobby, I repeat. What is your situation? Are you holding or have they broken through?"

"Who is this?" asked a groggy Bobby Ridger.

"The president and General Rexman. You've been giving us battle updates for the past two hours."

"Where is Annie? She's gone. Everything is blurry," stuttered Bobby.

"He's slipping in and out of consciousness. He's concussed, maybe even wounded," whispered the general to the president.

"Corporal Ridger, what is your status?" asked the general slowly and clearly. The firmness of his command activated an ingrained response in the former Marine.

He responded with slurred speech. "General, one of their grenades blew up part of the school bus I'm using for cover. I'm lying under the engine block. The bus is on fire and there is smoke everywhere. The gas tank hasn't blown yet but it won't be long before it does."

"Corporal, give me your visual status on the location of Gunnery Sergeant Miller and Major Daniels," said the general.

"Yes, sir. Hold on, let me look." The fingers of his left hand loosely gripped a pair of binoculars. With great difficulty, he rolled onto his stomach and inched his arms and elbows towards his chest. Ever so slowly, he gradually raised his binoculars to his eyes and searched the hillside. There was no sight of either Brice Miller or Chet Daniels.

"They're missing! Where's Annie?" he mumbled.

"I say again, corporal, give me your visual status on the location of Gunnery Sergeant Miller and Major Daniels," said the general more forcefully.

7:40 PM EDT (5:40 PM MDT)

"Wait! Wait! Yes sir, I see them. They're by the stone ledge, near the top of the hill. There are lots of trees and bushes, but I can see Chet clearly, he's in the open. Brice is behind him partially hidden by some trees. They're approaching a man who is lying against a log with a white flag fluttering near him. That's their command post. That's their leader. He's been directing their attack. Where's Annie?" muttered Bobby again.

"Corporal Ridger are you in contact with Gunnery Sergeant Miller and Major Daniels?" asked the general.

"Sir. I can hear them on my headset, but they can't hear me. My transmit function is busted. All I hear is them moving through the brush. Oh shit!" said Bobby.

The president and general heard the distant crack of a single shot over their satellite phone's speaker.

"What's happening?" commanded the general.

"The man on the ground was a decoy. He was dead. Their leader came out of the bushes twenty feet to Chet's side and got the drop on them. Major Daniels turned to shoot him but the bastard shot him in the lower body. The major is down!" cried Bobby.

Silence.

"Listen to me son. Help is on the way, but you've got to stay with me. Do you understand?" pleaded the general.

"Yes, general," said Bobby weakly. "Let's see. Their leader is yelling at Brice and the major. He demands the children come out from behind the buses."

"No, no!" cried the president over the speaker.

There was no response.

Bobby's eyes fluttered and he lost consciousness. As his head thumped against the paved road, his radio headset bounced off his head and settled atop the satellite phone.

Both the president and general craned closer to their satellite phone's speaker, struggling to hear the weak transmission. From Bobby's headset, they heard a distant voice.

"Never, asshole!" Followed by two distinct gunshots, the first louder than the second.

The gunshots stirred Bobby's consciousness. With a supreme effort, he raised his binoculars again towards Chet and Brice's position on the hilltop.

"Oh, God no!" cried Bobby.

"Report, report Corporal Ridger," demanded the general.

"He's hit! He's down! The bastard shot both of them at point-blank range with his pistol. Brice and the major are dead!" cried Bobby.

"Son, you've got to collect yourself," offered the general kindly.

There was no answer. Bobby had lapsed into unconsciousness.

The general repeatedly called for Bobby over the next few minutes, but there was no reply.

Ever so slowly, Bobby began to re-emerge from his unconsciousness. He first felt the cold pavement against his cheek and then noticed the absence of sound. His surroundings were totally silent. His blurred vision was like looking towards the sky from the bottom of a swimming pool. *Is this heaven? Have I died?*

His minds eye began to come to life as he studied a white tour bus that was parked at a crazy angle across the road from him. Feet, lots of feet were racing towards him from each end of the bus. Then, as if someone turned on the lights in a dark room, he realized what was happening.

Fuck, we're being overrun! He spoke animatedly into the satellite phone, "We're being overrun. We're being overrun."

There was no acknowledgement, other than "Bobby Ridger, come in. This is General Rexman."

Puzzled, Bobby looked at his phone and saw that his mute button was on. He fumbled with the key at first, but eventually managed to disable it. He was about to speak when a dozen feet appeared on the terrorist's side of the timber bunker. Kathy and Lynne, a pair of fearless and grandmotherly female bus drivers, had constructed the fortified bunker from discarded roadside shoring timbers between the second and third school buses.

7:46 PM EDT (5:46 PM MDT)

Suddenly, four loud blasts from a shotgun and the screams from dying men burst from the speaker. Startled, the president and general bolted upright from their hunched, cramped sitting positions.

"Empty!" said a woman's voice angrily. Her voice was as clear as if she were sitting at the end of the table.

"You die, infidel whore!" wheezed a man out of breath from running, his accent distinctly Arabic.

They heard a sharp thwack, a woman's muffled cry and the sound of a heavy object being dragged over what sounded like a pile of lumber.

"Shit, that was one of the female bus drivers with a shotgun. She and her friend were posted next to Bobby between the second and third buses, behind the timber bunker. They were the last line of defense for the children hiding below the retaining wall," said the general despondently.

Bobby whispered quietly into the satellite phone.

Radio static. "…on us." More garbled radio static.

"Was that Bobby?" asked the president.

"Couldn't tell. It was garbled," responded the general.

The sound of more footsteps and the shouts of al-Qaeda terrorists poured from the speakerphone. Next, they heard the distinctive, evil voice of the man who had struck the female bus driver. He spoke to his men in Arabic. Neither the president, nor the general understood a word he said, but from the reaction of his men they understood his meaning. The killing was about to begin. His men were stomping their feet and slapping their sides in excited anticipation of the bloodletting.

For what seemed like minutes, but was only seconds, the disquieting fog of imminent disaster lay heavy in the room. Both men's heads were bowed as if in prayer.

A young Marine corporal quietly slipped into the room and handed General Rexman a message. The general quickly scanned the message and pushed it across the conference table to the president. The president read it in a glance and sighed.

TOP SECRET

Flash Z Message

162346Z JUN 08

FM: NSA

TO: POTUS

CC: CJCS, CNO, CMC, SDHS, DFBI

SUBJ: Yellowstone Defense-Marines, civilians and 305-6th graders.

Weak transmission analysis; Cpl. Bobby Ridger reports... "They are on us. We've been overrun!"

A moment later, the president and general's worst fears were realized when they heard a loud voice proclaim, "Children of the infidel, you die," accompanied by the distant screams of children. Then, the horrific sound of deliberate gunshots... *crack... crack... crack.*

The president's large fist crashed into the speakerphone sending plastic phone parts flying in every direction.

"God damn motherfuckers will pay for this," swore the president.

CHAPTER 1
DENNIS, MONTANA

Late May 2008...

Bill Ridger stared angrily at the shredded remains of one of his young calves. In the chill of the Montana morning, steam rose from the calf's still warm body. It was a recent kill, no more than an hour earlier. *Just before sunrise*, he thought. *Even the coyotes hadn't had time to devour the remains.*

As Bill slowly walked around the carcass, he noticed that only a small part of the calf's liver had been eaten though the entire body had been savagely ripped apart. He also found only one set of wolf tracks that he thought peculiar. Wolves travelled in packs. This murderer was a lone grey wolf, most likely a male, who wasn't motivated by hunger, but bloodlust.

He saw from the paw prints that the wolf's right forepaw was splayed outward, which indicated a broken foot. It was impossible to know if it was a recent break, but he could tell from the uneven impressions of the tracks that it caused the wolf to limp. For some reason, possibly the wolf's injury or an overaggressive personality, this wolf had been forced out of its pack.

He knew a pack of wolves lived several miles away on Lone Mountain, but those wolves hadn't killed any ranch cattle in years because of the ample supply of game in the hills. The fifty or so calves and yearlings he'd delivered in the past eighteen months grazed openly on his 3,000 acre cattle ranch. He'd felt his cattle were safe from predators until this morning.

By 2008, the gray wolf population in Montana had exceeded its federally mandated recovery goal. However, that goal was achieved, in part, at the expense of unchecked wolf predation on Montana livestock. Neither federal legislators nor wolf loving environmentalists cared a lick about the cost of this policy to Montana ranchers. Nor did they care to acknowledge that a small percentage of wolves developed either a preference or a taste for livestock rather than their customary prey, which was wildlife. If this lone wolf staked his territory in this area and continued to slaughter Bill's cattle, he and his ranching neighbors would likely take matters into their own hands.

Bill's thoughts turned to his only son, Bobby, who was a skilled tracker and expert marksman. A smile brightened Bill's face as he recalled fond memories of hunting with his boy. It seemed like only yesterday when Bobby shot his first deer. He remembered that hunt with perfect clarity, especially when they approached the dead deer and he put his arm around his twelve-year-old son's shoulders. His comforting gesture helped his son cope with the unnerving sight of the innocent, dark eyes of the buck. Bill's father had helped him through the same childhood anguish a generation earlier. As he knelt beside the deer, he withdrew his field knife and began field dressing the deer. The animal's blood and guts spilled onto the cold ground. The butchery caused his son's lower lip to tremble. Large tears rolled slowly down his cheeks. As it had been for him, Bill, knew this was a difficult, first step for any boy on the road to manhood.

With a quiet, but firm voice, he explained to his son the procedures for dressing a deer. Gradually, his son collected himself. His closing comment to his son would guide the boys hunting philosophy for the rest of his life... *limit your hunting to food for your table and the protection of your cattle.*

Bill taught Bobby all he knew about hunting during the ensuing years, but it was a nearby rancher, Tom Youngblood, who elevated his sons tracking and hunting skills to an expert level. Bobby's first meeting with Tom Youngblood and his wife, Mary, occurred one cold and snowy winter night years earlier when Bobby was fourteen.

The stomping and heavy breathing of a horse caused Bobby to look up from his homework and peer through his bedroom window. Someone's escaped quarter horse was excitedly pacing near their barn. In seconds, he slipped on his winter coat and boots and raced through the house towards the barn. Before he stepped outside into the sub zero temperature, he grabbed a halter that hung on a hook by the kitchen door. The mare's eyes were wild with terror, her ears were perked and her nostrils flared. She'd been running hard and was wet with sweat.

Bobby knew that sudden movements or loud sounds from a stranger would spook the mare. He slowly approached the horse with his hand extended, palm up. The mare was skittish and snorting excitedly. After several long moments, the mare sniffed his hand. He unhurriedly moved his hand to the mare's white blaze on the horse's face and gently scratched it. Eventually, the terror in her eyes began to fade and her breathing eased. When he stopped his scratching, the mare nuzzled her head against his hand, as if to say, *don't stop.*

Inching closer, he began to speak gently to the mare and massage the mare's neck. Only when he could rub and pat the horse with both hands did he carefully take the lead rope off his shoulder and slip it over the mare's neck. After a moment of further calming, Bobby slipped the halter on. He led the mare into the barn and guided her into an empty stall.

Bill proudly watched his son through the kitchen window, as he settled the mare and led her into the barn. Bobby and his younger sister, Molly, both had a special touch with horses. He suspected they inherited that from their mother, Susie. His handling of horses was the complete opposite. He believed in brute force rather than soft whispers.

"Darn, it's cold," said Bobby as he entered the kitchen rubbing his bare hands.

"That mare belongs to Mary Youngblood. She loves that horse. I've tried calling them, but their phone is busy. If Mary finds that her mare has escaped, she and her husband, Tom, will search all night for her horse. We'd better return the mare right away before this snowstorm gets worse. They could be searching for her as we speak. I'll get my coat."

"No need for that, Dad. The Youngblood ranch is only a ten-minute walk from here. I'll be quick."

"You sure?"

"Yeah! No problem," said Bobby simply.

Fifteen minutes later, Bobby led the mare through the Youngblood's open barn door. A broken latch hung loosely from the doorjamb of an empty horse stall.

He led the mare into her stall and removed his halter. He grabbed two nearby brushes and gave the mare a quick brush down. After that, he replaced the mare's blankets on her back and checked to see if she had enough food and water before he slipped out of the stall and closed the stall door. After a quick search through the barn, he found a four-foot long 2"X4" that he used as a brace to keep the door closed.

Tom and Mary Youngblood were sitting quietly in their kitchen when they heard loud knocking on their front door. A young boy wearing a knit cap, covered with snow, greeted them when they opened the door.

"I'm Bobby Ridger. Your mare got loose. I just put her back in her stall," said Bobby shivering.

"Come inside. You're covered in snow and it's freezing," said Tom as took Bobby by the arm and led him inside towards the warmth of the kitchen.

"I'll get snow all over the place," said Bobby.

"Don't worry about that. Tom, you check on Breeze and I'll make hot chocolate for all of us. I'll call Bill Ridger and thank him for having his son return my horse," said Mary.

"Dad tried calling you, but your phone was busy," said Bobby as he placed his coat and halter over the back of a chair in the Youngblood kitchen.

Mary looked towards the telephone handset and sure enough the receiver lay on the kitchen counter top. She realized that she must have knocked the receiver off its cradle earlier that afternoon when she was rolling flour for fresh bread. She phoned Bill, thanked him and his son for returning Breeze, and asked if Bobby could enjoy a hot chocolate with them. Tom would drive Bobby home after their visit.

"That's fine with me, Mary. Bobby saw your horse running loose behind our house and he caught her. Don't keep him too late. It's a school night," said Bill as he hung up his phone and smiled. The Youngblood's didn't have any children. If Tom Youngblood took a liking to Bobby, he knew it wouldn't be long before the two of them were hunting together. He'd hunted with the man before and knew he possessed special hunting and tracking skills that could only have been passed down to him from his Arapaho ancestors.

Once Tom had returned from checking on Breeze, they settled into comfortable handmade chairs that surrounded a well-worn kitchen table, made of thick Douglas fir. A nearby wood-burning stove warmed them as it crackled with burning oak. Steam rose from their mugs of hot chocolate.

"The latch broke. I'll fix it tomorrow. Bobby did a good job of securing the stall door with a length of wood," said Tom.

"Bill told me over the phone that Bobby single handedly caught Breeze. She was running loose behind their house. She's my baby. You saved her! I can't thank you enough," said Mary seriously.

Bobby didn't respond. He was distracted by the Indian artifacts which hung from nearly every inch of the log cabin's walls... eagle feathers, spears, bows and arrows, tomahawks and ceremonial dress.

"How old are you Bobby?" asked Tom.

"Fourteen, sir."

"Please call me Tom. Do you like to hunt?"

"Yes, sir... er, Tom. I love to hunt," said Bobby as he sipped his hot chocolate.

Tom studied the boy's face and looked into his eyes, as he absently reached for several sprigs of sage that lay in a small, colorfully decorated pottery bowl in the middle of the table. He began to delicately roll the sage between the palms of his hands while he considered the boy's initiative.

He sees an excited, loose horse. It's freezing cold. He doesn't ask his dad for help, but takes it upon himself to catch the escaped horse. His father explains that it's our horse and he elects to return the horse, by himself, during a snowstorm in the middle of the night. We live one mile from his ranch. The road is not lit and he has never been in our barn. Not only does he return Breeze to her proper stall, but he also brushes her down and replaces her blankets. Finally, he closes and secures the broken stall door with a length of wood.

Very few grown men could perform those tasks competently and even fewer would do it for someone they didn't know.

Mary noticed that Bobby's eyes were focused on a buffalo headdress.

"Do you know the importance of that headdress?" asked Mary easily.

"No, ma'am," said Bobby politely.

"First name for me too, Bobby. I'm Mary," after a moments pause, she continued. "Your dad may not have told you this, but my husband and I are direct descendants of a long line of Arapahos. All the artifacts that you see hanging on our walls are authentic pieces that were handed down to us from our ancestors. We still use many of them at our tribal ceremonies."

She explained that buffalo headdresses were typically worn by only the bravest of the brave Arapaho warriors. Allegedly, the strength, power and courage of a rampaging buffalo was transferred to those who wore such a headdress.

"What about that spear with those feathers?" asked Bobby.

"Firstly, that spear is what we call a lance," answered Mary. "A lance is what our warriors used primarily to hunt game, like buffalo. In some instances, the lance was also used in battle for the protection and defense of our families. As to the eagle feathers, they represent different things to different tribes. For us, an eagle is the master of the sky and in some ways a connection to our ancestors in the heavens. Eagle feathers are extremely important to Arapahos. Those of us who are privileged to wear or display one or more eagle feathers hold a place of honor and respect in the eyes of our fellow Arapahos. Those feathers also represent wisdom, knowledge and freedom."

Mary continued to point out and explain to Bobby other important Arapaho objects that hung from the walls. In school, Bobby had studied the history of a few Western Native American tribes, but he'd never met a Native American in person. He sat transfixed as he listened to Mary's descriptions, his eyes the size of silver dollars. In closing, Mary explained that her husband was the last living descendant of a long line of Arapaho chiefs and shaman who lived and hunted throughout Southern Montana and Yellowstone National Park from the mid 1800s through the early 1900s.

"What's a shaman?" spouted Bobby.

Mary glanced at her husband before she responded. His eyes were closed and his head was swaying slowly from side to side. He was searching for Bobby's energy field. Most non-Native Americans gave little credence to this practice of connecting with another person's energy field or aura. However, Mary had often witnessed her husband's uncanny ability to connect with another's energy field. When this connection occurred, he experienced visions into that person's future. She was certain that Tom's ancestors had passed on to him very special powers.

Tom's head stopped swaying and his facial features relaxed.

"I think my husband sees something in your future. You will soon learn about the powers of a shaman!"

Tom's eyes were closed as if he were praying. His deep, rich voice maintained a slow lyrical meter as he spoke:

"I see that you love the prairies, mountains and rivers. You respect the life that lives there. First, you will become a great hunter. Next, I see that you will follow the path of warrior training because you have the heart of a lion. Only the strong survive this training. Battles here and in distant lands will test your courage and tear your body. Your most difficult battle will be in these hills where an Arapaho woman will come to your aid. She too is a warrior and she will repay your kindness tonight. Your greatest challenge will be healing your torn body and discovering contentment. Your warrior response to these trials is within you.

"Because you returned my wife's horse this cold, dark night, you shall be known from this day forward, to me and other Arapahos, as 'Dark Horse.'"

Tom Youngblood's unusual declaration unleashed a flood of questions in Bobby.

Were these the visions of an Indian chief or the ramblings of an old man? Battles in distant lands? An Arapaho woman will aid me? Healing my torn body and discovering contentment is within me? I'm Dark Horse? Can this shaman really see my future? What did all this mean?

Bobby sat motionless in his chair. He was confused and didn't know how to respond. At last, he simply blurted, "I really like to hunt."

Tom Youngblood smiled at the boy's response and said, "We will hunt and track together, Dark Horse. I will teach you much. But, now it is time for me to take you home."

Up until the day Bobby stepped aboard a plane bound for San Diego and the adjacent Marine Corps Recruit Depot, three years later, Tom Youngblood did teach Bobby much. They spent countless hours and days together in the nearby backcountry hunting, fishing, camping and tracking. When Bill Ridger could escape from his endless list of ranch chores… caring for injured cattle, repairing fences, fixing equipment, feeding livestock… and hunt with his son, he was amazed at his son's level of wilderness skills. It was as if part of him had become an Arapaho.

CHAPTER 2
THE HARD-BITTEN TEXAN

Jed Adams grew up on a thousand acre, South Texas cattle ranch located fifty miles north of the Rio Grande. From the time he was old enough to ride a horse, he helped his father and uncle tend the family's cattle. Minding cattle on hot, desolate and windswept brush country, which was better suited for horned lizards than long horn cattle, was hard work for the strongest of men. For a young boy, that work either hardened his body and mind or compelled him to pursue easier pursuits later in life.

By the time Jed neared his fourteenth birthday, he was five feet, ten inches in height, which was taller by a few inches than the average cow-hand in South Texas. His lean frame suggested that he was undernourished and weak. That observation couldn't have been further from the truth. He ate like a horse and his rock hard, one hundred and seventy pound body easily pushed out one hundred push-ups every morning, after chores, in less than two minutes. New acquaintances were surprised at his hidden strength when they shook hands with the skinny kid. His extraordinarily large and roughly calloused hand delivered a vice like handshake with relative ease.

One hot and cloudless summer day, not long after Jed's fourteenth birthday, Jed's dad decided that his son could handle several days of solo wrangling on the open range. As they were readying their tack for a day in the saddle, he simply declared, without any forethought, "About a dozen or so cattle have wandered south towards the Rio Grande. Take some food… biscuits, beef jerky and apples. You'll also need matches, a poncho and blanket, my pistol and an extra canteen of water. Bring them strays back." After a moment of uncommon reflection, he added, "Mind that southern trail. There's lots of rattlers that like to snooze in the shade of prickly pears."

In the first of many hot, hard and seemingly aimless cattle searches, Jed began to learn life's lessons the hard way. He wasn't more than a couple of miles from the family ranch, on the southern trail, when a rattlesnake did spook his horse and he was thrown head over heels into a gaggle of cacti and prickly pears. After extracting himself, inch by painful inch, from his thorny tangle, Jed re-mounted his horse and turned him back towards home.

His mother was outside hanging laundry on the line when she saw her son returning. His lower chin was trembling as he gingerly slipped off his horse and croaked, "Damn horse threw me. Can you help clean me up?"

She saw two-inch cactus needles sticking out of his back and two angry lines of prickly pear punctures along his left forearm. "You want to take a day off and heal up before your start your search?" asked his mother plainly.

"Nope, Mom! If you can just pull out those cactus needles and fix up my arm, I'll be on my way."

"You sure!"

"Yep, and please don't tell dad what happened."

Two days later Jed returned to the ranch droving fifteen cattle. After securing them in the ranch's corral, he gingerly walked into the house. His face was pale gray and stretched with pain. One eyelid, which often drooped when he was tired, was nearly closed.

"Those pricks and cuts bothering you, son?" asked his mother sympathetically.

"They're healing and bother some, but I must have hurt my back when I was thrown. My lower back is killing me," said Jed stiffly.

His mother walked into the kitchen and withdrew an aspirin bottle from a cabinet. She shook out three tablets and said, "Take these with a glass of water. Pull off your shirt and lay face down on the bed. I think we've got a bit of ice left in the icebox. I'll put it on your lower back. It should help."

Minutes later, Jed's mother settled herself on the side of his bed and gasped. Angry red splotches from the cacti needles covered Jed's back. She carefully set the ice, wrapped in a kitchen towel, on his lower back, and said, "Stay still. I'm going to get a wet cloth, clean up your back and apply more petroleum jelly to your cuts."

When she returned, Jed was snoring peacefully.

Those hard-bitten ranchers who lasted for more than a generation or two on the high plains of South Texas were, on the whole, an independent, tough and stubborn lot who were well accustomed to pain and adversity. Though Jed didn't spend a full generation in South Texas, his body and mind were clearly hardened on those high plains.

In 1968, Jed left the inhospitable environs of his family's ranch to pursue a degree in petroleum engineering at Texas Tech. Four years later, he graduated near the top of his class and began searching for work. Landing an entry level engineering job, however, with an oil company in 1972 was a tall order. Droves of Vietnam veterans were returning to Texas looking for work and the Texas oil industry was in the midst of a major slow down. Fortunately for him, his ingrained, South Texas willingness to tackle hard work paid off. He took an entry-level job as a roustabout with a small wildcat oil company in Lubbock, Texas that required a strong back rather than a sharp mind.

The wiry eighty-year-old West Texas wildcatter who gave Jed Adams his first job in the oil industry was a cantankerous sort. He routinely intimidated government examiners who inspected his oil rigs with the natural ease of a judge delivering a sentence to repeat criminal offenders. His most belligerent, and threatening, behavior, however, was reserved for those competitors who were stupid enough to drill a little to close to his oil rights. All of those offenders would readily agree, after their slightest transgressions, that the difficult, old man was not to be messed with.

The old man had outlived his wife and only son. His remaining passions in life were few, gambling his life savings on one wildcat oil well after another and sipping bourbon from a glass jar during a twice weekly, low stakes game of Texas hold'em with long time friends. During Jed's job interview, the old man and Jed were drawn together like kindred spirits cut from the same cloth.

Despite the old man's affection towards Jed, he didn't indulge him in the slightest. If anything, he erred in the opposite direction by assigning him the dirtiest and hardest jobs at his oil rigs. He was of the firm belief that any oilman worth his salt learned the business the bottom up. Further, he didn't want any of his long time employees to think that he was growing soft in his twilight years.

With a bottle of aspirin always at the ready should his lower back act up, Jed hauled joints of pipe, dug trenches and assisted the mud logger. The language of oil rig crews... jars, fish, traces, kicks, kills, pigs and pills... quickly became part of his everyday lingo. As the years passed, Jed's mentor passed on to him every piece of wildcatting knowledge and field intelligence he had acquired during his sixty-three years in the business. Jed realized, early in their relationship, that behind the old man's gruff exterior was a razor sharp, shrewd and calculating oilman's mind. By the early 1980s, the old man, not particularly talkative by nature, and Jed's conversations were brief and to the point, usually a *yeah, nah* or *BS*. They virtually read one another's mind.

On a hot July day in 1982, the old man collapsed beside a new wildcat rig while he and Jed were examining traces of oil on a drill bit. Jed and four of the wildcatter's long time employees quickly moved the old man out of the sun into the shade of the doghouse, below the rig's floor.

As one of the men moved towards the rig's radio set to call 911 for an ambulance, the old man raised his hand, "Don't bother with an ambulance, boys. I can tell I'm nearing my last roundup," rasped the old man as a crooked smile creased his leathery face. "Boys, I'm leaving my savings and wells to you men. Jed gets 50% and he'll carry on the business. I've divided the remaining 40% equally amongst the four of you. I hope you stay on with Jed. The other 10% goes to my poker buddies. This is all spelled out in my will which lawyer Hudson has at his office."

The wildcatter gasped for breath and choked. Jed raised his head slightly and gave him a sip of water. After several moments, the old man collected himself and looked into Jed's eyes as he spoke, "Jed you know the business. You understand seismic test lines and core samples better than me. You're also one of the very few men I've known who can walk a field and know by looking at the surface rock and soil that oil is not far below. I think you can smell that black gold!

"You also know how big oil can neglect oil opportunities. Them boys, as you know, have the knack of being sloppy and lazy. They write off reservoirs that aren't empty and they are way to quick to designate fields as unproven. When, not if, you hit your gushers don't ever, ever let the big oil bastards grind you down, especially their piss-ant landmen."

The old man winked and smiled at Jed. A moment later the light in his eyes began to fade and his body fell limp. A tear trickled down Jed's cheek as his hand tenderly closed the old man's eyes.

He died just as he wanted… beside his last wildcat oil well with his boots on and oil stains on his work shirt.

Jed and the wildcatter's four original employees stayed together for the next eighteen years as they enjoyed one success after another. In the year 2000, the same year Jed entered the political arena in Texas, he and his four fellow shareholder's sold their debt free oil rights, free water and pipeline rights to a big oil company for slightly more than one billion dollars. In addition to their cool billion dollar sale, they sold their infrastructure assets, existing pipelines, rigs, gathering facilities, rolling stock and the like, for another three hundred million dollars. The big oil buyer of Jed's gushing wells happened to be the underlying landowner who leased him the oil rights to these, supposedly unproductive, oil fields fifteen years earlier.

On the evening of Jed's oil company sale, Jed, his wife and his four partners, and their wives, assembled for a quiet celebratory dinner at the Capital Grille in Houston. Soon after they were seated at a semi-private table in the corner of the restaurant, the owner of the restaurant arrived with a fine bottle of chilled champagne.

"Mr. and Mrs. Adams, ladies and gentlemen, on behalf of my restaurant, please accept this congratulatory bottle of champagne. I find it very inspiring that honest, down to earth and hard working men, and women, who risk everything to build a business of their own are rewarded for their efforts. To your well deserved success," said the owner sincerely, as he popped the bottle of champagne and poured each one of them a glass of champagne.

After a brief toast, Jed thanked the owner for the champagne and asked him to remain at his side while he reminisced about a previous meal he enjoyed at the restaurant.

"The seeds of our company's success sprang from a business lunch I had here fifteen years ago. You were just starting out here as waiter, if I remember correctly. The oil company who bought us out, or back, today," said Jed lightly as he laughed and tipped his champagne glass to all those seated at the table, "had, at that time, just appointed a very inexperienced and unqualified individual to the position of vice president in charge of new oil field development. This was the individual who I met here that day for lunch. Fortunately for my partners and me, my lunch companion had a weakness for bourbon that you helped me exploit. The steady stream of tall glasses of good bourbon that you so efficiently served that day helped me gain his trust. It also opened the door to a relationship with his oil company. I believe there is a saying that describes such good fortune... 'Luck is what happens when preparation meets opportunity.' We were both prepared that day!"

"I remember when you walked through the front door and asked to be seated. You were early and your guest had not yet arrived. I noticed that your shirt collar was slightly frayed and your fingernails were clogged with dirt. It looked as if you just been digging in your garden with your hands," said the owner good-humoredly.

Those at the table laughed. Jed's wife interjected, "His fingernails were always disgusting. I made him carry a small scrub brush so he could scrub clean his fingernails in a restroom before he met with customers. Geez, you would have thought he was a grease monkey at a garage."

Everyone laughed except for one of Jed's partners who sat directly across from him. Everything about Jed's partner was big... his hands, forearms, upper torso and shoulders. His friendly face and innocent brown eyes belied has razor sharp mind. He was a giant of a man who neither said much nor missed much. When Jed's wife mentioned grease monkey his eyes lit up, as a smile began to curl from the corner of his mouth.

"Jed was an oil monkey, not a grease monkey. I have never, I mean never seen a man in a white collared, dress shirt enjoy scampering all over an oil rig like Jed. He'd fuss with the crane, drill bits, pumps, pipelines and mud pits. He was like a kid in a toy store every time he visited our rigs. Anyone else who wore a dress shirt... bankers, salesmen, consultants...

wouldn't come within fifty feet of a rig. Oil has a unique magnetism to nice clothes, but that never stopped old Jed," smiled the man.

"'Tiny,' you were and still are the best driller in the state of Texas. The first time I saw you, you were handling a thirty-foot drill string as if it were a fluorescent light tube. Drilling, training, supervising, organizing… you are hands down the best! To 'Tiny!'" said Jed as he raised his champagne glass in a toast to his trusted partner and friend.

After the owner left their table, they all enjoyed a sumptuous celebratory dinner together. Jed, and most of the others, devoured the house specialty, a large, dry aged Angus porterhouse steak, rare.

Over coffee, Jed announced, to the surprise of his partners, that he would be running for election to United States Senate. One of Texas' United States Senators had recently accepted a cabinet post in the current president's administration and the state was, thereby, holding a special election eight months hence to fill his remaining term in the United States Senate.

"I know it may sound a little corny, but maybe I can help make our country better. Y'all will be the first to hear my platform," said Jed, as the fingers on his right hand began to extend outwards, one by one. "First off, I'd like to change our absolute insane dependence on foreign oil. After that, I'll address the issues of more jobs, better educations for our kids and tort reform. Many of our politicians in Washington haven't a clue as to how many of their completely nonsensical laws discourage businesses from hiring new workers while needlessly increasing operating costs. Not a damn one of them had ever built a business, met a payroll or been sued for some unbelievably, frivolous matter. That has to be changed," he said.

Jed Adams was elected to the United States Senate in Texas' 2000 special election. From his very first days in Washington, he began to tackle his *to do* list as only a South Texas rancher and West Texas wildcatter could. In short order, his political prominence began to soar. Male and female, young and old, rich and poor, all liked him. His plain speaking, down to earth, common sense approach to all manner of legislation appealed to the countries voters. And, it was apparent, from his first day in office, that he was staunchly opposed to the extreme views of both political parties.

After three short years in Washington, he was elected to the presidency of the United States. To the country, he was a breath of fresh air.

He was an omnipresent "watchdog" over the mega Wall Street firms who would and could manipulate financial markets to their own advantage. For those woebegone legislators on the "Hill" who proposed a wasteful or senseless bill weighed down with "pork-barrel" riders, he was a merciless foe. All of these factors contributed to his unusually high and favorable presidential Harris Poll rating. It also gave him the clout to publicly ridicule and kill new or to be renewed legislation that came before Congress and had the earmarks of being overly gratuitous to those in the United States who chose not to work and foreign countries who turned a blind eye to terrorist training camps that thrived within their borders. For a country deep in debt, the days of mindless, out of control federal spending were over.

Because Jed was in many ways a political virgin on Capitol Hill, he unfortunately didn't understand or realize the depths to which his foes would descend to ruin his presidency and, in the process, place the lives of American children in grave danger.

CHAPTER 3
A SPECIALTY PRACTICE

Rod Turdlow parked his van in the handicap stall near the front door of the gas station. The station was less than one mile from the Helena airport on Custer Avenue and appeared to be doing a brisk business. After grabbing his crutches, which rested against the front passenger seat, he slowly maneuvered his bouncing, three hundred pound body out of the van. Even with the aid of his crutches, he could barely stand. In slow motion, he inched himself towards the van's rear sliding door. Once the door was open, he flipped his crutches onto the floor of the van and laboriously unfolded his wheelchair. His heart was pounding and his vision was blurred by the time he collapsed into his wheelchair. Sweat trickled down his forehead and he was gasping for air. After resting a minute, his breathing and vision slowly returned to normal.

If anyone could be categorized as a non-complaint and negligent type two diabetic, it would be Rod Turdlow. He avoided all forms of exercise, drank alcohol to excess and ate fried foods and pastries like there was no tomorrow. Contrasting sharply with his self destructive and unhealthy life style was an engaging and trusting personality. To those he met for the first time, his deep patrician voice, sincere gray eyes and friendly smile made a favorable impression. To his fellow "scammers" who knew him, it was a damn mystery how this fat, bald, white man with a round, clown like nose could so easily con the smartest people.

Turdlow noticed that there was a vehicle filling up at every gas pump and there was a steady stream of customers coming and going from the station's convenience store. It was obviously a very busy and profitable business. He wheeled his chair up the modest grade to the front door of the convenience store and punched the automatic front door opener. As he wheeled himself into the store, a young cashier who was serving a mother with an infant in a chest carrier interrupted her transaction and pleasantly asked him if she could help him. Three other patrons who were waiting behind the mother shifted impatiently.

"Yes, please. Where is the restroom?"

The cashier pointed to a sign in the back of the store that read "Restrooms."

"Do you need any assistance?" asked the cashier pleasantly.

"No, I'll be fine," said Turdlow.

He easily rolled his chair down the wide aisle that was at least six inches wider than federal ADA (Americans with Disability Act) requirements. He noticed that the end caps on each aisle were overflowing with merchandise that indicated strong, high margin convenience store sales. When he reached the "Mens Restroom," he turned his wheelchair back towards the cashier and began taking digital pictures of the convenience store counter, front door and aisles. He next wheeled his chair around and snapped several pictures of the restroom's entry door hardware. Secretly pulling out a tape measure, he measured the width of the restroom's door. So far, every ADA detail met or exceeded federal standards.

When he entered the men's rest room, he realized there was no need to take any further measurements. It was obvious to his trained eye that the sink was at the proper height, the hot and cold water handles on the sink met code, the hot water lines were properly wrapped with insulation and the handicap stall dimensions and fixtures exceeded the minimum ADA standards. He took a few more pictures and exited the restroom. He had no reason to use the facilities and was in and out of the restroom in less than thirty seconds. As he was leaving the store, he stopped at the cashiers counter and asked the helpful young cashier if the owner was present.

"Unfortunately, no. The owners, Dick and Betty Smith, were taking the day off," she said smiling.

She deliberately mentioned the owner's name so that he'd know who to ask for in the event he called back to compliment them on the service of their staff. She didn't mention that the owner's only child had a terrible case of spinal bifida and could only travel with the aid of a wheelchair. Nor did she elaborate on the owner's insistence that all their employees offer extraordinary service to their handicapped customers.

"OK," he said brightly, as he flashed her his trademark smile, and proceeded back to his van.

Once he was settled behind the steering wheel of his van, he picked up his three-ring notebook that lay on the front console. In the old days, he would have neglected this ADA shakedown prospect, particularly since their facilities fully complied with ADA standards. But, he'd recently relocated from Southern California to Montana and his start-up costs were greater than expected. And, he had joined forces with a very impatient investor-partner. The cash from even the slightest of settlements would be helpful.

With a pang of regret, he reflected on warm, sunny Southern California. Los Angeles and the surrounding smaller cities had been Turdlow's former home "turf." He had filed over 1,500 ADA lawsuits in that area over the past five years with nary a word of public outcry. His lawsuit mill was growing in leaps and bounds. The abundance of Hollywood liberals, grand standing politicians and deep pocket trial attorney's who aggressively opposed tort reform, of any kind, seemingly ensured that his predatory, shakedown lawsuit practice would last forever. ADA supporters, with a few exceptions like Clint Eastwood, jumped aboard the bullshit bandwagon because they erroneously believed that ADA legislation was perfectly written and good for all handicapped people. Had any of these misguided "do gooders" spent sixty seconds researching ADA legislation they would have felt otherwise.

In plain English, ADA regulations were impetuously conceived and badly written. Absent from their regulations were commonplace remedies for the slightest of infractions. With the absence of remedies, reasonable fines and an actual injury to a plaintiff, ADA regulations provided a legal form of extortion for ADA shakedown predators like Turdlow. Adding to this mess was the improbability of businesses, including every government office in Washington DC, to not only comply with, but even be aware of, the thousands of ever changing regulation minutiae. In short, ADA predators were driving an angry wedge between the relations of businesses of all sizes and their handicapped patrons.

As Turdlow's net wealth increased, two speed bumps appeared on his fast track to millions. First, federal judges and magistrates began to see through his and his colleagues burgeoning tidal wave of disingenuous ADA lawsuits. More and more of his ADA lawsuits were being summarily thrown out of court by these judges for the slightest of filing or pleading miscues. Second, a growing number of small business owners, if they could afford it, were stepping up to the plate and challenging his lawsuits. The cost of litigating an ADA lawsuit wasn't frightening them as much as it did in the past. And, since there was no merit to nearly all of the lawsuits he filed, Turdlow realized he had to be more selective about who he chose to sue.

Therefore, Turdlow elected to expand his predatory practice into the City of Compton, which was located just south of Los Angeles. He reasoned that because this was a lower income area, small business owners would be less likely to retain an expensive attorney to litigate their ADA defense. He was right on that count, but he didn't consider the alternatives to litigation in Compton. Only when the leader of the largest gang in Compton put a nine-millimeter pistol in his mouth and told him he had twenty-four hours to leave the state or *else*, did he realize the error of his ways. At first, he thought he could negotiate with the gang leader. However, when the gang leader explained to him that he already had two, very big strikes against him, he realized his options were few.

Strike one was encroaching on the gang leader's "turf" without obtaining his prior permission. That was simply an error in judgment, decided Turdlow. Strike two was his attempt to shakedown a woman who owned a hair salon and happened to be the gang leader's mother. That was sheer stupidity, he realized in retrospect, which could very well have cost him his life. Fortunately for him, by the time the gang leader tracked him down, the gang leader's mother had instructed her son to offer Turdlow a one time, free pass. Her merciful, Christian intervention provided him with a twenty-four hour grace period in which to pack up all his belongings and leave the state.

Returning his attention to the present, Turdlow opened his

notebook and made the following entries between the neatly spaced rows and columns:

Date and time: May 27, 2008 Arrived 1515 Departed 1523

Location: Dick Smith's Shell station 1427 Custer Avenue Helena MT

Type of business: Gas station with convenience store

Ownership: ___ Corporate _X_ Private Owners are Dick and Betty Smith

Pictures and measurements- Details attached

Comments: Meets all ADA standards; business is in top 5% of gas stations; pumps 300,000+ gallons per month; C-store does $100 K or more in sales per month; NOT A COMPANY STORE

Action: File suit for $250 K; run up legal fees and settle for no less than $50 K; grounds for suit -see "BS" file

The "BS" was short for bullshit. *It's just business Dick and Betty, nothing personal,* he thought, in a ridiculous attempt to console his warped conscience. However, he was quickly learning that it was *personal* with these Montana businessmen. He'd already been confronted by one angry defendant who stopped him on a public sidewalk with his six shooter holstered neatly on his hip. At least in Compton, California, they kept their weapons hidden.

He closed his notebook and drove to the Mobil station that was five blocks away. Four more prospective defendants were on his afternoon schedule before he met his business partner for dinner. Though he and his partner had a number of important matters to discuss, his biggest concern was meeting his partner on time. In two short months, he had learned that his partner was an extremely impatient, fastidious and violent man. Turdlow believed he should be on a heavy dose of anti-depressants. He was a walking time bomb. If need be, he would cut short his afternoon schedule so he could arrive early to his dinner meeting.

Several hours later, his wheelchair was parked at the open end of a dinner booth and he was sipping a margarita when his partner arrived. The man who pounced onto the bench seat opposite him was approximately six feet in height and had the trim, solid build of someone who worked out regularly in the gym. Black hair that was long and slicked back framed a sharp face that featured vacant, black eyes that seemed pinched together. He wore a stylish, lightweight leather jacket over a heavily starched white shirt that was open halfway down his chest. A necklace with a large, solid gold medallion hung loosely inside his shirt. His appearance would have been inconspicuous in West Los Angeles, but in Helena, Montana he stood out like a sore thumb. Turdlow viewed him as a bejeweled rat with oily black hair.

Turdlow had met the man a year earlier in Palm Springs, California. At the time, he was in the lobby of an Indian casino after indulging in their cut-rate buffet when the man approached him and offered to buy him a drink. His offer was more of a command than an invitation. Turdlow declined his offer, but when the man ignored his reply and wheeled him into the privacy of the bar lounge, he began to understand there was more to his offer than generosity. He introduced himself as Richie Smith and handed him his business card. It read that he was a consultant for Native American's gambling interests. The casino they were sitting in was one of his clients.

The manager of the casino had briefed Smith on Turdlow's background only thirty minutes earlier. Smith and the manager were sipping coffee after dinner when Smith made a derogatory comment about the whale parked at the dessert bar. The manager explained that he first met Turdlow years earlier when his scam ADA law practice was in its infancy.

"He tried to shake down this very casino. The guy didn't have a clue about U.S. jurisdiction on Indian land," said the manager laughing.

Smith's discussion with Turdlow lasted only a few minutes. The gist of Smith's message was that when, not if, Turdlow got run out of California, he could ensure that his specialty law practice would prosper in the fine state of Montana. He never learned how Smith knew about his practice, but at the time he didn't really care. It was all he could do to suppress laughing at the absurdity of Smith's proposition. *Who the hell would move from sunny Southern California to Montana?* Fortunately, he sensed that Richie Smith didn't like being laughed at. In time, he learned that laughing at Smith, no matter how insignificant the subject, could instantly ignite a maniacal rage in the man.

He saved the information on Richie Smith's business card in his Blackberry and called him a few minutes after the Compton gang leader pulled his nine-millimeter pistol out of his mouth.

Smith noticed the margarita cocktail that Turdlow was cradling in his hands.

"That shit isn't good for your diabetes," he said brusquely.

"Just one, after which I'll switch to iced tea."

"Yeah, yeah. Followed by fried chicken, ice cream and cake," added Smith sarcastically.

"So how is your day going or are you still recovering from a night of boozing?"

Smith's black eyes bulged like an angry gargoyle. No one talked to him like that.

"Fuck you, asshole! I can ruin your life in a New York minute. I know you're confined to a wheelchair because of your laziness and horse shit diet. Injured by a roadside bomb during Desert Storm… what bullshit! You didn't even serve in the military. Too fat, high blood pressure and diabetes. You're pathetic, especially when you dress up in your fake Army Special forces uniform with your phony medals. Rambo in a chair, poor baby!" sneered Smith.

"Why don't we get down to business!" suggested Turdlow, uneasily.

"Where do we stand on setting up the meth lab?" asked Smith.

"I've cut a deal with a reliable chemist I know. He has already bought supplies and equipment for our first batch of meth. He'll stay on site for two weeks while he teaches your buddies how to make the product. The chemist has his bags packed and he's ready to roll. He can be here within twenty-four hours. You'll have to tell me where the site is so I can give him directions."

Smith leaned back in the booth, his vacant, unblinking black eyes bored into Turdlow.

"Give me the chemist's name and cell phone number. I'll give him the directions. The fewer people who know the location of the lab the better," said Smith coldly.

Giving Smith the chemist's contact information would eliminate any remaining leverage he had with the bastard. Turdlow thought fast, "I don't have his cell phone number. He uses throwaway cell phones. He contacts me. I'll have him call you next time he calls me."

An evil smile curled Smith's lips and a warning bell clanged in

Turdlow's mind. Smith would kill him as soon as he was in contact with the chemist.

"Don't screw up the arrangement with this chemist. We can begin production at the lodge in the next couple of weeks. The current tenants will be out by then."

"Tenants! I thought this was a vacant hunting cabin."

Smith moved his face closer to Turdlow and growled angrily, "The tenants and the facilities are none of your God damn business."

The whole tenor of this luncheon meeting was turning from bad to worse. Turdlow spun his wheelchair away from the booth and headed for the men's room.

"We're not through here," barked Smith to the back of Turdlow's disappearing wheelchair.

"Restroom," responded Turdlow just loud enough for Smith to hear.

In the men's room, Turdlow splashed his face with cold water and took deep breaths. *Calm down. Think. Buy time. Change the subject of the conversation. Go on the offensive.*

Turdlow wheeled back to the booth several minutes later. Before Smith could say a word, Turdlow took an envelop from the inside of his coat pocket and slid it across the table to Smith.

"$10,000. My start up costs were higher than expected and it takes longer than I thought to settle my cases."

"Should I have a talk with a judge or two?" said Smith slowly.

"Shit no! They can't really expedite a settlement. Keep them out of this. I was referring to the defendants I'm suing. These Montana businessmen are stubborn people. I should have $15,000 for you next month."

"I see. Well don't sweat the 'feds!' Law and order in Montana is not high on Washington's list of priorities. Their local big mouth also owes me a few favors."

"Are you talking about the U.S. Attorney in Montana?" asked Turdlow.

"U.S. Attorney… I didn't say that! I'm just a simple government consultant for Indian affairs. No more, no less. Now, back to business. Next month, you'll give me $20,000. The $15,000 you owe plus the $5,000 makeup for this month."

With an unexpected rush of bravado, fueled by his high level of anxiety, Turdlow snapped, "Go to hell! We agreed that my start up costs would be deducted from my first month's payment."

"I've changed our deal. If you don't like it I'll find someone to replace you, like a real attorney who went to law school and passed the state bar exam. I don't give a shit about your start up costs or the status of your sham lawsuits. Think of my fee as a month to month license to operate."

"Replace me then! These sham lawsuits support your life style, Richie, and it's small change compared to the big bucks we'll take in together with the meth lab," said Turdlow weakly. He needed time to formulate a plan.

"You're on thin ice with me, Turdlow. Anymore payoff shortfalls and the ice could crack sending you to the bottom like a ton of bricks, which for you is an accurate description. *Capiche?*" said Smith threateningly.

Turdlow nodded his head in pained understanding as Smith stepped out of the booth and strutted to the restaurant's exit.

CHAPTER 4
CAMP PENDLETON, OCEANSIDE, CA,

Late May 2008...

Gunnery Sergeant Brice Miller stood erect at parade rest in front of his company commander's desk. He watched Major Chet Daniels leaf through his personnel folder. For the past six years, both men had served together with the 3rd Battalion, 5th Regiment of the 1st Marine Division, based thirty miles north of San Diego at Camp Pendleton, California.

The 3rd Battalion, 5th Regiment, referred to as the "3/5", is nicknamed the "Darkhorse" battalion. Its distinguished Marine Corps record includes participation in a number of legendary campaigns and battles that include, Belleau Wood, Guadalcanal, Peleliu, Okinawa, the Chosin Reservoir, the Battle for Hue, Fallujah and the Battle of Sangin.

"Gunny, I know you don't want to take a seat, but please do and relax. This meeting may last awhile. And let's use first names and drop the military formality for a few minutes. Is that OK with you?"

"Yes sir, Major Daniels," he snapped as he sat in the chair facing Major Daniels.

"It's Chet, OK."

"Yes, Chet," stuttered Brice somewhat uncomfortably.

Chet returned his attention to Brice's personnel folder. He noted that Brice had enlisted in the Marine Corps a couple of months after his graduation from high school. It was the day he turned seventeen years of age, August 30, 2001, which was also the minimum age for enlisting in the Marine Corps. He further read that Miller had scored in the top one percent of every written exam and physical test he'd taken in the Marine Corps. His high test scores, excellent performance evaluations and numerous combat commendations all contributed to his unusual promotion to gunnery sergeant at such a young age.

Chet doubted that he could have accomplished such a feat. When he entered the University of Illinois at seventeen, he remembered that simply attending classes and getting to football practices on time was a chore. Everything that Chet read in Brice's file confirmed what he, Brice's peers and Chet's superiors knew about Gunny Miller. The kid was truly one of a kind. *Kid,* he chuckled to himself. He was only eight years older than Brice.

Brice's first combat tour in Iraq was as a squad leader in Chet's platoon. During his first week in Iraq, he garnered the admiration and enduring gratitude of the freshly minted, 2nd lieutenant when he restrained Chet a half step before he stepped on an improvised explosive device (IED) that was carefully concealed at the base of a blown out doorway in a vacant building. Thereafter, Chet paid special heed to his young corporal's perceptive qualities in their ever changing and disconcerting urban war zone. It was amidst this combat setting that Brice's ascension through the Corps' enlisted ranks began to soar. During Brice's most recent tour in Iraq, he received a permanent field promotion to gunnery sergeant for meritorious action and served as the "gunny" of Chet's rifle company. His latest promotion combined with his earlier below the zone promotion to staff sergeant distinguished him as the youngest gunnery sergeant in the entire Marine Corps.

Shortly after their recent return to Camp Pendleton, Chet was also deep selected for promotion to major and Brice knew he was being considered for a slot as a battalion commander.

To an outside observer, it could have appeared that both men's early promotions were the result of some form of favoritism. That wasn't the case. Both men had been promoted by separate boards of review that independently knew, as did many Marines in the 1st Marine Division, that each man had routinely risked his own life during numerous missions to save and protect the lives of other Marines. They were clearly very courageous, as well as being smart, resourceful and, most of all, fierce as hell warriors.

Both of them looked as though they just walked off a United States Marine Corps recruiting poster. They were each approximately five foot ten inches in height and weighed a one hundred and eighty pounds of solid muscle. Both worked out religiously in the weight room, which was evident from their broad chests, strapping shoulders and powerful forearms. Small waists and narrow hips supported each of their impressive upper torsos. In addition to their weight lifting regimen, daily runs of five miles or more kept both of them in top aerobic condition. There was not an ounce of fat on either man. Physically, they could have been twins except that one was white and the other black.

Chet turned in his chair towards his office window. Through the window, he gazed wistfully at the tall grass on the Santa Margarita hills that was swaying gently in the breeze as the morning marine layer began to burn off. In some ways, he thought, those idyllic hillsides were like young, green Marines who were full of enthusiasm as they headed into their first season of combat. And, much like the seasons of the year, as the cool spring turned into the hot summer, both the green grass and the young Marines would lose some of their splendor as the heat from the sun or flying bullets relentlessly consumed their vitality. But, not all the tall grass, nor all the young Marines would succumb to the constant heat. Some Marines flourished under constant stress. Brice was one of those.

Chet thought back again to their first tour together in Iraq. An unusual incident occurred that Brice's men still humorously regarded. He'd sent Brice's squad deep into enemy controlled territory on a reconnaissance mission. As they were returning around 5:00 PM local time, they were ambushed while traversing the bottom of a rocky ravine. Enemy gunfire from both sides of the ravine pinned them down and escape seemed impossible.

Brice's last report to Chet over his radio was hard to hear because of the loud sound of background gunfire, "ETA [estimated time of arrival] at 'ex-fil' [exfiltration] site eight hours behind 'sched' [schedule]. Will require fast pick up and cold beer. Last comm. Radio dying, over."

Brice, as he would later explain, instructed a young private who was crouched beside him to pass the following message to his men, "Do not return enemy fire. Conserve ammo. Stay hidden behind the boulders. When total darkness arrives, disrobe except for t-shirts, skivvies, boots and weapons. Construct best dummy Marines with helmets, fatigues, packs and all else. Slither slowly and silently at least one hundred yards to the south end of the ravine to rally point. Arrive no later than 2300 hours. I will direct from there."

Unbeknownst to his men, Brice routinely carried an unusual home-made timing device that was a combination of a mousetrap and a small cooking timer. When the timer alarm went off, it activated the arm on the mousetrap that could release the safety lever on a grenade.

At 2300 hours, the instant flash and sound of a grenade exploded at Brice's former position. The enemy poured heavy gunfire into, what they thought, were trapped and dying Marines. When their gunfire was not returned, they began to inch themselves down the sides of the steep ravine. When they reached the bottom of the ravine, Brice's men heard them fire random shots into the shadows of dummy corpses.

When the enemy believed that all the Marines were dead, they flipped on their flashlights and began congratulating themselves. At that moment, Brice's squad, who now occupied the edges of the ravine above, poured killing gunfire into the hoodwinked enemy below. It was an incredibly simple ploy, but it worked and it saved the lives of the men in Brice's squad.

Once the helicopters had picked up Brice's scantily clad Marines and delivered them back to the safety of their firebase. The talk of Brice's unusual action spread like wild fire. It became known as the "skivvy patrol."

Chet remembered handing Brice his first of several cold beers at the firebase. He smiled and said good-naturedly to Brice, "You do know that asking for cold beer over an open radio net isn't an approved Marine Corps communication."

Brice's reply was not meant to be flippant, nor memorable, but it became so. "My men could hear my radio comm. We all thought that we were going to die, so I thought a little 'brassiness' might encourage them."

"'Brassiness!'"

"Yeah! Like big brassy… "

"I get it Brice," said Chet as he raised his hand.

Whether it was brassiness, a high level of creativity, an inherited warrior gene or some combination thereof, Brice was clearly endowed with a special skill set that improved the odds of survival of every Marine around him. Chet joined his hands behind his head, closed his eyes and rocked backward in his office chair and thought.

"Chet, are you OK?" asked Brice.

Holding his position, Chet answered to the ceiling, "I'm cogitating."

"Cogitating? I've never seen you like this before. Is cogitating a mental disorder?"

"No, it's not a mental disorder. I'm thinking about your separation request from the Corps. It's slightly unusual. I think I can confidently say that since Vietnam there has never been a gunnery sergeant, under the age of twenty five, who has made such a request."

A month earlier, at a Camp Pendleton "Wounded Warrior" dinner, Chet met Brice's high school football coach and surrogate father, Jack Powell. Hunched together over a table in a corner of the mess hall during most of the dinner, Jack discussed with Chet Brice's background as only a no nonsense Texas football coach could. Chet wasn't surprised at the similarity of Brice's background with his own.

Brice was born in a small, hardscrabble West Texas town that sat at the crossroads of a minor oil field. His mother died giving birth to him. His dad, who was an occasional roughneck in the oil fields, raised Brice. During his sophomore year of high school, Brice out hustled every senior on the football field and caught every pass thrown in his general direction. The other players liked him and it was obvious to Coach Powell that aside from his gifted physical skills, he was a personable, levelheaded young man. The coach also mentioned that academically he was an excellent student.

Home for Brice was a rusting singlewide trailer that he shared with his dad. That is, when his dad wasn't sleeping off a drinking binge in the county's drunk tank. As his father's drinking became worse, his confinement in the drunk tank became more frequent and his binges resulted in increasing violent behavior.. Once Brice entered high school, relations between father and son began to rapidly deteriorate. Brice's emerging growth as a strong, smart and clear thinking young man probably irritated the hell out of his lazy, unmotivated and often drunk father. He was becoming the man his father had never been, nor would ever be.

Increasing jail time and the sheriff's repeated warnings about his drunken behavior made no impression on Brice's dad. His first step out of the jailhouse, into the bright morning sun, was routinely in the direction of his favorite liquor store. After buying a cheap pint of whiskey, he'd start sipping from the bottle before he stepped out of the store. His wobbly shuffle towards his trailer park, down a rutted, dusty road, became a regular and pathetic occurrence.

By mid afternoon, the alcohol would cause mean, aggressive thoughts to boil in Brice's dads scrambled brain. When Brice returned home from football practice in the early evening and stepped into the trailer, he never knew whether he'd face an unconscious, snoring father or an incoherent, raging beast that was primed for beating the crap out of him.

The increasing frequency and severity of Brice's bruises and scratches concerned Jack. He and his wife, Judith, reached out to Brice. At first, they helped him with his studies and steered him towards odd jobs that provided him with all-important spending money. Occasional dinners at their house and gifts of clothing followed. All of which strengthened their relationship. Once Judith felt she knew and understood the boy, she suggested to her husband that they invite him to stay with them. Jack had been thinking along the same lines. They both had dreamed of having children, but a childhood injury that Judith suffered when thrown from a horse prevented her from bearing children. They asked Brice if he'd like to stay in their spare bedroom in the back of their house. He gladly accepted and the three of them quickly developed a close knit, familial relationship.

A year after Brice moved out of his father's broken down trailer, he heard from a friend that his father was being tried for an unprovoked, and near fatal, assault on a man in a local bar. Brice sent a note to the presiding judge recommending that the judge put his dad behind bars for life.

Once Brice joined the Marines, after graduating from high school, it wasn't long before he was dodging bullets and IED's in Iraq. Despite the constant dangers to his life and limbs, his contentment with his personal life was growing. He was surrounded with men who would risk their life to save his. His fellow Marines were truly like family and his best friend in the Corps, Bobby Ridger, was like a brother he never had. Daily letters and frequent *care* packages from the Powell's also gave him the comfort of knowing that his surrogate parents thought of him every moment of every day.

Though Chet's and Brice's backgrounds shared similarities, their hometown's couldn't have been more different. Brice's hometown was a hot, dusty and dry West Texas town with a rural population of approximately twenty thousand residents. Chet's hometown was East St. Louis, Illinois, which was a degenerating, urban battlefield, known as the "murder capital" of the United States in the late 1980s and early 1990s with a population of approximately forty thousand. During those years, East St. Louis was inhabited by three categories of black families. Those who were resigned to the status quo; those who were fighting to return the city to its glory of the 1950s and 1960s when jobs were plentiful in the meatpacking industry and eighty thousand residents prospered; and those who were dedicated to escaping. Chet's grandmother, Alice, who single handedly raised Chet from the day he was born, was determined to escape. She worked multiple jobs and saved every penny she could so that she and her grandson could escape the inner city decay of East St. Louis.

Chet spun his chair around until he faced Brice. He rocked forward and rested his forearms on his desk.

"Are you finished cogitating?" said Brice smiling.

"Yes, Brice, I'm finished. How's the therapy going on your hand, arm and neck?"

"Well, the 3rd and 4th digits of my right hand were successfully amputated and the stubs have healed nicely. There really wasn't much left to amputate so the surgery healed pretty quickly," said Brice indifferently.

"Digits! Is that what fingers are called? Can you hold a mug of cold beer with that hand?" said Chet shaking his head at Brice's gallows humor.

"No problem holding a beer mug and I can almost fit my whole hand inside the finger guard on my M-16. And… "

Chet raised his hand. He got the picture.

"How about the arm and neck?"

"The surgeons feel that they removed the last of the shrapnel in my arm last month. I've been getting regular therapy and lifting weights. The arm feels nearly good as new. As for the neck, I just have a scar. No nerve damage whatsoever. The scar looks like a 'hicky.' It should make the girls jealous," said Brice with a crooked smile pasted on his face.

"A 'hicky!'" Chet sat back in his chair and laughed. He paused a moment before turning more serious, "I'm glad to hear the arm is healing. Some of those arm injuries never heal properly. I've reviewed your discharge request and I'm not going to approve it. What I'd like to see you do is put your gear in storage and take some time off. Sixty days to be exact. I've reviewed your personnel folder and you haven't taken any leave in three years. You are going to lose some of that accumulated leave if you don't use it soon.

"Get away from the military. Climb mountains, travel through Europe, fish for marlin in Cabo San Lucas… clear your head before you decide to get out of the Corps. When you leave is over and if you still want to get out of the Corps, I'll approve your request.

"It would be a shame, however, to terminate your duty with the Corps. You have a very distinguished record. All your personnel reviews are excellent and you already have a box full of medals, including three purple hearts and a silver star. You've been involved in more intense combat in the last three years than most generals have in their entire career."

Chet recited from memory the *gallantry in action* highlights of Brice's recent Silver Star commendation, "On your last mission in Iraq, you lost two fingers from enemy fire and suffered life threatening shrapnel wounds to your neck and arm when an RPG (rocket propelled grenade) struck your HUMVEE and blew you out of your gun turret. Despite these injuries and while under heavy enemy fire, you crawled back into the gun turret of your burning vehicle and provided invaluable suppressing gunfire with your .50 machine gun against a well armed and advancing superior enemy force. Your gallant and quick thinking actions enabled the life saving rescue of two badly injured Marines that were trapped inside the HUMVEE. It also provided other men in your company invaluable time to reorganize themselves and beat back a well planned enemy ambush."

"Geez! I'm impressed. Really! I didn't think anyone remembered that stuff," said Brice. He smiled and added, " Well, that's all behind me now and I'm fully healed."

"Physically, but not mentally. I would also like you to meet with the base counselor regarding PTSD (post traumatic stress disorder) before you go on leave. I took the liberty of scheduling an appointment for you with him at 1500 hours tomorrow."

"Geez, Chet! I don't need any 'psycho babble' counseling. I'm fine. I couldn't be better," interrupted Brice.

"Well, that's bullshit! You forget that this is the Marine Corps, Brice, and there are no secrets in the Corps. The battalion's Senior Chief Corpsman mentioned to me that your platoon corpsman has been secretly slipping you 'meds' because you're having trouble sleeping."

"Lots of my men are getting psychological help, including me. I have horrible flashbacks of our tour in Fallujah several years ago. I was with you and Bobby Ridger when that IED sent us flying out of that house in Fallujah. I know Bobby is your best friend, and he got the worst of it, but that explosion rattled all of us."

Every time Chet thought or heard of that shit hole, Fallujah, he cringed. Though the urban violence there shared some similarities with East St. Louis, nothing could compare to the inhumane and cold-blooded havoc he'd seen the Shiites and Sunnis inflict on one another. Blowing up schools and mosques and, the lowest of the low, attacking funeral processions. The bastards were animals.

He took a deep calming breath and forced his thoughts of Fallujah aside as he looked at Brice.

Brice was silent and introspective for several moments before he calmly spoke, "So, I'm not the only one who relives those terrible images and sounds. They're brutal. They're the reason I submitted my discharge request."

"I thought so! None of us are invincible, Brice. Oftentimes our psychological wounds are worse than our physical ones. My personal opinion is if you take some time off you'll be OK. You don't have to leave the Corps to escape the nightmares!" said Chet.

"You think so?" questioned Brice.

"I know so! While you're on leave, if your sleeping disorders and flashbacks persist, our base counselor can arrange for you to see an approved civilian psychologist in most major cities. You need a break, my friend!"

Chet stood and moved towards the coffee pot in the corner of his office. Assuming their meeting was over, Brice snapped to attention and barked, "Yes sir, Major Daniels. I'll follow your orders."

Chet smiled and shook his head in disbelief. "Coffee, Brice?" he asked as he refilled his coffee mug.

"No thank you, major. Permission to leave, sir?"

"Nope! Sit back down. I've got a couple of other matters to discuss with you," said Chet pleasantly, as he returned to his desk and took a sip of his hot black coffee.

Smiling broadly Chet said, "First, the sixty days of leave is a suggestion, not an order. Second, before you go on leave, we should discuss your application for admittance to the United States Naval Academy."

"Annapolis! Is this a joke?" said Brice skeptically, unsure whether Chet was pulling his leg or not.

"Far from it. I'd been thinking about your prospective future as an officer in the Corps and was going to speak to Lieutenant Colonel Roy Adair, our battalion commander, about it. But, our regimental commander, Colonel John O'Brien, beat me to the punch. You may not know this but he's a graduate of the 'Boat School.' The colonel called a meeting a few days ago with Adair and me. I think he'd heard about your discharge request from the top sergeant. I suspect he was the one who also reminded the colonel of your record in the Corps. I don't know if you remember, but you saved the 'top's' brother's life in a firefight in Fallujah."

"Hmm, vaguely," muttered Brice.

"A 'hmm,' that's all you remember?" Chet stopped to collect his thoughts. Many young Marines under his command had preformed heroic acts and most all of them never gave it a second thought. Brice, however, was in a separate category all together. He began calmly, "You have saved many lives, including mine. I get that. But, let me remind you," he said, as his voice was rising, "that those individuals whose life you have saved, and all of their friends and family members, never forget those events. Read my lips, *they never forget!*"

Brice blushed and nodded silently.

"When we entered the colonel's office, your personnel file, high school transcripts and SAT scores were spread out on his desk."

"You're kidding?" asked Brice incredulously.

Chet continued, "Brice, I swear, it's the truth! This is the straight dope! The colonel looked at Adair and me like we were idiots. He said, 'This man belongs at Annapolis . His high school grades are excellent as are his SAT scores, though they are a few years old. He turns twenty-four on August 15, 2008.' He went on to explain that after speaking with the superintendent of Annapolis, who was his roommate there, that it was likely that Annapolis could provide you with an admission age waiver and a waiver on retaking the SAT exams if you submitted an application. All of this waiver business is, however, a onetime opportunity. In closing, the colonel told Adair and me, in no uncertain terms, that it would reflect poorly on our leadership skills if you didn't submit an application.

"I told the colonel that I'd been thinking of speaking with Lt. Col. Adair about the possibility of you applying to the Naval Academy because you were the smartest and most capable young sergeant I'd ever met. The colonel cut me off. He said that wasn't a question. He added that your qualifications were clearly evident. He instructed Adair and me, in no uncertain terms, to do everything we could to interest you in applying to Annapolis. We were then dismissed. Our meeting lasted less than sixty seconds."

"The coach and his wife have suggested I go to college in the past, but I've been so busy with my duties that I've never given it much thought," said Brice.

Chet cringed and said, "Cut that 'coach and his wife' reference. I've heard you say that before. They have names and you have a relationship with them. When they visited you several months ago, I had a long talk with them at the Wounded Warrior dinner. You think of them as your parents and they think of you as their son. Whether you make it official with formal adoption papers or simply reach an understanding with them, they'll feel better, as will you, if you call them Mom and Dad or Jack and Judith."

Providing family advice to his men wasn't one of Chet's favorite duties. He much preferred directing his men in combat. Chet's relationship with Brice, however, was different. He viewed his advice to Brice like that of an older brother giving advice to a younger brother.

"Next, most of my men are under the false perception that getting a college degree will lead them to a boring career cooped up behind a computer in a small windowless cubicle in a huge office building. That couldn't be further from the truth. There are plenty positions in lots of industries where you can get your hands dirty and have cold rain dripping down your neck. Real estate development, construction, oil drilling... to name a few. In the government sector there is, of course, the military. A college degree will give you the opportunity to become a commissioned officer in any branch of the armed services.

"We have worked and fought together, side by side, for the last six years. You know my job is far from dull. And at times, it's 'friggin' hair raising. I trust that I'll put my engineering degree to good use after I retire from the Corps. But, for now, my college degree gave me the opportunity to get an officer's commission in the Marine Corps and I love being an infantry officer.

"I know you can handle the academics and physical challenges at Annapolis. You might have to bite your tongue the first few years dealing with some of the petty bullshit from the upper classmen, but you can handle that. You've been through far tougher obstacles in the Corps than anything you'll see at Annapolis.

"I remember when you first joined my platoon. You had plenty of energy and enthusiasm, but no combat or leadership experience. Now, when I give you an order, you understand my objectives and grasp the big picture. When a mission breaks down for whatever reason, you have the uncanny ability to escape disasters. You are resourceful, decisive and tenacious. Your men look to you for leadership.

"Further, as you've been promoted, you've proved to be quite a task master to the men in your unit while being fair and approachable. You've also shown, by your example, that you would never ask them to follow an order that you wouldn't perform yourself. The combination of all these qualities is rare in a fighting man. Men like you are called leaders. I love them, the Corps loves them and Annapolis has a rich history of educating them. I know that you will do well at Annapolis. Quite well!"

In total silence, they sat looking at one another, considering what could be.

Finally, Brice broke the ice and said tactfully, "I'll think about it while I'm on leave." *PTSD counseling, the Powell's as real parents, Annapolis, my future, Chet sure has a knack of covering a lot of ground with very few words,* thought Brice. The wisdom of his advice had always been compelling, especially since it had also saved his life on more than one occasion.

CHAPTER 5
RIDGER ADVERSITY

January 2008...

Three years and two months after Bobby Ridger suffered a severe combat injury, he remained a virtual quadriplegic. His recovery was at a standstill. Saddened and frustrated with his son's lack of progress, Bill Ridger reached out to a long time friend, Dr. John Matthews, for advice. Matthews was semi-retired and working on a part time basis at the Bozeman Deaconess Hospital in Bozeman. Unbeknownst to Bill was his friend's area of expertise. Matthews was a nationally acclaimed spinal cord specialist who was frequently called upon by the Veterans Administration (VA) for advice regarding spinal cord injuries.

After speaking with Matthews over the phone, Bill Faxed Matthews a letter that he'd received from one of Bobby's doctors in which he described Bobby's condition. In general, the letter described the following:

Bobby Ridger lay in bed as a result of spinal cord injury that he incurred in November of 2004 while serving with the 3/5 Marines in the second battle of Fallujah. The explosion that caused his injury left him with an unusual trauma. His spinal cord was kinked in two places. Kinking was rare. It was caused by the hyperextension of the back and was referred to as a "stroke of the back." Blood vessels leading to the spine become kinked, like a garden hose, depriving the spinal cord of oxygen.

Usually, the blood vessels restored themselves and eventually provided all-important oxygen to the spinal cord. This often occurred within six months of the injury and it normally lead to the patient's full recovery. Unfortunately, in Bobby's case, there was nothing normal about his recovery.

Within two weeks of Bill's plea for help from his friend, Matthews thoroughly reviewed Bobby's medical history and consulted with the admitting doctors at Balboa Hospital (officially known as Naval Medical Center San Diego). He followed that up with a visit to the Ridger Ranch and performed a thorough physical exam of Bobby. Bobby's muscle atrophy, particularly in his spinal area, was of major concern to the doctor. Rigorous physical therapy was the only way to arrest the atrophy and restore those key muscles. Matthews retained, at his expense, an experienced Bozeman physical therapist to provide Bobby with weekly physical therapy treatments. During the three-hour sessions with Bobby, the therapist instructed the Ridger's and other family friends on how to administer basic daily physical therapy to Bobby.

Additionally, Matthews was able, with his VA relationship, to have Bobby enrolled in an experimental stem cell treatment program that was occurring at the VA Medical Center in Sheridan, Wyoming. In the case of the stem cell treatments, Matthews was of the opinion that the stem cells could help heal the damaged spinal cord and *jump start* the recovery of the kinked blood vessels. He also felt strongly that rigorous physical therapy could accelerate Bobby's recovery, though it would require a high level of patience from the young Marine. If healing did occur, it would arrive slowly, perhaps over years.

Matthews gave his physical therapist detailed written instructions for Bobby's follow-up care. The two main points were as follows:

Firstly, target Bobby's core muscles, particularly those muscles that are interwoven with his spinal area.

Secondly, if possible, identify and isolate those muscle groups that responded to therapy. Each volunteer that the therapist trained would be required to carefully note in a therapy log Bobby's condition at the start of each session plus describe what therapy they administered. This careful record keeping would be important in developing a clear picture of Bobby's baseline condition and identify those muscles that were coming to life. The team of volunteer therapists would then incrementally focus their therapy to nearby, connected muscle groups. As the muscle groups expanded, so too would the blood supply to those muscles and, theoretically, nearby nerve endings. With this approach, the doctor hoped to expand Bobby's nerve rejuvenation from head to toe.

Matthews thought Bobby's twenty-one year old sister, Molly, would be the perfect candidate to oversee Bobby's team of volunteer therapists. Bill Ridger wasn't so sure. Molly became the primary caregiver to her mother during her losing battle with pancreatic cancer when she was fifteen years old.

September 2002

Molly was scheduled to start her sophomore year of classes at the local high school in 2002. Instead, she talked her parents into agreeing to a homeschooling program, primarily so she could be with and help her mother, Susie, who was dying from pancreatic cancer. Susie had declined further cancer treatments and elected to spend her last months at home. Susie's husband, Bill, and her two children, Bobby and Molly, completely underestimated the time and effort required to care for a dying woman. Unfortunately for Molly, almost all of her mother's care fell on her shoulders. As a consequence, Molly's homeschooling program quickly fizzled and she had to repeat her sophomore year of high school the following year.

From Molly's perspective, repeating her sophomore year of high school didn't trouble her in the least. She could recall with perfect clarity how her relationship with her mother and her view of life changed for the better when she excitedly returned home with her high school principal's homeschooling approval tucked into her book bag.

As she approached the front porch and the entrance to the family's ranch house, she had the vague sensation that someone was watching her. She looked up towards the living room's large bay window that overlooked the ranch. Behind the window, her mother was sitting in a wheelchair smiling at her. Her smile beamed as she silently mouthed the words, "I love you."

Molly entered the house and stepped to her mother's side, "What a nice reception! I love you too, Mom!"

Once Molly was settled, her coat hung and her homeschooling books piled on the living room table, Susie asked, "'Honey,' would you mind making tea for us? Then, let's chat."

Beside Susie's wheelchair, in the living room, was a large electric hospital bed that had been delivered several days earlier. Adjacent to the living room, which faced south, was the open kitchen and behind that the dining room. Susie had specifically requested that her new bed be placed in front of the living room window. She wished to see the sun rise every morning and set every evening. She also wanted to be connected to her husband's and daughter's daily activities as much as possible.

Molly set two cups of steaming tea on a small side table between her chair and her mother's wheelchair.

Susie sipped her tea and organized her thoughts. "I see you brought home your homeschooling books. I guess that means I'll have to brush up on my algebra and world history. This program could turn into the student schooling the teacher," said Susie smiling. "If you feel, at anytime, that I'm failing you as a teacher or tutor, I want you to know that I will not be offended if you decide to rejoin your class at school. You shouldn't feel like this plan is set in stone."

As Susie gazed at her daughter, she recognized the determined set of Molly's jaw and the resolute focus of her emerald green eyes. When her daughter fixed her mind on something, she was like her husband, there was no room for compromise.

"We're in this program to the end. I want to be with you," said Molly firmly.

"OK, I appreciate that. I'll be the best teacher and patient I can, but towards the end I'll have my bad days. You'll hear me complain, moan with pain and cry. It won't be pretty. And occasionally, I'll forget to say 'thank you' for your help. That's why I'm thanking you in advance, Honey, for everything you'll do for me!" said Susie.

"And, I'm thanking you as well for understanding what I want to do," said Molly, as she stood and moved to her mother's side. She affectionately slipped her arm around her mother's shoulder and kissed her on the forehead.

"We'll be a great team!" said her mother, as she patted her daughter's arm. Tears began to well in Susie's eyes as she considered the commitment her daughter was making.

At first, Bill routinely checked on his wife every couple of hours during his fourteen-hour workday. But, as he witnessed the steady decline of his wife, he found it more and more difficult to visit with his soul mate and loving wife of thirty-five years. He lost weight, overlooked routine chores and wandered lethargically around the ranch as if he were in a trance. The agonizingly slow and painful death of his wife was sucking the life out of him as well.

Bobby visited with his mother daily, usually in the evening, and helped Molly with her extra caregiving chores, as best he could. Like his dad, he too wasn't emotionally suited to deal with the grim decline of his mother. Susie recognized his limitation and, so, asked him to read aloud poetry every night. She loved poetry and she loved it even more when her son read aloud her favorite poems. The poetry guided them both through difficult times.

For relaxation and a break from her caregiving responsibilities, Molly and her best friend, Penny Hoover, would often enjoy afternoon horseback rides together through the Ridger ranch and into the adjacent foothills. These rides typically occurred after Penny's high school classes and on the weekends. The Ridger ranch was situated between Penny's school and home. It was a convenient and simple matter for Penny to stop by her best friend's house virtually every day for a visit. A further draw to the Ridger ranch was to check on her quarter horse, Prince, who was boarded in their barn.

Penny was an incurable gossip who enjoyed sharing the daily high school news with Molly during their rides. For Molly, listening to her friend ramble on about the happenings of her friends in school was a wonderful and much appreciated change of pace. As her mother's health rapidly declined over the months, her growing dependence on her for virtually all of her needs was beginning to weigh heavily on her state of mind.

One evening while Penny and her mother, Lisa, were preparing dinner together, Penny commented on how distraught Molly was that afternoon. Molly had accidentally dropped her mother while trying to lift her out of bed.

Upon hearing of this incident, Lisa turned off her gas range, set the skillet of frying chicken aside, and turned to her daughter, "I thought Susie Ridger was simply recovering from the removal of basal cells on her arm?"

"Oh, no, mom, she's dying of pancreatic cancer. That's why Molly talked her parents into this homeschooling plan. She wanted to be with her mother during her final months."

Both mothers were friends, but their paths didn't cross very often. Lisa's nursing job had shifted from Dennis to West Yellowstone, so if they were to run into one another it was usually at a school function. And, now that Bobby had graduated from high school and Molly was being homeschooled, even that didn't occur.

Lisa put her hands on her hips and exhaled, "Damn, damn, damn! Call Molly and see if it's OK if I look in on her mother after your school tomorrow. I'll give Molly some nursing tips and I want you with me as well."

"Can we do this the following day? The weather is supposed to be nice tomorrow. Molly and I had planned a long ride into the foothills."

"No, this can't wait. Molly needs our help. Call her now, " said Lisa as she handed her daughter the phone.

The following afternoon Lisa, Penny and Molly all sat around Susie's hospital bed in the Ridger living room. After the two mothers exchanged a few pleasantries, Lisa got down to business.

"All cell phones off and give them to me," said Lisa firmly as she looked at the two girls. Despite a few grumbles, they handed over the phones.

Susie's eyes smiled and she said, "I can see you have experience with teenagers."

Over the next two hours, Lisa conducted a thorough, "on the job" nursing tutorial. Firstly, she covered Susie's daily needs. Cleaning, defecating, medicating, feeding, changing clothes, exercising, avoiding bedsores, writing letters to friends and entertaining. Lisa's resounding message to the girls... *you must think of and anticipate the needs of the patient.*

Secondly, she explained the physical side of nursing. This is how you turn, lift and move the patient. She's heavy... this is how you leverage your body strength. However, such and such a move will require two or more people. If your mother requires injections or has a problem with an IV system, call me.

Lastly, Lisa explained to the girls that Susie's mental state was almost as important as her physical needs. Keep her mind stimulated... read to her, review old photograph albums, tell her about your day, discuss the news of the day, ask her to tell you about her hobbies and interests, make sure her TV remote control is nearby so she can watch TV, download audible books on tape so she can listen to stories, sign her up for online education classes and, where possible, wheel her around the house and ranch in her wheelchair. Getting her outside of the confines of the house will do wonders for her mental health. She'll breathe fresh air, hear the birds chirp and see the horses wander around the corral.

When Lisa's tutorial was finished, she told her daughter that she wanted to speak with Molly privately. Both girls looked exhausted, neither of them was used to listening to a two-hour lecture.

"Mom, I've got my car. I'll go home and get dinner started. Take your time," said Penny.

"Shall wonders never cease! Maybe I should conduct weekly tutorials," said Lisa, surprised with her daughter's offer to volunteer for a household chore.

Lisa sat opposite Molly at the kitchen table. Susie was sound asleep. "Sweetie, cancer is a devastating disease. It's spreading throughout your mom's insides. If three experienced nurses moved your mother, I guarantee you she'd moan or groan in pain at some point, no matter how careful they were. She knows you're doing everything you can to help her. When you stepped outside to say goodbye to Penny, your mom told me how proud she is of you."

Tears began to well in Molly's eyes. One tear after another began to trickle down her cheeks. The trickle became a river and her chest heaved. Molly's emotional damn burst and her head dropped to the kitchen table, atop her folded arms. "I'm so afraid, so afraid... ... that I'm going to hurt her," sobbed Molly.

Lisa stood and moved to Molly's side. As she patted Molly's back, she whispered, "Sweetie, you're helping your mom through some very tough times. I'd say you're doing a great job!"

Molly composed herself momentarily before her emotions again overwhelmed her, "I don't know what to do? I've never done this before!"

"I'm available at any time. Just give me a call and I'll come to the house or give you advice over the phone. And, when the time comes for more caregivers to support your mom, we'll recruit them together. I know your mother's friends and neighbors. You won't be alone."

A few months after Lisa's first visit, the need for more caregivers occurred. As promised, Lisa contacted Susie's friends and neighbors and organized a schedule that provided nearly around the clock bedside care for Susie. This support group not only cared for Susie, but they delivered meals for the family, helped with the shopping, the laundry and even assisted Molly with her homeschooling when the need arose.

The last few days of Susie's life drained what little emotional strength remained in Bill, Molly and Bobby. Lisa, along with hospice volunteers from Lisa's church, tried to prepare the Ridgers for Susie's final moments, knowing full well that was impossible. When that moment did arrive, Molly lay in bed with her mother, cradling and comforting her frail ninety-pound body. Bill, Molly and Bobby were paralyzed with sadness, but thankful that Susie passed away with grace and dignity in the comfort of her home.

April 2003

Even though Bobby knew his mother's final days were nearing, when she passed away, he slipped into a state of depression.

It took the support of his family and numerous sessions with an adolescent psychologist before he began to slowly overcome the darkness that had overwhelmed his mind. Though the loss of his mother would always be a source of sadness for him, he was better able to manage his emotions.

Gradually, his outgoing, social personality re-emerged and his popularity among his fellow high school students returned. He fraternized with underclassmen, which his longtime friends and classmates considered a monstrous social blunder, and he consorted with upperclassmen, which they viewed as simply bizarre. What his friends and classmates didn't fully grasp was that Bobby was endowed with an insatiable desire to socialize with people of all shapes, sizes, ages and colors... and he didn't give a hoot what others thought of his relationships.

For the younger underclassmen who he befriended, he was their champion. His friendship was like a psychological elixir that helped them overcome issues with low self-esteem and a strong desire to be accepted amongst their peers. His popularity was such that they dubbed him, "Mr. Popularity."

Behind Bobby's magnetic and gregarious personality was also the mind of a master prankster. With his wide circle of friends, he was often privy to mountains of unsolicited, inside information on the activities of most everyone in school. He always knew who was dating whom; who was doing well in class and who was not; and who was grounded by their parents and why. With these guarded secrets in hand, he orchestrated one prank after another. He was especially merciless on those who were cheaters, arrogant or bullies.

One of his most famous pranks occurred during his junior year. Bobby learned that one of his classmates, who was known to cheat on exams through the use of text messages, was enjoying the sun in San Diego during spring break. His girlfriend, who was also a co-conspirator in his cheating ring, remained in Dennis so she could model apparel in her first ever Western fashion show. Bobby's informant was an attractive, but shy, girl in his sister's sophomore class who regularly modeled with Molly in the annual fashion. She explained to Bobby that the new model and her mother had somehow deleted Molly's name from the model invitation list, which created an unexpected model opening that the new girl now filled.

The day before the fashion show, Bobby arrived at the venue to watch the models rehearse. His informant was sitting patiently in a chair besides the runway as the older girls practiced their routines. Bobby sneaked into a chair behind her and whispered conspiratorially, "Patty, it's Bobby."

Patty turned around and smiled provocatively. "Hey, Mr. Popularity! What brings you here?" she whispered back.

"I like beautiful women and beautiful women model clothes. So… I came to see you and ask a favor?"

"Name it," said Patty enthusiastically.

"See if you can borrow *you know who's* cell phone for a minute. Give her some excuse… you need to call your mom for a ride home… or, whatever!"

"OK. I know I can get it. I'll meet you backstage."

"Perfect! And, don't worry about a ride home. I'll make sure my beautiful accomplice gets home safely," said Bobby as he winked.

Patty beamed.

Five minutes later, Patty met Bobby backstage and handed him the cell phone. In less than a minute, he changed the girl's cell phone settings and blocked her boyfriends cell phone number so she wouldn't receive any of his return calls or text messages. He next typed in a text message and turned the cell phone towards Patty so she could read the proposed text message.

Patty's eyes smiled as she said, "You're wicked!"

He sent the text message to the boyfriend and a moment later deleted the message from the girl's "sent" message folder. The text message read,

Buzz off! Bobby Ridger is way more fun than you. I love him and he loves me.

When the girlfriend didn't respond to her boyfriend's frantic calls and text messages, the flustered boyfriend panicked. He bought an expensive, last minute airline ticket and flew home the next day. He arrived at the fashion show just as his girlfriend was prancing down the runway, trying to keep her balance in six-inch stiletto heels. Broken hearted and distraught, he vaulted onto the runway and raced towards her. She smiled affectionately as he approached. Unfortunately for him, he wasn't thinking clearly and he misunderstood the meaning of her greeting. *She's happy. The witch is in love with Bobby Ridger!* Mumbling, fumbling and stumbling, he crashed into the girl and they tumbled together into the second row of chairs. He cursed, she screamed and the audience roared with laughter. Thereafter, the boyfriend became known as "Buzz" and the girlfriend as "Screech."

February 2008...

Molly was now three weeks into her second semester at Montana State University in Bozeman, Montana, as a full time, twenty-one year old, sophomore. Molly and her best friend, Penny, commuted to the university together and shared the daily expenses of the approximately one hundred-mile round trip drive from Dennis to Bozeman. During Molly's first two years at the university, as a part time student, she enrolled in a wide range of courses. Her goal was to explore subjects that she hadn't been exposed to in high school like economics, teaching, anthropology and environmental science. In the end, she decided to double major in Animal Systems and Equine Science, two courses of study that prompted her to attend Montana Sate University in the first place. Eventually, she planned on obtaining a doctorate degree in veterinarian medicine.

The sun had set and the temperature was rapidly dropping when Penny dropped Molly off at her house one Wednesday evening after returning from "State." Molly sprinted to the front door of her house and hastily stepped inside. Before closing the front door she noticed that the outdoor thermometer read 10 degrees. No snow was forecast, but it would be another chilly night. She marched to her bedroom, threw her book bag and down jacket onto her bed, quickly changed into more comfortable jeans and slipped on a warm, quarter zip fleece jacket.

She heard her dad organizing dinner dishes in the kitchen. Everyone was hungry, including herself. Her first stop, however, was to check on Bobby. She quietly opened his bedroom door and peeked inside. He was lying on top of his bed sleeping, fully clothed. She tiptoed to his bedside, leaned over him and kissed him on his forehead.

His eyes opened immediately and he greeted her with a broad smile. "I just clicked off the TV. I was watching the news. No happy news to report. I must have fallen asleep. Did you have a good day?"

"Very good. I'll tell you all about it at dinner. I also want to hear how your appointment with Dr. Matthews went. Close your eyes now and rest. I'll get you in about thirty minutes."

"Will do, 'Sis.' You're the best," said Bobby, as he smiled and winked at her.

In the kitchen, her dad kissed her on the cheek and gave her a big hug. "I've set the dinner table. What else can I help you with?"

"I was thinking I'd whip up spaghetti and meatballs. How about making a dinner salad! You're the best sous chef in Dennis."

"And, you're the best head chef," said Bill smiling.

As they alternately began to pull food items out of the refrigerator,

Bill said, "John spent a couple of hours with Bobby this afternoon. Much of that time he was administering physical therapy to Bobby. The two of them really get along well together. He firmly believes that daily physical therapy will help Bobby."

"That was nice of him. I like him. He's a pretty down to earth guy."

Bill continued tentatively, "John believes that you'd be the ideal candidate to oversee Bobby's team of physical therapists."

"Right," said Molly indifferently, as she began to boil water for the spaghetti.

She then rumbled through the pantry looking for garlic cloves. Next, she began searching for the brick of Parmesan cheese.

After several long minutes of silence, Bill's patience crumbled, "Well, what do you think?"

"What are you talking about?" replied Molly, as she tossed small slivers of garlic into a hot frying pan smeared with olive oil.

"Oversee a team of volunteer therapists? Well, do you want to do it? I know that it was hard on you during Mom's final months, and now you're immersed with your college studies," said Bill sympathetically.

"It's no big deal managing volunteers. I've already got six volunteers lined up and given them their schedules. If we need more volunteers, there are two others who are on my waiting list. I've dropped one class at State and explained to the registrar why. He said he'd give me full credit for that class against next semester's tuition. The registrar mentioned that if Bobby was interested, they could offer him fully accredited correspondence courses on-line. He could get an undergraduate degree while he's recuperating. And, listen to this, there are no tuition fees for wounded veterans like Bobby. State is a very veteran friendly school."

Molly paused for several seconds as she washed her hands at the kitchen sink and looked out at the barn through the kitchen window. "You know Dad, this is the second time in five years that we've had this same conversation and nothing has changed.

"I appreciate the fact that you're sensitive to my previous experience with Mom and that you are concerned about my studies, but you have to understand that you and Bobby are my family, my only family. There are no surviving grandparents, no aunts or uncles. We're it! You, Bobby and me. I love you and Bobby with every fiber of my being. All else is secondary," said Molly emphatically.

Bill stepped to Molly's backside and hugged her. Holding her firmly, he said, "You are just like your, mom, Honey. Total unconditional love when it comes to family. I feel the same way."

... five months later, late May 2008

As the weeks, then months, of Bobby's physical therapy progressed, it became clear to Molly that his daily therapy sessions were yielding not only positive physical results, but improving his mental attitude as well. When her brother had left Balboa Hospital in San Diego and returned to the familiarity of his home, he constantly fought bouts of depression. Molly and Bill, like most other families who welcomed a wounded veteran home, were unprepared and unaware of the psychological issues that they might have to confront. Isolated at a ranch in Montana, Bobby was no longer surrounded by a supportive peer group of other wounded Marines.

For Bobby, his social interaction with his team of volunteers was as rewarding, if not more so, than his physical improvement. He thoroughly enjoyed the camaraderie he developed with each of his volunteer therapists as they pulled, tugged and massaged his legs and arms. Bobby gave each of his therapists a friendly nickname such as the "the bender," "the muscle seducer" and "magic fingers." Each of the volunteers gave him hope for recovery and he, in turn, made sure each of them knew how appreciative he was of their efforts. His heartfelt compliments, coupled with his absence of complaints, kept all of them dedicated to his recovery.

Bobby's slow, but steady improvement encouraged his volunteers. Each of them, from Molly's girlfriends to his dad's ranching buddies, gradually witnessed a growing miracle... some of Bobby's muscles were coming to life! As he got stronger each of the volunteers got more excited. But, none were more excited than Molly, who spent the most time with him.

Bobby's military doctors believed that he would be bedridden for the rest of his life. *Well, those damn doctors were wrong*, thought Molly. With the help and guidance of Dr. Matthews, his physical therapist and her team of volunteer therapists, her brother could turn his head twenty degrees in each direction and could raise his arms six inches. If he regained the use of his upper body, which was still a big *if,* he could get around in a wheelchair and become independent.

Bobby would show those military doctors what he was made of!

Molly quietly stepped into her older brother's bedroom. The early morning sunshine spilled across his bed. He slowly turned his head towards her and smiled as she approached. His eyes were clear and there was color in his cheeks.

"How are you feeling this morning?" she asked pleasantly, as she wiped her brother's face with a warm, wet face cloth.

"A little stiff from yesterday's exercises. Your friend Penny awakened some muscles in my arm and abused a few others in my shoulders. She's got a future as an 'enemy interrogator.' She could pry the truth out of anyone!" he said as he lifted, with great effort, both arms six inches off his bed covers. His arms collapsed back to his side after a moment. "Progress!" he said smiling.

"Stiffness is good a good symptom. Have you experienced that before?"

"Not really. That feeling has just occurred in the past few days."

"Well make sure that you relay that information to your chief therapist, Gail Henderson. She'll apprise Dr. Matthews of that. I'll be back in a minute I'm going re-wet this face cloth with more warm water."

When she returned and wiped his face, his response was immediate. "Umm! That feels *sooo* good, Sis! I didn't sleep well last night," said Bobby.

"Bad dreams again?"

"Yeah, but these dreams are new. Sights as bright and vivid as watching high definition TV from a foot away. And sounds as loud as sitting in front of a ten foot speaker at an outdoor concert."

"What kind of sights and sounds?" asked Molly.

"All bad stuff. Sudden explosions, fire, men screaming, body parts everywhere. If I could only switch the TV channels in my brain to something more soothing like the CMT country channel, I'd be OK. A live concert with Carrie Underwood or Taylor Swift headlining would be ideal," he said with his broad, engaging smile.

The moment he mentioned "live concert" Molly was overwhelmed with self-pity. *Why can I enjoy a concert and not him? Why, why, why?*

She and Penny were going to a mid-July Brad Paisley concert at Jackson Hole. Each of them had been saving money for their tickets since the concert date had been announced eight months earlier, and they'd bought front row seats. She began to weep.

"What's up, Sis? Did I say something wrong?" said Bobby sympathetically.

"No, no," she choked. "It's just that Penny and I are going to a... " Her crying increased and her shoulders heaved.

"Oh, yeah! You're going to a Brad Paisely concert. You told me about that."

Trying to ease her discomfort, he said, "I like his music. He's got a great voice, but I'd rather see a foxy lady sashay around the stage with high leather boots and a loose blouse than a guy 'strumin and chewin!'"

Once she collected herself, she corrected her brother, "He doesn't chew!"

"Whatever!" he said smiling. "Listen, 'kiddo,' you're going to be late for school. Would you raise my back rest and turn on the TV for me before you leave."

"Any particular channel?"

"Anything but ABC, NBC or CBS!"

"Let's see. How about the Versus channel? They have sports and out-door stuff," she said calmly, with her steady composure returning.

"Perfect. I think Pro bull riding is on this morning! You know a couple of my high school buddies are on that circuit. Damn fools are going to get their heads busted by those bulls. Why would anyone ever want to ride a bull?" he said disapprovingly.

Her eyes rolled at that comment. *But, joining the Marine Corps, requesting an infantry assignment and jockeying for a unit that was headed to Iraq, where the 'action' was, that was OK.* As she slipped out of his bedroom, she shook her head in disbelief at her brother's crazy logic.

She quickly straightened up the single story, ranch style house. Dishes into the dishwasher, coffee turned off and steaks out of the freezer for dinner. The sound of gravel crunching on the driveway increased her pace. She plucked her lunch bag from the refrigerator and slid it into her knapsack. Took a quick peek at her profile in the hallway mirror and skipped out the front door to a waiting pickup truck.

Penny was behind the wheel of the aged pickup. Molly slid onto the bench seat and rolled down the window. Penny turned the steering wheel sharply and stepped on the gas. A hailstorm of gravel sprayed the Ridger barn as the two college sophomores raced down the driveway creating a cloud of dust in their wake.

Molly leaned forward and spoke to Penny, "Bobby's got feeling in his shoulders. They were sore this morning. He said you'd be a great 'enemy interrogator'... your hands could pry the truth out of anyone!"

"Hot dang! Maybe I should massage a little enjoyment out of his lower body when you give me the green light," said Penny provocatively.

"Just the upper body for now, OK!"

Though Molly laughed, she knew there was more than a sliver of truth in Penny's comments. She'd had a crush on Bobby years before he joined the Marines.

Molly slipped her favorite CD into the CD player and a moment later the first few chords of Brad Paisley's song, "Waitin' on A Woman" filled the cab. Both girls sang in unison with their favorite singer.

When they arrived at State, Penny sped into a parking stall amidst the young cowboy's section of the parking lot. As she jammed on her brakes, sleepy eyed cowboys wearing dog-eared canvas jackets, blue jeans, scuffed boots and well-worn Stetson hats scattered in every direction. With her tires smoking, she slammed the trucks transmission into "Park" and revved the engine until her tachometer redlined. She coolly slipped her foot of the gas pedal, flicked the trucks ignition off and dropped the keys into her purse. Since high school, teasing tongue-tied, introverted cowboys was her favorite way of starting her school day.

Turning towards her best friend, Penny grinned mischievously, "Got to have the full attention of these *boys* when we walk to class! They look a little lethargic this morning."

All male eyes scrutinized the two sophomores, especially Molly, who was seemingly a head taller than Penny, as they marched across the campus. Penny was a short dynamo with curly brown hair that framed a pretty, youthful face filled with freckles. Penny's slender frame scurried to keep up with Molly who, with her long legs, easily outpaced her as she gracefully strode to class.

At five-foot ten inches in height with long, muscular legs, Molly was a tall, physically strong woman. Much of her physical strength was the result of carrying out ranching chores, horse back riding and cattle. She was the state's female cattle cutting champ for her age group. In light of her family's health history, she was also serious about her health and those matters that influenced her well-being. Exercise and diet, friendships, volunteer efforts and, of course, her absolute commitment to family were imbedded in her DNA. And, like her brother, she too was a non-conformist who didn't give a damn what others thought of her.

Her demeanor, on the other hand, was just the opposite of her brothers. She was an introvert who tenaciously guarded her privacy. However, her physical attributes… silky red hair, ample cleavage, perfect complexion and a cover girl face… were such that she was the constant target of uninvited male attention. In an attempt to eliminate this attention, she wore clothes and accessories that, she hoped, would conceal her figure and face. Each item she wore, however, seemingly had the opposite effect. Baggy blouses weren't baggy in the right places. Extra large glasses magnified rather than masked her emerald green eyes. And, a well-worn Stetson, which allowed her to hide her silky red ponytail under its crown, invited total strangers to investigate the mysterious face that hid below the hat's wide brim.

Her biggest attention getter and major wardrobe gaffe was wearing blue jeans throughout the school year. When she squeezed into a pair of jeans, every muscle, from her calves to her butt, bulged. Sleepy young cowboys were far from sleepy when they observed Molly's long, muscular legs march to class. Their admiring comments were all very similar…

Man, 'ole' Molly looks like she was poured into 'dem' jeans. Hardly any need for a saddle with those riding legs. Yep and a looker to boot!

To those young cowboys on campus who watched her stride dispassionately to and from class, she was an enigma. Was she a stuck up snob or a solitary soul who kept to herself?

They didn't know that at twenty-one years of age Molly had more experience dealing with family tragedies and life's challenges than many forty-year old married women with families. Therefore, it was no wonder that she displayed little interest in dating immature, pimply-faced males who wore torn clothes, couldn't speak a complete sentence and thought it was cool to have Red Bull drooling from the corner of their mouths. As both her father and brother would attest, she was a *take charge* kind of woman who believed in steering her own life path rather than having other's influence it. Unbeknownst to everyone, except her best friend, Penny, she compared her relations with admiring male suitors like that of cutting cattle. She chose the bulls, the bulls didn't choose her.

CHAPTER 6
HELENA, MONTANA

Early June 2008...

A tall man, in his early thirties, gracefully stepped through the double doors of the Montana state capitol building into the brilliant, noontime sunshine. As he did so, his cell phone began to ring from the inside pocket of his sharply cut Western blazer. He glanced at the caller identification screen on his phone and groaned, *What now?*

As he pressed the cell phone to his ear, the distant caller said, "We've had an incident, boss."

Moving off to the side of capitol building's front doors to escape the droves of state workers who were pouring out of the building on their way to lunch, the man growled, "What kind of incident?"

Long blonde hair that was carefully coifed flowed over the collar of the man's blazer. His piercing hazel eyes, muscular shoulders and expensive silk shirt drew unabashed, second looks from nearly every woman who swept past him on their way to lunch. He was used to their gawking stares, it reinforced his narcissistic image of himself. He'd overheard his colleagues in the capitol building quietly refer to him as the "Dandy." He liked the moniker and thought it quite appropriate.

"We had to eliminate someone last night who threatened to tell the feds about the activities of your antisocial Arabs… er, renters," said the caller glibly.

"Shit! How did this someone learn about the Arabs?" asked Dandy.

"Junior met a 'working girl' in a local gin mill a couple of days ago. She was passing through town on her way to a convention in Seattle and one thing led to another. You get the picture."

"No, I don't get the picture!"

"They hooked up for a couple of days. Too much booze and sex. Junior ran his mouth off and the chick saw some of the weapons. She threatened to spill the beans if we didn't give her $5,000 in traveling money," said the caller.

"A couple of days! Wait a minute. This doesn't sound like your typical one night stand. And, how could she have seen the weapons? "

"He was shacked up with her at the lodge."

"The lodge!" screamed Dandy, as he turned his back to the front doors of the capitol building. His stomach tightened and bile rose into his mouth. After a several deep breaths, he regained control of himself and his volatile temper.

"Yeah! The Arabs were away for a few days in 'Vegas,' so Junior had the whole place to himself. They are returning to the lodge this evening along with a boatload of new recruits that they are meeting at the Bozeman Airport. By the way, Junior said that the conference center, next to the lodge, looks like a fucking armory."

Through clenched teeth, Dandy said slowly, "No more visitors to the lodge. Got it?"

"Got it!"

Suddenly, Dandy's temper flared and he barked, "The Bozeman Airport! God damn it! I told them to use major airports so they wouldn't be so damn conspicuous. You were with me when I told them that. Why the fuck didn't you say something?"

"Junior just told me of their plans one hour ago. I'll remind them," said the caller.

Exasperated, Dandy said, "Make sure he damn well understands."

What the hell did it matter which airport the Arabs used? There were Arabs everywhere these days. Dandy could be a real asshole, thought the caller.

In a calmer tone, he added, "I've heard that the Arabs will be leaving in a week or so. They are supposed to clean up and take all their weapons with them, but we should double check. I don't want any busy body asking questions about a thousand brass shell casings laying around."

"A thousand shell casings? That's a laugh. Junior said the place had more shell casings laying around then an an Army rifle range."

"Once they're gone, inspect the place. Make sure it's completely clean, as in no indication of their activities."

"Got it!"

" How was this 'working girl' eliminated?" said Dandy dully.

"Junior popped her last night. Made it look like a hunting accident, but there is a slight glitch."

" Slight glitch? How so?"

"Junior dumped her body in a deep gully near the trailhead of one of the state's hunting access points. He figured no one would find her body and, if someone did, they would think she went hiking and was shot accidently in a hunting accident."

"And, the glitch?"

"A wolf or coyote dragged her body into the trailhead's dirt parking lot last night. Several hunters found her body there this morning and called it in over a CB radio that was in one of the hunter's trucks. We heard the CB report."

"Then what?" snapped Dandy.

"When we got to the parking lot, there were two Montana State Highway Patrolmen investigating the crime scene. Junior said it looked like a hunting accident. The 'staties' and hunters didn't buy his story."

"Why not?"

"The woman was wearing flats, skimpy clothes and was shot in the forehead with a small caliber pistol."

"Thus, she was clearly not going for a hike nor was she shot with a hunting rifle. Why was the Highway Patrol at the scene?" interrupted Dandy with growing irritation.

"Junior called me last night after he dumped her body. He didn't want to leave her car near her body. I told him to drive the car back to the main road and park it about a mile from the hunting access turn off. I thought we'd make it look like a hiker had parked along the side of the road and simply vanished. It happens all the time. He left the car unlocked and set her car keys under the front seat. I picked him up at her car. No one saw either of us."

Leaving the victims car unlocked with the car keys under the front seat was amateurish, thought Dandy. A hiker would have locked up his car and put the keys in his backpack, or hid it somewhere on the vehicle. He had the distinct impression that this murder was very much a spur of the moment occurrence and that Junior was either drunk or high on drugs when all this happened.

"Why the Highway Patrol's involvement?" repeated Dandy.

"Oh, yeah. The main road is a state highway. The 'staties' were investigating her unlocked, abandoned car along the highway when they heard the hunters call over their CB radio. They decided to check the dead body to see if it was connected to the abandoned car."

"And… "

"The 'staties' found her driver's license along with some cash in her bra. The license matched the registration of the abandoned car. We said we thought it was a local matter, but the 'staties' said that it was a state matter since both the body and car were on state property. They had already called the state's homicide investigative unit and the medical examiner by the time we got there. They said the medical examiner told them to take the body to Dennis."

Dandy grimaced. It would be child's play for an investigator to check the tire treads from the dead girl's car and discover that the car had been driven to and away from the crime scene. His partners were idiots.

"Anything else?"

"No, that's it. Just thought you should know," said the caller.

"I have a couple of questions. Was there any kind of struggle before Junior put her to sleep?" asked Dandy.

"You bet! Junior said the bitch fought like a caged lion. She scratched the hell out of him. She calmed down, though, when he pulled out his pistol."

"Where will the body be taken?"

"To the old ice house behind the funeral home in Dennis. They have a small refrigerated morgue in there. The state medical examiner is suppose to examine her tomorrow."

"You've got a busy night ahead of you then. Get one of those lawn blowers and blow away all the tire tracks at the crime scene. After that, torch the ice house," said Dandy.

"Geez, boss, me and Junior was planning on riding our 'hawgs' tonight, followed by a few 'brewskis' at Mickey's bar."

"No. Cleanup the crime scene and burn down the icehouse. I'm concerned that there may be some evidence on her body that links her to Junior."

" I doubt it. He said he checked her pockets pretty good."

"But, obviously not her bra. My main concern is DNA evidence like skin, blood, sperm, saliva and hair that can connect Junior to her. The medical examiner will likely find plenty of Junior's skin and blood under her fingernails as a result of her fighting and scratching Junior."

"DNA evidence? They can't check for that shit in Dennis," said the caller cackling.

The caller was right about the capabilities in Dennis, but the state certainly had the technology and labs to check for DNA evidence. It would be a simple matter for either the medical examiner or state investigators to take the samples that interested them back to their labs in Helena for analysis.

"'Boy,' do you have a TV?" said Dandy on the verge of screaming.

Being called 'boy' riled the caller. The last person who referred to him like that ended up in the hospital. *When the time is right, Dandy will regret calling him 'boy,'* thought the caller.

"Yeah, a big 60-inch plasma HD screen. What's that got to do with anything?"

"Have you ever watched any of the 'CSI' shows on TV?"

"Once in awhile. I like the dude on 'CSI Miami.' He has cool shades and there's always lots of hot chicks on his show."

"Do you know what 'CSI' stands for?"

The caller had had enough of the 'Q & A' he said, "No man, we watch mostly porn and 'biker' shit on TV. You tell me, Dandy man, what does 'CSI' stand for?"

The Dandy's vision blurred and his face burned. He wanted to scream *crime scene investigation.* Both of his men in Dennis were liabilities. He knew that he would eventually have to eliminate them, but for now, he had to keep them in place and happy. He took several deep breaths before he spoke.

"Forget 'CSI!' How about I give you and Junior an extra $1,000 each to cleanup the crime scene and torch the icehouse? I realize that it's a last minute, extra effort that will cut into your riding and drinking time. I feel bad about that, but we just can't risk the possibility that the medical examiner or the state police discover evidence that links Junior to this woman's death."

"That's cool! Now you're being fair. We'll take care of it, boss. Later!" said the caller as he abruptly hung up.

CHAPTER 7
WEST TEXAS

After neatly folding all of his uniforms into his footlocker and depositing the locker in the Camp Pendleton storage facility, Brice drove back to his quarters. Sitting on the edge of his bunk, he kicked off his Nike's, slipped out of his hooded sweatshirt and lay back on his bunk. Wearing only his olive-drab Marine Corps tee shirt and jeans, he closed his eyes and within minutes was softly snoring. Seven hours later, at 2300 hours, his alarm clock woke him from a peaceful sleep. He was rested and ready for his nighttime drive to Texas. He'd called the Powells beforehand and explained that he was coming home for a few days to relax and discuss his future. Worried, they asked if everything was OK. He assured them that all was well.

He enjoyed driving at night, less traffic, fewer speed traps and no intrusions on his thoughts. Though he'd been stopped once before for speeding on Interstate 40, just outside of Amarillo, Texas, the trooper, a former Marine, released him with a warning. Many of the state troopers patrolling Interstate 40 between Camp Pendleton, Texas and Oklahoma were former Marines. They knew that their home states provided a great many new recruits each year to the Corps. As long as the trooper didn't smell alcohol on the man's breath, a simple, but stern, warning was the least they could do for these future warriors.

Taking the northern route home added over one hundred miles to

Brice's trip, but it was far more scenic than the southern route. The southern route, Interstate 8 and 10, ran directly east of San Diego through Casa Grande, Tucson and Las Cruces before crossing the West Texas border. It was flat, desolate desert country and he'd seen enough of those landscapes in Iraq.

The sun was rising as he approached Flagstaff, Arizona. This was his favorite section of the trip. He turned off the CD player in his Dodge Ram 1500 pickup and lowered his window a couple of inches. Cool, crisp morning air tinged with the fresh scent of pine filled the cab. Sunshine twinkled through thick stands of Ponderosa Pines. Neither Southern California nor West Texas had forests like these. The Northern Arizona scenery and sweet smelling, morning air infused him with a Zen like clarity as his thoughts began to form.

The coach and Judith? They aren't mere acquaintances. They are a compassionate couple who love me as if I were their natural born son. Fortunately, they've been patient with me. Chet is right! It's time for me to reveal my innermost feelings for them. I love and care for them as much as they do for me.

Bobby Ridger, my best friend. I think of you every day, buddy! I should have been more assertive in Fallujah. I should have entered that house first. I do the dirty work. I clear the way for my men. I should have taken the 'point.' Somehow, I'll make it up to you, Bobby! Damn, damn, damn!

Annapolis? Four years of academics, discipline and physical training. I can handle that. Driving boats isn't my thing, but being a commissioned infantry officer in the Marines would be a dream come true. The Marine Corps is my life, my family. Maybe I could even play football again. Wouldn't that be a blast!

Chet Daniels! Who would I be and what would I be without him? I'm a lucky man to have a friend and mentor like him.

A majestic red rock battlement loomed through his windshield and interrupted his thoughts. He'd lost track of the time. Pinion juniper had now replaced the verdant pines that were far behind. Surrounding him were red rock cliffs that were like sentries standing guard over the high desert mesas. Unexpectedly, a commercial billboard rose from the desert and stained the scenery. It advertised a hotel in Las Vegas with a picture of a beautiful woman lounging provocatively beside the hotel's swimming pool. Though the billboard was out of place, the image of the woman stirred his thoughts.

Hmmm! I've never had a steady girlfriend, even in high school. No time for that in the Corps. However, a girlfriend I could write and call occasionally while at Annapolis would be nice. Yeah! That would be great, but, as Chet would say, 'let's not get the wagon ahead of the horse.'

As he approached his hometown later that day, the sun was setting in a cloudless, brilliant orange-red sky. To the east, he could see the fiery chimney of an oil refinery. Oil pump jacks dotted the dry, flat landscape on both sides of the straight, two-lane road. Careful to avoid speeding since he was no longer on Interstate 40, he strictly obeyed the posted speed limits as he entered each small town. Except for some friendly leniency towards the local residents, the police strictly enforced the speed limits in these towns with expensive fines. With California license plates on his pickup, he would be a juicy target for a local cop whether he was speeding or not. In general, Texas lawmen viewed Californians as liberal elitists who thought they were above the law.

Brice's left elbow rested lazily on the sill of his open window as he entered his hometown. Perspiration pasted his tee shirt to his chest. It was already hot and summer hadn't fully arrived. He could see that not much had changed since his high school graduation, six years earlier, as he cruised by the vacant petroleum building, the aged, brick bank building and the downtown shops. It was a few minutes after 8:00 PM and the downtown area was deserted. Though it was quiet and peaceful, he found the absence of people unsettling. The saluting, greeting, meeting, waving, honking of truck horns and back slapping that was ever present in the military energized him and kept daily life stimulating. He hadn't thought of it until then, but he realized that he liked being around people. At that moment, he'd welcome the opportunity of tooting his horn or giving a 'thumbs up' wave to an immature teenager dressed in 'grunge' with spiked purple hair. Though the possibility of seeing someone like that in this town, he knew, was as likely as seeing a flying pig.

On his way into the residential area of town, he passed the mission architecture of the old theatre and the limestone high school built in the late 1930's. Turning onto the Powell's tree lined street, he passed one tidy, single story brick house after another. Judith Powell was sitting in a wicker rocking chair on the open air front porch of their brick house. As he slowly steered his truck into their narrow driveway, she dropped her well-worn bible on a side table and leapt to her feet.

Wearing an oversized sweatshirt and mid calf exercise tights, she raced barefooted to the open window of his cab. Her face brimmed with happiness and relief. *He was here... home... safe.* Moments later, Jack bolted out of the house. The three of them hugged and kissed. Jack grabbed Brice's duffle bag from the bed of his truck as the three of them walked arm in arm towards the front door.

On the porch, Brice paused, "This can't wait a moment longer."

Jack turned towards Brice, studied his solemn expression and was reminded again of his directness. There was not an ounce of deception or guile in Brice. "Let's hear it!" he said evenly.

Brice gushed a proposal, "Could we three become a real family? I'll change my name. I'll sign adoption papers. If it's OK with you, I'll call you 'Mom' and 'Dad' or do you prefer Judith and Jack?"

Judith's face blushed, her eyes expanded to the size of silver dollars and her legs began to buckle. Jack dropped Brice's duffel bag and grabbed her before she fell to the porch. While supporting Judith, he pried open the front door with one foot and suggested they move to the living room. Once Judith and Brice were seated beside one another on the living room couch, Judith began to wail, sniffle and laugh hysterically. Brice was equally unrestrained as he rambled unintelligibly in broken sentences. Jack sat opposite them in an overstuffed chair.

When Judith and Brice's outpouring of emotions slowed, Jack intervened, "OK! OK! Let's slow down. Brice, you're an adult now and no longer a minor so adoption is not necessary. You can change your name if you like, but we don't care about that. You can call us Mom and Dad or Jack and Judith or whatever you please. An adoption certificate or a name change won't have any effect on how much Judith and I love you."

Jack's simple, heartfelt declaration triggered another round of hysteria in his wife. Her head swayed from side to side and a torrent of tears tumbled down her cheeks. She clutched Brice's arm with a mother's 'never leave me' firmness and blurted, "Yes, yes, that's it. We do! We will!"

Jack smiled and studied the two of them. If there was any restrained, mother-son bond before, which he doubted, it was clearly gone now.

He closed his eyes, rested his head on the back of his chair and said a silent prayer of thankfulness. While Brice and Judith were gushing over one another like excited teenagers, Jack drifted into a tranquil daydream. When he came to, fifteen minutes later, Judith's head rested on Brice's shoulder, her eyes were closed and a dreamy smile filled her face. He stood, walked to the couch and gazed at his wife lovingly. She was his petite, vulnerable prom queen.

Brice eyes were open. He saw Jack's expression and winked. Jack tousled Brice's short hair with his hand and grinned. He leaned towards Judith and whispered softly into her ear, "It's OK, Honey. Brice is here. He's staying with us."

She simply murmured.

Jack straightened and spoke quietly to Brice, "I'll get the grill going. We're having steaks."

He was tending to his charcoal barbecue when he saw Judith amble by the screen door into the kitchen. At the kitchen sink, she splashed her face with cold water and dried her face with a hand towel. Brice joined her in the kitchen and soon the two of them were giggling like best friends at a high school dance.

When Judith placed Brice's oversized dinner plate in front of him, he tucked into his steak, baked potato and large green salad as if it was his last supper. During dessert, his eyelids grew heavier and his head began to nod. His twenty-hour drive and the anxiety of discussing his family proposal with Jack and Judith had caught up with him.

"Why don't you head to bed, Brice. You've had a long day," said Judith.

"Yeah! Dinner was great. I love you," mumbled Brice affectionately as he staggered towards his old bedroom.

He rolled onto his bed, fully dressed, and closed his eyes. Minutes later, when Judith looked in on him, he was snoring peacefully. She unlaced and slipped off his Nike's and laid a blanket over him.

Jack and Judith silently sipped coffee at their kitchen table. "He's worn out," interjected Judith.

"That he is. That boy has two speeds… fast forward and off. He needs rest and some of your great home cooked meals," said Jack smiling.

"I agree. I'll keep my eye on him, Dad!"

Jack stood and Judith moved into his open arms. Jack whispered into his wife's silky hair, "We're very fortunate Mom. Though I may be a little biased, I think he's one in a million. He's a very special young man."

"Yes, I agree. However, from all the letters he'd written us over the years, I was worried that his family of friends in the Marine Corps would replace us. I thought that we'd eventually lose him."

"Every young man or woman needs a home to anchor them. Though he's grown up fast, particularly in Iraq, we're still home for him. He knows he's loved and safe when he's with us. Despite his warrior exterior, he still has the heart and soul of a vulnerable young man. His Marine Corps family won't always satisfy all his emotional needs," said Jack.

"Yes, I see. I hadn't thought of it that way," murmured Judith as she again began to weep with joy against Jack's muscular, broad chest.

During the next four days, Brice indulged himself. With no scheduled duties or set commitments, he was free to do as he pleased. First, he slept. After two nights of ten hour, uninterrupted sleep, his nightmares began to abate. Strengthening his body was his next priority. At a nearby gym, he designed an exercise regimen for his damaged arm and hand. He complemented this therapy with strenuous exercises for his legs, back and shoulders.

To his surprise, he realized that a near empty gym, absent a hundred other young, alpha Marines jostling for exercise equipment, showers and sinks, was a very civilized experience. In the solitude of the gym, he remembered a tip passed on to him by a retired gunny sergeant who spent hours each day power lifting in a small gym near Camp Pendleton. The gunny's tip... listening to soothing classical music rather than the hammering of hard metal or syncopated rap music would improve your workouts. The "gunny" believed that classical music relaxed the mind and body, which thereby allowed the individual to better focus on specific exercises. Brice found that he particularly enjoyed the free flowing tempo of Mozart's music. When he finished his weight lifting, Brice laced up his running shoes and hit the sticky blacktop for a five-mile run in the hot, midday sun. An ice cold, invigorating shower completed his daily workout regimen.

On his way home, he enjoyed cruising through downtown. He noticed that many of the mom-pop retailers who had anchored the downtown shopping area for years seemed to be barely hanging on. Their window displays seemed skimpy and their "Clearance Sale" signs more prevalent. *Online shopping and a newly opened, regional Wal-Mart were probably killing their business,* he thought. A steady stream of customers, however, were still dashing in and out of the old Ekerd's Drug Store, which was now named CVS. Those were the obvious differences in the downtown retail area. That and, of course, all the storeowners were six years grayer than when he'd left town to join the Marines.

At home, he'd join Jack and Judith for lunch at their backyard picnic table, which was situated in the cool shade of an old oak tree. Now that final exams at the high school were over, Jack's science teaching responsibilities were minimal so he was able to linger with Judith and Brice over a leisurely lunch. Reminisces of prior high school football seasons and players usually dominated their light conversation. Jack and Judith did most of the talking during these meals. Brice would occasionally ask how a former classmate was doing, but for the most part he was simply listening and eating. When Judith served his favorite lunch of cold chicken, a large green salad and huge portions of steamed vegetables, he was especially silent as he devoured the meal. After a final glass of sweet, iced tea and a large bowl of sliced fruit, Brice would begin to glance covetously at the shaded, nearby hammock that swung invitingly from a large oak tree.

Jack and Judith quickly caught on to Brice's longings. As they stacked empty plates, he would offer to help clean up. They'd propose that he relax in the hammock. In minutes, he'd be sound asleep. Unbeknownst to the young Marine was the psychological healing he was experiencing in the safety and solitude of the Powell's quiet backyard. Thousands of miles separated him from the prospect of dodging enemy bullets, making snap do or die tactical decisions and dragging seriously injured men to safety.

Hours later, the sound of clinking pots and pans from the kitchen would stir Brice from his siesta. Once he'd rubbed the sleep out of his eyes, he'd saunter into the kitchen. He'd give Judith a hug and kiss on the cheek and apologize for not helping her cleanup after lunch.

"Brice, you're healing. Mentally and physically you've been through a lot. We all have times when we have to recharge our batteries. Resting and relaxing is more important for you now than helping us with a few dishes," said Judith affectionately.

He simply nodded and stretched. It amazed him how thoroughly refreshed he felt after an afternoon nap. Previously, he'd thought naps were the exclusive domain of old people. As much as he enjoyed the benefits of a nap, he knew he'd have to keep this little secret to himself if he returned to active duty. There was no doubt in his mind that the Corps would take a dim view of such slothful behavior.

In the kitchen, Judith enjoyed showing her sleeping giant how to cook and prepare salads. She knew most young men didn't have the slightest interest in preparing food, other than perhaps barbecuing steaks or flipping burgers while drinking beer. Brice, however, was different. Though he was curious about food groups and their preparation, he was particularly interested in nutrition. He peppered Judith with questions about calories, fats, sugars, fiber and protein. Clearly, he wanted to know what would make him stronger and healthier. She answered his questions using his truck as an analogy... fuel, octane levels, engine oil, batteries, exhaust and compression. He understood those concepts.

Though Judith knew Brice's gym workouts and running burned up large numbers of calories, it was hard for her to grasp his calorie burn rate while humping a seventy-pound, or more, backpack in 100 degree and higher desert temperatures. Physically, not many men could handle such demands. Add to that the daily mental stress of being responsible for a group of men who were your friends, getting shot at any moment or stepping on an invisible IED and it was easy to see how fourteen to sixteen months of continuous combat could stretch a young Marine's body and mind to its physical and mental limit.

Judith's dinner menu was a departure from lunchtime salads and fruit. It reflected the size of Texas... big steaks with big potatoes. Texas men liked their steaks blood red and they didn't like to be disturbed once their steak was set before them. Judith was accustomed to Jack's silence during dinner and Brice was no different. While sitting opposite Brice one night at dinner and nibbling on a small portion of her medium rare steak, Judith wondered if this dinner silence was unique to Texans. Then she remembered visiting her sister and her husband several months earlier in Oklahoma. 'Sooner' males partook in the same ritual.

After dinner, Brice and the Powells would regularly relax in front of the television and watch a rented movie. Brice knew that most of his fellow Marines would disapprove of his behavior. They, in sharp contrast, would likely spend their leisure time bar hopping while they consumed large quantities of alcohol. Burning up brain cells and turning one's guts inside out didn't appeal to Brice. He'd seen what it had done to his dad. His relaxing and mundane routine in the intimacy of the Powell household was just fine with him.

A front-page story in the town's weekly newspaper interrupted Brice's private and quiet visit. The article described the Marine Corps heroics of an alumnus from the local high school and it sparked a flood of personal appearance requests… dinners, speaking engagements and even an autograph signing at a Little League game. He asked Jack and Judith to screen the invitations. After dinner each night, the three of them discussed the pros and cons of each invitation. In the end, Brice realized that accepting one invitation over another would create resentment amongst a multitude of well-intentioned organizations. He elected to accept only one invitation and his choice was easy. He asked Judith to accept his high school's invitation to speak at their commencement service on June 3, 2008, which was only two days away. Everyone in town usually attended the service that was held at the school's football stadium. He knew exactly what he'd speak about.

The next morning Brice quietly slipped out of the house at 4:00 AM. He left a note on the kitchen table.

Hiking to the mountain for the sunrise. Back by mid afternoon. How about dinner at Cattlemen's Restaurant tonight? My treat! Love, Brice

Jack was the first to read Brice's note. He smiled knowing his wife would like Brice's hiking plans. The *mountain* was a two hundred foot rock formation on a prominent plateau. It was the highest natural formation within fifty miles of town and all the locals referred to it as the *mountain*. He and Judith had made the twelve-mile round-trip hike numerous times. Jack had even proposed to Judith atop the *mountain*. Watching the sunrise across the quiet, purple plains from its summit was always a renewing and sentimental event for both of them.

Jack made a mental note to make a reservation at the Cattlemen's Restaurant later that morning.

It was dark when Brice parked his truck next to the trailhead. When he stepped out of his truck, the sound of his boots crunching on the sandy, rocky terrain reminded him of the badlands of Iraq. Moving to the bed of his pickup, he pulled out a headlamp from his windbreaker and clicked on the red light. He lowered the tailgate and examined his hiking gear.

He was alone and the desert was silent. The fluttering wings of a nearby bird taking flight startled him. Involuntarily, all of his senses kicked into high gear. Adrenaline surged through his body and he froze.

What spooked that bird? Was there someone out there sneaking into his lines?

A moment later, he chided himself for the absurdity of his reaction. He forced himself to take several deep breaths.

Damn it! This is a recreational hike in West Texas. No need to watch out for infiltrators or ambushes. There will be no killing today! Easy now, take it easy!

His anxiety lessened for a minute before he found himself unconsciously scrutinizing his hiking gear as though he were heading into combat. Boots double laced and canteen full. Moving to his pockets he felt… flashlight in left cargo pocket, pocketknife and small compass in right cargo pocket and a couple of protein bars stuffed into the chest pocket of his light windbreaker. He subconsciously shook himself like a wet dog. All his gear was secure, nothing rattled. Some habits were hard to break.

He locked his truck, turned off his headlamp and folded his arms as he leaned against the side panel of his truck. He looked skywards, stars sparkled brilliantly in the dark sky. A sliver of the moon lay low in the western sky. It's shape reminded him of the crooked smile of one of his men. The air was clean and cool. He breathed deeply. Peaceful country.

With his eyes now acclimated to the darkness, the light sandy trail was just visible against the darker, bordering brush. His pace was brisk and silent as he weaved between the tumbleweeds and desert scrub brush. Forty minutes into his hike, the trail dropped into a deep gully. He pulled out his flashlight and cupped his hand around the red beam of the flashlight. Almost immediately, he shook his head in exasperation, *Damn, bright white light is OK!* He examined the trail. There was only one way down the steep slope of the gully.

How many times, in the blackness of the night, had he and his men waited silently at the edge of just such a gully, straining to hear the slightest of unnatural sounds? A hundred times, two hundred? His patience and caution had avoided disaster on a number of occasions. Quietly flipping the safeties off their weapons, his men would soundlessly inch their way down the steep trail following nothing more than the footsteps of the man ahead of him.

Standing at the edge of the gully, he thought of his men. He missed them. Suddenly, soft whispers rose from the empty desert behind him.

Sarge, hear any bad guys?

Do the choppers know the coordinates of our pick up point?

Is it my turn to take the point?

He paused before he spoke to the shadows.

Am I losing my mind, boys?

Heck, no Sarge! You always looked out for us. Now, it's our turn to look out for you. We can come and go as you please, Sarge, but rest assured, we'll always have your back.

He turned towards the voices, but there was nothing there. Those were his men. He recognized their voices. Was he losing his mind! Maybe he did have PTSD! As he continued his hike towards the *mountain*, their quiet footsteps followed him.

A half-mile away from the rock formation the eastern sky began to lighten. He reached the summit just as the sun rose over the horizon. The soft voices and quiet footsteps that had followed him disappeared into the purple plains. He rested against a large boulder, mesmerized by the heavenly canvas above. Oranges, reds and pinks spilled across the sky in an ever-changing palette of colors. Beauty, safety, solitude… and precious memories of best friends wounded or killed in action washed over him.

As he thought of his men, images from a dormant recess of his brain began to rise into his consciousness. The face of one man and then another appeared clearly in his mind's eye, two of his best friends. Each had died in his arms. Tears streamed down his face. His chest heaved. Years of repressed and sad memories of friends injured or killed in action poured from his soul. He stood and with outstretched arms roared at the heavens, over and over, "Why them and not me?" When his cries subsided, he collapsed against the boulder and spoke softly, "Boys, you deserve the attention, not me. I'm going to talk about all of you tomorrow at the commencement services. None of this public speaking or notoriety was my idea. After my speech, I'm going to visit Bobby Ridger. I'll send him your regards. I miss all of you."

*

The instant Brice opened the front door of the restaurant for Jack and Judith, he was relieved that Jack had made a reservation. The place was packed! The owner and his son, whom Brice had gone to high school with, rushed to his side. Wide smiles filled their faces as they each shook his hand enthusiastically.

"Brice, Cattlemen's is proud to have you and the Powells dine with us tonight. We've been expecting you and want you to know that the boys from the VFW (Veterans of Foreign Wars), our loyal customers and my restaurant are covering your tab tonight," said the owner as he turned towards Jack and Judith and flashed a wide, toothy smile.

Brice protested, "That's really not necessary."

"Oh, but it is and it's already been taken care. Please enjoy your dinner," he said as he performed an expert about-face and led them to the dining room.

Cattlemen's Restaurant was an institution in this small, West Texas town. The original steakhouse, built in the early 1900's, was destroyed by fire fifty years earlier. Fortunately, much of the memorabilia in the original steakhouse was rescued and it was now displayed throughout the larger, newer steakhouse. Décor aside, the main reason for the restaurants success over the years were its, moderately priced, but perfectly prepared, large servings of beef. Many of the steaks were eighteen ounces or larger. Some cuts were perfectly dry aged and others fresh from slaughter. All the dishes were accompanied with a huge Idaho russet potato and warm loaves of freshly baked bread. A single chicken entrée was the alternative on the menu.

The owner guided them along a wide corridor that led to the main dining room. Massive Texas longhorn skulls hung on each sidewall. Beneath each skull were signed photographs of area rodeo riders, team photos of the high school's state champion football teams and several oil paintings of West Texas landscapes. At the end of the corridor, the owner stopped in front of a 8"X10" framed, faded photograph of four men on horseback. Below the photo was a browned, newspaper clipping. The aged headline and article were nearly illegible, but Brice and the Powells knew the gist of the article. They had heard the story countless times before.

The owner tapped the frame with his knuckle as he spoke, "My great grandfather is on the far left next to two Texas rangers. The man on the right with his hands tied behind him was a cattle thief. In 1905, he stole cattle from my grandfather's ranch. The rangers and my great grandfather tracked him down and brought him in. The judge found him guilty the next morning and we hung the bastard that afternoon in front of the courthouse. Texans don't take kindly to thieves, especially cattle thieves."

The owner threw his shoulders back with an extra measure of pride as he finished his customary, but never tiresome, story of his family's contribution to West Texas justice. Jack and Brice thought there was also a subtle warning to first time customers that skipping out on your tab could be dangerous to your health. *His great grandfather's six-shooter was probably well oiled and loaded in a handy location near the cash register,* thought Brice.

Walking through the busy dining room, the owner directed them to an ancient wooden booth. The booth and tabletop were made of well-worn, oak planks. Red cushions adorned the benches and backrests. A dozen or so identical booths were located along the window line. These west facing window booths were the premier tables, especially at sunset. Other than a few distant oil rigs, a nearby cattle chute and a dilapidated blacksmith shack, the diners could enjoy an unobstructed view across the plains. The sun he'd seen rising fourteen hours earlier was now dipping below the horizon.

Before Brice could seat himself, the Marine Corps hymn boomed from the restaurant's sound system. A dozen older men wearing VFW caps stood and began singing the hymn. Brice stepped towards the nearest man and put his arm around his shoulder.

"My singing's not the best," said Brice.

All the other restaurant patrons stood as well, nearly a hundred in total, and joined in the singing.

"Who cares about the tune! This song is about Marines and 'esprit de corps.' Semper fi!" bellowed the man as he sang, off tune with the others.

After the singing, Brice rejoined the Powell's and slid into the booth next to Judith. "Well, well," said Judith, as she wiped the tears from her eyes with a Kleenex. "That was a first for this town."

Jack was shaking his head laughing. "I haven't seen those guys expend that much energy in the last twenty five years. They were really worked up." He looked at Brice and added, "...and deservedly so!"

Brice smiled absently. The camaraderie and excitement of the moment caused him to reflect upon *friends not present*. Grief stabbed at his warrior heart. He turned away from the diners and gazed wistfully westward through the large bay window. Daylight's journey was near its end. Only a sliver of red, gold brilliance lit the horizon. Solemn, purple shadows stretched across the peaceful prairie.

The day is done, boys, but not my memories. You men were truly the best!

During their dinner, a steady stream of Jack and Judith's friends, Brice's former classmates and total strangers stopped by their table to chat and offer their appreciation for Brice's military service. Between visits, they devoured perfectly cooked, rare porterhouse steaks. Once dessert and coffee were served, the restaurant owner strategically positioned himself near their booth to redirect many of the now inebriated well-wishers to the bar. It gave Jack, Judith and Brice time to chat in private.

"After my speech at the high school tomorrow, I've been thinking of leaving for Dennis, Montana to visit Bobby Ridger," said Brice.

Though the Powells hoped Brice would stay with them a few days longer, they knew a visit with his closest friend, Bobby Ridger, would be good for both young men.

"I know he's been on your mind," said Jack agreeably. "Anything particular you want to discuss with him or will this just be a social visit?"

Brice sipped his black coffee and took a few moments to collect his thoughts. "I still feel awful about what happened to him. I should have been the first one in that house in Fallujah. A squad leader leads from the front."

Jack mentally shifted gears from surrogate father to football coach. During twenty-five years of coaching young men on the football field, Jack had become adept at dealing with their impressionable psyches. Never would he nor his coaches ever point to an individual's dropped pass, fumble or missed field goal as the reason for the team's loss. Though a breakdown on the field may have occurred at an inopportune time, he would always patiently explain to disgruntled teammates, boosters or the news media that there were a hundred other plays during the game which influenced the game's final outcome.

His constant mantra was that football was a team sport consisting of eleven individuals. Each individual played to the best of his abilities within the framework of a team. All of them, at one time or another, during the course of a game would make a mistake. To expect otherwise was unrealistic. As a team, they would win together and lose together.

In this context, Jack asked firmly, "Who was the point man at that time?"

"Bobby!"

"Was it his job to enter the house first?" asked Jack.

"Yes."

"Was it your job as the squad leader to position the rest of your men?"

Brice didn't respond.

"In countless letters to us, you've described your responsibilities in situations like this. The importance of setting up a mobile perimeter is to protect your rear and ensure your men aren't being drawn into a trap or ambush from the enemy hiding in the other buildings, rooftops and alleys," said Jack as he paused and looked hard at Brice.

Brice's mind churned with gruesome memories. The chaos, confusion and viciousness of urban warfare that could, and often did, explode in the most benign of settings could bend and break the psyche of the toughest Marine. Brice's head dropped and his shoulders slumped.

"Yes," said Brice in a whisper.

"Did you have any indication there was an IED in the house?"

"No. We even heard a baby crying inside," said Brice.

"OK. Listen carefully, I'm going to say three things," said Jack dispassionately. "First, in football, business or combat, all a coach, a manager or squad leader can ask of his team is that they perform their assigned duties to the best of their ability. Assigned duties! A football lineman isn't assigned the task of returning punts or kick-offs. His job is to block for running backs who can return a kick one hundred yards for a touchdown. A corporate secretary isn't responsible for deciding major deal points during the final negotiations of a multi-million dollar business transaction.

She or he is on the transaction team to ensure that their company presents accurate information to the opposite party.

"A squad leader, like you at the time, received countless hours of field and classroom instruction on how to lead your men. You also advanced through the ranks based on your actual performance. As a squad leader, you were in charge of the tactical deployment and fire control of three four-man fire teams. I know that all good Marines lead by example, but that doesn't mean a squad leader, or for that matter your company commander, Captain Daniels at that time, is the 'first one through the door' into an enemy stronghold. I know you were the 'first one through the door' at one time, but as a squad leader your responsibilities and 'assigned duties' changed, they became broader in scope. You were responsible for the lives of twelve men.

"Second, shit happens! I've coached hundreds of games and thousands of practices. Players will block and tackle exactly as I've coached them and injuries still occur. Head injuries, blown knees and broken bones. My point is that injuries are a part of football, failed transaction negotiations are a part of business and casualties are a part of combat. You did everything by the 'book' in Fallujah to the best of your abilities and a bad thing happened. There are no guarantees in life.

"Third, there is the issue of survivors guilt! Major Daniels explained the ramifications of this emotion to Judith and me during our last visit with you at Camp Pendleton. He explained that it's OK to tell an injured friend from your squad or platoon, us or whomever, how you feel about the circumstances surrounding their injury. It helps the healing of your friend and it will help you as well. Keeping your feelings bottled up inside can be destructive. Talking about matters like this is a sign of strength, not weakness."

Brice sat still as he considered Jack's advice. He had heard much of this same counsel before from Chet and his counselors at Camp Pendleton, but it felt more authentic and less instructional seated intimately in a restaurant booth in his hometown with Jack and Judith. Survivors guilt, be it for Brice or anyone else, was no minor matter. It could become a gnawing, festering reaction that for some ended in suicide. Unbeknownst to Brice, the other men in his squad battled the same sense of guilt. They all repeatedly questioned their actions on that fateful day. *Why Bobby Ridger and not me? Was he strong and I weak? Was he brave and I scared?* The answer to their second-guessing lay in Jack's earlier admonition… shit happens!

A single tear rolled down Brice's cheek. Judith put her arm around him as she began to cry. It was hard for Jack to imagine the mental anguish a young Marine suffered when a close friend was injured or worse, died. The tough, Texas high school football coach kept a stiff lower lip as tears welled in his eyes as well, and he reflected on the trials of combat for a young man in his late teens or early twenties.

What these young Marines go through is unbelievable. Accounts of their courage and bravery are headline news in every newspaper, magazine and TV news broadcast in the country. But, until you see a Marine's emotions with your own eyes, you don't have a clue about their strength of character or the bond these men have with one another.

Time passed slowly for each of them as they struggled with their emotions.

Judith finally broke the silence. "No more tears tonight. My tear ducts are bone dry," she said as she held Brice's arm tight to her side.

Brice nodded silently and smiled at both Jack and Judith. Before he could agree with Judith, his cell phone rang. The caller identification was Major Daniels. His posture stiffened and his mind shifted to Marine Corps bearing.

As he moved to leave the booth and speak in private, Jack raised a hand indicating he could stay. "You can take the call here if you like. It's OK with us, if it's OK with you!"

Brice relaxed, resumed his seat and answered the call. "Yes sir, Major Daniels," said Brice firmly.

"Brice, let's use first names again, OK!"

"Yes sir, er, yes Chet."

They exchanged idle chitchat. How was your drive? Have you been able to relax? Getting any local news media attention? Do the Powells have new titles?

"I'm with 'Mom and Dad' now at a restaurant. I took your advice. Thanks, Chet."

"Please send them my best regards. Am I interrupting your meal?"

"No, we were just having coffee and a good cry."

" A good cry. Are you feeling OK?" asked Chet tentatively.

Brice smiled as he looked at Jack, "I'm feeling better now. I was talking with Mom and Dad about what happened to Bobby Ridger and… ." After a moment's hesitation and a deep breath, he added, "Dad gave me much the same counsel as you have."

"Shit happens!" said Chet.

"Exactly."

"Struggling with survivors guilt is no minor matter. In time, you'll get better," continued Chet.

"I know."

"Are you keeping busy? Clearing your head? Resting and relaxing?"

"Listen to this daily routine," said Brice smiling. "Three great home cooked meals, ten hours of uninterrupted sleep, a light workout in an empty gym, nightly movies at home on a big couch and no commitments."

"It sounds like what I've been recommending you do for the past three years."

"We're getting the 'red carpet' treatment tonight at a local steakhouse, Cattlemen's. The restaurant and the local VFW paid for our dinner. And tomorrow, I've been invited to be one of the speakers at my high school's commencement service."

"What will you talk about?" asked Chet.

"Character!"

"Why am I not surprised? I'm sure your talk will get everyone's attention. Listen, on a separate note, I wanted to check with you to see if you've given any further thought to Annapolis?"

Brice unconsciously straightened in his seat and said firmly, "Yes, sir, I have. I'd be honored to attend, if they'll have me."

Jack and Judith exchanged questioning glances.

"That's great news, Brice. And, here is even better news. Col. O'Brien just called me. The superintendent of the academy personally reviewed your application and said he had an opening for you in the class of 2012 if you decided that's what you wanted. So, you're in! O'Brien will be quite pleased to hear of your decision. "

"Really, 'no bullshit, GI?'" blurted Brice.

Chet laughed deeply, " 'No bullshit, GI.' However, there are a couple of matters you have to take care of. One, O'Brien, not Annapolis, would like you to schedule an appointment with a psychologist at the VA

(Veteran's Administration) outpatient clinic in Bozeman, Montana. I've got the name of the psychologist which I'll text you. I think the colonel wants to be doubly sure that he's not sending a half-crazed 'Rambo' type Marine to his alma mater. It's a lot of hooey if you ask me, but orders are orders."

Brice laughed at the thought and said, "A VA 'shrink' in Bozeman!"

"A psychologist! Take it easy. This is a formality. You also get paid for doing this along with travel time to and from the psychologist's office. For a one hour appointment, you save at least a couple of days of leave," said Chet.

"A couple days of free leave! That's nice! I appreciate you looking after my best interests."

Chet laughed aloud at Brice's reply. *The kid still didn't get it! If someone saved your life, common sense dictated that you would naturally be indebted to that person for the rest of your life.*

"Gunny, there is a very long list of Darkhorse Marines at Camp Pendleton, myself included, who will look after your best interests until their dying day," said Chet sincerely.

"OK, OK! I get the picture," said Brice casually.

"I wonder if you really do!"

"Whatever! I'll schedule the appointment, but how did you arrive at that location?"

"I figured you were going to see Bobby Ridger in Dennis, Montana and Bozeman is less than an hour away. It was simple."

"You can read my mind Chet," said Brice innocently.

"And you mine. One other thing, and you may not like this, but you must report back here to Camp Pendleton by June 24 so we can give you your new orders and transportation vouchers to Annapolis."

"June 24! That's three weeks from now. I thought I had sixty days of leave?"

"You did! But enlisted inductees muster at Annapolis on June 30."

"Is this a remedial summer school class for the enlisted men?"

"Hardly, Brice. It's the United Sates Naval Academy. There is no such thing as summer vacation at a service school. You and all the other plebes, enlisted men and otherwise, will report on or close to June 30.

Your formal induction into the Navy will be on July 2, 2008. According to O'Brien, you'll spend 99% of your first year at the academy."

"Chet, you sometimes feel like a big brother. I appreciate everything you've done for me. I'll make it back to Camp Pendleton by June 24, and I'll meet with the 'shrink' in Bozeman."

"I like you thinking of me as a big brother. Like a little brother, you just need some guidance from time to time. I'll call O'Brien back. Lt. Col. Adair and I were worried the colonel might force us out of the Corps if we couldn't persuade you to go to Annapolis. I'm glad it didn't come to that."

"You're kidding right!"

"Hey, this is the Marine Corps. Marine Corps colonels are used to having their way," said Chet smiling over the phone.

"I get the picture," said Brice.

A soft ring tone interrupted their conversation.

"Got to take this call, Brice. Guess who?"

"The colonel. Please thank him for me."

"Will do. Bye."

Jack and Judith looked intently at Brice.

"Honored to attend, remedial summer school, VA psychologist in Bozeman. Do you mind filling us in, Honey, on what's going on? Are you OK?" asked Judith cautiously.

"I hope you haven't volunteered for some super secret, suicide mission," said Jack with a note of concern.

Brice laughed heartily. Both Jack and Judith looked at one another questioningly. Even the restaurant owner turned to see what caused Brice's loud outburst.

Playfully, Brice turned to Jack, "Would you say attending Annapolis is suicidal?"

"It depends on what you'd be training for? That's a very secure place. It's not an open campus like the University of Texas," said Jack tentatively.

"What if I studied at Annapolis?"

"Studied what?" probed Jack.

"Seamanship, history, nuclear engineering… "

"Nuclear bombs! Oh no!" erupted Judith in horror.

Brice's hearty laugh exploded again.

"OK. Hold on everyone. I'm not going to teach bomb making, nor am I going to learn how to make bombs," said Brice lightly.

"Thank God!" sighed Judith.

"I've been accepted to the United States Naval Academy as an incoming plebe."

Jack and Judith looked at him with blank faces. They still didn't comprehend what he'd just said.

"Once I'm inducted, I'll be a first year midshipman," said Brice.

"But you're a gunnery sergeant in the Marine Corps! I don't get it," said Jack.

"Each year the service academies… Annapolis, West Point, Air Force, Coast Guard… accept 98% of their incoming freshman class from graduating high school applicants. The other 2% are active duty enlisted personnel whom their division commanders have nominated and who meet their service academies entrance qualifications. As you know, the Marines are part of the Navy. In my case, my regimental commander, Col. O'Brien, nominated me for admission to Annapolis with endorsements from my battalion commander, Lt. Col. Adair, and my company officer, Major Chet Daniels."

"Do you take the entrance exam on June 30, followed by remedial summer school classes? Oh, I hope you get in!" gushed Judith.

In deference to Judith, Brice politely contained his laughter.

"If you and Jack remember, once I moved in with you during my sophomore year in high school, I made the honor roll every semester. I also received high scores on my SAT exams that I took my senior year. Annapolis waived my requirement to take their entrance exam and accepted me based upon my high school grades and prior SAT scores."

"But didn't you say something about summer school to Major Daniels?" asked Jack.

"Yes, I did. But it's not summer school in the traditional sense. It's plebe summer, which is physical training and indoctrination into the Navy. I'm required to attend it like all other incoming inductees. I check into Annapolis on June 30, and will be inducted into the Navy on July 2. Just about one month from now. I hope you can come to my induction at Annapolis. It's a big deal. You're invited."

Jack's face brightened for the briefest of moments before his steely gaze returned, "Tell us more about this VA 'shrink' in Bozeman!"

With a serious expression, Brice began, "I've been having problems sleeping because of flashbacks and nightmares. Before I left Camp Pendleton, I met with both a psychologist and a psychiatrist on the base to discuss it. According to them, my nightmares and flashbacks were caused by my cumulative combat experiences and physical exhaustion. They and Major Daniels believed that if I took sixty days of leave, it would help me decompress mentally while I regained my strength. I hadn't taken any leave in years. I was about ready to lose some of my accrued leave anyways, so it seemed like a 'win win' proposition all the way around. In retrospect, I can't believe how worn down I was. I feel like a new man now."

"Flashbacks and nightmares. Oh dear!" said Judith as she took Brice's hand in hers.

"The good news is that in the last few days I haven't had any flashbacks or nightmares. Taking this leave and staying with you has done wonders for me both mentally and physically. I've also quit taking the sleeping pills they gave me. "

"These flashbacks and nightmares sound like a serious matter," said Jack.

"Well, I've learned more about them from counseling. And yes, they can be very serious. The message I got from both the psychologist and the psychiatrist was somewhat the same. The mind is like a muscle. It needs exercise and rest. I haven't rested mine in years. Further, it can be damaged like any other body part. In which case, it needs time to recover and strengthen itself. The recovery time for each person is different as is the emotional trauma that caused it. Some soldiers recover quicker than others and some never recover. All of this falls under the broad category of PTSD, which stands for post traumatic stress disorder. In my case, my doctors and Chet Daniels felt that I had mild symptoms of PTSD which were aggravated by physical fatigue."

"Did your doctors explain to you that these flashbacks and nightmares may never completely disappear?" asked Jack.

"Yes, they did. However, their thinking was that if I simply took a month or so of leave, my flashbacks and nightmares would likely disappear. They also stressed, like you did earlier tonight, that openly discussing my feelings and emotions is quite therapeutic."

"You're following their advice," said Judith with motherly concern in her voice.

"Yep, I already feel like an invincible Marine again," he said grinning.

"Not so fast! 'Likely disappear!' Why then the visit with the VA 'shrink' in Bozeman?" asked Jack inquisitively.

"Just precautionary! Col. O'Brien may have called in a few favors on my behalf to get me admitted. He wants to make sure he's sending a 'stable plebe' to Annapolis." Brice preferred the use of "stable plebe" rather than Chet's reference to a "half crazed, Rambo Marine."

"OK! I hear what you're saying, Brice. That's all great news. But, in the future, listen to your body and mind! They will tell you when they need a rest," said Jack evenly.

"Yes, Dad. Can you and Mom make it to my induction?" asked Brice excitedly.

"Brice, are you saying that you've been accepted to Annapolis and that you will start classes there on July 2?" asked Judith cautiously.

"It's actually summer training, followed by classes in the fall. But, yes Mom. I've been accepted!" said Brice.

Judith turned her head into his shoulder and hugged him tightly. Magically, her tear ducts were refilled and tears of joy streamed down her face.

"Brice, I can't tell you how proud Judith and I are of you. This is wonderful news! Wild horse couldn't keep us away. We'll be at your induction," said Jack.

"I'm really stoked up about the opportunity. I've also decided to try out for the football team. I might be their first ever three finger receiver!"

With that comment, Jack saw in Brice his old self, "This deserves a toast!"

Slipping out of the booth, Jack clinked his coffee cup with a spoon and stood on a chair.

"Ladies and gentlemen. Thank you so much for your warm reception for Brice tonight. We thank all of you for your generosity in hosting our dinner. Our meal, as usual, was delicious. Brice has just received a cell phone call with news…

The crowd quieted instantly.

"…he has been accepted to the United States Naval Academy and will report to Annapolis at the beginning of July."

"Hoorah, hoorah!" screamed the veterans. Patrons cheered, feet stomped and someone began singing "Anchors Aweigh."

*

Brice skipped up the few steps to the temporary stage assembled in the middle of the football field. Dressed in snug jeans, highly polished cowboy boots and a freshly ironed white, short-sleeve dress shirt, he walked purposefully towards the lectern. As he crossed the stage, he smiled and nodded at the mayor, city council members and several tenured teachers who were seated along the back of the stage. Once at the lectern, the high school principal made a few introductory comments, then handed him the wireless microphone.

With his head held high and standing ramrod straight, Brice calmly studied the faces of the young and old who were gathered in the football stadium. Graduating seniors wearing caps and gowns sat on folding chairs in front of him. Behind them, on the field, the underclassmen were seated. Sitting on the stadium benches were family friends and relatives of the graduating seniors. There was also a large contingent of people from nearby towns who had no connection whatsoever with the graduating seniors. They came, like many others, to hear what Brice had to say.

Stepping casually to the center edge of the stage, he smiled easily. The senior girls were transfixed with his rugged handsomeness. Short blond hair, laser like blue eyes and a smile that could melt the heart of any teenage girl. The girls elbowed one another and rolled their eyes. His physical build awed the boys.

Geez, how'd he fit those shoulders into that shirt? Look at those forearms! Totally ripped, thought the boys.

"This is a special day for all these seniors. Today, they embark on a new path, the 'commencement' of life's next chapter. For the boys, life will offer further education, military service, fast cars, worldwide adventures, a satisfying job, hard earned money, a wife and family. For the girls, they'll have similar options except they'll have a husband and they'll bear the children. They'll have more interest in fashionable clothes than fast cars, and probably prefer to settle down in a home of their own rather than travel the world in search of adventure. All of you will start your new life thinking that you are invincible. I know I certainly did when I sat where you are sitting six, short years ago," began Brice.

He paused and shifted his full attention to the graduating seniors and underclassmen, "However, each of you will experience varying levels of success and failure as your pursue your goals. You will learn that happiness and despair will be fleeting and capricious. During the difficult times, some of you will find shelter in your faith, some refuge in drink or drugs and others will build walls to insulate yourself from life's disappointments.

"I hope my comments today about character will help all of you, including the boys in the back row. "

Brice's eyes bored into four fourteen-year old, immature freshmen that sat slumped in their seats, oblivious to his speech. They were passing a digital camera between themselves, an amusing picture of one of their classmates held their interest. The crowd followed his eyes to the four students. Each of the boys blushed with embarrassment as they straightened in their seats. Brice smiled, *nothing like a little peer pressure to keep everyone's attention.*

Maintaining his gaze on the boys, he continued, "I too sat in that back row at one time with my buddies, goofing off and inattentive. At that time, I had absolutely no idea what character meant. Was it a form of knowledge? Did it come with age? Was it a reflection of one's wealth? It's none of those. I believe that three things form one's character:

1. Understanding the true meaning of friendship.

2. Knowing the difference between right and wrong. For me, this also includes understanding the difference between good and evil.

3. Developing the inner strength to stand by your beliefs.

"The bible, Greek philosophy and the Marine Corps have all contributed to my understanding of character.

"John 15:13 in the 'good book' says quite a bit about the meaning of friendship

Greater love has no one than this, that he lay down his life for his friends.

"Laying down your life! Are you kidding, cowboy! Isn't that a little extreme!

"In your environment, a high school friend can oftentimes be someone who will simply write an English paper for you, provide a false alibi to your parents or copy you on a text message. That is your sole measure of a friend... nothing more! Those are superficial gestures.

"In the Marines, the lives of approximately forty men in my platoon are dependent on the actions of their fellow Marines. In combat, when events deteriorate, which they often do, I have absolute faith in knowing that my platoon, and those platoons on my flanks, will follow their orders. Though I may not know everyone in these other platoons, I know that they will lay down their life protecting me. I also know that my men will do the same for them. Is this loyalty, honor, courage or sacrifice? It's all of these virtues and it builds friendships, close friendships. These are friendships that will last a lifetime, through thick and thin. How many of you have friends like this?

"In the past five years, I have had four of my best friends lay down their life protecting me and my men. Two of these men died in my arms. I was totally unprepared to deal with each of these tragedies. There are no classroom courses, no psychologists that can prepare you for the loss of a friend. Only the loving grace of God and the support of surviving friends can help you deal with such a heart breaking experience. In my case, my faith, my fellow Marines and my adopted parents, Jack and Judith Powell, supported and guided me through my despair.

A friend is always loyal, and a brother is born to help in time of need. Proverbs 17:17

"If you remember nothing else from my talk today remember this... friendship is measured by deeds... not by something as meaningless as a text message!"

Jack squeezed Judith's hand and whispered in her ear, "Brice is impressive."

"He has the full attention of 1,000 people. Did you know he could speak in public like this?"

"Are you kidding? He was as he said... just like one of those boys in the back row when he was here in school," said Jack.

"God and the Marine Corps have done wondrous things to our boy," said Judith quietly. She held Jack's hands tightly as they, and the entire stadium crowd, listened spellbound to Brice's Marine Corps experiences and his personal beliefs.

His closing comments were especially impressive.

"Every day we hear cool sound bites on TV or 'YouTube' from our alleged leaders in Washington or those financial giants on Wall Street... 'I'll go to bat for this person! I'd share a foxhole with him! You can take this to the bank!'

"Politicians, TV broadcasters, businessmen and our peers voice these empty and 'catchy' sound bites daily. But, when an adverse event occurs, the 'catchy' sound bite vanishes and we're flooded with compromising escape clauses... 'The situation has changed! New information has come to light! You misunderstood my meaning!'

"In short order, the 'back pedaling' begins. Self-preservation guides these individuals rather than the best interests of their constituents or stockholders. For me, the shame and guilt of compromising my beliefs so easily would be worse than death itself. The Greek philosopher, Epictetus said it best, 'The greatest injury a man can suffer is that administered to himself.'

"The United States would be a far different place today if our leaders and soldiers didn't stand strong for what they believed in. Our founding fathers, like George Washington, Ben Franklin, John Adams and Thomas Jefferson opposed English tyranny and risked the hangman's noose standing up for what they believed was best for their fellow citizens, not what was best for them. Likewise, soldiers routinely put their life on the line to protect the life of fellow soldiers, or for the success of their mission. Their life is subordinate to what they believe in because they, like Epictetus, know full well that compromising their beliefs would be worse than death itself.

"In closing, we are measured by our deeds," emphasized Brice. "We perform these deeds based on the composition of our character... our willingness to lay our life on the line for our friends, knowing what's 'right' and standing firm in our beliefs. Life's passage is not an easy path, but with solid character, I promise you, your walk through life will be rewarded and comforted."

The audience, who had been riveted to Brice's every word, gradually emerged from their trance like state and began to stand and cheer. Seniors threw their caps in the air. The four freshmen hooted, "Brice, Brice!"

Adults stood and clapped. Jack and Judith laughed and cried. Then, the normally stoic principal raced to Brice's side, grabbed the microphone from him and uncharacteristically screamed over the public address system, "That's one of our boys! That's one of our boys!"

The quiet, indecisive teenager who joined the Marine Corps directly from high school six years earlier had become a changed young man. Drill instructors, boot camp, combat, casualties… his and others… had left its mark on Brice. Brice had also left his mark on those who had heard his speech.

Hours later at the Powell's house, Brice was standing in the bed of his truck securing his duffle bag with his last tie down. He gave a final tug on a knot and hopped lightly to the ground.

Judith handed him a large paper bag. "Lunch, dinner and treats!" she said smiling. "We love you Brice," she said as she hugged him fiercely and began to cry.

"Thanks, Mom. I love you too! I'll see you soon at Annapolis," said Brice as he gave her a comforting pat on her back and turned towards Jack.

Brice and Jack embraced one another for several moments. When they separated, Jack extended his hand to Brice. He held Brice's hand firmly as he looked proudly into his eyes and said, "Son, that was an inspirational speech from an inspirational man. We're very proud of you and we'll be at Annapolis for your induction. Have a safe trip, and give Bobby Ridger our best wishes."

"I will! I love you both," said Brice as he released Jack's hand and quickly slipped into his truck before he too was overcome with emotion.

He carefully backed his truck out of their driveway, honked his horn and waved as his truck pulled away from the curb.

Like thousands of other military parents before them, Jack and Judith stood, arm in arm in their driveway, waving goodbye, crying and silently praying for the well being of their son as he disappeared around a bend in the road.

CHAPTER 8
DR. MATTHEWS

Early June 2008...

Molly burst into her brother's bedroom with a full head of steam. Matthews was leaning over her brother, checking his heartbeat with his stethoscope. Her father stood on the opposite side of the bed with his hands resting on the bed's guardrail. Bill raised an eyebrow at his daughter's agitated state. Her face was flushed and she was nearly out of breath. She was never late for the doctor's visits. These late afternoon appointments didn't conflict with her school schedule and she always had a question or two for the doctor regarding Bobby's physical therapy. He'd speak with her after dinner, something or someone had upset her.

"I'm sorry I'm late Dad, doctor. Something came up. How's he doing?"

Matthews straightened his six foot four inch frame and looked at Molly. He was dressed in his usual worn jeans and scuffed cowboy boots. His buttoned down blue dress shirt provided the only hint of his professional background. In his late fifties, he had jet-black hair, which was graying at his temples, large brown eyes and a boyish grin that never disappeared. He was the epitome of a down to earth, friendly country doctor who still made house calls.

"I think the Veteran Administration's experimental stem cell treatments are helping. Bobby has some feeling in his hands and arms, he's able to move his head from side to side and he has minor feeling in his shoulders."

"I've noticed his movements, but what does that mean? Will he be able to walk someday?" she asked.

"I just don't know. The latest MRI's and CAT scans I've studied still show that there is no blood supply to the spinal nerve endings that were injured. Those nerve endings are still dormant. However, other parts of his spinal cord, which were traumatized, have fully recovered. Some of these muscle groups are taking over the work of those muscles that are non-responsive. It's apparent that physical therapy is clearly working." He paused to consider his closing prognosis, knowing a patient's optimism could perform medical miracles.

"I think further improvement is a real possibility."

Bill and Molly stood motionless at Bobby's bedside, each digesting the news in different ways. Bill Ridger was hopeful his son could someday motor around the ranch on an ATV (All Terrain Vehicle) equipped with special hand controls. Molly's goals for her brother were more modest. If he could dress and feed himself, she thought he'd feel better about himself. He'd enjoy greater self-esteem and a higher level of self-respect. If that improvement occurred, she believed he'd be more likely to get out of the house to visit a friend's house for dinner or even go to a restaurant. Prior to his injury, her brother was like a human hummingbird as he dashed around town in his decrepit pickup truck visiting his wide circle of friends. Though she hoped he could return to his old self, for now, she'd be pleased if became more self-sufficient and occasionally got out and about with the aid of a helper.

Bobby spoke first, "Well hot dang! Molly don't get rid of my free weights and Dad start oiling Mom's old wheelchair. That's great news, 'Doc.' If I talk the VA into a double dose of stem cells, will that speed up my recovery?"

"Stem cell therapy is still very much at an early, experimental stage. I'd suggest you and your family do all you can to encourage the VA to simply continue those treatments. The government isn't too keen on stem cell therapy. Shower them with praise for the miracles the treatments are providing you. Perhaps that will improve their opinion of stem cell therapy and expand their therapy to others in similar situations." He would have said more about the government's out-of-date and prejudiced view of stem cell treatments, but this was neither the time nor place to voice his personal opinions.

"In closing, your hard work, Bobby, and the hard work of those who are helping you are yielding positive results. Keep up the good work. I'm proud of your effort," said Matthews sincerely.

Bill and Molly saw the doctor out and returned to Bobby's bedroom.

"Well, that's encouraging news, son. Molly, if the VA vacillates on further stem cell treatments, let me know right away. Our U.S. Senator Tom Smith is a good friend who I served with in the Marines. I know he would lobby the VA on behalf of Bobby, if it comes to that."

"I'll keep my eyes and ears open, Dad. His next treatment at the VA Medical Center in Sheridan, Wyoming is in six days. Bobby, when does your friend come to visit?" asked Molly.

"Let's see. He was the commencement speaker last week at his high school in Texas. After that, he left for the Grand Canyon. In Iraq, he talked constantly about hiking through parts of the Grand Canyon and Zion National Parks. He's visiting those places on his way to our ranch. From what he said in our last phone call, he should arrive here the day after tomorrow. Is it OK if he stays with us for a week? I already asked him. He said it was fine with him if it worked for us. He could sleep on the pullout sofa bed in the study," said Bobby.

"Good with me! Do you think he would mind driving you to Sheridan for your stem cell treatments? It would be nice if we gave Molly a couple days off of nurse duty," said Bill.

"Oh, Dad! It's no bother at all taking Bobby to the VA. The folks there are real nice and the VA has a cut rate lodging deal with the Holiday Inn right next door," said Molly.

"I'm sure Brice would do it. We might even go 'clubbing' in our free time!" said Bobby playfully.

"Let's see how Brice's schedule looks before we get to excited about this field trip. By the way, is he much of a hunter or tracker? We've got this grey wolf problem. I was thinking maybe he could put in a couple of days looking for this wolf while he's visiting," said Bill.

"Dad, he's a guest. We can't put him to work… "

Bobby interrupted Molly, "Hold on. First, Brice is a Texan. Texan's will tell you that they're expert at everything. I don't think he's had much experience tracking four legged animals, but he's clearly an expert at hunting and tracking two legged insurgents. I can show him the ropes. Molly and Brice can strap me into the jeep and I'll give him some tracking pointers while we tour the ranch. Second, getting out of the house, now that the snow has melted and it's warming up, will be good for me. I've got a bad case of cabin fever. Lastly, Brice won't have a problem taking me to Sheridan. We'll take the long way to Sheridan through Yellowstone and I'll show him the sights. It will be a fun guys trip for both of us," said Bobby.

"Well, take this slow and easy, Bobby. Brice will, after all, have some input. Further, you can rest assured, I'll be behind the wheel on any jeep excursions you plan on the ranch. I'll see you both later for dinner. I've got to run into town for a pick up at the feed store," said Bill as he left Bobby's bedroom.

"Well, Mr. 'Ants-in-your-pants,' you're sure feeling frisky. I'm anxious to meet your friend, Brice. I hope he doesn't faint when I show him how to adjust your catheter, bathe, feed, medicate, massage and dress you. The two of you knock yourselves out. I'll enjoy a couple of days off," said Molly.

"Molly, I wouldn't be healing without you. Physically and emotionally you've been a savior. I can never thank you enough," said Bobby passionately.

"Hey, hey, let's not get too emotional. You would have done the same for me. And by the way, sport, you've still got a long way to go before you're doing 'wheelies' in Mom's old wheelchair."

"I know, but the doctor gave me renewed hope. Damn, I'm happy!"

Molly smiled at Bobby and leaned over him and kissed him on the cheek. She whispered, "I'll work your butt off. You'll be in wheelchair races before you know it."

As she stepped through his bedroom door to leave, he said, "He's a 'hunk!'"

She turned slowly, "A what?"

" A 'hunk,' you know, a stud! He'll melt your heart, Sis."

She just shook her head and laughed as she walked towards the kitchen thinking, *boys will be boys.*

CHAPTER 9
BAD CONDUCT

Bill Ridger was a short, stout and powerfully built man with swept back, curly salt and pepper hair that framed a strong, friendly face. His son, Bobby, often joked that his, six foot, father looked like a human Abrams tank. There was a sliver of truth in the comparison. Bill's wide shoulders supported a head that swiveled like a tank turret and his thickly muscled arms were seemingly the same diameter as a tank's cannon. When he stomped across an open pasture, he left a trail much like a tank tread as his powerful legs chewed through knee high grass and the uneven ground. Bobby also thought his dad dealt with life's problems much like a tank, straight ahead with steely resolve.

Molly's view of her dad differed. She believed her father could have enjoyed a successful career on the stage had his formative years occurred in say Los Angeles, rather than Montana. His gravelly voice, warm brown eyes and noble facial features, which projected an aura of strength and courage, would have been an instant hit in Hollywood. And, his cute, dimple chin could have swooned legions of female moviegoers. She regarded him as a cross between John Wayne and Kirk Douglas.

Molly and her dad were in the kitchen cleaning up after dinner when Bill casually asked her why she was late for Matthews' visit, "What happened this afternoon? You're never late for John's visits."

Molly folded her arms across her chest and turned towards her father.

Her facial muscles tightened and her body stiffened, it was obvious that she was upset about something.

"Skip Dower! He stopped Penny's car again as we drove into Dennis. I think the creep has our Montana State class schedule."

"Did he cite Penny for any traffic violations?" said Bill over his shoulder as he placed several dishes in a kitchen cabinet.

"Heck no! He never does. It's the same old routine. He parks his cruiser by the traffic intersection at the north end of town, near the market. When we drive through the intersection, he pulls in behind Penny's car and turns on his lights and siren. He swaggers up to her car window, leans his elbows on her open windowsill and starts rambling on about his sexual fantasies. It's as if he expects each of us to beg him for sexual favors at the nearest motel. He's a sick pervert!"

Bill's slow temper began to roil. His head turned slowly towards his daughter, "You know his dad is the sheriff?"

Molly nodded.

His eyes turned darker and narrower as he continued, "We didn't even have a police force until three years ago when the city became incorporated. I've heard from some of the ranchers that they've recently found the Dowers snooping around their property. When they've confronted them, the Dowers would cite them for some drummed up zoning violation. The ranchers suspect they're angling for some free beef or free rent on an outbuilding where they can set up some illicit activity. I've told the city council members countless times that you can't have incompetent police officers running around town acting like they own the place. I hate to think what would happen if they had to investigate a serious crime. They're idiots."

Molly responded, "Well, since you mentioned serious crime, let me give you my take on Sheriff Dower and his only son. They're supplementing their income in some manner. The father just bought a new $30,000 Harley Davidson, and Skip invited Penny to Las Vegas for an all expenses paid weekend trip… shows, gambling, new clothes, the whole nine yards. Penny told him she had a steady boyfriend and passed. But he knows she doesn't have a boyfriend and he's starting to hit on me."

"Do you think the Las Vegas offer was simply big talk?"

"Nope. Penny's aunt, who is an accountant in West Yellowstone, heard an interesting story from an accounting client who owns a bar there. One of the client's barmaids got roughed up on a weekend trip to Las Vegas with a young deputy from our town. Apparently, there was some talk of rape charges being filed, but that ended when the barmaid's checking account became $5,000 richer and she decided to move out of the state."

"Damn, I was afraid of this. It sounds like Skip is a clone of his old man. I went to school with his father, Fred. He was and still is an overweight bully who views himself as something of an Adonis, which is quite a stretch. He barely made it thru high school because he could hardly read or write.

"He was a biker back then and hooked up with some white supremacy group east of Great Falls. The feds broke up the group and arrested just about everyone for making bombs or some such thing. The feds found sticks of dynamite in Fred's motorcycle bags, but he claimed they were road flares. His buddies, who were behind bars, couldn't stop laughing when they heard his *road flare* explanation. Apparently, Fred really thought they were road flares. The feds decided not to arrest him because he was so stupid.

"Keep me posted on what you hear and don't encourage Skip in any way, not that you would. I'm having lunch with the mayor tomorrow and will update him on Skip's latest offences," said Bill sourly.

CHAPTER 10
THE DRIVE TO BOBBY'S HOUSE

After leaving the Powell's, Brice drove non-stop to a modest motel seventy-five miles south of the Grand Canyon National Park. Other than a few stops for gas, coffee and bathroom breaks, it had been a tiring seven hundred and fifty mile drive. When he steered his truck into the motel's parking lot, it was nearing midnight and a major thunderstorm was furiously peaking. Heavy rain rattled the cab of his pickup, and bolts of lightening filled the sky. With his windshield wipers operating at full speed, he inched slowly through the lot as he searched for an open parking stall. Recreational vehicles, pickups overflowing with kids bikes and family vans were everywhere. Finding the last open parking stall, he parked and ran through the rain to the motel's office. The motel clerk sadly explained that there were no rooms left and none to be had nearby. She'd already tried placing several families who had sought a motel room earlier in the day.

"Summer vacations are in full swing. We're full. It will be like this for the next three months," said the tired clerk plaintively.

Brice spent the night dozing uncomfortably in the cab of his truck, while being awakened intermittently by thunderclaps that were very reminiscent of incoming artillery fire. The next morning, he awoke early and rubbed his red eyes until his vision cleared. Unfolding his stiff body from the rear seat of his pickup, he rolled out of the rear door of the cab and stepped briskly to the adjacent diner. After drinking a quart of hot black coffee and picking at a bizarre looking omelet stuffed with mystery meat, he returned to his truck and headed to the Grand Canyon.

It was a few minutes before 9:00 AM when he parked at the El Tovar Lodge near the South Rim of the Grand Canyon. It was a cool, cloudless morning with clear weather forecast for the balance of the day. Perfect weather for his eighteen-mile round-trip hike to the bottom of the canyon floor and back. He slid out of his truck and stepped onto the grass berm that surrounded the parking lot. With his back to the historic hotel, he stared, mesmerized, at the beauty and grandeur of the Grand Canyon that was spread before him. Heavy rains from the prior night's thunderstorm had washed and scrubbed the air. As he breathed in the clean, crisp morning air, his spirit tingled with the anticipation of his hike.

Though he was anxious to see Bobby, he had a feeling it might be awhile before he had such an ideal opportunity to visit two of the west's most famous national parks, the Grand Canyon and Zion. His detour to the Grand Canyon and Zion would only delay his arrival to Bobby's house by a couple of days. He'd visit a third national park, Yellowstone, after his stay with Bobby.

Three dog-eared copies of *National Geographic* with cover stories on each of the parks lay in the passenger seat beside him. He'd studied the magazine's pictures and read the stories describing each of the parks countless times while stationed in Iraq. While on patrol, their vivid pictures and descriptions provided him a degree of vicarious comfort as he regularly humped seventy pounds or more of water, gear and ammo in the unrelenting desert heat. At night, whether on patrol or in the barracks, sound sleep for Brice was at best a fitful proposition. These park images were his only defense against a nightly procession of violent dreams and flashbacks that assaulted his mind.

Moving back to his truck, he lowered the tailgate and began to anxiously get his gear together for his hike. A couple of cars away a middle-aged couple were reloading their car after checking out of the lodge. The man walked over and introduced himself to Brice. He had seen the Camp Pendleton parking decal on Brice's truck and said that he was a recently retired Marine gunnery sergeant. Brice explained that he too was a gunnery sergeant and, in short order, they learned that they had several friends in common.

Brice's new friend briefly described his three three-day hike and camping trip into the canyon that he and his wife had finished the previous night. But, before the man could delve deeper into the details of his hike and their common friendships, his wife walked over an introduced herself.

"Son, I overheard you say that you are a gunnery sergeant in the Corps. I know my husband could spend hours bending your ear about his adventures in the Corps and what friends you have in common, but that conversation will have to wait for another time.

"I love my husband dearly. We've been happily married for twenty-five years, but he often thinks of me as one of his boot privates. I, on the other hand, think of him as my aide-de-camp.

"Despite being drenched in the rain last night during the last hour of our climb, we thoroughly enjoyed a wonderful, but tiring, three-day round trip down and around the canyon. I've had a thirty-pound pack on my back for much of that time. I want to get back to our home in Oceanside, California as soon as possible, take a long, hot bath and sleep for 48 hours in my warm and cozy bed," said the woman imperiously.

Brice was unconsciously smiling at the man's wife as he contemplated her comment about twenty-five years of contented marriage to a Marine Corps "gunny" sergeant.

Geez, that could be a world record, he thought.

Her husband started to speak, but she flashed him a stern look and stuck her open hand inches from his face. Her 'stop' signal silenced him in mid sentence.

"I overheard you say you're making the round-trip hike in one day. OK, this is the 'straight dope.' Get rid of those blue jeans and get into your 'PT' (physical training) shorts. Apply Vaseline between your toes and other body parts that could get chaffed. Fill up your water bottles, and don't forget to re-fill them at the bottom of the canyon. Otherwise, you'll never make it back to the top of the canyon's rim. Here, you'll need these hiking poles.

"Get on the shuttle over there," she pointed to a group of people standing by a bus stop several hundred yards away. "From the shuttle drop off to Yaki Point is a couple of miles. From there, follow the signs to the South Kaibab Trail, which will take you to the bottom of the canyon. Once you get to the bottom, follow the River Trail. There are some interesting Indian artifacts along the way and you'll pass the Phantom Ranch. Don't dally too long at the bottom of the canyon or you'll find yourself hiking in the dark on narrow trails with loose gravel that are inches away from thousand foot drop-offs. There's a lot to see and explore in the canyon, but you won't have time to see everything in one day. You can do that on your next trip. I recommend you take Bright Angel Trail back to the top of the rim."

"Thank you, ma'am. I appreciate your advice and let me pay you for the poles," said Brice.

"That's not necessary. A Marine Corps wife gave them to me when we started our hike from this same parking lot several days ago. They were a life saver," she said. Turning to her husband, she added, "Mr. 'Tough Guy' here thought hiking poles were for sissies. I had to drag him up the trail the last two miles."

"That's not entirely... " began her husband until he was interrupted again by his wife's raised hand. She pointed her index finger towards their car. Amusement sparkled in Brice's eyes as he watched her direct her husband with silent hand signals. They were the same signals he and his men would use during a combat mission.

"Fred, start the car! Get the air conditioning going. We're leaving." Like a young recruit who had been reprimanded by his drill instructor, Fred waved weakly to Brice over his shoulder as he headed to his car.

She turned sweetly back to Brice, "This is a beautiful hike. However, don't underestimate for one moment the difficulty and time it takes to hike eighteen miles. The temperature will be over one hundred degrees by the time you reach the bottom of the canyon. The 'killer,' however, will be the overwork your knees suffer. First, they'll restrain your body as you descend the five thousand feet to the canyon's floor. After which, you'll put opposite stress on them as you reverse course and trek upward to the canyon rim. Ice your knees and take a couple of Ibuprofen when you finish your hike. Have fun!" she said as she abruptly did an about face and marched to her car.

At the shuttle drop off, the congregation of people was like a meeting at the United Nations... Japanese snapping pictures, Europeans with the latest hiking equipment and Americans in sneakers and baseball caps. Most of the visitors were only hiking a couple of miles to Yaki Point, a lookout that offered unbelievable views of the canyon. Despite numerous signs explaining the risks of hiking further to the bottom of the canyon, a group of unprepared, overly enthusiastic sightseers, on impulse, elected to join Brice on his hike to the canyon's floor... parents with a gaggle of young kids, teenagers in flip flops and older folks in dress shoes. A park ranger strategically situated a mile or so beyond Yaki Point reminded everyone again of the risks of proceeding further. Though his officious warning was generally ignored, the sight of other ill equipped, inexperienced and gasping hikers limping up the trail generally convinced the unprepared to reverse course.

Stepping to the side of the trail to let a large group of over zealous hikers pass, Brice braced himself with his hiking poles and studied the canyon below. He could hardly wait to finally touch and see some of those images that had safeguarded his sanity... the canyon's eroded and towering limestone walls, it's ancient trails, crystal clear spring waters and the power of the great Colorado River as it continued its timeless erosion of the canyon floor.

Five minutes after passing the last returning hiker, Brice came to a series of blind switchbacks. He was attentive to both the steepness of the trail and the constant distraction of the canyon's magnitude and splendor. It was easy to see how an overly enthusiastic camera bug could neglect his surroundings and simply walk off the trail to his death as he snapped one photograph after another.

Suddenly, the distinctive and vile odor of cigarette smoke whipped his senses into high alert. It was the smoke from those cheap Iraqi cigarettes. If he'd been on patrol, he would have given silent hand signals to his men and released the safety on his rifle. As it was, he carefully inched around the next switchback and peaked at three young men in their early twenties who were animatedly speaking Arabic with one another. He studied them for a minute. Each of them was unshaven and wore street clothes. They were pointing to different areas of the trail above and below them. One of them was making notes on a small map. They didn't appear to be armed, but there was no doubt in his mind what the bastards were up to.

He heard a soft whisper in his ear. It was the voice of his radioman, Corporal Don Whistler, who died in his arms in Fallujah. *A haji recce! No doubt about it. They don't appear to be armed, but I'd be careful. Shall I call headquarters?*

Brice turned. There was no one behind him.

We're on the same page, Whistler. No calls for now, thought Brice.

Moments later, the sound of laughing hikers coming down the trail behind him interrupted his thoughts. He stepped aside for two couples in their mid twenties. Two attractive women, both strong and athletic, dressed in tight fitting, spandex exercise shorts and armless tee shirts led their husbands down the trial. All four of them were immersed in conversation as they briefly smiled and whisked by him. He opened the blade of his survival knife, held it upward against the inside of his wrist and slipped into step behind the group. The three Iraqi men stood contemptuously in the middle of the trail, their posture surly and sullen.

In seconds, the two girls leading the group were amongst the three men on the narrow trail. One of the women bumped into the smallest man, who was sucking on one of his foul-smelling cigarettes and deliberately blocking her path.

When she was twenty feet beyond the man, she raised her arm, flipped him the bird and said, without turning back, "This is a fresh air hiking trail, not a smoking break room. Don't smoke or hog the trail, asshole!"

Brice let the two couples continue. As he knelt to one knee, pretending to tighten a bootlace, he glanced back at the three men. The man who had been bumped was being restrained by his two companions. He was convulsed with rage at the disrespectful behavior of the uncovered female infidel. Familiar Arabic blasphemies poured from his mouth. After calming the infuriated man, the three of them slowly headed upwards, towards the rim of the canyon.

Something bad was brewing, but what magnitude and when was the question. The three men didn't appear to present any imminent danger. He decided to continue his hike and reconsider the matter later. For now, he would indulge all of his senses in his trek to the canyon floor.

At nearly every switchback turn, he stopped and took one photograph after another of the multi-colored canyon walls. At the clearly marked viewpoints, he compared the sights before him with his copy of the

National Geographic geological pullout that he had stuffed into his pack. The pullout denoted, in multiple dimensions, the two billion year geological creation of the Grand Canyon... ice ages, volcanoes, lava and erosion. From a geological perspective, it was stimulating to see and understand on site the geological science of the canyon's creation. What was difficult for him to grasp was the time frame, two billion years of nature's work.

At the bottom of the canyon, he withdrew another set of papers from his pack. It was a three-page summary of John Wesley Powell's explorations in the Grand Canyon that he had Xeroxed at the Oceanside library before he left Camp Pendleton. Spellbound, he read of their expedition. Three months exploring and riding down the Colorado River in twenty-foot dories! Portaging the dories around some of the larger rapids when they could and running those rapids that they couldn't escape. Sitting a stone's throw from the raging Colorado River, he simply shook his head in wonderment at Powell's tenacity and adventuresome spirit.

He could have spent days studying and exploring the canyon. The Colorado River, verdant side channels, Native American petroglyphs and shear cliffs that exposed millions of years of history. Everything about the canyon fascinated him. He was sorely tempted to stay longer in the canyon floor, but the difficulty of an uphill, nine-mile trek in hot weather outweighed his temptation. When he reached the Grand Canyon's rim, three hours later, he was exhausted.

Thank God for those hiking poles!

It didn't take much of an imagination to see how an inexperienced, unfit and ill equipped hiker could get into a dangerous fix on that nine mile uphill climb. If they were not properly hydrated before they started their climb and they carried insufficient water with them, trouble could easily turn into death. He'd seen it happen before to men unprepared and unaccustomed to the hot wastelands of Iraq.

Back at his truck, Brice changed into a dry tee shirt and shorts. Slipped on his ever so comfortable sandals and spread his soaked hiking clothes in the bed of his truck under a light cargo net. In the El Tovar Lodge convenience store, he bought an inexpensive Styrofoam cooler, a bag of ice for his knees, three quarts of Gatorade, a large plastic wrapped hoagie, a bottle of Ibuprofen and an extra large bag of trail mix. He was anxious to start his journey to Zion National Park where he would next experience smooth sandstone arches, spires, domes and hoodoos.

The sun was low in the western sky as he drove east then north along the Grand Canyon rim. The canyon's immensity was overwhelming… a mile deep and eighteen miles across at its widest point. It stretched across the flat plains as far as the eye could see, seemingly carved towards the core of the earth eons ago. It was easy to see why Native Americans felt a mystical attachment to this natural wonder. After just a single day of hiking in the canyon, he too felt a primal connection to the place.

With daylight fast disappearing, in the middle of a desolate desert, he decided he'd spend the night sleeping in the bed of his truck. Seeing a washed out dirt road that led to a hilltop 200 yards back from the road, he shifted his truck into four wheel drive and left the pavement. Once he reached the peak of the hill, he turned his truck in a tight circle, leaving the truck's front wheels on a slight downward slope, headed back towards the dirt road. He'd gotten stuck so many times off-roading that the maneuver was like second nature to him. It eliminated the possibility of getting his wheels stuck in loose sand or getting his drive train hung up on a boulder. In the morning, if his truck wouldn't start, he could simply release the brakes and jump start the truck as it rolled down the hill.

He lowered his tailgate, inflated his camping mattress and unfolded his sleeping bag. Sitting on top of his sleeping bag, he first began to massage his aching calves and thighs. After ten minutes of kneading those sore muscles, he softly rubbed his feet and knees. Both knees were warm to the touch. Most of his recent hiking in the Marines had been on level deserts. His eighteen-mile round trip to the bottom of the Grand Canyon and back to the rim was the opposite of flat terrain. Every step of the nine descending miles pounded his knees and hips; and jammed his toes into the front of his hiking boots. In days, he knew dead toenails would begin to fall off his black and blue toes. The nine ascending miles tested his gluts and those muscles surrounding his knees. He couldn't imagine how bad he'd feel if he hadn't used those hiking poles to cushion his descending steps and use his arms and shoulders to assist every ascending step. He pulled two plastic bags out of his daypack and filled each bag with ice from his cooler. When he placed a bag of ice on each of his swollen knees, his pain began to subside.

As darkness blanketed the hilltop, Brice stretched out on his sleeping bag with his head resting easily on both hands. He'd drunk two quarts of Gatorade and eaten the hoagie within an hour of leaving the Grand Canyon. During his drive, he nibbled on the bag of trail mix. He was drowsy, but not particularly hungry. Warm, gentle breezes washed over his body and comforted him. He stared at the pinpricks of light that dotted the clear, black sky. These heavens looked down peacefully upon his quiet retreat.

On the opposite side of the world, it was far from quiet and peaceful. His thoughts drifted to his fellow Marines stationed in the badlands of Iraq. Those on night patrol would just be returning to their firebases as the sun began to lighten the dark eastern sky. They'd be dog tired, caked with dust and famished. If they had engaged terrorists, they'd be decompressing after the adrenaline rush of their firefight. They might also be battling the emotional trauma of seeing one of their friends injured or, worst of all, killed in action.

Be safe and strong my brothers, prayed Brice as his heavy eyelids slowly closed and his mind began to wander. In moments, he fell into a deep sleep and dreamt about Indians painting the history of their people on the walls of the Grand Canyon.

Two days later, he was one of the first early morning visitors to arrive at Zion National Park's Visitor Center. He had previously heard the local weather forecast on his trucks radio and was pleased to learn that it would be a perfect day for hiking. No rain forecast, clear skies and temperatures in the mid 80s. He was hopeful the "Narrows" would be open for hiking. Rain as far away as thirty miles could quickly swell the banks of the Narrows rendering it impassable. Park Rangers closely monitored weather conditions throughout Southern Utah for just such flash flood possibilities. To his delight, a chalkboard note at the visitor center confirmed that the Narrows was open for hikers.

A shuttle bus was the only means of motor transport along the canyon floor during the parks busiest season, spring through fall, to the Temple of Sinawava at the north end of the canyon. Brice took a seat next to a window that gave him a perfect view of the park as it followed the Virgin River past Zion Lodge, the Grotto, Menu Falls and the trailhead to Angels Landing. Whereas the Grand Canyon looked as if it had been quarried layer-by-layer by giant bulldozers, Zion's steep red sandstone walls appeared as though they were shaped by a sculptor's knife with its sweeping curves and smooth, circular depressions.

Another significant difference between the two parks was their widths. The Grand Canyon was eighteen miles across at its widest point. Zion was generally not more than a half-mile across. The Narrows, at certain places, was only a few feet wide.

At the Temple of Sinawava, the shuttle emptied approximately forty sightseers. All of them were greeted by an otherworldly setting. Red rock cliff faces merged together to form a perfect amphitheater. Brice took several pictures in an attempt to capture the majesty of the setting. Knowing that a camera had its limitations, he paused for several tranquil minutes to engrave the colors and shapes of this natural temple upon his memory.

He next followed the well-worn "Riverside Walk" trail northwards for a mile towards the Narrows trailhead. Once the trail disappeared into the Virgin River, nearly everyone turned back to the bus stop. His plan was to hike eight or so miles upriver. Sixteen miles round trip, it would be another glorious, though exhausting day.

From the river's bank, he studied the moving water. The river water was clear and visibility to the river bottom was good, except in places where the water was moving fast. Foam and water turbulence limited his visibility. Tentatively, he stepped into the river and shuddered. He couldn't believe that the water was so cold, especially in light of the ambient air temperature. Steadying himself with his hiking poles, he took a minute to acclimate his feet and legs to the cold water. He was dressed in quick dry, synthetic clothes... a lesson he'd learned from his Grand Canyon hike... and wore his high cut combat boots. He also had his indispensible hiking poles and carried a daypack that was filled with two quarts of water, several protein bars, a set of dry clothes and his low cut Nikes. Anyone less equipped than this wouldn't last long while wading blindly against the river's cold current and straining to scamper over and around the slippery, wet rocks.

He reached the area of the Narrows called "Wall Street" after two hours of tiring and foot numbing wading. Above him, the sheer red sandstone walls curled and rose to over fifteen hundred feet. At ground level, the canyons walls narrowed to twenty feet. In some places, the clearance was only a few feet. Never had he felt so small or so insignificant as he looked upward at nature's creation. As he turned his gaze downward to the water that churned around his knees, it was hard to imagine that this small creek could provide the force and power to sculpt this geological miracle. It was no wonder that the Narrows was widely considered the most impressive slot canyon in the world.

After Wall Street, the canyon walls widened. The river dashed around moss-covered boulders and plunged into emerald pools of quiet water. Sunlight peaked from atop the canyon's rim and painted a montage of reds, purples and various shades of orange upon the canyon walls in a continuous kaleidoscope of colors. Swaths of green, from gardens clinging impossibly from smooth canyon walls and slices of blue from cobalt skies above added depth and contrast to the ever-changing tableau of colors.

Several rock climbers caught up with Brice as he rested on a boulder, beyond the river's banks, massaging his cold feet. Laden with ropes and rock climbing gear, they enthusiastically described the technical climbing that lay ahead. Curious to see what they were talking about, he slipped on his boots and gear and joined them until they reached their destination… a one thousand foot, sheer vertical sandstone wall. The climbers carefully laid out their gear on a gravel bar and explained that they had enough gear for an extra climber, if he was interested. Though he had received a day or two of rock climbing training in the Marines, he could see that this undertaking was far beyond his skill set. If he were to take a risk, he preferred it be with his brothers in arms on a combat mission. Risking his neck with a couple of strangers on a death-defying lark, in which he had little training and no experience, just didn't make sense. He kindly declined their offer, citing fatigue. *Perhaps another time*, he thought, as he decided that it was also time to return to his campsite. Hiking for miles against a cold river current, with a rocky bottom, and scrambling up, over and around the large boulders was more demanding and debilitating than he had ever imagined.

Once he returned to his pickup, which was parked in his designated parking spot in the Watchman Campground, he changed into dry clothes and slipped on his flip-flops. Hopping into the bed of his truck, he unfolded a beach chair and positioned himself so he faced the day's last rays of sunshine. His body and feet began to warm. It was another day of spectacular hiking through another wondrous national park. He gazed absentmindedly at fellow hikers and tourists who were ambling back to their cars and campers. All of them were animatedly talking about the sights they'd seen and when they'd next return to the park.

A slow, steady stream of vehicles trickled out of the park, headed south on Highway 9 towards St. George, Utah. Brice's tired eyes rested on the diverse parade of vehicles leaving the park… convertibles with tops down, huge RV buses towing smaller vehicles, pickups packed with bikes and camping gear, station wagons with storage racks on the roof and, of course, a *to be expected* aged and dented sedan spewing oil and fumes. *That $100 clunker is probably carrying teenagers returning home from their seasonal summer job of serving cokes and hot dogs to the tourists,* he thought. As the car approached, the driver threw an empty coke can out his window. A moment later, the front seat passenger tossed a crumpled cigarette pack out his window. Both acts were unusual in such a pristine park and it drew his full attention. As the car drove slowly past him, he studied the three passengers. They were familiar faces. Not the same three Middle Eastern characters he'd seen in the Grand Canyon, but clearly some of their buddies and from the same neighborhood.

Brice left the campground early the next morning, after a fitful night of sleep. During a mid morning breakfast in Provo, Utah and a second cup of coffee, he mulled over his second sighting of suspicious characters. He took a last gulp of coffee, left several bills on the countertop that covered his tab and tip, and headed for the exit. When he reached his truck, he leaned back against the tailgate and raised the collar of his windbreaker. Though it was early June, a cool, crisp breeze blew towards him from snowcapped peaks of the Wasatch Mountains, just a few miles to the east. He organized his thoughts and speed dialed a familiar number on his cell phone.

Later that afternoon, Brice walked into the busy lobby of the Gray Wolf Inn in West Yellowstone, Montana. Both receptionists were busy checking in several large, extended families. One of the receptionists, an attractive girl in her mid-twenties, saw him approach and said regretfully, "We're full."

"I called ahead. The name is Brice Miller, for a single room."

The receptionist unabashedly checked Brice out from head to toe:

broad shoulders, handsome face, and traveling alone. His looks were a welcome relief to the long line of impatient, middle-aged men with cigarette stained teeth, beer guts and a gaggle of loud, unruly children. She turned her attention to her reservation list. "Gotcha, Brice! We'll hold your room. This is our peak check-in time. Here's a free pass to the 'Grizzly and Wolf Center' across the street. Take your time looking around and I'll check you in when you return," she said with a pleasant smile.

"Thanks," he said as he returned her smile and slid the pass off the counter.

"Hey! I'll take ten of those passes for my family," snapped the man who was standing in front of the receptionist, in the midst of checking-in.

"No," said the receptionist without hesitation.

"We're customers!" said the man's wife in an equally demanding, but shriller manner.

"Those passes are for guests who we unfortunately inconvenience. Furthermore, there are five, not ten people in your party. By the way, your credit card is 'maxed out.' Do you have another card we can use, sir?" said the receptionist coolly.

Brice shook his head in disbelief as he headed toward the lobby's exit. Both the husband and wife were rude. If one of his men had spoken to him like that, he would have knocked him on his ass in a New York second. Perhaps, he was better suited for military life than the civilian world after all. Corporal correction appealed to him.

Moments later, he was pleasantly surprised when he entered the Grizzly and Wolf Center. The center was bright, airy, extremely informative and relatively new. Instead of finding a dark and aging display of taxidermy with a few stuffed animals propped next to dusty descriptions of the animals, he found that the center was part museum and part zoo. The zoo area contained a viewing area for a group of gray wolves, a large simulated habitat for grizzly bears, and a caged area that held falcons, owls and a bald eagle. The bears were immense, with heads and paws larger than he expected. He read that they could weigh up to eight hundred pounds and, standing, they could reach a height of up to eight feet. They could run thirty miles per hour, and a mature grizzly's skull could be three to four inches thick.

The size and speed of grizzly bears peaked Brice's military curiosity.

Who would survive if an angry grizzly charged an experienced hunter who was armed with, say, a .308 semi-automatic rifle that was loaded with 220-grain bullets? Major factors that would influence the outcome included distance to the target, terrain, the hunter's physical condition and level of preparedness, time of day and the weather. How far away was the bear when he charged the hunter? Did brush and trees interfere with the hunter's shot? Was the bear charging uphill or downhill? Was the hunter winded from climbing uphill through heavy brush? Was the hunter's rifle locked and loaded? Was it getting dark, or was there full daylight? Was it windy or rainy? Lastly, if the two met in a surprise encounter, like a Marine coming face to face with an armed terrorist in a dark alley in Iraq, who would that favor? In a dark alley, he knew that the winner, rather survivor, was usually the one who reacted the fastest, kept his composure and performed as he was trained.

If the hunter saw the grizzly charge him on a clear, level field at a distance of sixty to seventy yards away, he'd give the edge to the hunter. However, if it was a close-range, surprise encounter in heavy brush, the bear's physical size, speed and familiarity with the terrain would give him the advantage. The hunter's only chance of survival, if it were indeed a surprise encounter, would be if he could clearly place two to three shots on the charging bear's bobbing head, in a matter of seconds, at a minimum range of forty yards. That would be a tall order for the best of hunters, and he had serious doubts that he could perform such a feat. He filed this thought in his memory bank... *watch out for grizzlies, especially in close quarters!*

Moving to the wolf viewing area, he became fascinated with the interaction of ten wolves; eight young ones who were born in captivity and two adults who were recovering from injuries. After ten minutes of viewing the wolves, behind the safety of a heavy chain link fence, he could see that they had the lightness afoot of a coyote, the sinewy strength of a mountain lion and the playfulness of little kittens. However, his fleeting impression of the wolves' playfulness soon disappeared when he witnessed the roughhousing of two young males rapidly escalate into a fierce confrontation. Snarling with bared, razor sharp teeth and hackles up, each wolf slowly backed up eight to ten feet until they were nearly twenty feet apart. With heads bowed, like a sprinter in the starting blocks, the ferocity of their snarling peaked and, without warning, they leapt at one another as if they had been shot out of a cannon. In an instant, they collided mid-air and slammed to the ground locked in a savage tempest of biting, growling, clawing and kicking. There was no doubt that they would have fought to their death had not both adult wolves and several of the other young males intervened immediately. The pack separated the two wolves and kept them apart until both wolves calmed down and retreated to separate ends of the viewing area where, beneath shade trees, they both flopped to the ground and began licking their wounds.

Astonished by the ferocity of the two young wolves, Brice picked up a brochure off a display table and began to read about the genealogy of gray wolves. He learned that they could live to ten years in age, weigh as much as eighty pounds, hunt for miles on end at a trotting pace of six miles per hour, accelerate up to forty miles per hour for an attack and leap fifteen feet or more onto their prey.

Yes, that leaping part was believable. He had just seen two still-developing, young wolves leap ten feet from a stationary position.

They usually traveled in packs while protecting territories that encompassed fifteen to twenty square miles, which they marked with their scent and by howling. And not surprisingly, they enjoyed the top spot in their food chain. If a wolf was traveling with a pack, his only real threat, as unlikely as this was, would be from a human. Aside from a wolf trap or poison, Brice could easily see that someone who was hunting a wolf had to be an experienced tracker, a tireless hunter and an expert marksman.

One piece of information that really surprised him was that gray wolves could decimate a coyote population. He had firsthand experience hunting those wily critters in Texas, and couldn't imagine any animal species threatening their numbers.

By the time he returned to the Gray Wolf Inn it was after 6:00 PM and the attractive receptionist who he met earlier had left for the day. Standing in front of the reception counter, he set his overnight bag on the floor along with a plastic bag full of barbecued ribs that he'd just picked up at a nearby restaurant. Without any lines, his "Check In" progressed quickly and ten minutes later he was sitting back on a queen size bed, in a clean room, munching on ribs and watching ESPN's Sports Center on

TV. Eleven hours later he awoke refreshed and walked several blocks to the *Running Bear Pancake House.*

He found a secluded window booth in the back of the restaurant, took a seat and opened the menu. It was early, only one other customer sat at the counter. Chicken fried steak with gravy and biscuits was the breakfast special. That *artery clogger* wasn't what he had in mind. He was rubbing the sleep out of his eyes with the back of his knuckles when a waitress appeared at his side.

"Coffee?" said an attractive and athletic looking waitress in her mid forties.

"Please!"

"You know what you want, 'Hon?'" asked the waitress as she filled Brice's coffee mug.

"Oh yeah, a tall stack of blueberry pancakes and a large orange juice. I've been looking forward to some pancakes since I drove by your restaurant yesterday afternoon," said Brice as he lifted the mug of steaming coffee to his lips.

The waitress wrote down his order on a pad and said, "I noticed you when you came in. Clean cut, walking like you're marching. Are you a Marine?"

Brice set his coffee mug on the tabletop and looked up at the woman. "Yes ma'am, I am. Why do you ask?"

"My son is in boot camp at the Marine Corps Recruit Depot in San Diego," began the waitress tentatively. After a moment's pause and a deep breath, her restraint dissolved and she began to gush excitedly, "It's just me and him. His dad walked out on us when he was born. He's a good boy, but not particularly motivated. He was a good student in high school. I thought he would go on to college after graduating last year, but he seemed to have lost interest in everything. I don't know what happened to him, but he was just drifting."

He lifted a hand and stopped her. "Since it's early, and the place is almost empty, why don't you pour yourself a cup of coffee and sit with me," suggested Brice kindly.

Once she was seated opposite him, Brice continued, "Now, we are in no hurry. Relax and tell me about your son."

"Football seemed to keep him motivated. Games in the fall and weight lifting during the winter and spring. After his last game, he seemed lost. No goals, no purpose. I was worried about him. After seeing some of those Marine Corps ads on TV, I thought they could jump start his life. I drove him to the Idaho Falls recruiting office ten weeks ago and told him to sign up, which he did. Your haircut and posture reminded me of the Marine recruiter who signed him up." Her eyes filled with tears and she held her head in her hands. "I hope I did the right thing?" she sniveled.

Brice took both of her hands in his hands, looked her square in the eye and said evenly, "Two things. One, after boot camp, your son will be a different person. His increased level of maturity and responsibility will be the most obvious changes. But, in time, you will find that your son has set goals for himself. You can rest assured that he'll be a highly motivated person after boot camp. Two, if you have any questions about his military classification, where he's being stationed or the battalion he's assigned to, please give me a call. I'm Gunny Miller, at least for the next few weeks until I'm inducted into the Naval Academy as a plebe. Here's my cell phone number," said Brice. He borrowed the waitress's pen and wrote his name and cell phone number on her order pad.

"Thanks for telling me these things and offering to help me, Brice," said the woman softly, before an attack of hiccups interrupted her.

"Easy now! You're doing fine," said Brice smiling.

After several long moments, the woman regained her composure and said, "You've been very kind. My name is Kristine Haze. One last question, did you say that you're going to the Naval Academy?"

"Yes."

"How did that happen? Didn't you also say that you're a gunnery sergeant," asked Kristine curiously.

"Yes, I did. I am a gunnery sergeant, but each year the Naval Academy, like the other service academies, accept a small number of applicants who are already serving in the military. That's how I was accepted. There are tests to pass and required recommendations from their superiors, but if those details fall into place any enlisted man or woman, your son included, could prospectively apply to the Naval Academy."

"Hmm! That's very interesting. The Naval Academy and West Point recruited my son to play football for them. He was an all-state offensive tackle who is six foot three inches tall and weighs two hundred and fifty pounds of solid muscle. That is according to his high school football program. I went to all of his games." Kristine massaged the side of her head, as if trying to erase the memories of her son's indecision, "He just ignored their letters and phone calls."

"How were his grades?" asked Brice.

"He had the second highest grade point average in his class of two hundred and twenty five students."

"Did he take the SAT exams?"

"Yup! He scored in the ninety-eighth percentile in both math and English. I told him he should look into those schools, but what teenager listens to their parents. I better put your breakfast order in before it's lunchtime."

"What's your son's name?"

"Brian, Brian Haze," she said over her shoulder, as she headed towards the kitchen.

Brice sipped his hot coffee. It tasted wonderful. Two days of hard hiking and two days of frenzied driving had left him drained. After another long, slow sip the coffee's warmth spread through his body and he began to feel energized. Smiling inwardly, he thought, *It won't be long before the Marine Corps transforms another aimless teenager and rewards a hard working, single mother for her foresight.*

Brice lathered his pancakes with farm fresh butter and doused them with Vermont maple syrup. He dove into the pancakes as if it were his last meal. Kristine smiled at his concentrated eating when she, unnoticed by him, refilled his coffee cup. He reminded her of her son's voracious appetite and mealtime silence of a few years earlier. She much preferred that to his latest picky eating habits and his ridiculous discussion of video games.

Propped comfortably against the window in his corner booth, with his empty plate of pancakes pushed aside, Brice reflected on his days of hiking in the Grand Canyon and Zion. He removed his dusty digital camera from his sweatshirt pocket and began viewing the many pictures he'd taken in the parks. The pictures transported him back in time. The colors, the geological shapes, the sounds of the rivers and the solitude of the places, they all appealed to him at some undefined primal level.

When he finally slid out of the bench seat in the pancake house, he looked at his watch. Surprised at how quickly the time had passed, he uttered to no one in particular, "Two hours!" He looked at the check that Kristine had left on his table and plopped enough cash on the table to cover the tab and a generous tip. He looked for Kristine, but she was nowhere to be seen.

As he opened the coffee shop's exit door, he heard the clatter of dishes as someone hustled to a stop behind him.

"You take care, Brice. I'll be calling you," said Kristine with an armful of hot breakfast plates.

Turning he said, "Please do. I want to hear how Brian is doing."

After Brice checked out of the Gray Wolf Inn, he threw his overnight bag into the front seat of his truck and leaned against the front panel. He opened his cell phone and speed dialed Bobby Ridger's home phone, expecting to speak with Bobby's sister or father.

"Hello, this is Bobby!"

"Geez, Bobby is this you or is this a recording?"

"This is a new fangled, state of the art telephone recorder which is voice activated. I can answer calls with a voice command or simply let the call get recorded. It lets me to talk with friends, order groceries and invite lady friends to the house. It's a splendid invention. The only thing it can't do is give my best friend a hug."

"You sound great Bobby. I mean it. Really great!"

"Well shoot… I am great! Nothing's really changed other than I can't move. And even that's changing. Where are you?"

"I'm just leaving West Yellowstone," said Brice.

"Hot dang! You're about forty-five minutes away. The directions to our ranch are simple. Follow the signs out of West Yellowstone to U.S. Route 287, which will take you north towards Dennis. After thirty or so miles, you'll see a sign for the road to Sphinx Mountain. Exactly five miles north of that turnoff, you'll see a ranch entrance arch made with old timbers. Our Ridger Ranch cattle brand, double R's, hangs from the cross timber. There's also a large mailbox out front with an American flag painted on its side. That's our place. Come down the drive and park by the house. The front door is unlocked. I'm the only one home now. My bedroom is straight down the hallway to the back of the house. I can't wait to see you."

"Me neither, buddy. Can I bring you anything?"

"Nope. I'm all set. We've set up a place in the house where you can stay. Drive safe."

"I'll see you in a few."

His best friend sounded like his same old self. Cool and casual with not a care in the world. Bobby could light up a room with his broad smile and non-stop quips. A smile filled Brice's face as he reflected on the good times with Bobby… exercising in the gym together, going out on the town with him and even learning to surf together on the beach near Camp Pendleton.

A couple of minutes later the four-block downtown area of West Yellowstone was far behind. Travelling westbound, he tried to identify familiar landmarks, but then remembered that when he arrived in West Yellowstone the previous afternoon he was traveling in the opposite direction through a thunderstorm. Suddenly, the highway sign for the entrance ramp to U.S. Route 287 North whizzed by his windshield. He glanced in his rearview mirror and saw that no one was behind him. Braking hard and wrenching his steering wheel sharply to his right, he realized, a second to late, that he had totally misjudged the speed of his truck and the acute angle of his turn. Skidding sideways, on two wheels, with his brakes and tires smoking as if they were on fire, he saw that he was leaving the paved road and headed towards an overgrown landscaped area. He straightened his truck out a moment before it flew off the pavement and violently bounced into waist high tumbleweeds and thick brush. Dust and dirt flew over the hood of his truck temporarily blinding him. Though it seemed like minutes, only a few seconds had passed before his visibility cleared and he saw that he was feet from the paved entrance ramp. With a loud crash and thud, he landed onto the entrance ramp.

A truck driver who had seen Brice's bouncing, skidding dust storm, while driving towards Brice on the opposite side of the highway, pumped his air horn and gave Brice a smiling thumbs up wave. Brice waved back sheepishly at the driver as he corrected his steering and cautiously drove his truck along the last hundred feet of the entrance ramp. Had he not added skid plates to the underside of his truck to protect his engine and drive shaft, he knew that he'd be sitting behind the wheel of a badly damaged vehicle with a broken axle and steam gushing from a crushed engine block.

This ain't a slow moving, high riding, armored HUMVEE, big boy, thought Brice as he attempted to collect and calm his jangled nerves.

As his composure returned, the natural beauty of the valley began to unfold before him. Roadside wild flowers were bursting with color and knee high, green grass danced languidly with the morning breeze. White puffs of cotton seemed to float on invisible air currents from one flowering cottonwood stand to the next. On his right, snow capped mountains rose steeply from rolling hills into cloudless blue skies. Curving valleys and high meadows peeked alluringly between the white-spired sentries that overlooked the valley floor.

The famous Madison River flowed on the left side of the road. With his elevated view of the river from his pickup, Brice could see that the river was running near or over its banks in most places. It was high, fast and dangerous water. He'd overheard a couple of fly fishermen in West Yellowstone complain about their cold spring and how it had delayed the runoff of that winter's heavy snowfall. The river was now one hard rushing riffle after another. There were no drift boats on the water and he saw only a few fly fishermen who were carefully positioned close to the banks, in protected pockets of water, casting to back eddies or inside river seams. He suspected those gutsy fishermen might be enjoying good fishing in light of the number of salmon flies that smeared themselves on his windshield. The reddish flies were the size of large grasshoppers and were prized morsels for hungry trout after a long, cold winter.

At times, the river flowed boldly in full view. But, like a flirtatious woman, it would unexpectedly meander away from the road and disappear below flat, grasslands into hidden, secret riverbeds. This magnificent scenery with its colorful flora, snow caped mountains and racing river was a sharp contrast to the dry, flat and dusty landscapes that he was so accustomed to in West Texas. "Big Sky" country was love at first sight.

Brice passed the Sphinx Mountain road sign and checked his odometer. Exactly five miles later he recognized the Ridger mailbox, with its American flag painted on its side, and turned his truck onto their driveway. He passed through open wrought-iron gates and beneath a fourteen-foot timber arch. The gates met split rail fences and the arch was solidly built with large oak beams. From the center of the arch hung the prominent Ridger Ranch cattle brand, two overlapping "R's." Hail and lightning in the summer and blizzards and high winds in the winter had taken their toll on the aged beams and rusting steel cattle brand. They both looked as if they were a hundred years old.

A cloud of dust followed him as drove slowly down the rutted dirt driveway towards the ranch house and red barn. Cattle grazed lazily on each side of the drive. In a corral attached to the barn, several horses nickered as he parked in front of the weathered, single-story ranch house. An aged Willy's Jeep was parked just inside the open barn doors.

He climbed two steps to a broad, covered front porch that faced west. Several bentwood chairs were neatly arranged along the side of the house. Through the screen door, he saw that the front door was halfway open. There was neither a doorbell nor a doorknocker.

"Hello, anybody home? It's Brice Miller," he said loudly.

"Brice, come on in. My bedroom is in the back of the house, straight down the hallway past the staircase," said Bobby.

The screen door closed with a slap and Bobby heard footsteps walking down the hallway. Brice was greeted with a low growl as he stopped abruptly at Bobby's open bedroom door. A mid-sized dog lay against Bobby, his teeth bared. The dog had pointed ears and a short, blue-mottled coat with tan markings. Though Brice had been around dogs his whole life, he'd never seen a dog with these features. The longer he studied the animal the more he questioned whether it was indeed a dog. It looked and acted like a wolf.

"Good to see you, Bobby. I hope your… er, dog has eaten recently. It looks and sounds as if he'd like to make a meal out of me," said Brice cautiously.

Bobby grinned broadly at his best friend and said, "You look great good buddy. Just great! This is Blue. He's an Australian cattle dog. He's rather protective and territorial. He'll rip your arm off if you don't make a nice first impression. Walk in slowly and let him smell a couple of knuckles on your hand. Give him a big smile and don't show any fear."

"That's easy for you to say. I'll offer my three finger hand so if things go bad I'll still have one good hand."

Bobby affectionately rubbed a few inches of Blue's stomach with his left hand as he spoke in a calm, friendly manner, "Blue, this is my best friend, Brice. Treat him nicely!"

Brice took a deep breath and stepped slowly towards Bobby's bed. When he was an arms length from Blue, he calmly extended the back of his right hand. Blue sniffed his three knuckles and moaned softly, as if saddened by Brice's injury. He softly licked Brice's hand in an apparent attempt to heal his injury.

"You have a new friend."

"That's a relief. I had second thoughts about extending my injured hand. If he chomped off the three fingers on that hand, it would have been weird getting a medical discharge from the Marines because of a dog bite."

"I don't think he would have taken all three fingers in one bite. He has a small mouth and his teeth have dulled over the years," said Bobby with a chuckle.

"Unhuh," grunted Brice, as he smiled.

Bobby and Brice stared at one another, motionless for several moments. Memories, both good and bad, flooded their minds. Wordlessly, these brothers in arms reunited. Blue saw tears of compassion fill the corner of Brice's eyes. He moved to the other side of the bed so his master's friend could take the place he had warmed.

CHAPTER 11
AWFUL LAWFUL

Bill Ridger was casually strolling along the sidewalk of Dennis' main street. It was warmer than usual for an early June day and he had a few minutes to kill before his 1:00 PM lunch meeting with the mayor. He paused outside the local sporting goods store to inspect their sidewalk, clearance sale display. The store owner's yellow Labrador lay peacefully in the warm sunshine beside the display. Seeing the shopper, the dog flopped his tail in a friendly greeting. Bill leaned down and scratched behind the dog's ear. As Bill did so, a marked down winter camouflage jacket hanging from a peg just inside the store's front door caught his attention. He stepped inside the shop to examine it. While checking the size of the jacket, the docile Labrador behind him yelped in pain. Turning, he saw the dog licking its side and heard muffled laughter. Someone had kicked the dog. An instant later, he saw a man's foot give the dog a second vicious kick.

Bill rushed outside and found himself face to face with the town's two uniformed policemen. Fred Dower, the sheriff, and his deputy son, Skip. Both men were six foot, four inches in height with muscular arms and flat faces that were highlighted with perpetual sneers. Flabby, soft bellies sagged pathetically over the tops of their trousers, hiding their wide police belts. Each man was chewing on a toothpick and laughing at the cowering dog. Their flushed, red faces indicated that they had been drinking.

When Bill stepped closer to them, his impression was confirmed. They both reeked of alcohol.

"You drink your lunch again, Fred? And now you're kicking friendly dogs," said Bill angrily.

Fred slurred, "The dog tried to bite me. He doesn't belong on the sidewalk. I could have the dog taken away and put down. I could also lock you up little man for interfering with my duties."

A crowd of townspeople quickly circled the three men and dog, all of whom had seen the sheriff maliciously kick the dog.

"Listen sport, there are a dozen people here who saw you kick this resting dog. He didn't try to bite you. You attacked him. Everyone in town pets this dog when they pass by. The city allows dogs on sidewalks and in shops. You're a pitiful excuse for a policeman!"

Fred's hand went for his holstered pistol and the crowd gasped. Skip Dower quickly restrained his father's arm.

"OK, OK, this was an accident. Let's all calm down. My dad must have accidentally stepped on the dog. No one's hurt. We'll just move on," said Skip as he attempted, unsuccessfully, to steer his drunken and enraged father away from the store.

Fred Dower's threatening move towards his sidearm triggered a dormant, but ingrained response in Bill that had been hammered into him during his days in the Marine Corps. In an instant, his cool, calm nature dissolved. With eyes blazing and fists balled, he took an aggressive step towards the sheriff, fully intending to knock the living daylights out of the cruel bastard. Fortunately for the sheriff, an attractive, older woman, who was standing in the crowd, anticipated Bill's response. She quickly jumped between the two men, bumping Bill slightly to the side in the process. The unexpected presence of a third party surprised him.

As Bill turned his attention to the newcomer, the woman's animosity exploded. She forcefully drove her forefinger into the sheriff's chest and barked, "Freddy, you were a troublemaker when you were in my 11th grade class thirty two years ago, and you've gotten worse with age."

The woman, Emma Austin, was a retired teacher and a leading voice on the City Council. She was a remarkably fit, one hundred and ten pound retiree in her mid sixties who filled her days hiking the local mountains, exercising at the YMCA and volunteering at the local Humane Society.

"Don't ever abuse an animal like you just did, or you'll find yourself behind bars. Go back to your office and sober-up," she said with a final, forceful forefinger jab to his chest.

Fred began to object when his son said, "Yeah, yeah, we're leaving. You hoity-toity 'grey hairs' think you own the place!"

"We do own the place! And, both of you can be replaced," said Emma angrily.

Skip whispered, "dyke bitch," inaudibly under his breath. He began to pull his father away from the crowd when he nearly collided with a young salesman who marched out of the sporting goods store pulling a heavily loaded handcart. An unshaven, swarthy man in his late thirties followed closely behind the salesman.

"Hey, Ajani! How ya doin'?" slurred Fred.

Ajani ignored Fred, turned away from the group and quickly moved to the rear of a Ford Explorer that was parked fifteen feet away at the curb. He moved in a suspicious crouch that suggested he was hiding something.

Bill looked at the handcart. It was loaded with four cases of 5.56X45 mm NATO ammunition cartridges. Each case was filled with 1200 rounds.

Ajani was fumbling with his car keys when Bill stepped in front of him. Smiling, Bill said, "Hunting or target practice?"

"Ajani's my friend. He's a hunter," belched Fred.

"That's nice. What are you hunting, Ajani?" asked Bill easily.

"Ah, bears!" said Ajani with a strong Arabic accent.

"What kind of bears?"

"Grizzlies!" interjected Fred.

"Grizzlies are protected! You can't hunt them, but even if you could, this ammunition wouldn't stop one," exclaimed the young salesman.

"Dad's confused. Ajani is using the ammunition for target practice and maybe turkeys," offered Skip.

"Yeah, turkeys! Just like the ones I have to deal with everyday," laughed Fred as he began to hiccup.

Ajani quickly loaded the cases of ammunition into the back of his Ford Explorer. With his head down, he scurried to the driver's door and slipped into the drivers seat. He drove away from the curb with the overly attentiveness of a newly licensed driver. Or, thought Bill, *someone trying to avoid unwanted attention.* In the meantime, Skip grasped his father's upper arm firmly and the two of them began to shuffle away.

Bill watched the Ford drive south, out of town, towards West Yellowstone. Emma glared at the Dower's as they staggered away towards the police station.

Several moments later, Bill turned to Emma and said appreciatively, "Thanks Ms. Austin for intervening. I was on the verge of doing something I may have regretted."

"I suspect that *something* was something every resident in town would like to do to those losers."

"You're right. But I think our best solution is what you suggested… replace them," said Bill.

Fred Dower had been running roughshod over the town's peaceful citizenry since he became the town's first sheriff three years earlier. Police conduct went from bad to worse when Fred hired his son, Skip, eighteen months into his term. Within thirty days of his appointment, Skip allegedly molested a fourteen-year-old girl following her late afternoon music lesson at the high school. According to the girl, she was walking home from school when Skip stopped his squad car beside her, and ordered her into the car where he proceeded to fondle her breasts. Skip claimed the girl came on to him.

It was a classic "he said, she said" case. The girl's parents elected not to file charges against the police department, though everyone in town believed the young deputy was guilty of, at the very least, lewd behavior with a minor. In light of Skip's continued harassment of his daughter, Molly, and her friend, Penny, there was no doubt in Bill's mind that Skip preyed on women.

"I hear you're having lunch with the mayor in a few minutes to discuss this very issue," said Emma.

"Yes, Ms. Austin. Fred is a mean, bad-tempered jerk whether he's sober or not. His son on the other hand… " said Bill, as he paused to collect his thoughts. "I think he's a sick pervert who preys upon women. His stalking and harassment of younger women in this town is escalating."

"Billy, you're old enough to call me Emma. The mayor has asked my new boyfriend to join you for lunch. You'll like him. He's a retired Marine Corps colonel who lost his wife of thirty-five years to cancer several years ago. He's an avid fly fisherman from San Diego who decided a change of scenery might help him overcome his grief."

"Would he consider becoming the sheriff?"

"I doubt it, but he's willing to do whatever he can to help the town."

"That's good news. I look forward to meeting him," said Bill.

"Good luck with resolving our problem with our two rotten cops. They have antagonized everyone in town. And say hello to my new sweetie," said Emma, as she abruptly marched across the street to the coffee shop to meet her girlfriends over coffee and spread the latest gossip.

Five minutes later, Bill stood beside the front door of a restaurant watching the mayor's SUV pull into a parking stall. The mayor and three others exited the SUV. Bill knew the mayor and one of the other three. He was his close friend and hunting buddy, District Judge Bill Bramley. Mayor Murph Hayes introduced him to the other two new faces. One was the head cop in charge of the Montana State Highway Patrol in Helena, Alan Fischer, and the other was Emma's newest flame, Col. Jan Dank. They filed into the restaurant, followed the mayor to a semi-private alcove in the back of the dining area and sat at a well-oiled oak table.

Mayor Hayes pulled from the table's centerpiece a small chalkboard on which was scribbled the daily specials. He quickly perused the chalkboard and passed it to Fischer who was sitting next to him.

"The city's official dining room. I see that the filet mignon and lobster are missing from today's specials. However, all of their sandwiches and burgers are excellent, as is their salad bar," said the mayor lightly.

After a few minutes of menu review and small talk, the five men gave their lunch orders to their waitress.

The mayor spoke first, "I appreciate all of you taking time out of your busy schedules to meet with me. Especially, Alan Fischer who traveled here from Helena. Our number one problem in Dennis is our two policemen, Fred and Skip Dower. Father and son are both loose cannons who should be behind our jail's cells rather than managing them. It's like the fox guarding the hen house.

"When we became an incorporated city about three years ago, and left the protective umbrella of the State Highway Patrol, our city charter specified that we could appoint, rather than elect, a sheriff. As a newborn, independent city, we had a number of start-up costs that we hadn't anticipated. We cut costs in areas that we shouldn't have. Our most imprudent cut involved the annual salary for sheriff. Our advertised salary on our Internet job posting was far below the norm for a city our size. No one expressed interest in the position other than our own homegrown moron, Fred Dower.

"As our start-up costs disappeared, we enjoyed an influx of second homebuyers and, hence, an increased level of property tax revenues. We had enough room in our budget to bring Fred's salary up to a competitive level and cover the cost of another full time deputy. Not surprisingly, Fred hired his son who, rumor has it, had just been kicked out of the Army with a bad conduct discharge. The two of them have systematically harassed and intimated just about everyone in town. The judge will describe some of their offenses," concluded the mayor.

Judge Bill Bramley began to detail the Dowers offenses. "Shortly after Fred was appointed sheriff, a number of residents appealed traffic citations. When Skip joined his father on the police force, the appeals expanded to zoning infractions from many of the ranchers. From there, the appeals grew to citations for public behavior. In general, all of the resident's appeals were valid objections to the Dower's improper and indiscriminate use of their authority."

"Whoa!" said the mayor. "Zoning infractions? I never heard about that. They aren't responsible for that."

"Originally, the Dowers used the threat of zoning infractions to extort free beef from the ranchers. But, things have gotten worse recently and several ranchers suspect that the Dowers are now trying to acquire an isolated outbuilding, on a rent free basis, where they can set up some sort of shady operation," said the judge.

"Jackasses," grumbled the mayor.

"There's more. Six months after Fred's appointment, as I became swamped with appeals and protests, I invited him into my chambers for a discussion about his duties and his police powers. He didn't listen to a word I said. He said he didn't care a lick about our liberal laws. He was going to run his department the way he saw fit. His exact words were... 'I'm the law around here now. What I say and do shall not be questioned. If you or anyone else messes with me it might not be good for their health.'"

"He threatened you?" asked Fischer.

"Yes, and he's warned me as recently as one week ago about dismissing anymore of his citations. I think he's full of hot air, but now that his son has joined him, that changes the dynamics of the situation. The son is the one I worry about. He influences his dad and I get the sense that he's an unbalanced young man. The appeals continue to grow. None of his citations cite a civil infraction. Under the comments section of the citation, father or son simply scribbles in the alleged offense... disrespectful to police officer, restaurant serves bad food, property owner prohibits public hunting and fishing on his property, rancher leaves farm equipment outside his barn, shop owner's prices are to high, etc. In general, I'd say the Dower's goals are to shake down the merchants, ranchers and citizenry for cash, free goods and services. If anyone balks, the Dowers simply cite him or her. The Dower's personal agenda is what guides them, not police protection for our community," said the judge.

"Sounds like two real bad apples," said Jan Dank.

Then, Bill Ridger chimed in, "I hate to add fuel to the fire, but I, like the judge, am particularly concerned about the behavior of the son, Skip. His stalking of young girls in town is escalating. First, there was his molestation charge of a fourteen-year-old girl who was walking home from school a year or so ago. Now, he has targeted my daughter, Molly, and her best friend, Penny. He parks his cruiser by the traffic light on the north side of town and waits for them to return home from their classes at Montana State. When he spots the girl's vehicle, he pulls them over, for some bullshit reason and plants himself at the driver's open window. He makes lewd suggestions to both girls and intimates that he could make life difficult for them if they don't accommodate him."

"Oh, Christ! This is getting out of hand," complained the judge.

"Well, listen to this! Molly's best friend, Penny, has an aunt in West Yellowstone who is an accountant. A client of her aunt's, who owns a bar there, told her that one of their barmaids was roughed up by a young deputy from Dennis during a weekend trip to Las Vegas two weeks ago. There was talk of rape charges being filed against the deputy, but the girl suddenly left town with an extra $5,000 in her checking account. Since there is only one young deputy in Dennis, it's got to be Skip. Further, he proposed the same Las Vegas trip to Penny, several times, in the last month during his phony traffic stops," added Bill.

Alan Fischer, the top man with the Montana State Highway Patrol, had been listening attentively to the complaints. He was a handsome, well-built man of medium height in his early fifties with a short, military type haircut, laser like brown eyes and an inscrutable demeanor. A short hitch in the Marine Corps thirty years earlier helped finance his college education at Montana State University, Billings campus, where he majored in law enforcement. After graduating from college, his first assignment was a posting to Montana's highways in the vicinity of Dennis. During that posting, which lasted ten years, he developed a friendly, but professional relationship with Judge Bill Bramley.

Because of the vastness of Montana and the large number of small towns throughout the state, most of whom couldn't afford to staff a full-time police department, the Montana State Highway Patrol was tasked with overseeing law enforcement in these towns. Additionally, federal law enforcement agencies often asked the state, which meant the Montana State Highway Patrol, to police and investigate federal matters. Dennis, Montana, fell into the "small town" category up until three years earlier when they became an incorporated city and appointed their first sheriff, the troublesome Fred Dower.

In the late '80s, Fischer was promoted to the officer in charge of coordinating all intra-agency federal matters on behalf of the Montana State Highway Patrol. Because of his diligence and thoroughness in performing his duties in his new position, the Montana State Highway Patrol was selected as the first nationally accredited Highway Patrol in the country. The governor of Montana, Aidan Barrett, and many of the state's part time legislators felt strongly that Fischer's high level of professionalism played a key role in this selection. It was this national highway patrol accreditation that thrust Fischer into the top post at the Montana State Highway Patrol.

"Have you had any local increase in drug dealing, rowdy biker activity or hate crimes?" asked Fischer evenly.

"Yes on the biker activity. Usually the bikers hang out on the weekends at a tavern several miles out of town on an empty stretch of the highway. However, in the last year or so, they have migrated into town. Fred and Skip are both bikers. They may have encouraged that relocation," said the mayor.

"No hate crimes at all. We had an unusual influx of Middle Eastern types this past winter, which was strange. We have no skiing, snowmobiling or hunting opportunities to draw tourists of any background to town during that time of year," added the judge.

"An hour ago, I was involved with Fred and Skip in an incident in front of the sporting goods store," said Bill. "Fred was drunk and kicked the yellow Labrador that lies in front of the store. We had words, but just as the Dowers were leaving, a salesman from the store nearly ran into Fred with a handcart. The handcart was loaded with four cases of M-16 ammunition, 1200 rounds per case."

"What the fuck!" burst the normally tranquil mayor.

"It gets worse. I confronted the man and asked him the ammo was for. He said, with a very thick Arabic accent, it was for hunting grizzlies."

"Grizzlies? They're protected! Everyone knows that," said the mayor incredulously.

"Not this guy. Fred and Skip both knew the man and called him Ajani. Skip corrected the man's story and said his ammunition was for target practice and possibly hunting turkeys," said Bill.

The men sat in silence for several long moments as they each digested this latest news.

Fischer broke the silence. "Let's look at the facts. Firstly, I checked on Fred's background before this meeting and I know that he was involved with a white supremacy group twenty-five years ago. His pals went to jail for planning a bombing and somehow Fred got off the hook. I don't know anything about his son, but I will follow-up with my Washington contacts on the details of Skip's bad conduct discharge from the Army. Drunk and disorderly conduct is the basis for most bad conduct discharges from the military. However, if his discharge was related to his predatory nature towards women, you are dealing with an altogether different and worrisome matter. My experience with predators is that their behavior rarely improves. If anything, the bastards get worse over time.

"Secondly, both father and son have clearly abused their police powers and are probably leveraging their position of authority for their personal benefit. Thirdly, someone or some group is paying for trips to Las Vegas and $5,000 in hush money," added Fischer.

Bill interrupted Fischer, "According to my daughter, Fred also just bought a new $30,000 motorcycle."

Fischer reflected a moment on this latest news before he continued, "Lastly, I am really bothered by Bill's latest observation of this Ajani guy purchasing four cases of M-16 ammunition. Damn, an M-16 isn't a hunting rifle, especially for bears. It's an automatic assault rifle."

Lot's of easy money for two bad cops and, now, their relationship with a Middle Eastern outsider who just bought 4,800 rounds of M-16 ammunition. This is just the tip of the iceberg. Something bigger is brewing, thought Fischer.

Fischer continued, "Independently, and this information is to be kept confidential between the five of us, I've received disconcerting reports from my highway patrolmen in this area. The Dowers have stopped them and told them they have no business in or around Dennis. They pointedly told my patrolmen the same thing they said to the judge... they are *the law* in Dennis and to stay off of their "turf." I'm afraid what all of us are seeing might be the indications of a bigger problem."

From his jacket pocket Fischer pulled out two Highway Patrol reserve badges and placed them on the table. He turned towards the judge and spoke, "I have the authority to appoint reserve deputies to the Highway Patrol. When a smaller community, like Dennis, already has a police department in place, I normally steer clear of local law enforcement issues. However, in this case, there appears to be a very fundamental problem... the 'foxes' are not only guarding the hen house, they're already in the hen house. I'd be willing to take the unusual step of deputizing two local individuals to my highway patrol. These deputies will keep me personally apprised of what's happening locally. I don't want local matters to go from bad to worse. Also, I suggest you consider firing the Dower's for cause as soon as possible.

"These deputy appointments will be unpaid, volunteer positions that I'll review every three months. Judge do you have any recommendations now or would you like to discuss this further with the mayor? The fewer people who know about this the better."

"The mayor and I discussed this possibility earlier this morning. We have two candidates in mind. One has already said he'd be willing to volunteer if the need arose. The other, Bill Ridger, knows nothing of our earlier discussion," said the judge, as he nodded towards Bill.

"What do you say, Bill? We need someone like you in this temporary position. Someone everyone in town knows and trusts," said the mayor.

"My plate is pretty full running the ranch, taking care of my son and, now, keeping tabs on my daughter's whereabouts. Who's the other volunteer?" asked Bill.

"Col. Jan Dank. Unlike you, he hardly knows anyone in town, which I think is a positive. He can operate below the radar. Neither the Dowers nor any of our local busy bodies know him. He's a retired Marine Corps Col. with twenty-five years of distinguished service to his credit. General Chuck Hay, USMC (retired), who grew up in Dennis and who just recently relocated to San Diego spoke very highly of Col. Dank. Further, Jan told me that during his last two stateside tours, the base military police reported to him so he has some prior law enforcement experience. Jan, why don't you tell the boys a little bit about yourself and what you've been doing in Dennis since you arrived here," said the judge as he turned to Jan.

Jan was a lean man, six foot three inches in height, with thinning blonde hair and intense gray eyes. His bulging, muscular shoulders, slight limp and crooked, pug nose suggested that he had been involved in his share of fistfights of over the years. In fact, his crooked, pug nose was the result of numerous broken noses that occurred during Golden Gloves championship bouts as a youth and later bouts as a perennial heavyweight boxer on the Marine Corps boxing team. His limp, however, was not the result of any boxing, but rather from a Viet Cong bullet to his hip during violent battles in and around Khe Sanh, Vietnam in 1968 when he was in command of a platoon of Marines.

A unique quality of Jan's life, which began in the Marine Corps, was his daily devotion to exercise. He was an early morning gym rat. His uncompromising workout routine began every morning at 5:30 AM sharp with five minutes of strenuous stretching, followed by sixty minutes of station-to-station weightlifting. He concluded each workout with ten minutes of punching the speed bag until his sweatshirt was soaked.

He slowly and rhythmically began each speed bag session with a gentle tap of the teardrop bag with the back of one of his gloved hands. As his punching speed increased, his mind began to concentrate on the coordination and speed of his hands, arms, shoulders and torso while his body monitored the ebb and flow of his stamina. Sad thoughts of loved ones lost, his wife and best friends in the Corps, were absent from his mind when he was focused on the speed bag.

When he punched the speed bag machine gun style, his hands were a blur and his rhythm much like a fast drum roll. At the conclusion of each of his workouts his body was physically drained, but his mind was energized and refreshed. A psychologist might liken it to the "high" a runner experiences after a long, strenuous run. Endorphins are released into the runner's body which, in turn, gives the runner a euphoric sense of contentment. Whatever the cause of the euphoria, Jan was addicted to the end result. He thought it ironic, however, that he had to all but physically collapse before he could appreciate the joys of daily life.

"I retired from the Marine Corps twenty years ago as a full bird colonel and settled down with my wife at our home in Carlsbad, California, which is near Camp Pendleton. For fifteen wonderful years after my retirement, my wife and I travelled to places that we'd always dreamed about seeing. Both my wife and I were avid hikers. We trekked through the Alps in Europe, the Milford track in New Zealand and the John Muir trail in the Sierras, fantastic country and wonderful times. Three years ago my wife learned that she had cancer, an undetected cancer that had spread into her lymph nodes. She died six months later. The light of my life... gone!" said Jan, as his voice cracked and his head sank.

He collected himself after a few moments and continued, "We didn't have children and there were too many sad reminders of happier times with my wife in San Diego. So, I sold the house, furniture, everything about a year ago and moved to Dennis. During my first summer here, I spent much of my time fly fishing on the Madison River. The last five months, I've winterized my thirty year old, new house. I did this in the middle of the winter, which is something I wouldn't recommend, especially with the kind of winters you have.

"The only people I know locally are a couple of fellow fly fishermen who I've met on the Madison River, my girlfriend, Emma Austin, who I met at the gym and those helpful folks who work at Ace Hardware. Emma has been a lifesaver. With the loss of my wife, she's filled a huge void in my personal life. We've been constant companions for the past six months.

"Neither my eyesight nor my body is as strong as it once was, but I still have strong passion for putting bad guys in their proper place. Once I finish installing the last thermal window in my house, which should be by 1600 hours this afternoon, I will have plenty of free time. I'd be honored to help you out."

"That's all I needed to hear from a fellow Marine. Ooray! I'm in! I look forward to working with you, Jan, on our covert mission," said Bill smiling.

"Men, I've got to get back to the office. Alan, thanks for coming to meet with us. You'll have our town's full cooperation on this matter," said the mayor as he picked up the lunch tab and headed towards the cashiers counter.

"I've got to get back to my chambers as well. Alan, I trust that you may have some paperwork and instructions for both Bill and Jan. If you need any administrative help, my office is yours," said the judge.

"Thanks, judge. I'll stop by your office after I finish up here and make you copies of Bill and Jan's official deputy paperwork for your records," said Fischer.

Fischer considered the backgrounds of Bill and Jan before he addressed them. Were they younger, less experienced men he would have kept them on a short leash and micro-managed their activities from Helena. Fortunately, there was no need for that with these two volunteers. The judge had told him privately before lunch that both Bill and Jan were trustworthy and clear thinking men. He was also pleased to hear of Jan's former military police experience. That could be a real asset. His sixth sense also told him that he didn't have the luxury of time to investigate, from Helena, the criminal activity of the Dowers in Dennis.

"I'd like both of you to keep confidential what I'm about to say. It's not that I don't trust the judge, the mayor or your family and friends, but the longer we keep your deputations secret, the longer your activities will be productive. Eventually, word of your deputations will get back to the Dowers and their confederates, whoever they may be, and I may be pressured to end or curtail your efforts.

"These are the activities which lead me to believe something *big* is brewing," said Fischer as he ticked off the issues with the fingers on his right hand.

"Brazen actions- The Dower's warnings to my highway patrolmen to stay away from Dennis. Only an idiot or someone with money and highly placed political connections would make that kind of threat.

"Snooping around ranches- They are looking for a secret hiding place to either make something illegal, or store something illegal. My guess is that they're looking to set up a meth lab. Damn meth labs are everywhere. Keep your ears to the ground with respect to all things meth related... large purchases of decongestants at your drug stores, meth being sold at the schools, new faces in town hanging out at bars sipping beer or soft drinks.

"Lots of pocket money- Fred and Skip Dower are on someone's criminal payroll and it's not penny-ante amounts. I don't sense that any kind of full-scale regional meth lab is up and running yet, but I'm concerned about the source and purpose of this upfront money.

"New faces in town- Any influx of new faces in this small town should draw your attention, especially if there is no reason or purpose for these folks to be here. Bill, your report on this fellow named Ajani is particularly disturbing. Please check with the owner of the sporting goods store on Ajani's ammunition purchases

"Skip Dower's female relations- I'm going to look further into his Army record, if I can, and see what I can learn there. Aside from probably being a lousy soldier, I suspect it may reveal a history of violence towards women. I'll also check the National Sex Offense Registry. Like you Bill, I have the uneasy feeling the bastard is a sexual predator.

"You can call me at the office or on my cell phone at anytime for any reason... information, questions... just call! The dumbest question is the question not asked! However, calls to my office might raise eyebrows in my department and I'm leery of someone on my staff listening to my conversations. I prefer that you call me on my cell phone, if necessary. Lastly, though I can't authorize you to carry a hand gun, I recommend you get a hand gun and a license to carry it."

"I have a license for my Glock. I carry it when I'm out on my ranch. It's for critters. I also have several rifles for bird hunting and game. I have licenses for all of them," said Bill.

"My .45 caliber pistol is licensed and I have a couple of sniping rifles which are licensed. The rifles are the same models that I used in the Marine Corps," added Jan.

"You were a sniper in the Marines?" asked Fischer.

"Early on, yes. I haven't shot my rifles at a range though in probably ten years," said Jan.

"OK, well I hope you won't need them. With respect to using a handgun, as a volunteer deputy, neither of you are authorized to brandish, present or use your handgun in the course of your investigative activities. However, if you or any other innocent party is threatened by someone using a dangerous weapon... pistol, rifle, knife, crowbar, etc.... you may use your weapon for protective purposes, and as my deputy you shall be protected under Montana law. I'm going to give each of you a copy of our Highway Patrol Regulations Manual. I want both of you to read it and send me a signed affidavit confirming that you've done so within the next few days.

"In closing, the most important piece of advice I can give you is that the criminal mind is cunning. It is unpredictable and it can be very violent. Don't let your guard down and always err on the side of caution," said Fischer.

He handed the two men badges, the manuals and their deputy volunteer agreements. They each signed a badge receipt and volunteer deputy form.

Outside the restaurant, Bill and Jan watched Fischer cross the street and head to the judge's chambers.

"He's a no nonsense guy. I like him," said Jan.

"Me too. The sooner we rid ourselves of the Dower's the better," said Bill with an edge in his voice.

"I share Fischer's concerns that something bigger is brewing. There is way too much weird stuff occurring." After a brief pause, he added, "Emma texted me just before we met you for lunch today. She described your confrontation with the Dowers."

Bill regarded Jan with a look of surprise.

"Word does travel fast these days with texting on our cell phones. Emma is quite a lady. She was my 11th grade teacher many years ago. Say, why don't the two of you come to our house for dinner tomorrow night.

I'd like to introduce you to my daughter and son. And, I'd like to catch up with Emma. I've just waved and nodded to her in the past five years, but I have never stopped to really talk with her, or thank her for visiting and helping my wife during her battle with cancer. I know my wife really appreciated all her support. You're a lucky guy," said Bill sincerely.

"I know I'm lucky. She's a beautiful person. I'd be lost without her. I'll check with her and let you know if we can make it for dinner. I look forward to working with you," said Jan as he extended his hand.

Bill looked him square in the eye as they exchanged a strong handshake, "I feel the same way, 'pardner!'"

CHAPTER 12
MOLLY AND BRICE

Molly stood in the open barn door of the Ridger ranch with her hands on her hips. Late afternoon sunshine spilled across the barn's hard packed, dirt floor. She studied the scene before her. Her brother was strapped into her mother's old wheel chair and his Marine Corps friend was hidden beneath the hood of their jeep. Bobby was offering his friend one repair suggestion after another... clean the spark plug points, adjust the carburetor screw and make sure the battery connections are good. Though she was elated to see her brother involved with the restoration of his favorite vehicle, she was concerned about his level of ambition. It was only a few days earlier that Dr. Matthews said he was strong enough to sit in a wheelchair.

"How're you doing 'Mr. Ants-in-your pants?'"

Bobby slowly turned his head a couple of inches towards his sister. "We've been busy, Sis. The house is wheelchair friendly again. Brice re-installed the front door threshold shims and the plywood ramp that we used for Mom. And, we're now fixing the jeep. It wouldn't start so I asked Brice to check a few things under the hood. I have to keep a close eye on him because he doesn't know much about engines," said Bobby flashing a playful smile.

"Don't know much about engines, huh? Other than you, who knows anything about a 50-year-old engine? Everything in here is backwards.

By the way, I can see someone has performed some pretty shoddy work. There is nothing but electrical tape holding this engine together. I wonder who did that, 'Mr. Fix-it?' By the way, are you talking to yourself or is someone else here?" grunted Brice as his arms and shoulders twisted around the engine block.

"My sister, Molly, is here. I'll introduce you once you've finished your work."

Brice emerged from beneath the jeep's hood a minute later with an oily rag in one hand and a wrench in the other. He looked towards Bobby's sister who was still standing inside the barn door. With the sun behind her, all he could see was the outline of her fully formed body. She, on the other had, had the benefit of a million candlepower of sunshine to scrutinize her brother's friend. His scruffy jeans and boots, with loose laces that dragged along the dirt floor, reminded her of the disheveled teenage boys in high school. As her eyes moved upwards to his oil smeared, skintight tee shirt, she was impressed with his muscled stomach and large shoulders. Few college males, and even fewer high school males, possessed such a striking physique. This was a well-built, mature man.

Brice stepped to the side, out of the sunlight, which marginally improved his vision. As he smiled easily to the outline of the female figure, still hidden by the brilliant sunlight, he said, "Hey!"

His simple comment coupled with his rugged good looks and warm, dimpled smile caused Molly's heart to skip a beat, a first for her. His piercing blue eyes and short blonde hair added to his allure.

Bobby was right. He is a 'hunk!'

Molly stepped out of the sunlight and moved towards Brice. When she was within arm reach, she extended her hand for a handshake and said tentatively, "I'm pleased to meet you, Brice. Bobby has told me a lot about you. You're one of his best friends."

Brice could now clearly see Molly and her extended hand. His body and mind froze. He'd never been this close to such a beautiful woman. Molly's silky red hair, which hung loosely over her shoulders, framed a perfectly sculpted wholesome and eye-catching face. He didn't comprehend anything she was saying or doing.

"Huh!" mumbled Brice, with his arms glued to his side.

Bobby could hardly contain his amusement with their awkward

moment. He suspected that they would like one another, but he wasn't expecting immediate fireworks. This was puppy love at its finest.

"Wipe the grease off your right hand, 'Sarge.' Introduce yourself to Molly and shake her hand," said Bobby snickering.

Brice's muddled mind eventually grasped Bobby's simple, but affected, suggestion.

"I'm Brice, Molly, and I'm very pleased to meet you as well," he blurted, as he vigorously shook her hand.

After several awkward hand pumps, Molly pulled away from Brice's grip and frowned at her grease-covered hand. She reached for the rag Brice held in his opposite hand.

Seeing the grease smear, Brice asserted, "Oh, let me!"

"No, let me," said Molly, as they each tugged on opposite ends of the rag.

"Oh, let me!" sang Bobby melodramatically.

As if on cue, they each released the rag. When they simultaneously stooped to retrieve it, they collided and instinctively grabbed one another for support. Both their faces reddened with embarrassment.

"Already groping!" laughed Bobby.

Brice and Molly's self conscious restraint crumbled and uninhabited laughter filled the barn.

*

After dinner that night, the Ridger's and Brice lingered around the dinner table chatting lightly and drinking coffee. Every so often, Brice would raise Bobby's coffee mug so he could sip his coffee through a straw. Brice performed this simple gesture with the natural ease of a family member who had been helping Bobby eat and drink for years.

Bill had met Brice once before. It was just prior to one of Bobby's many surgeries at the Naval Medical Center, San Diego. From their brief discussions at the time, Bill suspected that Brice felt responsible in some way for Bobby's injuries. After hearing his son's account of that fateful mission, he knew that any lingering guilt his friend harbored was completely unfounded. He also knew, from his own personal combat experience, that it was one thing to be told that you bore no responsibility for a fellow Marine's injury and another to feel it in your heart.

Aside from being enamored with Brice, Molly was surprised at his interaction with her brother. They seemed to think the same thoughts and say the same things. It was as if they were twins. Sometime during dinner, while Brice was helping Bobby with his meal, she also realized how thoughtful and compassionate he was. Beneath his rugged exterior was a sensitive man.

"Brice, you're welcome to stay with us as long as you like," said Bill.

"I appreciate that, sir, but a couple of things have come up at Camp Pendleton and I can only stay a week, if that's OK?" said Brice.

"Please call me, Bill. A week is fine. If your schedule changes you are welcome to stay longer."

Brice nodded his head, "I appreciate that Bill. I'll let you know if things change."

"Only one week! I thought we agreed on two weeks," complained Bobby.

"I know, I know. I feel bad about this. We'll just have to pack two weeks of activities into one," countered Brice kindheartedly.

Now was not the time to bring up the whys and wherefores of his shortened visit. When they were alone, he'd apprise him of his acceptance to the U.S. Naval Academy.

"There are a couple of jobs that Bobby and I have discussed. I'm hoping you can lend a hand!" said Bill lightly.

"Absolutely. I'd be pleased to help out."

"There are two things. One, I have a problem with a lone wolf that's begun preying on my cattle. He killed a second calf just a few hours ago. When I came home this afternoon, I saw the vultures circling and found the dead calf only one hundred yards away from our driveway."

"A killing in broad daylight, close to our driveway. That's a bad sign, Dad. Not only is that wolf bloodthirsty, but he's fearless," said Bobby.

Brice noticed the serious look of concern on each of the Ridger's faces.

"I was hoping you might be able to spend a few half days tracking this wolf. It's unlikely you'll even see him, but I'd like to give it a try before I organize a large scale hunt with my neighbors. I have a .308 caliber Remington rifle that you can use," said Bill.

"No problem. Though I have to admit, I've never tracked a wolf or any animal for that matter before."

"That's what Bobby said. I've made arrangements for one of my ranch neighbors, Tom Youngblood, to come by our ranch tomorrow morning at 6:00 AM to give you a few tracking lessons. Tom's part Arapaho. He taught Bobby how to track. He'd like to get rid of this wolf as well, but he's tied up for the next week, or he'd join you on the hunt."

"Wait a minute! I'm an expert tracker. I can show Brice the ropes," interjected Bobby.

"Yes, you are. But even if you were strapped into the jeep your range would be limited. And, the jeep isn't working."

"Brice and I fixed the jeep this afternoon," said Bobby quickly.

"Unhuh! You and Brice have been busy? OK, I'll strap you into the jeep tomorrow morning and you, me, Brice and Tom will visit the latest kill site. We'll see how you handle the ride," said Bill, as his eyebrows arched curiously. For the first time since Bobby's injury, a spark of genuine hope raced through his heart.

Damn, if Bobby could ride in the jeep, I could have my son with me again as I performed some of my daily ranch chores. Maybe there was a God after all.

"That won't work, Dad. Brice can't go into the hills alone. He doesn't know the lay of the land. Nor is it safe to hunt alone in unfamiliar country. You know that!" said Molly firmly.

Bill sipped his coffee and thought. As usual, his daughter's level of common sense was spot-on. His plan might be a little too ambitious.

"Your right. Perhaps I should wait until Tom's available, and then organize a large scale hunt."

"No. Let's do this. You, Bobby and Tom can ride out to the site in the jeep and Brice and I will saddle up and meet you there," said Molly.

"I wasn't thinking along those lines. I was thinking Brice would track the wolf on foot." After a moments pause, he continued, "I don't even know if he can ride a horse and don't you have classes tomorrow?"

"I'm a Texan, I can handle a horse. I entered a few cattle roping events at local rodeos when I was in high school," said Brice grinning.

"Dad! You know I'm not taking any summer classes. I've been busy running errands for you all day long for the past week. Brice can ride the 'grey.' His foot is fully healed and we'll take it easy. Tracking a wolf on foot would take forever, and in the end the wolf would win. Brice is about the same size as Bobby. He can use his saddle, chaps and boots if that's OK with you," said Molly, as she looked towards her brother.

"It's OK with me, but take care of my tack. I plan on using it again," said Bobby seriously.

"I'll take care of your gear, but may I remind you how you handled some of my gear. It took me a week to clean my grenade launcher after you used it in Fallujah," said Brice.

"Yeah, well, I was busy writing letters to Molly, telling her what a nice guy you were," said Bobby smiling.

The romantic reference never registered with Bill, though Brice and Molly both blushed.

"It's settled then. I'll have breakfast ready at 5:15 AM. Brice can you dress Bobby? He'll have no problem telling you how to do it. Dad can you find some belts and cushions so we can strap Bobby firmly into the jeep?" asked Molly authoritatively.

Tom Youngbood arrived at the Ridger house the following morning at 6:00 AM with his golden retriever, Arrow. The Ridgers and Brice had just finished a busy hour and a half of hustling through morning ranch chores, devouring a large breakfast, and strapping Bobby into the passenger seat of the jeep. Molly and Brice were mounted on their horses, each with rifles held in leather scabbards attached to their saddles. The rifles were identical .308 caliber Remingtons with scopes. Stuffed into the saddle bags on Molly's horse was lunch, several bottles of water, a waterproof topographical map, compass, binoculars, extra ammunition, one of the ranch's long range two-way radios and two light-weight rain shells.

"Morning Tom, this is Brice. He and Bobby served together in the Marine Corps. He's from Texas and is an experienced rider. He and Molly are going to do the tracking today," said Bill as he waved an arm in the general direction of Molly and Brice.

Brice dismounted and stepped towards Tom Youngblood.

"Pleased to meet you, Mr. Youngblood. Bobby's told me a lot about your tracking expertise," said Brice as he extended his hand for a handshake. The small, wiry man in his early forties with jet-black hair and deep-set, dark eyes ignored his hand and stepped close to Brice. His face suggested only a hint of his proud Arapaho heritage.

Tom's head was cocked at angle as he patiently studied Brice's face.

He saw and felt in him many of the same energy fields he recognized in Bobby Ridger years earlier. The spirit of brotherhood and the force of the warrior were clearly apparent. His strongest power, however, was that of a chief who would one day lead his people. *This is a very special man*, he thought.

Still ignoring Brice's extended hand, he put his hands on Brice's shoulders and said, "Good man and friend!"

Tom's unusual greeting left Brice momentarily speechless. "Uh, thanks!" he finally said.

Bobby smiled knowingly, *Old Tom is still checking those energy fields.*

"Nice, real nice. Let's head out to the site. Tom, why don't you hop into the back of the jeep. The dogs can run along beside us. The site is only a quarter of a mile away," said Bill formally, somewhat at a loss for words after Tom's unusual behavior.

As Bill slowly approached the carcass of the dead calf, Tom jumped out of the jeep and ran forward to the kill site. He directed Bill to a parking area ten feet away from the carcass. Tom didn't want the jeep to disturb any of the wolf tracks, but he did want Bobby nearby so they could inspect the kill site together. He believed that having him involved in investigating this lone wolf would help his healing.

"Watch out for my traps. I laid several out to keep the coyotes away from the carcass, but I didn't set them. I didn't want the coyotes to disturb the site," said Bill.

"I see them," said Tom as he picked up the unset traps and tossed them into the back of the jeep.

Tom called to Molly as she and Brice approached on horseback. Pointing to a tree thirty yards away, he said, "Molly, would you and Brice tie your horses to that tree. And tell Blue to keep Arrow away from this area. We're trying to preserve the wolf tracks."

Molly and Brice tied their horses to a low hanging tree limb. She then gave Blue a voice command and hand signal to "stay and guard."

Blue watched Molly and Bobby's friend walk towards the parked jeep. His ears stood upright, another of his calves had been killed. He tried to see which calf it was, but Bill blocked his view. When Bill stepped around the carcass, he caught a brief glimpse of the bloodied face of his favorite calf. That calf was the smartest one in the entire herd, and he often helped him drove the others.

Blue's blood boiled as he considered the loss of another calf, *These are my cattle. My job is to guard them and I have failed!*

Blue's ancestors were a mix of the English sheep dog, the Australian dingo and other unknown canine breeds. The sheep dog enjoyed inherent herding instincts and the dingo, which lived in the wild, possessed a high degree of hunting and survival skills. These skills likely originated from their cross breeding with the wolf family.

Beginning in the early 1800s, the Australian cattle rancher required a working dog that could keep up with his long hours and was comfortable droving cattle. Generation by generation, Blue's ancestors were crossbred with other canine breeds to fine tune and improve their cattle droving abilities. The result of all this cross breeding was a dog like Blue who enjoys protecting and droving large numbers of cattle, likes a good challenge, has no fear of predators or horses and who looks like a wolf.

Blue reflected on his master's behavior the previous night, *He didn't scratch behind my ears when he entered the house. He was probably upset with me because another calf had been killed. That's the second time in the last couple of weeks that I have failed him.*

When he went into the kitchen, he didn't fill my food bowl. He always does that first. Instead, he picked up the strange black shoe from its cradle and sent a signal to the Indian to come to the ranch this morning. But, why did the Indian have to bring his dog, Arrow?

How can the Indian tolerate such a good for nothing dog? Indians know that dogs are supposed to work! That dog acts like a cross between a lumbering Saint Bernard and a brainless Afghan hound. Arrow doesn't know a thing about tracking. The only thing that stupid dog does is chase those furry yellow balls and sometimes not even that. He's a jerk!

Suddenly, Blue saw the gathered group point towards the hills. The Indian and Bill then spoke to Molly and Bobby's friend.

Molly is going to lead the hunt for the wolf. That's why she strapped the hunting rifles to the horse saddles this morning. She and Bobby's friend are going after the wolf.

The Indian is here to give them tracking instructions. Because Bobby can't track anymore, the Indian is explaining to Bobby's friend what's involved in tracking a wolf. What a waste of time that is! Wolves are smart. They can easily hide their tracks.

To get this wolf, they need me to follow the wolf's scent. The only animal odor humans can smell is a steaming pile of fresh dung from a few feet away. Even at that distance, they often don't recognize the odor and they step in it!

After a couple more minutes of sitting, Blue could no longer control his impatience and barked angrily.

Hey, don't forget me! I'm your best tracker! I can lead Molly and Bobby's friend to the wolf.

Blue's thoughts turned inward, *When I catch sight of this wolf, there will be no stopping me. I will rip his throat out in a minute. His warm blood will taste like honey.*

Arrow misinterpreted Blue's bark. He thought it was a sign that Blue wanted to play. Arrow gave Blue a goofy, playful nudge with his head that indicated he wanted to play.

Hey! I don't want to play. I want to track that wolf. I'll teach you not to bother me when I'm thinking about work.

In the blink of an eye, Blue gave Arrow a sharp, painful warning nip on his hindquarter. Arrow yelped like a baby.

By the time all those surrounding the carcass looked towards the dogs, Blue was sitting with his back to them, obediently watching the horses. Slowly, he looked over his shoulder at them, cocked his head to one side and pointed his ears, as if to say,

I didn't do anything!

Tom turned back to the calf's carcass and resumed his patient tracking explanation.

"You now know what the wolf's tracks look like. His tracks are almost identical to Blues, except a little larger. His normal stride will be longer as well, say thirty inches. When he's running his stride can be up to eight feet long, and he can run up to forty miles per hour.

"Once he senses that you're tracking him, it will become almost impossible to follow him. He will zip along rock ledges or travel down the middle of a flowing creek. In a wooded area, like the foothills above the ranch here, all he really has to do is trot away from his trackers. His normal, effortless trot is twice as fast as yours on horseback. If you're lucky and he's a little careless, you might get, at best, a 300-yard shot at him.

"Wolves have excellent hearing, eyesight and sense of smell. They are smart and have no natural predators other than man. He's lived in the wild forever, and he's a formidable hunter." Tom paused a moment for emphasis before discussing two specific issues about this particular wolf.

"There are two things about this wolf that I don't like. One, he's alone which means he didn't get along with his pack of wolves. The Cedar Creek wolf pack lives nearby, but none of that pack hunts alone nor are any of them as big as this wolf. Look at the size and depth of this paw print," he said pointing to a deep impression in the soft ground.

"I'll bet this wolf weighs 125 pounds. Lone wolves, like this one, are usually males, and usually very nasty. Not only with their own kind, but also with whoever crosses their path.

"Two, though he ate part of the calf, it looks to me like he crushed some of the calf's bones. This is one angry wolf.

"I'll take a few pictures of the carcass. I'm sure that the Fish and Game Department will agree with me that this wolf is dangerous and needs to be killed.

"One other point, which is very important," said Tom seriously, as he looked directly at Brice.

"Do not, under any circumstances, ride below any rock ledges. Wolves are expert at doubling back and setting up an ambush. Unless you want a wolf on your back, keep an eye on what's above you."

Brice nodded.

"Also, I recommend you take Blue with you for your tracking. You'll see why in a moment. Molly, please call him over!" said Tom.

Brice watched Molly turn towards Blue and give him a hand signal.

Blue raced to the kill site and skidded to a stop. As he inspected the calf's carcass, his anger increased. He emitted a long, mournful cry and thought, *Oh, my poor young helper. He broke all of your bones. I'll bet that wolf knew we were friends. He probably saw you lick and clean my ears from time to time. I'm going to kill the bastard!*

After his cry, Blue took several deep breaths before he began to feverishly paw and sniff the ground. The wolf's scent covered the area and it told him that a change had come over this wolf since his first killing.

From the scent at the first kill, Blue determined that the wolf was a large, aggressive Alpha male who was living on his own. This latest scent, however, was different. In addition to the odor of bloodlust, the odor of pain and anger were now present. These three odors and the manner in which the wolf had killed his friend were a call to battle.

After I rip your throat out, I'll piss all over your sorry ass!

"See the paw scrapes that Blue is smelling. The wolf marked an excessive number of spots around the calf with his urine and spread his scent around. That's a form of taunting. The wolf knows your dog is guarding the cattle, he's challenging his leadership," said Tom.

"Oh, shit. I don't want to risk losing Blue. He's part of the family and he's the best cattle dog around," said Bill.

"Until Blue and this wolf engage in battle, this wolf will make a steady diet of your calves. However, I have a sense that this wolf is old and injured and not much of a threat to Blue. I think Blue can track him down in a day or two. When he finds him, I expect that he'll tear him to pieces. That is, unless these two riflemen do the job first. Your horses look fresh and ready to hunt," said Tom in closing.

CHAPTER 13
SENATOR LEONE

Alan Fischer walked briskly into Ruby's restaurant at a quarter past noon. His jaw was set with angry creases. He was not fond of luncheon meetings. In his opinion, they were a waste of his time and the taxpayer's money. If a politician had something to say to him, he believed they could damn well say it over the phone rather than dance around the issue during two hours of cocktails and a heavy meal. He knew, however, that the popularity of these luncheons, especially at Ruby's, would never disappear because they provided the politicians with a cozy, dimly lit setting in which they could discuss both borderline and outright illegal schemes.

In Montana, the state legislature convened for a ninety-day legislative session every other year. Twenty per cent of the state legislators were businessmen, the rest were farmers or ranchers. Fortunately, for the people of Montana, the majority of the farming and ranching legislators were hard working, honest folk. Farming and ranching in Montana was a "24/7," all encompassing proposition that left little or no spare time for outside activities, like consulting. For those who didn't pay close attention to what they were doing on their farm or ranch and did dabble in other activities, they eventually failed at both.

The businessmen who served in the legislature were the ones who needed watching. They enjoyed more free time and flexible schedules. Those who were inclined to cloak their scheming under the title of "Appearance Stipend" or "Consulting" knew that these fees were bribes, plain and simple.

Nick Leone was a businessman, and the majority leader of the State Senate. He had called Fischer earlier that morning and demanded that he meet him for lunch. *Important business*, he explained, as Fischer silently groaned.

June 10, 2008 was not a convenient day for a two-hour luncheon with a drinker. Fischer had been awakened at 1:00 AM by his graveyard supervisor. His office had just received a FBI "High Alert" message regarding possible terrorist attacks in or around the National Parks. He'd ordered the supervisor to immediately send out the information to all his area leaders with instructions for them to call him five hours later. He'd been on the phone with each of them since 6:00 AM. He was also expecting a similar "High Alert" message from Homeland Security, but that never occurred.

Montana was a large state with limited law enforcement resources. Fischer discussed the specifics of his customized plan with each of his area leaders. In short, he told them to concentrate their attention on the major roads throughout the state, especially those that led to and from both Yellowstone and Glacier National Parks. Small town conflicts and back country disputes would have to take a back seat to this terrorist alert for the time being. He also told each of them, in no uncertain terms, to keep the nature of this threat confidential. That meant no blabbing to wives, girlfriends, drinking buddies and, most of all, state legislators. If Leone had gotten wind of this threat from one of his men, Fischer swore he'd find out who he was and he'd reassign him to a graveyard patrol in the coldest and most remote part of the state.

Fischer first met the man fifteen years earlier when the thirty-year-old Leone was newly elected to the state senate. His family was well known throughout the state's political circles, and he supported a conservative platform that appealed to most Montanans. His uncle, who was the majority whip of the state senate at that time, appointed him to the all-important Department of Justice Committee. Leone was now the chairman of that committee. Since the Highway Patrol reported to the state's Department of Justice, Fischer had to endure the meddling of the uncle and nephew in Highway Patrol matters for years. Though it was well known throughout the state that the Leones had a proclivity for subtly manipulating and bending the laws of Montana for their personal gain, it didn't seem to hurt their re-election efforts. In Nick Leone's case, his flowing brown hair, bedroom eyes and perfectly chiseled white teeth, which beamed like a floodlight when he smiled, also contributed to his popularity. He especially appealed to the ladies and he knew it.

Nick's uncle retired from the state government several years earlier, amidst his shadowy involvement with Jack Abramoff, Indian gaming matters and tribal leaders holding positions with the Bureau of Indian Affairs. That left just the nephew in office, but he wielded more political clout than his uncle and was proving to be the shiftiest of the Leone clan. And, he had his sights set on becoming the next governor.

Before he stepped into the dark interior of the restaurant, Fischer's right hand moved to the left breast pocket of his Western shirt. Without unbuttoning the pocket, his fingers found the outline of his thin recording device. His index finger found the protruding record button, which he surreptitiously slid to the *on* position. Shifty state legislators, like Leone, falsely believed that they were safe from electronic recording devices once they had left the state capitol building.

Inside the restaurant, Fischer stopped to let his eyes adjust to the dark setting. After several moments, he located Leone standing in the rear of the restaurant, partially hidden behind a plastic palm tree. He was whispering into the ear of a twenty-something waitress whose breasts were spilling out of her revealing black blouse. When Leone made eye contact with Fischer, he waved to him and simultaneously handed the girl a scrap of paper, no doubt with his phone number, which she unabashedly tucked into her push-up brassiere. Fischer knew the bastard was married and had three young children.

When he arrived at the booth, Leone extended his hand for a handshake while his other hand affectionately slapped Fischer softly on the back of his right shoulder. To an outsider, the greeting had the appearance of two men who were best friends.

Though Fischer spoke with Leone often over the telephone, he realized that he hadn't seen him up close in perhaps a year. Middle age, a diet of rich food, too much booze and little physical activity were apparent from Leone's flushed face and bulging waistline. His once rich and flowing brown hair was now thinning and graying prematurely. Fischer also noticed food stains on his whacky tie. His tie depicted dolphins jumping through the ocean surf. Fischer smiled hospitably at Leone. He was aware that Leone was far from *whacky*, he was as cunning as a fox. His tie was a poor attempt at disarming his adversaries.

"I'm glad you could make this last minute luncheon meeting. Can my favorite waitress, Tammy, get you a cocktail? I'm having a gin and tonic," oozed Leone, as he and Fischer sat across from one another at a small table.

"No, thanks. I'll have an iced tea and the Caesar chicken salad. I've got a lot going on in the office," said Fischer curtly.

Leone studied the top man at the Highway Patrol for a moment before he responded. He knew Fischer was highly respected throughout the law enforcement community, both within the state and at the federal level. What troubled him most about the man, however, was his complete indifference to a little extra cash for a favor. He had approached him on several occasions to fix drunken driving charges for friends and he'd been bluntly rebuffed each time. He was a "nut case" with high moral standards who would work his tail off in the Highway Patrol for the next ten years, after which he would retire on the state's paltry pension. Clearly, he had more scruples than common sense. He was hopeful that this time, a little extra cash for "Consulting," might change his stubborn inflexibility.

Leone smiled insincerely at Fischer before he spoke. "It sounds like we are busy! I'll have the salmon with a Caesar salad. Oh, and I'll have another one of these," he said, as lifted his empty cocktail glass and shook it in Tammy's direction.

"What's on your mind senator?"

"Alan, please call me Nick! We've been friends and colleagues for fifteen years. There's no need for formalities."

"OK, Nick! What's on your mind?"

Damn, this guy may be a hard nut to crack. The son-of-a-gun is all business, thought Leone. Nevertheless, his uncle's frequent dictum, "everyone has a weakness," kept him shamelessly determined.

Leone leaned towards Fischer in a conspiratorial manner and spoke quietly, "I've been working with a very reputable and successful energy company in London. They are quite serious about expanding into the United States in a big way. They extract oil from shale oil, and also explore for natural gas fields. They already hold options on a number of promising tracts in

Wyoming, but they are very secretive and adamant that no one learns they are in the market. It has been their experience that if someone discovers their interest in a geographic area, the price of nearby, prospective mineral tracts skyrockets."

Leone paused in midsentence when Tammy arrived at their table with their drinks. She conspicuously rubbed one of her breasts against Leone's shoulder as she set his fresh drink in front of him. After she left the table, Leone continued unfazed as if every woman he came in contact with couldn't resist rubbing her breasts against his body.

"Several months ago, I was invited to London by the executive in charge of this company, for the purpose of being briefed about his company's plans in the United States. During our meeting in his office, he explained that their first step is to set up and train a security department that would keep nosey neighbors and prying eyes away from their exploration activities. Related to this training issue is their need of a nearby airport to accommodate trainees and staff who will be traveling to and from their training center.

"Since the company was so concerned about secrecy, I told him it didn't make sense to train their security department in Wyoming. That would simply raise their profile in the state. I suggested they consider a neighboring state, like Montana. Additionally, I specifically recommended they consider Dennis, Montana because of its distance from our capital's meddlesome news media and its proximity to a well-connected, small airport, the West Yellowstone Airport. After they discreetly checked out Dennis, they contacted me and said that Dennis was the perfect small town for them. They were so delighted with my understanding of their goals that they persuaded me to provide them with further assistance as a paid consultant."

Fischer sensed the direction of this not so subtle conversation. He also knew that Leone needed very little, if any, persuading to become a paid consultant.

"As part of my consultancy, I retained the police sheriff in Dennis, Fred Dower, and his son and deputy, Skip, to very quietly and confidentially secure a remote location for my client's training efforts. The Dower's found a secluded property for my client and everything has been running smoothly until you arrived in Dennis several days ago and deputized two local men to investigate the Dower's activities."

Leone's knowledge of his recent deputations angered Fischer. Though he remained impassive, he swore he'd find out which insider leaked Leone this information. He also wondered about the origin of the leak. *Did it come from his office in Helena or Dennis?*

As Leone continued his elaborately conceived deceit, he omitted those facts that he thought would discourage Fischer's cooperation.

First, there was no security training force to be trained because there was no London energy company. That is, unless, one accepted the tenuous proposition that because the individual Leone met with was a Saudi prince whose entire wealth was derived from existing oil fields in Saudi Arabia, he was an energy company.

Second, the executive he met with wasn't an executive of anything. He was an extremely wealthy Saudi prince and Muslim. According to the prince, he was a devout Muslim who was anxious to personally thank and entertain American clerics, in the United States, for spreading the loving and compassionate teachings of Allah throughout their country. The location of these altruistic get togethers would have to be at a secluded, private estate near Yellowstone National Park and would occur over a period of four months. The prince added that nearby, convenient air service to Las Vegas would heavily influence his site selection.

Lastly, his meeting with the executive, rather the prince, didn't occur in an office. It took place at an exclusive brothel in London where both Leone and the prince spent more time in the arms of thousand-dollar-a-night hookers than discussing private estates in Montana.

When the prince approved Dennis as an ideal meeting and entertainment locale, Leone immediately tied up a "corporate" retreat on the outskirts of Dennis that every real estate buyer of substance in Montana knew of because it had been on the market for years. He told the prince that he, coincidently, had just purchased a private estate in Dennis that fit his exact needs. It was a five year old, six-suite lodge, with an adjacent conference center for meetings. The estate was situated on a slightly remote, but beautiful, fifty-acre parcel.

The lodge had been custom designed and built for a "high tech" company as a wilderness leadership center for their executive management. Unfortunately, the company went broke before the executives could hone their team building and corporate survival skills. Fortunately for the prince and his guests, explained Leone, the place had never been occupied and he would be honored to rent it to him. Further, there were frequent flights from the nearby West Yellowstone airport to Las Vegas. Leone quoted the prince a ridiculously high rental rate, and an enormous security deposit, for a minimum one-year lease term.

After patiently listening to Leone's pile of bullshit, the prince had one of his henchmen check out the lodge before he signed the rental agreement. From his henchman's report, he learned that Leone hadn't owned the Dennis lodge when he made the offer to rent it to him. He also learned that the lodge was as Leone described, but that it was so damn remote that, under the best of summertime weather conditions, it took a good twenty minutes of careful, slow driving along deeply rutted dirt roads to get to the property from the main road, U.S. Route 287. For the remaining nine months of the year, the property was virtually inaccessible to all but snowmobiles and four-wheel drive vehicles, which was why there had been no buyer interest in the foreclosed bank property for the past three years. Little did Leone know that the remoteness of the property was more of a prerequisite for the prince than a liability. Though the prince only intended to occupy the property for four months, it fit his needs perfectly.

Leone's closing on the property, via a Grand Cayman shell company, occurred several days after the prince forked over to Leone a substantial amount of cash for prepaid rent and a security deposit.

Fischer nodded wordlessly as Leone concluded the description of his client's needs. Leone's expressions… his greedy smile, the frequent and intimate use of Fischer's nickname, 'Al,' and his constant touching of Fischer's forearm… made his skin crawl. The setting also offended him… mid-day cocktails in a hidden corner of a dark restaurant with a buxom waitress who was falling all over the married Leone. But, what really tested his self-control was Leone's request that he join forces with the Dowers. He was certain they were up to no good. However, if Leone thrust them into an alliance with him, perhaps he could discover proof of their past crimes before they committed new offences.

Only one question remained. How much money would Nick offer him to buy his cooperation? He didn't have long to wait.

Leone withdrew a fat envelop from his coat pocket and slid it towards Fischer.

"I'd like to retain you, from one *consultant* to another, to oversee the Dower's activities. The Dower's strong suit is police matters. The energy company may have need for some local administrative support, in which case I thought you would be the perfect candidate."

Leone stopped talking as he watched Fischer open the envelope and loudly count out fifty one hundred dollar bills.

Mindful of the importance of clearly recording his next statement, Fischer emphatically said, "So, Mr. Nick Leone, you're giving me five thousand dollars to help Fred and Skip Dower in Dennis interface with this energy company during the training of their security department in Dennis, Montana."

"Not so loud! This is a highly confidential matter!" cautioned Leone, as he raised his index finger to his lips.

Fischer ignored Leone's request. "Is this energy company and their security department legitimate?" continued Fischer over the din of the restaurant.

"Absolutely. I've thoroughly checked them out."

Leone's superficial background check of the prince did reveal that much of the prince's wealth was related to his interest in Saudi oil, but that was the case for thousands of royal family members in Saudi Arabia. In truth, the prince's only interest in energy in London was to direct the driver of his Bentley to the nearest petrol pump.

Had Leone disclosed the actual use of the lodge to Fischer, he knew it would unnecessarily draw attention to his offshore acquisition of the lodge and the Muslim renter. *Why rock the boat*, he thought. He wasn't breaking the law by renting his property to the prince, or exposing the good people of Montana to any public safety issues. What harm could come from accommodating an apparently, benign religious retreat. *Not all Muslims were bad!* With a clear conscience, he simply misrepresented the lodge's use. Had Leone not been blinded by the good fortune of his real estate deal and taken just a few more minutes to perform a more thorough "Google" search of his renter, he would have discovered that the prince's Muslim faith was far from benign.

"Is this the entire retainer?" boomed Fischer.

"Sshh! No that's half. You'll receive the other half once you relieve your two newly appointed deputies in Dennis of their badges," said Leone firmly.

"Why do that? Both men are smart, respectable Marine Corps veterans. They could be an added resource for the Dowers."

"No, that won't work. The fewer people who know about this confidential security training center the better. You and the two Dowers will be the only three in Dennis who know what is occurring at the lodge," said Leone with all the sincerity of a rattlesnake.

"OK, whatever you say," said Fischer.

"You'll rescind those deputy appointments?"

"Absolutely, as soon as I get back to my office."

A greasy smile blossomed across Leone's face. He'd found Fischer's weakness. *Cash for "Consulting," not cash for fixing penny-ante traffic violations. Perhaps, he has more than one weakness.*

While he was on a roll, Leone continued his seedy probe, "Tammy gets off early today. Would you like to meet her for an afternoon drink at her place?"

Bold! The little prick was bold, thought Fischer.

"I can't. Like I said, I'm busy."

"Well, just let me know when you have some free time and I'll see if I can arrange some female companionship for you. White, black, Asian, young, mature… even two if you like!" he said coarsely.

Fischer's opinion of Leone went from bad to worse. The scumbag was probably involved in a broader range of illicit activities than he originally suspected. When he had the time, he'd take a closer look at Leone's businesses. He pulled his cell phone out of his pocket under the pretext of having received an urgent text message.

"Oh no! Got to go, Nick. It's an emergency!" said Fischer, as he quickly stood, nearly knocking over Tammy who had silently arrived beside their table and was juggling their lunch plates.

"But you haven't eaten 'darlin,'" she said affectionately.

A cool breeze greeted Fischer the moment he stepped outside the restaurant. He took several deep breaths of pure, fresh air before he undid the top two buttons of his shirt. He shook the collar of his shirt several times in hopes the breeze would cleanse him of his recent association with Nick Leone.

CHAPTER 14
TRACKING

Molly gently pulled on the reins of her horse. As her horse glided to a stop, she turned to Brice and said, "If Blue doesn't pace himself one of us will have to put him across our saddle for the ride back to the ranch." Dismounting, she handed the reins of her horse to Brice and hopped atop a large boulder that overlooked a heavily wooded gully below the trail. The sound of Blue's thrashing and racing through the dense underbrush was apparent. After several calls for him to *come,* his head finally poked out from behind a tree and he gave her an irritable look.

"Blue, come!" she said firmly as her eyes bored into his.

He didn't move.

What now? I am locked onto the wolf's scent. He's not making the slightest effort to hide his tracks and I found one of his hideouts in this gully. He's bleeding which means that he's either injured or sick. Just a couple of more hours at this pace and I'll have him in my sights.

"Blue, come," repeated Molly.

OK, OK! But, just a short water break, thought Blue as he effortlessly scampered to the top of the gully and loped easily to Molly's side. Despite his powerful desire in resuming the hunt, his wagging tail and eager eyes reflected his primary goal of pleasing and obeying his master.

"Good dog," said Molly as she petted him and fed him several pieces of kibble.

"'Take time,'" she commanded. He understood her command, despite emitting a low whimper of displeasure.

"What does 'take time' mean?" asked Brice who was in the midst of dismounting from his horse.

"Basically, slow down. Sometimes Australian cattle dogs can get overly enthusiastic when directing or protecting their herd. The cattle sense this and they get stressed. In this case, I think Blue may have formed a relationship with the dead calf we looked at this morning. Perhaps, he feels responsible on some level for the calf's death and is anxious to right a wrong. When he sets his sights on something, it's nearly impossible to change his mind," said Molly.

"So, he could overly exert himself," said Brice.

"Absolutely! Right now, he's on a mission. I think we should all take a little break. We've been in the saddle for over two hours and I wouldn't mind stretching my legs."

Brice tied both horses to a small tree while Molly dug into her saddlebags.

"Here you go!" she said as she tossed Brice a water bottle.

She knelt beside Blue, in the shade of a nearby grassy meadow, and poured water into his collapsible water bowl. He noisily slurped up the water.

"Not too thirsty, are we?" chuckled Molly sarcastically.

The first part of their hunt was up ever steepening hills which Blue tackled effortlessly as he skillfully tracked the wolf along animal trails and through heavy brush. Occasionally, they crossed an open meadow like the one they were in now. The early morning cloud cover had burned off, revealing a brilliantly blue sky. Far below them, the Madison River meandered through the green valley floor. A nearby stand of cottonwoods swayed lazily with the light morning breeze, their dew laden leaves sparkling in the sunshine.

Brice's eyes turned to Molly who was lovingly stroking Blue's head and whispering sweet somethings into his ear. Blue's eyes closed and his tail wagged. *You're a damn lucky dog,* he thought jealously.

As if hearing his thought, Molly looked at him and smiled. His heart skipped a beat. She was one of a kind, an unusual combination of horse-woman, hunter, rancher, caregiver, homemaker and, of course, cover girl. He returned her smile as he tried to calm his quaking heart. He walked stiffly towards her and settled timidly in the grass beside her. He petted Blue's back and, at a loss for words, simply said, "He's quite the tracker!"

"Are you feeling OK, Brice? You looked flushed," she said flirtatiously as her eyes locked on his.

"Oh, yeah, I'm fine! I'm loving this. I mean it's a nice ride. I mean I like the feel of this," said Brice awkwardly.

"What does it feel like?"

"Huh! What does what feel like?" he stammered.

Her look puzzled him. It was as if she hadn't heard a word he'd said.

"Can I kiss you?" she asked softly.

He nodded feebly.

She gently slipped her hand behind his neck and slowly pulled him towards her. Though she kissed him lightly and tenderly, Brice felt as if he'd been jolted with a 1,000-volt charge of electricity.

Leaving her hand on his neck, her warm lips whispered into his ear, "I like you, Brice."

"I feel the same about you," he said in a raspy, low voice.

Their kissing and petting, tentative and respectful at first, quickly increased in intensity. Tongues explored, hands caressed and breathy murmurs were exchanged as their bodies embraced one another and they rolled together in the high grass. Were it not for Blue's loud, persistent barking and several paw slaps to Brice's backside, their passion might have progressed further. For the moment, Blue's obsession with the wolf prevailed.

Molly and Brice slowly separated from one another and sat, side by side, in the middle of the meadow. After a minute, their breathing returned to normal and their sweat streaked faces regained their natural color. Molly buttoned her blouse and Brice tucked his shirttail into his jeans.

Molly looked hard at Blue. "OK, Blue, you win! But, once you get this wolf, you better behave or I'll tie you to a tree," said Molly as she playfully elbowed Brice in the ribs.

Humans are so weird, thought Blue.

If a male and female human like one another, they perform the strangest rituals… whispering to one another, holding hands, sucking one another's tongues, groping each other, rolling around together… it's such a waste of time. When I meet a female that I'm attracted to, I'll do a little sniffing then it's down to business!

Those two could roll around in the grass all day and accomplish nothing. This is not the time for petting or whatever they're doing. We've got work to do!

"A very distant tree!" added Brice as he stood and offered his hand to Molly who was still sitting in the grass. He easily pulled her upward and into him for one last, long kiss before they headed to their horses.

Time seemed to stand still as the two of them rode languidly beside each other, indifferent to Blue's frenetic sniffing and searching. For them, the wolf hunt was irrelevant. The euphoria of their first intimate encounter consumed their thoughts. After a time, they came to a narrow animal trail, which required the horses to travel in single file. Molly turned towards Brice and gave him a seductive smile and wink before she "clucked" aloud and gently nudged her horse ahead of his with a light tap of her heel against her horse's flank.

Brice's heart almost exploded. He was in love, madly in love.

*

They rode for another hour and a half in near silence. When there was a clear opening in the trees, Molly would stop and point out prominent peaks and valleys. She showed Brice the valley where the local elk herd wintered and a hillside where bighorn sheep could often be seen.

They were about to leave the tree line of a south-facing peak when Molly again reined her horse to a stop on a level draw between two rock ledges. It was 11:15 AM and the high, midday sun felt warm on their shoulders. Blue was twenty yards ahead of them and heard the horses stop. He looked back at them questioningly as Molly gave him the hand signal to *come*.

"It's windy atop that high rock ledge. This is a good protected place to stop for a bit of lunch. We started early this morning and I'm ravenous," said Molly.

"Ravenous, that sounds exciting," said Brice with a raised eyebrow.

Molly smiled provocatively at Brice's leading remark and said, "Nourishment first and perhaps something else afterwards."

"Let's hurry up and eat then!"

Molly's head tilted backwards as she laughed heartily. "'In for a penny, in for a pound!'"

"That's me! All in, Brice."

"OK, that's good to know. While I get lunch ready, why don't you tie up the horses to those trees near those boulders."

"I'm on it! Should I keep an eye out for rattlesnakes?" asked Brice seriously.

Molly thought about that question for a moment before responding. "In Texas, you have diamondback rattlers. Our snakes are primarily prairie rattlers that are tamer than your diamondbacks and they usually live in lower elevations, like prairies. We're at about 7,000 feet above sea level. It's a little high for them up here, but better safe than sorry. I'd keep your eyes open."

As Brice walked the horses the horses to the trees, he turned his head to Molly, "How come you know so much about rattlesnakes?"

"When you live on a ranch, you learn about predators and snakes. I also just studied reptiles in one of my classes at Montana State," said Molly as she spread out their lunch on a blanket.

Brice returned to Molly, dropped to the blanket and sat crossed legged. They both began eating in silence, each surprised at their hunger. Turkey sandwiches, pickles, chips and a couple of apples were a tasty break after their long ride. Brice broke the silence by asking Molly about her horse riding competitions. He'd seen her numerous blue ribbons hanging in the den of the ranch house. She, in turn, asked him about his prior deployments. It was light, unaffected conversation, very much like that of a happily married couple.

After Brice finished his meal, he leaned back on his elbows and stretched. "I am a little stiff. It's been awhile since I've ridden a horse for that long. How are you feeling?"

"I'm good, but I do more riding than you."

"How much longer should we follow Blue? I can see that he won't quit until he gets that wolf, which could be days from now."

"You're right about that. I think there might be a hunting cabin nearby, with dirt road access to the main highway. We could trailer our horses to the dirt road tomorrow, save ourselves hours of riding and resume Blue's tracking from there. Let's take a look for the cabin from up there," said Molly as she turned and pointed to a rock ledge that rose to a ridge about one hundred yards above them. "We'll take our binoculars and rifles with us. We should be able to see for miles from up there. Perhaps, we'll get lucky and spot the wolf."

While Molly was feeding the apples to the horses, Brice withdrew the rifles from the scabbards and was in the midst of checking them when he stiffened. A familiar sound sent a warning signal to his brain. He suspended his rifle inspection and turned his head while he aimed his right ear in the direction of the sound. He covered his left ear with his left hand, closed his eyes and listened intently. There it was again.

"Molly, did you hear that?"

"Hear what?"

Without getting Molly unnecessarily excited, he said, "A sound like someone was throwing pebbles at us!"

"Pebbles? Maybe rocks just shifting in the heat of the day," she said as she too stopped to listen.

A moment later they both heard the same sound.

"That's not shifting rocks," she said as she looked at him questioningly.

"I think those are spent bullets, but I don't hear any rifle shots," he said.

"The wind is blowing away from us. When we get to the top of the ridge, I bet we'll feel a twenty-mile per hour wind against our back. That could muffle gunshots, especially if the shooter is some distance away. Plus, the wind can really whip through the breaks in the hills, which would further reduce any sound," she said.

The number of spent bullets that were falling against rocks increased. One of the spent bullets tumbled to a stop nearby. Brice picked it up and said, "Let's get out of here, we're standing in someone's line of fire."

After moving the horses a safe distance away, Brice ejected a .308 round from one of their Remington rifles and compared it to the spent bullet he had just picked up. While Molly looked on, he held the spent bullet next to the .308 round.

"The bullets are virtually identical. Considering the volume of spent bullets that are rattling around us, my guess is that this is a spent 7.62 bullet from an AK-47. Some collector or nut job probably firing an AK-47 on full automatic, rather than a hunter taking careful aim at a target," said Brice.

"What should we do?" said Molly nervously.

"The spent bullets aren't ricocheting off the rocks. They're dropping to the ground, which means that these bullets are at the end of a high trajectory shot. They don't have much velocity, but you still wouldn't want to get hit in the head with one. Stay close to me, keep your head down and crouch low as we climb to the ridge. I think we'll probably see a couple of old 'geezers' burning through a $100 of ammo with automatic rifles in the valley below us," said Brice casually.

Molly gave Blue a *down stay* signal as she and Brice low walked to the top of the ridge crest, each carrying a pair of binoculars and their rifles. They lay together in a prone position studying the down slope of the ridge. Scree and a few small trees marked the uppermost reaches of the ridge. About a mile below them the terrain changed. Mature trees and heavy brush became more prevalent. No sign of life… no wolf, no humans. But, they could now clearly hear the muted sound of distant automatic gunfire.

"I can't tell where that gunfire is coming from," said Brice.

Molly swept her binoculars across a distant hillside, several miles to the east, where a cluster of thick, tall trees swallowed a grassy meadow. "I see three or four vehicles parked at the east end of that fire trail where it enters the tree line," said Molly as she extended her arm and pointed.

"It looks like two white vans and a heavy duty pickup with a 'low boy' trailer behind it. Whoever is shooting brought along several ATV's," said Brice.

Molly's binoculars next spotted a building.

"I think I see their camp. It looks like three or four ATV's are parked by a hunting lodge. It's hard to see through the trees," she said pausing for a moment. "It's just to the left and a hundred yards below that tallest tree. Do you see the lodge?"

"I got it, but I can't see very well. There are too many trees in my line of sight. This ridge turns directly towards them. I think if we stay below the crest and get a little closer, we'll have a clearer and more direct view of the hunting lodge. We'll also be out of their direct line of fire," said Brice.

"You're the expert on this stuff. I'll follow you," said Molly warily.

"Maybe the shooters are firing at an animal that they saw. It could be the wolf that we're tracking. If so, their gunfire may have turned him our way. Let's keep our eyes open," added Brice.

They returned to the horses and walked them eastward, along the reverse slope of the ridge, until they came to a shaded area besides tall brush. It was a good spot to tie up the horses while they studied the lodge from a concealed position. Molly put Blue on a *down stay* near the horses before she and Brice carefully crawled to the crest of the ridgeline.

From their new prone position, they had a clear line of sight to the lodge. The shooting had ceased. They could now clearly see six ATV's and a large group of men. The sight before them transfixed both of them.

"I know this place now. It's the 'high tech' lodge and conference center that's been for sale for years. But, I don't understand what I'm seeing. There are lots of hunting rifles leaning against that tall building, which is east of the lodge. It looks like a high ceilinged gymnasium. About twenty men are performing what looks like yoga exercises on mats near its front door. Hunters aren't into yoga, especially when they are on a hunt. They are all wearing skullcaps and none of them are dressed for hunting. The lodge looks like it's equipped with a satellite dish and several TV antennas. None of this makes sense to me," said Molly.

Brice didn't respond. He was rapidly moving his binoculars from one area of interest to another, and she could tell he was tense.

"Brice, what's going on?" implored Molly.

He didn't hear her question. All his attention was on the lodge until he, unexpectedly, turned to her and whispered, "Signal Blue to us?"

"Sure, but why?" asked Molly worriedly.

"I'll explain in a minute, but first get Blue."

Molly turned to Blue. His ears were upright as he eagerly awaited her signal to *come*. Once she gave him the signal, he sprinted across the forty yards that separated them in seconds. Molly extended her hand, like a traffic cop, as Blue belly flopped into a *down* position between them.

"Molly, I think the dead body of the wolf we've been tracking is west and below us on the side of that steep peak that juts upward from the valley. My guess is that the shooters from the lodge caught him in the open. They may have previously wounded him, which would account for the reason why he so viciously retaliated against your young calf."

"That makes sense. Earlier this morning, when Blue was hot on the wolf's trail, I think I saw him occasionally sniff at what looked like drops of blood. It could have easily been a prior wound that reopened," said Molly as she searched through her binoculars for the wolf's body. Blue instinctively rose from his *down* position and followed Molly's eyes. When they'd both mentioned the word *wolf*, he'd understood what they were discussing.

"I see him. Yep, he's dead."

When Blue caught sight of the wolf lying on the steep peak, his ears tilted up and forward, his hackles rose and he emitted a fierce, low growl. After several moments of intense scrutiny on the wolf's bloodied, lifeless body, he realized that his quarry was dead. Slowly, his body relaxed and he dejectedly slunk back to the ground. *Damn, someone else killed the wolf!*

Molly stroked Blue's head and whispered, "That'll do! Good dog, good dog."

"Now that our hunt is over, let's get off this ridgeline. I don't think they saw us," said Brice in a serious tone. They inched backwards on their stomachs until they were hidden from sight.

"What do you mean, 'they didn't see us?'" asked Molly anxiously.

Brice put his hand on her shoulder for comfort, "It's OK, we're safe now. You can relax." Rather than comforting Molly, his comment had the opposite effect.

"Brice, don't indulge me! What did you mean when you said, 'They didn't see us!' Those guys don't look like 'geezers' or hell's angels or skinheads shooting ammo for the fun of it. Most of them looked like young boys. Who the hell are they?" demanded Molly.

"Those boys are Muslims terrorists. And, they aren't performing yoga exercises. They are saying their mid-day prayers.

"Those rifles you saw aren't hunting rifles. They're automatic assault weapons. They have a mix of M-16's and AK-47's. I also saw several .30 caliber machine guns on tripods next to the shed. Those antennae are not for TV, they're for long-range communications. And, I think that satellite dish is for large bandwidth microwave transmissions. Two lookouts are guarding the trail to the lodge. There may be more. That's a terrorist training camp," said Brice solemnly.

Molly's eyes widened to the size of saucers. "Are you… " she began.

Brice interrupted her, "Positive! I recognized three of the older guys. I ran into them during my hike in the Grand Canyon last week. They're probably training young recruits."

Brice opened the flap of his shirt pocket and pulled out his cell phone. At their current location, high on a ridgeline, his cell phone showed excellent reception. He was about to dial '911' for the local police department when Molly grabbed his wrist.

"Whom are you calling?" she asked.

" '911'… the local police," he said.

"No. They could be mixed up with these guys. I'll explain later," said Molly.

"You're kidding."

"No, I'm not, Brice. Let's call my dad on the two-way radio. The head of the State Highway Patrol just deputized him so that he could keep a close eye on our degenerate police force, a father and son who are bad guys. Put your cell phone away," she said firmly.

Molly ran to the horses and pulled the radio out of her saddlebag. Brice followed her to the horses.

"Turn the *squawk* volume down. We don't anyone to hear us!" he said.

Molly gave him a hard look, as if to say, *I'm not a dumb teenager.*

Molly spoke quietly into the radio, "Dad, please answer. Please answer. This is an emergency." She released the transmit button and they waited.

Twenty seconds later Bill Ridger answered, "I hear you Molly. Are you and Brice OK? Where are you?"

"We're OK, I think! We're on the ridge overlooking that 'high tech' retreat, the fancy place that's been for sale for years. It's way back in the hills. Probably four or five miles from U.S. Route 287. You know the place?"

"Affirmative. Geez, you've covered a lot of ground. You better turn back. You'll be lucky if you make it back here before nightfall."

"That's the least of our concerns. I'm going to let Brice explain," said Molly as she handed the radio hand set to Brice.

"Bill, I have a positive visual sighting on approximately forty to fifty

Middle Eastern terrorists armed with M-16's, AK-47's and several .30 caliber machine guns. They're using the hunting lodge as a training camp. Do you copy?"

"I read you loud and clear. AK-47's and .30 caliber machine guns! Shit! The internet and travelling 'gun shows' sell those guns like they're candy bars," ranted Bill.

Bill, and most likely every other Montanan, was a responsible hunter and target shooter. He owned several rifles for hunting and a couple of pistols for target shooting, all of which he kept locked up in a gun safe when not in use. However, he knew that it was child's play for any ex-felon, nut case or terrorist to obtain just about any weapon or type of ammunition that they desired through the Internet, unregulated gun shows, straw buyers and private sellers. The sale of illegally trafficked firearms was soaring. He didn't know how the government could put a stop to these illegal sales. But, he, like most of his friends, became incensed when brain dead liberals discussed "gun control," and characterized all gun owners as either unstable or criminals.

After several moments, Bill calmed himself and continued, "This is not a secure transmission. I will immediately notify the appropriate authorities. Are you in the open or concealed?"

"We are concealed on the reverse side of a ridge, just north of their location. Approximately two kilometers above them and four kilometers to the west," said Brice.

"Do you have the two Remington rifles with you?"

"Yes, sir!"

"Don't hesitate to use them, Brice. Montana state law gives you the right to protect yourself?"

"I understand. By the way, the terrorists killed your wolf."

"That's a small consolation, in light of your troubling sighting. Get back here as fast as you can," ordered Bill as he abruptly terminated the call.

*

After breakfast the next morning, the Ridger's and Brice sat leisurely around the breakfast table sipping coffee.

"Dad, how did the Homeland Security agents sound yesterday when you called in our sighting?" asked Molly.

"Concerned and very interested! They said they would call in your intelligence immediately to their superiors in Washington, DC," responded Bill.

"Good. Something bad is brewing. I trust the feds will nip it in the bud. I know the Corps would," said Brice.

"You got that right. Damn terrorism! It's like an infection. If you don't clean it up, properly treat it and keep an eye on it, it's going to get worse. That's a law of nature. By the way, Sis, do I still have a physical therapy appointment with Gail Henderson this morning at 10:00 AM?" asked Bobby lightly.

"Yes! She confirmed the appointment by email earlier this morning. I was thinking that while she's here with you that I'd take Brice into town and show him around."

"That's a nice idea. He's supposed to be on leave and yesterday wasn't exactly an *off day* for him," said Bill.

"Yeah, good idea. While you're in town Sis, would you mind picking up a box of .22 long rifle ammo for me? I was thinking that Brice could help me with a little target shooting. I haven't handled a rifle since Fallujah," said Bobby.

"Target shooting, huh! Do you think that's a little ambitious, son?" asked Bill.

"I can raise my arms six inches, move my head from side to side and I have some feeling in my trigger finger. I'm good to go!" smiled Bobby.

"I see. Why don't you start with just the prone firing position? Brice, do you mind helping him?" asked Bill.

"No problem at all. I'd be pleased to do it," replied Brice.

Two hours later, Brice and Molly were casually walking down the main street of Dennis. The sun peaked through mountains of cumulus clouds, and the temperature was in the mid-60s. It was a pleasant morning for a stroll and many of the shops were just opening. Molly slipped her arm inside of Brice's arm and smiled inwardly as she noticed his face redden. *My boyfriend is blushing.* She liked that.

They entered the sporting goods store that had just opened and Brice began browsing. Molly stepped to the counter and scrutinized the boxes of ammunition that were on the shelves behind the counter. The owner of the store recognized Molly and approached her from behind the counter, "Hi, Molly. Looking for something?"

"Yes, please! A box of Remington .22 long rifle cartridges."

"You 'betcha,'" said the owner as he turned towards the shelves.

As the owner turned away from her, a shadow crossed the counter and she felt the presence of a large man at her side. A moment later, she felt the stranger's arm wrap around her shoulders. The man wore a neatly pressed tan, short sleeve shirt. She noticed that the man's forearm was heavily muscled, and on it was the tattoo of a bird. His arm began to squeeze her uncomfortably. There was nothing sociable about the embrace. Slowly, she turned to look at the stranger. It was Skip Dower.

"Get your hands off of me," snapped Molly, as she struggled to escape his embrace.

"I like it when bitches squirm," he whispered, as he tightened his grip.

"You're hurting me," protested Molly.

By this time, Brice was now standing behind Skip. He heard Skip's lewd remark and he also saw a sick look of pleasure cross his face as he hurt Molly. In an instant, Brice clasped Skip's opposite arm with both his hands. One hand grabbed his upper arm and the other hand firmly clenched his wrist. In a blur of rotating arms and hands, Brice rolled Skip's arm over in a 270-degree arc while he bent Skip's wrist inwards, towards his forearm. When Skip doubled over, Brice released his upper arm and applied pressure to his elbow. Skip's elbow joint was locked in position. With a modest amount of levered pressure, Brice easily pivoted Skip to the floor, face down. Skip's face was red with rage. He kicked out at Brice who easily sidestepped the kick. Brice applied more pressure to Skip's bent wrist, and he whimpered in pain.

Brice leaned over Skip until he was inches from his face, "You will apologize to Molly, or I will break every bone in your hand and arm," said Brice menacingly.

"Let me go you asshole. I'm the law. I'll have you thrown in jail," spat Skip.

Before Brice could respond, an older gentleman stepped to Brice's side and spoke authoritatively to the deputy. "No, you won't Skip. I witnessed your disgraceful conduct. As of this moment, you are suspended from the

Dennis police force, further you may face other charges depending on what Molly Ridger decides," said the Dennis district judge, Bill Bramley. Bramley knelt beside Skip, withdrew his city issued revolver from its holster, and slipped his deputy badge off his shirt. "You are a disgrace to the uniform and a cancer in this community. Get out of here before I lock you up myself," said the judge angrily.

Brice released Skip and he stood shakily. After straightening himself, Skip stood defiantly in front of Brice. Without taking his eyes off of Brice, he pulled a scrap of paper out of his pocket and threw it on the counter.

The sporting goods storeowner picked up the paper and read it. It was an order form. A moment later, he slid the form back across the counter towards Skip and said, "I don't abide those who treat ladies like you just did. You, your dad and your pal, Ajani, can take your business elsewhere. I'm not filling anymore of your orders, especially for cases of 5.56X45 mm NATO cartridges."

AK-47 ammunition, thought Brice.

"Did you say, *cases?*" asked Brice, as he turned towards the storeowner.

"Yes! They've been buying eight to ten cases of ammunition every few weeks for the past couple of months," said the storeowner.

Brice nodded in silent understanding.

He turned back to Skip. Brice noticed Skip's forearms. One forearm had the distinctive tattoo of the U.S. Army's 101st Airborne Division, a screamin' eagle. The other forearm had a ragged scar that Brice recognized as a knife wound.

Molly was still visibly shaken, and the judge was only slightly more composed. Brice, on the other hand, was calm and curious. In a strange way, this highly charged confrontation was, for him, like another day at the office.

"You serve with the '101st?'" Brice asked evenly.

"Yeah! What's it to you?" replied Skip belligerently.

"You serve with them in Iraq?"

"Of course."

"Fallujah?"

"Yeah, what's with the questions, jarhead? I've heard one of Ridger's pussy friends was in town visiting him. You that pussy?"

"Fallujah two?"

"Yup, you want my autograph. You a REMF?" taunted Skip.

Brice knew that REMF stood for *rear echelon motherfucker*. It was someone in the military who, though far from the action, could make combat more difficult and dangerous for those on the frontlines.

"That a knife wound?"

"Affirmative! I got real intimate with a haji dickhead during the second battle of Fallujah. I won, he lost!"

"I believe that I know you," said Brice with a perceptive smile.

"How so asshole?"

"The 101st was only deployed for the first battle of Fallujah. They were stateside at Fort Campbell, Kentucky, refitting during the second battle. I know that because Bobby Ridger and I fought with the 3/5 Marines in the second battle.

"I bet that the only fighting you did during that time was with other inmates in the Fort Campbell stockade while the 101st was processing your bad conduct discharge from the Army. And that's probably where you got your knife wound. Even the inmates couldn't stand you!

"The 101st is a fine fighting outfit, and they don't tolerate losers like you. You have loser written all over you. That's how I recognized you," said Brice darkly.

Skip stepped towards Brice. With his eyes ablaze and his face beet red, he said, "You're a dead man walking." He pushed the judge aside as he angrily stomped out of the store.

CHAPTER 15
TWO DUDES

Richie Smith sat quietly on a park bench, hidden from the mid-day sun by the shade of a tree. He had considered calling his partner in advance to set up a meeting, but thought better of that. His partner was a clever bastard. A surprise visit might disarm him and work to his advantage.

From a distance of seventy yards, Smith was admiring the Greek neoclassical architecture of Montana's state capitol building when he saw his partner exit the building and receive a cell phone call. The call lasted five minutes, and it clearly upset him. When the call ended, his partner slapped his cell phone closed so forcefully that its clamshell lid flew off. *Bad news*, thought Smith. He wondered if it had anything to do with their deal.

His partner was distracted, and didn't notice him as he marched by the park bench. Smith waited until he was well past before he growled at his back, "Hey, 'Dandy,' remember me?"

His partner turned in surprise and rushed to his side. Smith could see that he was visibly annoyed.

"Damn it, Smith. Don't you know how to follow orders? We only meet in private, not in public. For Christ's sake, this couldn't be a more public place. I'll call you later tonight!"

"The chemist arrived in the area as scheduled on June 11th. That was two days ago, and you haven't returned my phone calls. I get a little paranoid when my partners don't call me back promptly. What's the status of moving into the lodge?" asked Smith malevolently.

"I've been busy, Smith. I'll call you later tonight. Get out of here," snapped Dandy.

"Let me remind you, Dandy man, that you are extra baggage in this deal. In a New York minute, I could easily walk over to Nick Leone's office and explain to him the meth lab plans for his lodge that you have cleverly arranged behind his back. I'm sure I could also cut a better deal with him than I have with you. I call the shots, not you!" warned Smith.

"Leone would never involve himself with a drug deal. Don't fuck with me Smith! It could be unhealthy for you."

"Unhealthy for me? Dandy, I think you've forgotten who's the boss, and who's the peon," said Smith as he stood and stepped to within inches of Dandy.

"You don't intimidate me, little man!" said Dandy as he squared his broad shoulders.

Smith's lightening quick move surprised Dandy. Before he realized what had happened, Dandy felt the edge of a sharp knife pressed against his throat.

"*Little man!* I don't think that was meant as a compliment. Dandy, your bullshit bravado may scare the poor slobs who work in your office, but it has the opposite effect with me. You're lucky we're in a public place. If it were anywhere else, you'd have a slit throat, and I'd enjoy watching you drown on your own blood."

Dandy's eyes bulged with fear.

"You get my meaning Dandy?"

Dandy nodded his head.

"Cat got your tongue, tough guy?"

"I understand," warbled Dandy.

Smith stepped away and withdrew his knife, which quickly disappeared into the side pocket of his jacket. He calmly returned to the park bench and patted the bench seat beside."

"Sit!" commanded Smith. A moment later, he continued, "Now, where were we? Oh, we were talking about the scruples of your boss, Nick Leone. Let's see, he would never involve himself in a drug deal, but an easy $300,000 in cash for a ninety-day rental of his lodge to a terrorist group is within his moral standards. Maybe if I educated him on the prospective rate of return of a meth lab investment, he might change his mind," hissed Smith.

"Terrorists! What are you talking about? It's a religious retreat," said Dandy, thunderstruck by Smith's assertion.

"Please, Dandy man! You forget that I'm one of the premiere government consultants in the Western United States. You and Leone's government cronies pay me lots of money for my brains and real world intelligence. I also possess, as you just experienced, superb powers of persuasion."

After flashing Dandy an ominous smile, Smith continued sarcastically, "A Saudi billionaire wants to thank U.S. clerics for spreading the word of Allah. Will they also discuss the virtues of world peace? Really now! Is that the best Leone could come up with? His *renters* include three battle hardened al-Qaeda terrorists, who are on both Interpol's and the FBI's "Most Wanted Terrorists" list. They are training a group of 60 or more teenagers how to aim, fire and reload AK-47's, M-16's and .30 caliber light machine guns. The kids are pawns, soon to be, most likely dead pawns that believe that if they sacrifice their life for Allah, they'll go straight to paradise where they can 'get it on' with seventy-two virgins.

"These assholes are burning through at least 10,000 rounds of ammo every week, and draining the ammunition inventory of every gun shop within a hundred miles of Dennis, Montana. Come on!

"One word from me to a friend in the local U.S. Attorney's office and you and Leone will spend the rest of your life playing tick-tac-toe on the wall of a federal prison cell," said Smith menacingly.

The color in Dandy's face began to drain.

Dandy's expression caused Smith to chuckle. After savoring Dandy's discomfort for several long moments, he said, "Let me guess? Leone conned you. You bought his bullshit story about a religious retreat. I don't know what rental details he had you handle, but I'm guessing your signature is on enough rental documents for Leone to claim that you were the one who arranged and consummated the rental agreement with the terrorists. Your name may even be on a phony offshore deed that you unwittingly signed."

All the color in Dandy's face had now disappeared and his face was white. He looked as if might faint.

"You and Leone are quite the pair. He conned you on the lodge rental, and you conned him on the meth lab setup. It's the old 'double cross!' Some business practices never seem to change," cooed Smith, as he shook his head in disbelief. "Tell me when my chemist can move into the lodge and set up our lab."

Smith learned that the renters had unexpectedly stayed over several days and were now planning on leaving the lodge on Sunday, June 15. Dandy had made arrangements with his two associates in Dennis to inspect the lodge and grounds Sunday afternoon to ensure that the site had been thoroughly cleaned. They would send Dandy time stamped digital pictures of the cleanup. Per Leone's instructions from earlier that morning, Dandy would confirm with Leone, via a call to his new cell number, that the renters had departed and that the site was clean.

"If all goes well with the cleanup, the chemist can move in on Monday morning, June 16?"

"Yes, but let's make it for Tuesday, June 17. My associates in Dennis are not the most reliable. I promise that I'll call you right away if there are any further delays," said Dandy respectfully, as the color in his face began to return.

"Good. I'll need directions to the lodge," said Smith.

Dandy stood and handed Smith a folded slip of paper. "That's a map of the Dennis area with the lodge's location marked with a 'X,'" said Dandy cautiously.

Smith opened the paper and studied the detailed map. "Planned ahead, I see! Were you expecting me?" said Smith cynically. "Do you know why Leone instructed you to leave a voicemail on his new cell phone? He's smart and he's careful. He doesn't want to be connected, in any way, with the lodge if there is a subsequent government investigation into his relationship with this prince. If there is any criminal 'blowback,' you are his scapegoat! Would you like a suggestion?" said Smith smugly.

Another wave of panic washed over Dandy, draining what little color had returned to his face. Leone had trapped him. The prospect of enduring years of hard time behind bars paralyzed him. In response to Smith's offer, all he could muster was a feeble nod.

"Rather than telephoning Leone with the lodge's cleanup confirmation, you should send him an update via email to his government office. In the email, you should say something like this…

'… per your instructions, your investment property has been thoroughly cleaned. See the attached pictures. The renter left you a case of wine with a thank you note. See the attached scanned note.'

"The note, along with the prince's signature, which you'll forge, should read:

'I enjoyed doing business with you. Your lodge was the perfect venue for my Muslim mission. Thank you for renting it to me. Allah Akbar, Saudi prince… '"

Gradually, the color began to trickle back into Dandy's face as he began to understand the implication of sending such an email to Leone.

Yes, that's perfect! Build a paper trail! It would support my contention that I didn't have any ownership stake in the property, and that I knew nothing of the terrorist training.

"He'll be pissed," said Dandy weakly.

"Yes, of course. However, if you explain in your best illogical, 'government speak' that you were simply trying to perform a thorough job, he'll understand. He won't like it, but he'll understand," said Smith.

An evil smile slithered across Smith's face. *The bastard is gloating! He enjoys screwing people,* thought Dandy.

Dandy mistook Smith's trademark sneer. He wasn't gloating. He was simply pleased with his latest manipulation. The breadth of his influence was expanding, which, after all, was his profession. Unbeknownst to both Dandy and Leone, Smith had a paid informant in Leone's office that would forward him a copy of Dandy's email to Leone. The email would be a nice addition to his Leone-Dandy blackmail library.

CHAPTER 16
EXERCISE AND DIET

Rod Turdlow's eyes squinted in the bright, mid-day sunshine as he walked unimpeded out of the gym towards his van. The fact that he could walk without the aid of a walker for more than ten feet without gasping for breath was a tribute to his new diet and exercise regime. Two hours in the gym every day and the absence of fried foods, sweets and booze had helped him shed twenty pounds since his last meeting with Richie Smith. Though his weight and degree of fitness were still far short of normal levels for someone his age and height, he was beginning to feel healthier.

With his diminishing cravings for fatty and sugar laced foods, and his gradual withdrawal from a slew of medications prescribed to combat his high blood pressure and early symptoms of diabetes, he was also beginning to think like an intelligent adult. With his newfound level of consciousness, he began to realistically assess his current station in life. The first matter that he addressed was his relationship with Richie Smith. He knew Smith was many things: a scam artist, a blackmailer and an influence peddler. Those activities, however, weren't unusual for your run of the mill criminal. What Turdlow could now see with perfect clarity was that Smith was also, in all likelihood, a cold-blooded killer. If he were to reinvent himself and set new life goals, his first step would be to eliminate Smith before he eliminated him.

If he succeeded in eliminating Smith, his next step would be a change of vocation. His days of practicing law in Montana were numbered. Small businesses in Montana weren't acquiescing as easily as those in California to his bullshit, nit-picking ADA lawsuits. Further, the judges and magistrates in the federal courts in Montana seemed to be far more intolerant of the shabbily written ADA legislation than their counterparts in California. With no cure provisions for the slightest of ADA infractions, these judges found creative ways to dismiss his ADA scam lawsuits faster than he could draft them. Furthermore, if the lawsuits did go to trial, his plaintiff damages were a pittance compared to his former California rulings.

Adding to the collapse of his law practice was his recent notification, from the Montana Bar Association, that they were suspending his temporary practice of law while they investigated the legitimacy of his California law degree. With only a phone call or two, he knew they could easily learn that the academic credentials he had submitted to them were fake. Richie Smith had, no doubt, apprised someone at the Bar association of this fact.

As he thought about his goals for the future, he began to contemplate the possibility of killing two birds with one stone. If he was going to eliminate Smith, *why not take over his businesses in the process!* This would require extracting from Smith a boatload of information about his consultancy practice and the details of his meth lab setup, prior to killing the man. The blackmail details Smith had on the U.S. Attorney in Helena would be profitable. However, what could really jumpstart his new career would be to learn how Smith pocketed millions from the Indians in Montana and Southern California.

His rational conclusion was relatively simple. He'd have to torture Smith to get the information he needed. But, what form of interrogation should he employ and where should it be done? His lack of medical training, weak physique and aversion to screaming, begging and pleading limited his options.

One afternoon, after an unusually energetic morning workout, Turdlow was reclining on his threadbare bed in a cheap motel room that he'd rented for the month. Not sure whether he felt like taking a nap or watching TV, he indifferently began to surf through the TV channels. To his delight, he came across a re-run of one of his favorite movies, *Dances with Wolves*. Turdlow's attention level grew when Lieutenant Dunbar, played by Kevin Costner, decided he was going to stay at the remote and abandoned Fort Sedgewick. Dunbar had traveled to his posting with a derelict teamster, Timmons, who was delivering a wagon full of supplies to the garrison. Dunbar invited Timmons to stay with him at the fort, but Timmons had had enough of the hot, dry plains. A plan began to form in Turdlow's mind.

Turdlow moved closer to the television as he intently watched the movie scene unfold. Timmons also had no interest in spending another minute with the young, daft lieutenant. His supplies had been delivered and, as far as he was concerned, he'd fulfilled his contract. Despite the presence of hostile Pawnee Indians in the area, he elected to return home, alone, with his wagon and team of horses. Pigheadedness trumped common sense.

Yes, that's it! thought Turdlow. Timmons fateful decision was the answer to Turdlow's interrogation dilemma.

CHAPTER 17

YELLOWSTONE

Monday, June 16, 2008, 9:00 AM MDT (Mountain Daylight Time).

Brice and Bobby waited in the large, one room airport lounge as they watched an all black, unmarked C-130 aircraft taxi into a staging area five hundred feet north of the passenger terminal at the West Yellowstone Airport. There were no other scheduled arrivals or departures at that time on that Monday morning so the small airport waiting area was empty.

The rear ramp of the aircraft lowered and both boys recognized Major Chet Daniels, wearing jeans and a polo shirt, as he stepped from the ramp to the tarmac. A man in a suit quickly approached Chet and they each presented one another with their identification credentials.

Brice said to Bobby, "I bet the 'suit' is FBI."

"Yup, he sticks out like a sore thumb. They have no concept of how to dress inconspicuously. No one wears a suit in Montana. By the way, did Chet ever tell you why he wanted to accompany us to Sheridan, Wyoming? Do you think it has anything to do with my stem cell treatments at the VA center?" asked Bobby.

"I have no idea why he decided to join us. I've asked him, but all he gives me is military 'mumbo jumbo' regarding classified matters and a need to know."

The FBI agent waved to an airport employee, who drove up to the unmarked aircraft's rear ramp towing a baggage-carrying cart. Chet watched as two of the flight crewmembers loaded three very large and heavy duffel bags onto the cart. Once the cart was loaded, the FBI agent sat next to the driver and directed him to the secure FAA service entrance that was out of sight from a couple of idle airport employees.

Several moments later, Chet walked through the deplaning door into the terminal.

"Good to see you again, Major Daniels" said Bobby, lifting his right hand a few inches off the armrest of his wheelchair in a friendly greeting.

"Bobby, you look great. You look a lot healthier than the last time I saw you in Fallujah, when we all got blown out of our boots. I'm so sorry you got the worst of it. I should… "

"Say no more! As I've told Brice a 1,000 times, I was the point man that day. It was my job to be the first one in that house. Not you, not Brice. I appreciate your compassion and concern, but we should all move on if that's OK with you major?" said Bobby kindly.

"Absolutely, Bobby. And by the way, let's all use first names while we're wearing 'civies.' Please call me Chet."

"Right on, Chet!" said Bobby with his trademark smile.

Brice extended his hand to Chet and said, "Good to see you, Chet. The plane, duffel bags and your presence all have the makings of a 'Top Secret' mission. What's up?"

"Why don't I discuss that with you and Bobby in the privacy of your pickup. Bobby is cleared to hear everything I have to say," said Chet formally.

Brice turned to Bobby, and they exchanged knowing looks. *Some Marine Corps matter was afoot.*

"I'm parked just outside," said Brice as he pointed to his pickup truck that was parked on the other side of the terminal's bay windows, in a handicap stall.

A minute later, they stood beside Brice's pickup. Brice carefully lifted Bobby into the front passenger seat of his Ram 1500 quad cab pickup and buckled him in. He collapsed Bobby's wheelchair and set it in in the bed of his truck. Chet seated himself comfortably on the rear bench seat.

Chet began to speak when his cell phone rang. The caller identification read "Grandma."

He looked to Brice then Bobby, "Do you boys mind if I take this call, it's from my grandmother?"

They both nodded their assent.

Chet spoke briefly with his grandmother:

"Yes, I'm fine… A surprise! Oh, that's great news! I'm so happy for you. When is the wedding date?… Unhuh, sure, I should be able to make the date. I'll be stateside in the fall. I'd like to hear more about your fiancé, but I'm a little busy now. I just landed at the West Yellowstone airport in Montana on a special mission… What, you say he flew into West Yellowstone yesterday… Your 'honey bear' is going to hunt black bear near Cody, Wyoming!… Retired from the Army, that's nice… Yes, it's too bad I missed him by a day… OK, I'll look for him. A big, light colored black man with a beautiful smile. I'll call back tonight… No, I won't forget. Love you!"

He rolled his eyes as he closed his cell phone and exclaimed, "She still thinks of me as an immature teenager."

"Are you?" teased Brice.

Chet turned slowly towards Brice, raised an eyebrow and flipped him the bird.

"OK, Gunnery Sergeant Miller, I have been ordered to give you the following message, in person, by the Commandant of the Marine Corps," said Chet officiously as he withdrew a 3X5 note card from his buttoned shirt pocket and read:

"The President of the United States, the Commandant of the Marine Corps, the Department of Homeland Security, the FBI and the entire 1st Marine Corps Division at Camp Pendleton extend our heartfelt thanks and appreciation to you for your timely and accurate information, which you dutifully passed on to your superiors, regarding suspected terrorist activity that you observed in two national parks. Your field intelligence contributed greatly to the country's arrest and apprehension of three groups of terrorists who were headed to Bryce, Zion and the Grand Canyon National Parks yesterday afternoon. These terrorists were heavily armed with weapons and explosives that were intended to kill and maim innocent U.S. citizens."

Chet returned the 3X5 card to his breast pocket, and added, "As you probably heard on the late news last night, Homeland Security and the FBI stopped and arrested these bastards yesterday afternoon. You did good work, Brice. You saved innocent lives."

"We partied last night, and overslept this morning. We hadn't heard any of this. Brice is in love with my sister, Molly," interjected Bobby.

A blushing Brice added, "What about their training camp in Dennis that Molly and I discovered several days ago?"

Chet looked puzzled. He, his superiors at Camp Pendleton and the Commandant of the Marine Corps had been copied on all the top secret communications from every law enforcement and security department in Washington regarding their plans to be on the lookout for possible terrorist activity in or around the national parks in the Western United States. There was no mention of a known terrorist training camp in Dennis in any of the message traffic.

"Piss, shit, fuck. Which government agency did you pass this information to?" asked Chet uneasily.

"Brice and Molly were on horseback deep into the back country tracking a wolf four days ago when they called my dad on our two radio. My dad and I were sitting at the kitchen table when Brice's call came in. He said it was large camp with about fifty Middle Eastern men who were firing AK-47's, M-16's and .30 caliber light machine guns. My dad immediately called the Department of Homeland Security in Fort Harrison, Montana over our land line," responded Bobby somberly.

Chet thought for a moment before he re-opened his cell phone and pressed a speed dial number. Several moments later, his call was answered, "3rd Battalion, Lt. Col. Adair's office, this is Gunnery Sergeant 'Hammer' Stephens speaking."

"Hammer, this is Major Daniels, is Lt. Col. Adair available?"

A moment later Chet's battalion commander at Camp Pendleton, Lt. Col. Roy Adair, came on the line, "Roy, its Chet. I just got off the C-130 in West Yellowstone, and am sitting in Gunny Miller's pickup with Bobby Ridger, outside the passenger terminal. As ordered by the commandant, I read them the message I was given. Neither Miller nor Ridger had heard about yesterday's arrests. They were partying."

Brice and Bobby could hear Lt. Col. Adair's loud and expected response over Chet's cell phone.

Brice mouthed quietly to Chet and Bobby, "I'm on leave. I'm suppose to party!"

Bobby nodded his head and smiled.

"Yes, yes, I understand. I know, but listen to this. Brice and Bobby's sister, Molly Ridger, were on a backcountry horseback ride four days ago when they discovered a terrorist training camp. Brice called in his report immediately over a two-way radio to Bobby Ridger's dad. He estimated that there were fifty Middle Eastern men in the camp and that they were firing AK-47's, M-16's and .30 caliber machine guns. Bobby was with his dad when he received the radio transmission and he confirms that his dad called the Department of Homeland Security in Fort Harrison, Montana and reported the discovery," said Chet.

Chet jerked the phone away from his ear, a loud torrent of obscenities streamed from his cell phone.

Gradually, the profanity subsided and Chet cautiously inched the cell phone closer to his ear.

"Yes. Yes. I'll keep my cell phone charged and close by. Thanks, Roy."

"What was that all about?" asked Brice.

"Lt. Col. Adair was in charge of briefing the Department of Homeland Security on your field intelligence. He spoke numerous times directly with the Secretary of the Department Homeland Security, Lowell Preston III, regarding your observations in the national parks. Preston didn't utter a word about your discovery of a terrorist training camp near Dennis," said Chet.

"That's odd," said Brice lightly.

"Very fucking odd!" said Chet not so lightly. "Adair is going to call Preston to discuss this new development. I'm sure that our regimental commander, Col. O'Brien; our 1st Division general and the commandant will also be on the call."

"Heads should roll at Homeland Security! Someone was asleep at the wheel. I wonder how the president will react once he hears about this," said Brice sardonically. A moment later he continued, "It's nice to see you

Chet, but what brings you to West Yellowstone in an unmarked C-130? Couldn't you have told me all this over the phone?" asked Brice casually as he drove his pickup towards the FAA service gate. "And, what the hell is in those duffel bags? From the grunts those flight crew members made lifting them, I'll bet they off loaded a 1,000 pounds of gear," added Brice.

"Those bags weigh closer to 1,300 pounds. The plane's loadmaster weighed them before we took off. Further, I was ordered not to discuss these matters with you over the phone for a number of reasons. As the reality of multiple terrorist threats unfolded, it occurred to the Commandant of the Marine Corps that your level of common sense and observation far exceeded those of just about everyone else's in Homeland Security, the FBI and the National Parks. In light of this, the commandant directed our division general to have someone with a level of competence, equal to or greater than yours, accompany you on your national park sightseeing tour. Col. O'Brien selected me for this grand assignment. I feel like a glorified baby sitter!" said Chet irritably.

"Equal in competence?" interjected Brice, as he and Bobby both grinned.

"Greater! Far greater, meathead," replied Chet forcefully. After a moment, he continued, "As I was saying, if during your sightseeing you were to observe any other unusual activity, the commandant suggested to O'Brien that you, now we, should be *appropriately armed*. O'Brien hand-picked all the weapons and equipment. We're armed to the teeth!"

"Hey, this is turning into quite the field trip to Sheridan. This has the feel of a combat mission," said Bobby grinning.

Chet turned towards Bobby, "I hope to God it doesn't turn into a mission, Bobby. But if it does, Marine, we will be the most heavily armed three man fire team ever assembled!"

After they loaded the duffel bags onto the bed of Brice's truck, Brice covered them with a tarp, which he pulled from a storage box bolted to the bed of his truck.

They exited the airport and headed south, towards the town of West Yellowstone, on a quiet, two-lane road. It was a clear, crisp morning with the early sun peeking through tall pine trees that lined each side of the road. Morning dew glistened off pine needles at the treetops, while a thinning morning mist swirled between their shrouded trunks. Chet took little interest in the beauty of their surroundings. His stony silence and body language told Brice that he was stewing. Something was bothering him.

"From what you told us Chet, the feds caught and arrested all the terrorists yesterday. They might have preempted all the threats had they moved on their training camp earlier, but that didn't happen. Unless I'm missing something, the threats are over. Our military top brass will probably scream and shout at a few civilians who dropped the ball, but we're out of that *loop*. Your arrival with a small armory seems to be an after the fact overreaction. What's troubling you?" said Brice evenly.

Chet collected his thoughts. His response was tinged with concern, "Brice, you've done an amazing job uncovering these terrorist plots during your leave. But, damn it! Don't tell me we're out of the *loop*. There are a number of things about this terrorist action that don't make sense to me.

"First, a bona fide visual confirmation by two parties of an active, 'guns blazing' Middle Eastern terrorist training camp on U.S. soil doesn't get investigated?

"Second, all the terrorists were intercepted south of their targets, on state highways in conspicuous white tour buses. Dennis, Montana is approximately nine hundred miles north of the Grand Canyon, and approximately six to seven hundred miles north of Bryce and Zion."

"You seem to be quite familiar with those distances," observed Brice.

"When you called in your report on suspicious terrorist sightings in the parks, I studied the interstate highway maps for the Western United States to see where you had been and where you were headed. I specifically remember the distances between the Grand Canyon, Zion and Bobby's home in Dennis, Montana," said Chet thoughtfully.

"Shit, the terrorists that were intercepted were travelling north! They weren't coming from Dennis. Those distances are too great to transport terrorists and their weapons undetected in white tour buses on state highways. They have to stop for gas, food and bathroom breaks. Someone would have seen suspicious activity and alerted the authorities," added Brice.

"Exactly! That leads me to believe that there was a second terrorist training camp south of the Grand Canyon," said Chet.

"The Dennis training camp would ideally support an attack, say, in Yellowstone," replied Bobby, as he said what they were all thinking.

After a several minutes, Brice suggested, "Do you think Bryce, Zion and the Grand Canyon were diversions?"

"No, I don't think so. All three groups were heavily armed and most of the young *martyrs to be* were high on drugs. They were clearly headed into battle," answered Chet.

"There is no reason to stagger their attack dates. That eliminates their element of surprise, and increases their risk of being caught by increased security at all the national parks," said Brice.

"I think I know what happened," said Bobby evenly. "Remember that terrorist attack in Fallujah which intelligence got wind of beforehand? Intelligence had intercepted and decrypted a message that was forwarded through Mexico. We set up and waited for the bad guys and they didn't show."

"Yeah, I remember that. They misinterpreted the time of their attack. They arrived twelve hours late," said Chet. "But, twelve hours have passed since we rounded up yesterday's terrorists."

"Yes, but what if their instructions were sent from a country like Iran or Pakistan westward to the United States. Their time runs ahead of us, which could explain the wrong day. Add to that the possible confusion over PM instead of AM, and you've got a 24-hour error. These guys struggle keeping track of their local time," said Bobby.

"You're right! That makes sense, Bobby. Let's see," said Chet looking at his watch. "It's nearly 10:00 AM (MDT) now. Yesterday's arrests went down around 4:30 PM in this same time zone. The terrorists were probably getting ready for a 5:00 PM jump-off." Chet mulled his options for a few moments, "I'll follow-up with Adair no later than 3:00 PM (MDT) local time to see what he has learned. Hopefully, we'll hear that the Department of Homeland Security rounded up all those bastards prior to yesterdays arrests, and elected to keep it secret for some strange fucking reason," said Chet heatedly.

"That's all you can do for now, Chet. We'll keep our eyes and ears open as we travel through the park, but like I said before, we're out of the *loop*," said Brice soothingly.

"When I'm with you Brice, we're never out of the *loop*. For that matter, we always seem to be in the God damn center of the *loop*," said Chet irritably.

Brice and Bobby laughed.

"Assholes!" howled Chet.

"Now, now, Chet! Watch your temper. You need some rest. You probably had to get up pretty darn early this morning to catch your flight. And, I know those C-130 seats aren't the most comfortable. Close your eyes and relax," said Bobby as if he were speaking to a child.

"You're both big assholes!" murmured Chet, as he closed his eyes and tilted his head back against the headrest.

Ten minutes later, Brice's pickup rolled to a stop at the West Entrance of Yellowstone National Park. A park ranger sauntered from the ranger's hut to his open window. The ranger noted the defense department sticker pasted to the lower left hand corner of Brice's windshield. Entrance fees were waived for active duty military personnel. He asked for Brice's military identification card, which Brice withdrew from his wallet and handed to him. The ranger casually examined Brice's photo identification photo and took a quick, cursory glance at the tarpaulin that covered the duffel bags in the bed of Brice's pickup. Satisfied with his inspection, he returned the identification card to Brice and waved him indifferently into the park.

"Business as usual for these park rangers," said Brice.

"Shit! They should be on high alert, especially after yesterday's terrorist arrests at Bryce, Zion and the Grand Canyon. This is not good," said Bobby.

"No, it's not. But, at least, we won't have to spend half the day in handcuffs explaining why we were entering the park with a small armory in the bed of Brice's truck," said Chet with a feeling of relief.

Bobby knew that neither Chet nor Brice had ever visited Yellowstone National Park. Though he could talk for hours about the park's wonders, he elected to remain silent. He'd let the natural beauty of the park arouse their interest before launching into a discussion of his beloved park.

After their first mile or so into the park, a river emerged on the north side of the road. Brice first spotted the smallish river as it magically appeared from distant sagebrush. On its northern bank, a small herd of elk was wading indifferently through its waters. As the river turned closer to the road, the prairie grasslands evolved into green meadows. Pines and cottonwoods sprinkled the banks of the shallow, gin clear water. At times, it was difficult to tell in which direction the slow moving river was gliding. Only the occasional presence of a white water riffle told Brice that the river was meandering westward.

"Bobby, is that grass I see growing in this creek?"

"Not exactly," began Bobby. "Those are weeds. This river is formed by the Gibbon and Firehole rivers, which are not too far from here. Both of those rivers have geysers in and around them. We'll actually see steam wafting from the surface of the Firehole in twenty minutes or so when we drive beside that river. All that geothermal activity heats the water, as does the summertime heat. The net result is that all the native water plants grow fast and furious in the summer. Another effect from this warm water is that the trout lay low in the summer and don't really move around or feed much until it gets cooler in the fall."

"What river is this?" asked Chet.

"It's the Madison," replied Bobby.

"This is a much smaller river than the section that runs in front of your ranch," said Brice.

"You're right! We are near its headwaters plus the river picks up an awful lot of water from various watersheds as it travels towards our ranch. The dammed Hebgen Lake and Quake Lake being the biggest contributors," answered Bobby.

Several miles further, the road crossed over the river. North of the road, a steep hillside, much of it rock fall, rose to form an irregular butte. Along the butte's ridgeline, the burned remains of naked, limbless trees were clearly visible.

"Does that butte have a name?" asked Brice.

"Yes, it's named Mount Haynes," said Bobby.

"It's an interesting formation. Those dead trees along the ridge almost look like tall, crooked crosses in a cemetery. It's like a natural monument dedicated to the cycles of nature," said Brice thoughtfully.

"Hmm! I never thought of Mount Haynes like that, Brice. But your description fits. As we drive through the park, I'll point out the effects of the 1988 fire that burned about one third of Yellowstone. The cycles of nature and the geological composition of the earth are evident everywhere," replied Bobby.

"Are those buffalo at the base of the rock fall?" asked Chet.

"Yup! We'll see lots more of those 'big boys' during our visit today," said Bobby.

"Just what exactly will we see today?" asked Chet, as his interest in the park began to grow and his thoughts of terrorists receded.

"In a couple of miles, we're going to turn south on the Grand Loop Road and head towards Old Faithful and Lake Yellowstone. We could spend days exploring the park, but I thought for today, we'd drive by the major highlights of the southern part of the park so we can make it to Cody, Wyoming before nightfall. We'll check into a motel there and have time for a nice dinner together. On our way back, we can take our time and explore the northern part of the park including the Grand Canyon of Yellowstone," said Bobby.

"There's a grand canyon in Yellowstone?" asked Chet.

"Yes, it's a miniature version of the real thing, but, nevertheless, very impressive. Yellowstone is a huge park, about 3,500 square miles, with amazing diversity... steaming rivers, geysers, mud volcanoes, waterfalls and an immense lake. And, lots of wildlife, buffaloes, black bears, moose, wolves and eagles.

"We'll check in on Old Faithful on our drive today. If we're lucky, we might arrive just before it erupts. It erupts about every ninety minutes. After that we'll head towards Yellowstone Lake, the Lake Yellowstone Hotel and the mud volcanoes. The lake is the largest in the world above an elevation of 7,000 feet. Most of the buffaloes hang out a short distance from the mud volcanoes. We'll exit the park through the east gate on our way to Cody," said Bobby.

"You know a lot about the park, Bobby, did you work here?" asked Brice.

"No, but our Boy Scout troop hiked and camped out in nearly every square mile of the park. And, Tom Youngblood's Arapaho tribe lived in the park at different times. He knows this place like the back of his hand."

"Who's Tom Youngblood?" asked Chet.

"He's a cattle ranch neighbor in Dennis. He and his wife are both Arapahos. Tom taught Brice how to track a wolf a couple of days ago. We had a problem with a wolf that was killing our cattle. Brice discovered the terrorist training camp while he was tracking the wolf with my sister," answered Bobby.

"Un, huh! Anything else I should know about Arapahos or wolves while we're on this trip?" asked Chet suspiciously.

"Nope, other than Arapahos are great people," said Bobby.

"I'll second that. Is Tom a tribal shaman?" asked Brice.

"No, but his father was, and I think he inherited some of his father's gifts," said Bobby.

"What is a shaman?" asked Chet.

"He's like a visionary for a tribe of Indians. He has dreams in which the spirits tell him things. It's somewhat like a prophet. Tom believes that Brice has these special powers," said Bobby.

"Really!" said Chet sincerely.

"Yeah! For example, Brice predicted that a large, black bird would fall from the sky and deliver a princely black man to us today. And that this black man would protect us and guide us safely through Yellowstone, while he silently communicated with the buffaloes," teased Bobby.

"I've heard enough! I don't know if you two planned this skit in advance or if it just comes naturally, but you can skip any further mention of shamans and special powers. Bobby, how about sticking to the *National Geographic* version of what's in Yellowstone," said Chet, annoyed that his two young traveling partners had again gotten under his skin.

"Yes sir, Major Daniels!" barked Bobby, still giggling.

The next three hours flew by. Chet and Brice were totally captivated by the wonders of Yellowstone. The steaming rivers and buffaloes particularly intrigued them.

"Geez, I didn't realize that buffaloes were so big. I can't imagine taking one of those down with a bow and arrow while riding a fast moving horse," said Brice.

"Strange beasts. Their front end is the size of a rhino and their butt and rear legs look like they were designed for a goat," said Chet.

"They're one of the top attractions in the park. You sure don't want to frighten or annoy them. When they get up a head of steam, they're very dangerous. They've gored tourists and rolled cars," said Bobby.

"I can see that. Some of those tourists we saw today seemed to have a death wish. I'll keep my distance, thank you," said Chet.

After seeing the large herd of buffaloes just north of the bubbling mud volcanoes, Bobby suggested that they turn around and start working their way toward the park's east exit. When they reached the Fishing Bridge near the lake, Brice turned his pickup east on Route 20. It was a few minutes after 1:00 PM and Bobby wanted to get a head start towards the exit. Late afternoon traffic during the summer months in the park could be dreadfully slow, especially if one got caught behind a slow moving RV or school bus.

During the first few miles of their eastward drive, the 1988 fire damage was clearly visible on every southeastern hillside. After twenty years of new growth, the largest trees had only reached a height of ten to fifteen feet. Bobby explained that it would take at least fifty to seventy five years of growth for the new trees to be indistinguishable from those trees that were spared by the fire.

The grade of Route 20 gradually increased as the road ascended into a more mountainous area. In many places, the road was literally carved from the side of a granite mountain. Occasional construction stops gave Chet, ever the engineer, time to more closely examine the road construction. He was impressed with the road's design.

"Man, this road could wash out in a day of a heavy rain or winter runoff without proper foundations and drainage for lots of fast moving water. I see they've got massive drains every couple of hundred feet with very stout channels above and below the road. They've also added retaining walls everywhere. I'm impressed," said Chet.

"I think this road has been closed more often than it's been open for the very reasons you mentioned. Seven or eight years ago they decided to rebuild it properly so that it would last. The band aid fixes never worked," explained Bobby.

After driving through Sylvan Pass, the north side of the road gradually changed from shear granite walls to steep, heavily wooded hillsides. Lush green pastures and gentle hills unfolded on the south side of the road. A postcard-perfect river... Middle Creek... rapidly churned as it tumbled through the pasture below them. Traffic moved slowly at fifteen miles per hour, when it wasn't stopped, and school buses full of active young kids were both ahead and behind them.

"These buses are full of 6th graders from Cody, Wyoming. As part of their graduation from elementary school, their school district treats them to a two day, overnight trip into the park. Park Rangers lead tours of the park and help them set up a campsite near one of the park's lodges. It's a great experience for the kids, though somewhat exhausting for their teachers and chaperoning parents," said Bobby.

"That's a nice way to learn about nature, animals, birds, the science of geothermal activity. I sure didn't have anything like that when I was in grade school," said Chet enviously.

Chet glanced at his watch, 1:24 PM (MDT). In a little over ninety minutes, he'd give Adair a follow-up phone call. Hopefully, he'd learn that Homeland Security had indeed shutdown the Dennis training camp and arrested the terrorists.

His mind, however, continued to analyze the chain of events. *If Homeland Security or another federal agency had moved on the training camp in Dennis, it would have provided solid evidence of the terrorist's intentions. With that hard information in hand, all those federal agencies, which were simply on alert for possible terrorist activity, would have responded in a completely different manner.*

His battlefield instincts told him something was amiss. But, what?

A nervous tic rippled across Chet's left cheek as he unconsciously rolled up the sleeves of his long sleeve shirt. He absently turned to view the scenery while his mind considered one terrorist scheme after another. The idyllic sight of lush green hills and the sparkling, clear river that flowed below the road began to unconsciously calm him. His worried thoughts gradually dissolved and his eyelids grew heavy. In minutes, he was peacefully snoring.

CHAPTER 18
TALK, RICHIE

Monday, June 16, 1:30 PM (MDT)

Rod Turdlow sat patiently in his wheelchair in the middle of a remote, gravel parking lot two miles from the nearest paved road and ten miles from the nearest ranch. He was waiting for Richie Smith to arrive. Overgrown weeds, empty beer cans and used condoms littered the area that was surrounded by a thick wall of mature trees. His handicapped van was parked haphazardly twenty feet away. The only access to the isolated location was from a seldom used, rutted dirt road. In addition to being remote, it was a difficult place to find. Two large boulders, beside the lightly used single lane secondary road, marked the nearly undetectable dirt road turnoff. Turdlow had learned of the location from the tattooed and nose pierced teenage girl who worked at the front desk of his gym. She said it was the ideal place to party in total privacy.

Richie Smith also liked the idea of meeting Turdlow in an isolated, out of the way location. It was also the perfect setting for him to accomplish several of his objectives with his cheeky, slow-moving partner. The move in date for the meth lab operation was scheduled for the following day, Tuesday, June 17, and he had yet to receive from Turdlow any of the chemist's contact details, other than a brief text message on his phone that read, "chemist arrived." Everything Turdlow did irritated the hell out of him. Once he got the chemists contact information from Turdlow, he would shoot the bastard. As Smith's SUV bumped along the pitted dirt road that led to his rendezvous with Turdlow, he touched his nine-millimeter Glock that was resting comfortably in the inside pocket of his jacket and smiled.

Turdlow heard Smith's SUV approach. He peeked into the brown paper bag that rested on his lap to ensure that the two unopened Twinkies packages hid his TASER gun. Two empty Twinkies wrappers, which he'd licked clean, were also in the bag. He deliberately tossed one to the ground, ten feet in front of his wheelchair. The other he left in plain sight on his lap.

Smith pulled into the lot and parked his Explorer next to Turdlow's van. He exited his SUV, and slowly ambled towards Turdlow. He stopped twenty feet from Turdlow, his hands rested on his hips. The Twinkie wrapper that lay on Turdlow's lap was suddenly caught by the wind and settled at his feet. Smith picked up the wrapper and inspected it.

Shaking his head in disgust and extending the Twinkie wrapper towards Turdlow, he said "Damn Rod! This shit is going to kill you, especially with your diabetes."

"Oh, don't say that! You know me. It would take a lot of self-control to eliminate sweets from my diet. Maybe I'll start a new diet next week," said Turdlow deferentially. His response was designed to upset Smith, which it obviously did.

Despite his deadly plans for Turdlow, Smith couldn't control his response, "Jesus! Why the fuck wait until next week? Start today!"

Turdlow needed to draw Smith closer to effectively shoot him with his TASER.

"Today?"

"Yeah, now!" said Smith forcefully as he absentmindedly stuffed the Twinkie wrapper into his pant's pocket.

"Hmm! That's a major commitment. I'll need help. You're my best friend. Will you help me?" whined Turdlow. "Here! You take these last Twinkies," said Turdlow as he pulled the two unopened Twinkie packages out of the paper bag and placed them beside the bag.

Turdlow returned his hand into the bag as if retrieving more Twinkie's. Carefully, he slipped his hand around the grip of the TASER gun.

In the meantime, Smith stepped forward to the wrapper Turdlow had previously tossed to the ground, ten feet away. "Shit! You're making a mess. Put your trash in the bag," said Smith, as he bent over to pick up the second wrapper.

As Smith straightened, his wary black eyes saw the grip of a TASER emerge from Turdlow's paper bag. Reflexively, he leaped backwards and went for his Glock.

Turdlow's trigger finger was a split second faster than Smith's. The TASER'S probes sank firmly into Smith's chest and 50,000 volts of electricity coursed through his body. At first, his black eyes bulged at Turdlow in anger and then with acute pain. All of his muscles were incapacitated and he shook uncontrollably. He collapsed and began to flop on the ground like a fish out of water. Turdlow held the trigger in the fire position as he stood from his wheelchair and walked slowly towards Smith. He pulled a six-inch blackjack from his side pocket and firmly slapped it across the side of Smith's head. Only when Smith's head sagged and his eyes closed did Turdlow release the TASER'S trigger.

Turdlow picked up Smith's fallen Glock and stuffed it into the side pocket of his windbreaker. He patted down Smith's body, and felt a hard oblong object in one of his pants pockets. It was a switchblade knife, which he removed and deposited into the other side pocket of his jacket. He roughly jerked the TASER probes out of Smith's chest and rolled him onto his stomach. He withdrew a hand full of heavy-duty electrical ties from his hip pocket and doubled cuffed Smith's legs and arms. When all the ties were firmly secured, he dragged his partner into a sitting position against a nearby tree.

He rolled his wheelchair to a spot ten feet in front of Smith. Continuing with his carefully planned interrogation, he moved to his van where he retrieved a foot long bundle of slender implements that were wrapped in an old towel. He set the bundle on the ground next to his wheelchair, and next removed a large bottle of water from the knapsack that hung from wheelchair back.

Smith moaned as Turdlow splashed water over his face. His head and shoulders swayed sluggishly from side to side. Turdlow's blackjack had left a welt on the side of Smith's head that was now the size of a small banana.

Turdlow poked the hot welt with his index finger and his partner whimpered. Smith slowly regained consciousness.

"Richie! Open your eyes, Richie. It's time to start our meeting."

"Huh! Where am I? What happened? God every muscle aches. My head. Geez, was I shot in the head?" slurred Smith with unfocused eyes.

"No my friend. You're fine. My TASER zapped you with just a few volts of electricity, and I gave you a baby tap with my blackjack. Take some deep breaths and open your mouth. I'll give you a drink of water."

Smith opened his mouth and turned his head upwards as Turdlow turned the water bottle up side down. Smith gagged on the rush of water. A moment later a stream of water and vomit flew from his mouth.

Smith's eyes began to regain focus. "Damn, Turdlow! Are you trying to drown me?"

Smith's level of awareness was gradually returning. Turdlow's earlier comment about his TASER and blackjack began to have meaning. He tried to move but realized his legs and hands were tied. He shook his body violently trying to free himself, but the ties held firmly. Meanwhile, Turdlow returned to his wheel chair, sat down and casually crossed his legs.

"Richie! You're going to hurt yourself if you try to get free of those ties. I'll let you go after our little talk," said Turdlow in a soft, ingratiating manner.

"Turdlow. if you don't release me in the next sixty seconds, I'll shove that TASER up your ass."

"I have no doubt, Richie, that you'd do that and more. For example, I found this loaded Glock in your jacket pocket," said Turdlow as he withdrew the gun from his windbreaker.

He pointed the pistol at Smith's head, "Were you going to shoot me Richie, after I gave you the name and phone number of my chemist? That wouldn't have been a nice thing to do to your partner. Partners are supposed to work together, not double-cross one another."

Smith was silent as he stared down the wrong end of the Glock. He tried to think of a way to escape. His head throbbed.

"Listen Turdlow, I had no intention of shooting you. I carry that Glock all the time to defend myself. I'm in a dangerous business. If you want a cut of the meth lab business perhaps we can work something out, but first remove these ties. I'm losing the feeling in my hands and feet. Come on, buddy, cut me loose."

"Buddy! I didn't realize we were buddies. You were mean to me the last time we met. I got the distinct impression during that meeting that you'd get rid of me… er, kill me… the moment I gave you my chemists contact information. If you'd told me we were buddies, we could have avoided this awkward situation. Oh, well! What to do?"

"C'mon Turdlow. You know me. I get a little agitated from time to time and overreact."

"Overreact! Yes, I'd say that's accurate." Turdlow began to smile in anticipation of his partner's response to his next words, "Richie, have you ever thought of getting anger management counseling? I think it would improve your overall personality and communication skills."

Smith's black eyes bulged and his face contorted into a cruel, menacing grimace. "You motherfucker," he roared. "I'll give you ten seconds to cut me loose or so help me, I'll skin you alive, and slowly cut you into small pieces. You'll beg me to kill you."

Turdlow ignored the threat, picked up the bundle from the ground and set it on his lap. He unfolded the towel and examined two slender steel objects, and what appeared to be a rock.

He picked up one of the items, showed it to Smith and declared, "Hunting knife for field dressing animals." Meticulously, he returned it to the towel.

He displayed the second item. "Razor sharp scalpel. Best instrument for skinning… or scalping!" chuckled Turdlow, as he carefully returned it too to the towel.

He held up the last item for Smith to see, "Sharpening stone in case the blades get dull." After he set the stone on the towel, he refolded the towel.

"'Cut me up into small pieces,' you say," said Turdlow. "I thought you might like to do something like that to me. So, of course, I came prepared. However, after I found this switchblade knife in your pocket, I can see that my advance preparation was… ah, overkill. Get it?" laughed Turdlow as he twirled Smith's knife in his fingers. "Obviously, the tables are turned now, but you can rest assured that I won't be doing any… ah, field dressing on you… so long as you cooperate. I just have a few questions for you, after which I'll cut you lose and we can go our separate ways. Fair enough, good buddy!"

"Go to hell, Turdlow. I bet you get queasy carving a roasted chicken. You haven't got the balls to step on an ant. Now cut me lose!"

"Sorry Richie, no can do. You're hostility is not helping your cause. You really should consider counseling," said Turdlow derisively. A moment later, he continued, "My first question. Indian Consultancy- How do you screw the Indians out of their money?"

Smith remained silent, his face flushed with anger.

"Would you like me to repeat the question?"

No answer.

Turdlow unfolded the towel on his lap, and selected the scalpel. After placing the bundle on the ground, he stood and walked towards Smith. Stopping just a few feet from Smith, he looked down unsympathetically at his captive.

Smith's face reflected surprise, as he watched Turdlow effortlessly walk towards him. His surprise turned to apprehension when he saw the scalpel, which Turdlow held at his side. A ray of sunshine that had slithered through the wall of trees glinted off its sharp edge.

"This is called role reversal," said Turdlow assertively.

The TASER and blackjack had muddled Smith's thinking. Until the last few moments, he hadn't wondered how he had been moved against the tree or how Turdlow had maneuvered his wheelchair across the uneven parking lot. Now that he was thinking more clearly, the reality of his predicament was setting in. Turdlow had lost at least thirty pounds, and he could walk. The bastard's been working out in a gym. His thoughts began to race, *What did he say about the scalpel and skinning or scalping?*

Turdlow saw a trace of fear dance across Smith's eyes. A moment later, it was replaced with his customary macho outrage. "Fuck you, Turdlow," he spat.

"Did you ever watch the movie *Dances with Wolves?* Kevin Costner plays the part of an Army officer, Lieutenant Dunbar."

"Yeah, a couple of times. So what?" said Smith warily. "What's with the scalpel?"

"In the movie, the U.S. government is taking over Indian land in the west. They are, like you, screwing the Indians at every turn. There is a scene in the movie where the Pawnee's take revenge on the U.S. government by attacking a white man. The man they attack is a teamster named Timmons, who had taken supplies and a Lt. Dunbar to a remote Army outpost situated in the middle of ancient Pawnee hunting grounds."

"Yeah, yeah. I get it! The poor Indians strike back. Big fucking deal!" said Smith with his usual irreverence.

"No, I don't think you do get my point. Timmons is an irascible sort who doesn't listen to anyone's advice. He's obstinate, like you. He decides to leave Lt. Dunbar at the abandoned Army outpost and return to his home base. Lt. Dunbar cautions him about the dangers of crossing hostile Indian country alone, but he blows him off. Much like you blew off my questions during our last meeting"

"You got that right, ace. You better put that scalpel away before you hurt yourself," said Smith menacingly.

Without any warning, Turdlow grabbed a thick thatch of Smith's greasy black hair and jerked his head backward. Placing the tip of the scalpel against Smith's forehead, he drew the scalpel along Smith's scalp, just below his hairline. The scalpel easily sliced through Smith's skin. Blood began to trickle down his forehead into his black, evil eyes.

"Ah, ah! What the fuck!" gurgled Smith, who was stunned by Turdlow's swift attack.

Smith's vanity and ego revolved around his thick, black, wavy mane. He'd spent thousands of dollars over the years conditioning and pampering his hair. Then of course, there were untold hours combing it *just so* in front of a mirror. He viewed himself as a forty year old, teen idol. All the ladies said his pompadour was better looking than that of John Travolta's in "Grease." And now this asshole, Turdlow, was messing with it.

Finally collecting himself, Smith screamed, "Stop you motherfucker! What the fuck do you think you're doing? I'll kill you!"

"I'm taking my first coup. You know what that means, right."

"Coup! That's a prize. A scalp that a warrior takes for killing the enemy," said Smith, his voice breaking.

"Correct! That's what happened to Timmons when he neglected Lt. Dunbar's advice, and crossed hostile land on his own. The Indians scalped him! Don't you see Richie? Our relationship is very similar to theirs."

"Stop, God damn it!"

Turdlow ignored him. As he continued slicing, he said, "Your scalp will be my first coup. That is unless you talk, Richie."

"OK, OK, I'll talk."

"Everything," said Turdlow as he wiped the bloody scalpel across the front of Smith's shirt.

Turdlow returned to his wheelchair and retrieved from his knapsack several bandages, and a small tape recorder. The bandages temporarily stopped Smith's bleeding. He moved the wheel chair nearer to Smith and sat.

As he started the recorder, Turdlow smiled downwards towards Smith, "Let's start anew. How do you screw the Indians out of their money?"

Smith's initial answers weren't particularly forthcoming or especially insightful, which required Turdlow to provide occasional prodding. Jabbing his finger into Smith's hot welt on the side of his head, or ripping the bandage off his forehead clarified his responses. However, when Smith became reticent, extending the incision along his scalp proved to be a surefire means of loosening his tongue.

Turdlow wasn't familiar with the names and positions of all the crooked congressmen in Washington DC that Smith recited from memory. He did, however, clearly understand the simplicity and magnitude of his scams, which screwed not only the Indians, but also every American taxpayer.

In general, the lobbyist's activities were much like selling insurance. A lobbyist would explain to a prospective Indian tribe or corporate client that they could "insure" that the federal government would favorably rule on the client's request... be it a tax break, the approval of a casino or waiver to sell technology to foreign governments. Just like an "insurance policy", this meant that the lobbyist's clients' desired goals were never at risk. The cost to the client for the lobbyists "insurance" was exorbitant consultant fees. These consulting fees were then liberally distributed by the lobbyist to the appropriate key congressional chairman who would "insure" that a last minute, unintelligible and supposedly benign rider (i.e. the client's "insured request") was added to a bill or appropriation being first approved by his committee, and later, in rubber stamp fashion, by the entire congress.

Another source of income for the lobbyist was the commonly

accepted practice of overbilling. Months,' or even years after the lobbyist's services had been performed and they had been paid in full, the lobbyist would re-bill their client for former services rendered, especially if certain economies prevailed. These certain economies were often excessive, windfall profits that their clients experienced by virtue of the favorable governmental legislation these lobbyists had snuck through congress. When the client understandably objected to the overbilling, the lobbyist would artfully characterize the overbillings as a "re-examination fee" for the illegal services they had previously provided. In short, the practice was a slick form of corporate blackmail and the fees were simply hush money.

The list of Smith's clients, or more accurately industries, staggered Turdlow. The list covered not only Indian gaming, but healthcare, telecommunications and foreign governments. Turdlow wasn't surprised when Smith confided that he originally learned the "ins and outs" of lobbying while working for the infamous lobbyist, Jack Abramoff, who was currently in prison serving time for multiple convictions of defrauding Indian tribes and casinos, corruption of public officials, tax evasion and mail fraud. Smith had managed much of Abramoff's regional field liaison with Indian tribes in the Western United States until Abramoff had been sent to prison.

Smith further explained that though the federal government had investigated him, they elected not to prosecute him because they had so little evidence against him. He also added that they viewed him as little more than a lowly bagman for Abramoff.

What the federal investigators didn't realize about the lowly bagman was that he had a photographic memory. Smith knew the details of every past and future Abramoff legislative scam in his Western United States region. So when the Justice Department, and the duplicitous congress, witnessed the country's outrage with Abramoff's practices, they elected to perform their duty and prosecute the bastard. The threat of criminal prosecution, rather than an inconsequential fine, sent shock waves through the boardrooms of nearly every lobbyist inside the beltway. When the gavel fell and Abramoff was sentenced to prison, the shock waves turned to panic as all of Abramoff's clients and competitors ran for cover and began formulating revised business plans.

The real possibility of hard time in prison and or the loss of a government pension were the "big sticks" Smith used to extort money from both past and "work in progress" Abramoff clients and fixers. For the fixers, primarily bent public officials, they had, in virtually every case, already squandered their dirty money. And, why not? They expected the dirty money train to run forever. In these cases, Smith acted like a bank receiver who designed a payment plan for a bankrupt client. His threat of public exposure motivated all of them to return their dirty money payoffs, with interest, to Smith on a regular, monthly payment schedule.

For the dirty clients, primarily corporations and large trade groups, who were benefiting from ill gotten, but favorable legislative rulings, they required Smith's special attention. Smith knew it was only a mater of time before the various legislatures that had been duped realized the error of their ways and reversed prior favorable rulings. With this category of clientele, Smith was dealing on matters that were time sensitive. His course of action was simple. On the heels of the Abramoff sentencing, he immediately demanded large sums of up-front hush money from the deep pocket corporations and trade groups. For those that balked, he threatened immediate high profile, public exposure at a very sensitive and unfavorable time. He knew that million dollar hush money payoffs were inconsequential to the public relations damage they would incur if the national news media began to publicly dissect their indiscretions.

If any of the clients or fixers continued to balk, Smith sent them an email with incriminating excerpts of videos, with the audio tracks, that he had secretly filmed during their prior meetings. Without exception, all of his customers cooperated with him.

"Water! I need water," gasped Smith.

This time, Turdlow slowly tilted the water bottle into Smith's mouth, which allowed him time to swallow the water.

After learning the location of Smith's millions in savings, which were in the form of bearer bonds, Turdlow said, "You're doing fine, good buddy. A few more questions and I'll release you."

"Promise," said Smith weakly.

"I promise, Richie. Now tell me about your network of local players and what you've got going here in Helena. It must be something significant for you to move from Palm Springs to this place," said Turdlow.

Smith gave a feeble attempt to remain silent. When Turdlow violently ripped the bandage off of Smith's forehead, it had the desired effect.

"OK, OK, I'll talk, but please re-bandage my scalp first. I don't want to lose my hair," pleaded Smith.

Thereafter, Smith sang like a bird into the recorder. He was blackmailing a key administrative manager with the Montana Highway Patrol, a handful of prominent chairpersons in Montana's state senate and just about everyone in the U.S. Attorney's office in Helena. There were also a large number of lesser, bent public officials who were located outside of Helena. With one last prodding incision along Smith's scalp, he disclosed the hidden location of all of his incriminating evidence against these individuals. Turdlow now possessed a treasure trove of information that far exceeded his wildest dreams.

Damn, thought Turdlow, his ADA scams were petty ante crimes compared to the schemes that Abramoff was running. He could also see how Abramoff was able to leverage his resources with the likes of Smith working for him in the field. Corrupting governments was obviously quite a profitable business.

Smith's head drooped to his chest. He was getting weaker. Turdlow knew Smith wouldn't last much longer.

"Last question, Richie. What's the location of the meth lab ,and who owns the lodge?"

Smith's voice was barely audible as he answered these final questions. The lab was to be set up in a lodge on a remote ranch on the outskirts of Dennis, Montana. The owner was someone named Leone in the Montana state senate. Leone was aided by crooked sheriffs in Dennis, a father and son team named the Dowers. And, there was someone in the Montana Highway Patrol, he began, until he toppled, unconscious to his side. Turdlow knew he couldn't revive Smith. He was near death.

Turdlow cut the ties restraining Smith's legs. Next, he cut his pants free in the vicinity of his right thigh. With his scalpel, he made a deep incision high on the inside of his right leg. Blood spurted from Smith's severed femoral artery.

"I was going to scalp you Richie, but a promise is a promise. Your hair will look good in an open casket, that is, if you're at all recognizable after the vultures and wild animals finish with you," said Turdlow aloud as he began to clean up.

Once the site was clean and his van packed, he knelt beside Smith and pressed his fingers against the side of his neck. No pulse, Smith was dead. He cut the ties from Smith's raw, bloodied wrists, pulled the bandages off his forehead and stuffed the bloodstained items into a trash bag. By the time his van left the dirt road and pulled out onto the single-lane paved road, a thunderstorm had rolled into the area and it was raining hard. His footprints and tire tracks at the crime scene had already washed away.

CHAPTER 19
THE AMBUSH

Monday, June 16, 2008 1:39 PM (MDT) Mountain
Daylight Time... 3:39 PM (EDT) Eastern Daylight Time

Once Brice had driven through the Sylvan Pass, the vertical granite walls on the north side of the road were displaced by heavily wooded, steep hillsides. Despite the distraction of Bobby's non-stop commentary on Yellowstone and Chet's light snoring, the lay of the land pricked Brice's sense of vulnerability. He ignored both of his passengers and focused on his surroundings. His truck was boxed in amongst a line of five school buses full of young kids. Their movement along the exit road was at a "stop and go," snail's pace. This was typical traffic during the peak season in Yellowstone.

The line of slow moving vehicles presented the perfect ambush target for an enemy imbedded on the hillside. Below the roadbed were gently rolling, grassy pastures that provided no cover whatsoever. The Middle Creek sliced through the pastures and the nearest tree line was at least a half-mile from the road. If he were in Iraq, he would have stopped the vehicles and dispatched several scouts to check out the hillside before proceeding. Though he continued to remind himself that he wasn't in Iraq, the fact that the Dennis terrorists might still be in the wind clearly troubled him.

As his truck approached an empty, unwashed and dilapidated white tour bus that was parked at an unusual angle, on the opposite side of the road, his combat senses began to quicken. When he was fifty feet from the bus, he could see that its rear end was blocking westbound traffic. Inching closer, he noticed that the bus's engine had just recently been turned off, exhaust fumes still drifted from its tail pipe. There was no sign of a bus driver who would normally be redirecting traffic around his bus or, at the very least, placing caution cones on the road behind his bus. And, there was something about the color of the tour bus that sent a warning signal to his brain that he didn't quite grasp. His grip on his steering wheel tightened. Was he driving his friends into the kill zone of a classic ambush, or was he truly suffering from PTSD?

A sunglass reflection from a rock outcropping 200 yards above him, on the steeply wooded hillside, caught his attention. A moment later, he saw the flash of an explosion fifty yards ahead, amongst a stand of tall trees at the base of the hillside. He screamed "ambush" just as the shock waves from the explosion rocked his pickup. Bobby and Chet bolted upright, instantly alert. Like a string of firecrackers exploding in quick succession, innumerable blasts rocked his pickup. Over a dozen hundred foot tall lodge pole pines and several larger Douglas firs, their trunks expertly blown away, fell lazily across the road fifty yards ahead of him, narrowly missing the hood of the first school bus. A number of smaller trees, caught in the downfall, combined to form a massive wall of tree trunks and limbs, fifteen to twenty feet high. The road ahead was completely blocked. Seconds later, another round of blasts occurred behind him. From his rear view mirror, he saw the falling tree scene repeat itself behind the fifth, and last, school bus.

June 16, 2008 1:45 PM (MDT)... 3:45 PM (EDT)

The falling trees and explosions caused all the vehicle drivers to come to a stop. Five school buses, four passenger cars and Brice's pickup were trapped. Brice immediately shoved his gearshift into "Park" and ran to the bed of his pickup. Seconds later, Chet was beside him. They quickly moved the three large duffel bags to the protected side of the bus behind them. Combat experience guided their every move. There was absolutely no doubt in either of their minds that this was a carefully orchestrated ambush.

Chet immediately unzipped one of the duffel bags and handed a M-16 automatic rifle to Brice. He took one for himself and grabbed two magazines. After seating his magazine, he chambered a round and tossed the other magazine to Brice, who immediately slammed it into his rifle.

"Unbelievable! A damn ambush in Yellowstone Park," said Chet.

Brice moved to the edge of the road and examined the retaining wall that supported the roadbed.

Turning to Chet he said, "How about I stay with Bobby and cover the open road while you evacuate the two buses and car in front of us. There is a three-foot drop below the retaining wall behind us. The drop is deeper in a couple of places. It will provide good defilade protection for all the school children and civilians."

They both moved back to the concealed side of Brice's pickup. Chet spoke to Brice, but loud enough so that Bobby could hear as well.

"Atta boy, Gunny, always thinking one step ahead. I'll tell the teachers to get all the kids below this wall ASAP. I'll instruct them to take their jackets and water bottles, but no cell phones. Same goes for the civilians. We'll try to keep a lid on this ambush for the time being. Once everyone is safely below the wall, I'll instruct the bus drivers to pull their busses into the emergency lane and close up, bumper to bumper. I'll tell the civilians to leave their vehicles in the road where they are. If the enemy has heavy weapons, the buses won't offer much protection, but at least they won't be able to see our movements," said Chet.

"I like it," said Brice.

"Brice, while I evacuate the first two buses, call Lt. Col. Adair at Camp Pendleton on one of the satellite phones that's in this duffel bag. Give him a situation report."

"Aye, aye, Chet," said Brice.

"No cell phones is smart. We'd have hundreds of kids posting pictures and videos of our defensive set up in minutes. Everyone could see them, including the bad guys," said Bobby.

"That, plus anxious, and understandable, calls to parents would trigger a tidal wave of media attention that would be closely followed by a cluster fuck of an uncoordinated call to arms. Every nutcase within a hundred miles of here would throw a case of cold beer and a pile of automatic weapons into his pickup truck and race to our rescue. No one would know who's who. Christ, we could have park rangers getting into firefights with white supremacists," said Chet.

"Well, you won't have much time to keep that tidal wave in check. I'm sure the cell phones and digital cameras of those folks just outside of the fallen trees are busy," added Bobby.

"Shit, you're right! Brice, you better get on the horn right away," said Chet over his shoulder as he moved towards the lead bus.

Just as Chet left for the bus, Brice spotted a smallish man emerge from behind the dilapidated tour bus. A black ski mask covered his face and he carried an AK-47 automatic rifle. He kneeled and raised his rifle to his shoulder aiming at an older man who'd just gotten out of a car that was sandwiched between the two buses ahead of them. The older man shuffled along the road towards the lead bus, curious about the explosions and fallen trees.

"You die infidel!" laughed the man with a distinctly Arabic accent.

"Shooter on the road," said Brice as he instinctively brought his rifle to his shoulder, quickly aimed and fired. Chet and Bobby heard two nearly simultaneous shots.

The shooter's shot went astray as Brice's headshot hit home. The older man jumped back a foot.

Brice waved and yelled at him, "Come to me for cover."

The old man's legs moved like a young sprinters.

Chet immediately returned to Brice's truck and spoke to the old man, "Anyone else in your car?"

Out of breath, the man stuttered, "No, just me! What was that?"

"A terrorist trying to ruin your day. This is an ambush." Turning to Brice, he said, "I'd better get back to business and you'd better call Adair. These are the damn terrorists you saw in Dennis," said Chet, infuriated at the incompetence of Homeland Security.

1:51 PM MDT (3:51 PM EDT)

After the exchange of fire, an older, gray haired, female teacher exited the third bus less than ten feet behind Brice's pickup. Her face was taut with terror.

"My God, what is happening?" she said.

With a steady, confident voice, Brice gave her the same instructions that Chet was delivering to the first two buses, "Ma'am, please immediately move all the kids in your bus to cover below this retaining wall. The kids take only jackets and water bottles, no cell phones. Everyone will be all right."

His assurance seemed to calm the woman. She nodded and stepped back into the bus and began instructing the kids.

Brice opened the front passenger door of his quad cab, carefully lifted Bobby out of his truck and lowered him to the roadbed so that he was sitting upright against the protected, front wheel of the third bus. He rearranged the duffels bags, crammed with weapons, to provide Bobby with extra sitting support.

"Perfect head shot, buddy. I can see you haven't lost your touch," said Bobby.

"Yeah! Listen, can you oversee the teachers? Make sure all the kids get below the retaining wall. Answer any of their questions and keep them calm," said Brice, while he was dialing Adair's office at Camp Pendleton on a satellite phone.

"Will do, Brice," said Bobby.

1:53 PM MDT (3:53 PM EDT)

A friend and fellow gunnery sergeant smartly answered Brice's satellite phone call.

"Hammer, this is Brice. Is Lt. Col. Adair available?"

"No, he just stepped out for a moment. I think he went to the personnel office. Are you OK, man? You sound amped up, and I recognize that no bullshit edge in your voice."

"Hammer hit the record button for this call."

"Recording Gunny"

"Major Daniels and Bobby Ridger are with me, as are five school buses full of kids and four carloads of civilians. Terrorists in Yellowstone National Park ambushed us about eight minutes ago. We were heading east out of the park on Route 20 towards the east exit when terrorists blew up trees in front and behind our line of vehicles. I think we're about five miles from the actual east exit of the park. The bad guys are hidden on a steeply wooded hillside above us. I believe that they arrived in an older, white tour bus that is parked on the opposite side of the two-lane road from us. Their bus could have easily transported forty to fifty terrorists.

"Fortunately, there is a protective downhill retaining wall below the level of roadbed. We're having all the kids and civilians take cover behind that retaining wall. We have the weapons and gear that Col. O'Brien ordered Major Daniels to bring with him. One enemy is dead. The attacker was in the midst of shooting an unarmed civilian male when I shot him. Once you round up Lt. Col. Adair, please have him call us back. I've got to go Hammer," said Brice.

"I'm on it. Take care buddy," said Hammer as the call went dead.

Chet returned moments later, out of breath from running, "The buses ahead of us are starting to close up against this bus behind us. How about moving your pickup to the rear of the column so we have a clear line of sight from this center position. I'll cover you while you drive your truck to the rear of the column."

"Good idea. I just got off the phone with Hammer. Adair wasn't in the office. I gave Hammer a situation report that he recorded. He's going to get the colonel, and he'll call us back," said Brice.

"Right on! Give the civilians and bus drivers, in our rear, the same instructions we gave to those in the front of the column. The buses close up together, bumper to bumper, in the emergency lane," said Chet to Brice's back as the young gunnery sergeant slipped through the passenger door of his truck and bounced across the front bench seat into the driver's seat.

Seconds later, Brice's truck roared to life. Because the buses boxed him in, he pulled out of the bus column into the center of the road and braked hard. The instant he jammed his automatic gearshift into "Reverse" a torrent of .30-caliber machine gunfire tore up the roadbed five feet ahead of his front bumper. His right foot crushed the gas pedal to the floor, his tires screeched and smoked, as he raced backwards to the last bus in the column. Bullets pinged into the side of his truck and shattered his windows. Luckily for him, the machine gunners were inexperienced. Once he was past the last school bus, he braked hard and a cloud of burning tire rubber enveloped his truck. Brice leapt from his driver's seat and sprinted to cover behind the last school bus.

He skidded to a stop as he rounded the rear of the last bus. He was face to face with a young, female teacher in her mid-twenties. Her arms were folded across her chest, and she gave Brice a stern look that reminded him of being caught in a school hallway without a hall pass. "What's this bullshit, cowboy?" she asked calmly, but forcefully.

After nearly bowling the woman over, he studied her for a moment. She was of medium height with a strong, lean physique much like that of a long distance runner. Her shiny black hair was cut short and swept to the side. She was cute and attractive, and her no-nonsense demeanor reminded him of Molly.

"Terrorist attack. I'm a Marine gunnery sergeant, and am working with Homeland Security and the FBI. I believe all the school kids are the target of an armed terrorist attack. Get all your kids out of the buses and have them take cover below this retaining wall," he instructed as he pointed to the three-foot drop at the edge of the roadbed.

"Make sure they take only their jackets and water bottles, no cell phones. The same goes for the civilians in the cars. Once all the kids are below the retaining wall, please have the bus drivers move their buses into the emergency lane and close up, bumper to bumper, with the bus ahead of them. The cars stay where they are. I'm putting you in charge of this rear section of vehicles. Please explain this to all the civilians and school-teachers. If you run across anyone who can handle a rifle let me know. When you're finished back here, please report to me behind the third bus," said Brice, hurriedly, but with resolve in his words.

"I'm an expert shot, sarge. I can help you," she said as she began to give instructions to the teachers who had begun to gather around them.

"I'll need all the help I can get. Stay safe and keep your head down," added Brice.

1:57 PM MDT (3:57 PM EDT)

When Brice came running up to Chet and Bobby from the last bus in line, he noticed that the first and second buses had closed ranks with the third bus. Bobby was sitting on the road, repositioned against the right front wheel of the third bus. Chet was dressed in camo gear, wearing an armored vest and strapping on a pistol belt, which held a holstered Glock. Camo clothing, communication equipment, automatic weapons and pistols were carefully arranged atop the tarp from Brice's pickup. Boxes of ammunition, grenades and body armor were neatly stacked beside them on the asphalt road.

Brice carefully studied the gear… two secure global satellite phones, a six man radio head set net, four hand size binoculars, six M-16 automatic rifles, four M-40A3 sniper rifles with day scopes attached (two with suppressors), four attachable night scopes for the sniper rifles, four Benelli combat shotguns, four M-32 multiple grenade launchers, six .357 caliber Glock pistols in holsters with belt, one M-249 light machine gun (SAW-squad automatic weapon), a case each of both fragmentary and smoke grenades, several field first-aid kits, boxes of ammunition for all the weapons, camouflage clothing and, lastly, body armor for eight people.

As Brice buttoned a camouflage jersey over his short sleeve shirt, he said, "Thank goodness Col. O'Brien knows his weapons and gear. It's now an even fight."

"We'll see!" grunted Chet.

Ten feet away, two female bus drivers who looked to be in their mid-sixties, were building a reinforced firing bunker in the narrow gap that existed between the second and third buses. There were using discarded timbers that the school kids found laying at the foot of the road's shoring. The timbers were similar to railroad ties, though thicker, and had previously been used to shore the old section of the road. The two women carefully slid one timber after another across the narrow gap while staying hidden behind the buses. It was apparent to the three Marines that these women had done this before. The base of the protective bunker was four-timbers wide and the vertical walls were three-timbers deep. A line of school kids, similar to a bucket brigade, were passing the timbers up to the roadbed.

"Great idea, ladies. Have you done this before?" asked Chet.

"Lots! You ever build a duck or deer blind? You sure as hell don't want the dang thing to collapse on you during a thunderstorm. It can ruin a good hunt," said one of the drivers.

"Your friend suggested it. He heard the kids talking about the timbers that were stacked against the road's retaining wall," said the other driver, who nodded towards Bobby.

"Good thinking, Bobby," said Chet.

"These women deserve the credit. They're the ones doing the heavy lifting," said Bobby.

Chet tapped Brice on the shoulder and waved him towards Bobby.

Kneeling on one knee, next to Bobby, Chet spoke quietly to both Marines, "I looked at the area maps before I flew in. There are just a few nearby Air Force bases, but they're manned for long range, strategic air defense. None of them have aircraft designed for close air ground support, nor do they have any combat troops. I also didn't see on the maps any nearby cities with a large enough population to support a SWAT team. We may have to hold on for quite some time before the cavalry arrives. I trust we'll hear back from Adair and probably even the commandant shortly.

"I'm going to move to the front of the second bus to take their call. I don't want the kids and civilians hearing my conversation. In the meantime, Brice, I'd like you to develop a defensive plan and recruit anyone you think can help us. Let's pass out as many weapons as possible to the civilians. I think we'll need all the firepower we can muster," said Chet.

"Should we arm some of the school kids?" asked Brice. "A few of the boys look like they are big enough to play varsity football in high school."

"I've been thinking about that. Every one of them probably owns a .22 rifle for hunting rabbits and messing around. Shooting people is, however, an all-together different matter. I'd use them only as a last resort."

"Will do. Maybe a couple of them could chuck smoke grenades?"

"Yeah, I like that. See who you can sign up," suggested Chet.

"Bobby, I'd like you to be in charge of our command post, which we'll set up by the front end of this third bus and the timber bunker. It's in the center of our line of defense and has good visibility. You'll handle all incoming communications, supervise our civilian fighters, spot for Brice and me and snipe at all targets of opportunity. We'll find someone who can help you, but you'll be in charge. Can you handle that?" asked Chet.

"Yes, sir," said Bobby assertively. Having Major Chet Daniels assign him an important job nearly brought tears to his eyes. After Fallujah, he was certain his fighting days with fellow Marines were over. But, through this strangest of circumstances, he'd been given another opportunity to be a fighting Marine once again. He'd make damn sure that Major Daniels' trust in him was well placed.

"Defensive plan and recruiting… I'm on it, Chet. I'll also find someone to assist Bobby," said Brice.

"Good. These headsets are active, one for each of us. Let's stay in touch," said Chet as he handed a headset to both Marines.

With his orders and briefing completed, Chet stood and stepped towards the weapons and equipment. Brice watched him as he crammed ammunition and grenades into every pocket of his camo jersey and pants. He grabbed a M-16 with one hand while his free hand tucked a satellite phone into the armpit of that arm. With his free hand, Chet reached for his most prized weapon, the multiple grenade launcher, which Brice noticed was loaded with six 40mm high explosive Hellhound grenades. As Chet lumbered forward towards the second bus, Brice smiled. His boss' constant mantra to his men before every combat mission was "never ever be outgunned" by the enemy. As usual, his boss was leading by example.

2:05 PM MDT (4:05 PM EDT)

After Brice donned an armored vest, he picked up a second vest. Crouching beside Bobby he said, "OK Marine, can you lean you forward and I'll give you a little extra protection."

After slipping Bobby's arms through the armored vest, Brice said, "I'm thinking that Chet and I should go on the offensive and attack the bastards from their flanks. Maybe we can pin them down. But first, we need to put together a team to help you secure your command post. Hopefully, there are some volunteers amongst the teachers, bus drivers and civilians in the cars who can handle a rifle. I met a young teacher at the rear of the column who offered to help. She says she is an expert shot. I'm going to ask her to help you. Are you OK with that?"

"Well, that depends on her age and looks. If I'm going to risk my life fighting these terrorists, I'd like to make an impression on a comely young lass," said Bobby smiling.

Brice was pleased to hear Bobby's former bluster and braggadocio resurface, "You haven't changed one bit, Ridger. Always thinking about the opposite sex. But put those thoughts on hold until we get out of this mess. Got it?"

"Got it!"

As Brice stood and turned away from Bobby, the young teacher he'd just spoken of strode up to him. Two burly men who looked to be in their fifties closely followed her.

"Have all the buses and vehicles been evacuated?" asked Brice.

"Yes. All the kids, teachers, bus drivers and civilians in the cars in the rear of the column have been evacuated, sarge. These two men offered to help," said the teacher as she waved her hand at both men.

"Good work. My partner evacuated the front of the column. Do you have any idea how many kids and adults we have below the retaining wall?" asked Brice.

"There are exactly 305 6th grade kids, ten teachers, myself included, five volunteer mothers and five bus drivers. All five of these buses are from Cody, Wyoming. It's our entire 2008 6th grade field trip contingent. I also counted six adult civilians from three passenger cars behind this bus. That's a total of three hundred and thirty one individuals, but it does not include the number of people in your truck or that car at the front of the line of buses." After a moment, she added self-confidently, "Escape and retreat doesn't look promising."

Brice raised an eyebrow. He sensed an element of experience in her concise report. In a neutral, calm voice, he asked, "Why do you say that?"

"I've walked the entire length of the retaining wall, end to end. The retaining walls, at both ends, terminate at deep ravines. Actually, they are sheer vertical cliffs. No way of climbing down. Lateral escape isn't a possibility. As far as a direct retreat to our rear… " The young teacher pointed to the terrain below and beyond the retaining wall, "…as you can see, this high plain levels out, fifty feet from this retaining wall, until it reaches that tree line, a half mile away. There is no cover between here and there, plus there is a river that cuts through the plain. You can see that the river is about two hundred yards away, and it runs parallel to this road. It's hard to tell from here how wide or deep that river is, or how fast moving it is. But, I'm sure it's freezing cold. It may be difficult, if not impossible to cross.

"We could wait for nightfall and make a run for it so long as the terrorists don't have night scopes. Unfortunately, we are just a couple of days away from the year's longest day of the year, June 21. It won't start to get dark around here until after 9:00 PM, which is nearly seven hours from now," concluded the teacher.

"Ma'am, that was damned fine intelligence. I am truly impressed," said one of the male volunteers that stood beside the young teacher.

Brice hadn't had a free moment to study the ends of the retaining wall nor scrutinize the leveling off of the slope to his rear. This teacher and the two female bus drivers, who were building the bunker, were providing an unexpected, but quite productive level of experience and intelligence.

He let out a soft whistle as he considered the implications of the teacher's detailed briefing and his own observations:

- The terrorists held a superior position on the hillside above them.
- They had, at least, one .30 caliber machine gun that fired on him when he moved his truck.
- There was no avenue of escape during daylight or nearby armed reinforcements.
- Chet's initial concern was now a reality. This was the contingent of forty to fifty terrorists that he and Molly had seen days earlier at the remote hunting lodge in Dennis and he knew, damn well, that they were armed with automatic weapons. The white tour bus that was parked opposite the school buses had delivered them.

"The *white* tour bus, shit!" exclaimed Brice in frustration. That was the color of the buses that the intercepted terrorists had used. That was the warning signal his brain had received, but hadn't understood. No matter, it wouldn't have changed anything, but it was a compelling reminder that he'd best get his shit together. This was war.

Brice and the two other Marines in his truck, and the old man who he'd saved earlier, raised the total count of trapped individuals to three hundred and thirty five, of which ninety percent were eleven-year-old kids. This clearly wasn't any spur of the moment, haphazard terrorist attack. The bastards had carefully planned and executed this ambush.

As he was considering this latest information, both bus drivers suspended their bunker building and moved to the side of the young teacher.

As Brice began to speak, one of the bus drivers exclaimed, "Annie is a champion shooter!"

"Yeah, she's in the newspaper all the time… best female shot in all of Wyoming, Montana and Idaho," boasted the other driver.

"So that's how you know about fields of fire and cover. Good, very good! By the way, my name is Brice Miller. What's yours?" asked Brice, as he extended his hand towards Annie.

The bus driver closest to Brice seized his hand and shook it firmly, "I'm Kathy Wardein."

"Lynne VanderMeid," said the other driver, as she too shook Brice's hand in quick succession.

Finally, Annie griped Brice's hand and shook it with surprising strength, "I'm Annie Youngblood."

"You're Annie Youngblood… 'Little Raven!'" said Bobby from his sitting position.

"Little Raven! How do you know my Arapaho name?" asked Annie, clearly surprised.

"Your uncle told me, Tom Youngblood. He taught me how to hunt and track. Our ranch is next to his in Dennis."

Bobby and Annie's eyes locked. A flicker of recognition slowly spread across Annie's face.

"You're Bobby Ridger? The Marine hero who was injured in Fallujah. You're 'Dark Horse!'" said Annie.

"The one and only! You visited our ranch about twelve years ago for a picnic. You slapped my face!" said Bobby.

After a few seconds of thought, Annie countered, "You tried to kiss me and I refused your advance. You chased me around your barn. When you caught me, you got what you deserved."

Bobby blushed, "I was out of line."

"Unhuh… " grunted Annie, not quite convinced of the sincerity of this long overdue apology. "My uncle said you were bedridden."

"Well, as you can see, I'm not. My range of motion is improving," said Bobby as he wiggled his legs and lifted his arms six inches.

"Dark Horse and Little Raven, I hate to interrupt you, but this reunion will have to wait. We've got more pressing matters. Annie, I met your uncle several days ago at the Ridger Ranch. He taught me how to track a wolf," said Brice.

"Oh! You were the one who discovered the terrorist training camp!"

"How did you know that?" asked Brice suspiciously.

"Bobby's dad, Bill, mentioned it to my Uncle Tom and he told my dad about it. I thought the government rounded up all of those terrorists yesterday at Zion, Bryce and the Grand Canyon," said Annie.

"I thought the same thing, but as you can see, that's clearly not the case. Based on my observations of their training camp in Dennis, and the size of that tour bus across the road from us, I believe that we are opposing as many as forty to fifty terrorists, possibly more. However, they are not all experienced. From my observations, many of them were inexperienced teenagers who hardly knew how to load their weapons." After a moments thought, Brice added, "Let's keep all these details to ourselves. I don't want to worry the civilians or the kids more than necessary."

As he gazed at his group of volunteers, Brice spoke in a direct, factual manner, "Let me introduce myself to all of you and explain why I'm here, and why we have all the weapons and equipment you see laid out behind you on the road. My name is Brice Miller and I'm a gunnery sergeant in the Marine Corps. My company commander is Major Chet Daniels. He's the black man in camouflage clothes who is crouched behind the bus ahead of us. He is in the process of contacting our battalion commander at Camp Pendleton on a secure global satellite phone with our status report. Once that is accomplished, our battalion commander will forward that information up the chain of command. In very short order, I expect that the Commandant of the Marine Corps, Homeland Security, the FBI and the National Security Council will all be apprised of our situation.

"Sitting against the wheel of the bus is my best friend Bobby Ridger, apparently also known as Dark Horse, who served in the Marines with Chet and me. As you can see, he is still recovering from combat wounds suffered in Fallujah.

"On my way to Bobby's house in Dennis, Montana, I visited both the Grand Canyon and Zion for day hikes. During both of those hikes, I observed the activity two separate groups of suspicious Middle Eastern types reconnoitering each park. I forwarded my observations on to my superiors at Camp Pendleton. My observations may have contributed to our government's successful interdiction yesterday of terrorist attacks in Zion, Bryce and the Grand Canyon.

"While staying at Bobby's house in Dennis, his sister and I also discovered a terrorist training camp in the backwoods as we were hunting a wolf that was preying on the Ridger cattle. Bobby's dad called that intelligence into Homeland Security. However, someone apparently dropped the ball.

"In light of yesterday's interdictions, the Commandant of the Marine Corps decided that while I was traveling through more national parks that I should be accompanied by an additional rifleman, and be properly armed. A few hours ago Bobby and I picked up Major Chet Daniels, along with all this weaponry, at the West Yellowstone Airport. We were headed to the Veterans Hospital in Sheridan, Wyoming for Bobby's stem cell treatments when this ambush began," concluded Brice somberly.

"Brice, let me introduce you to these two gentlemen who offered to help. This is Al Edwards. Al is a retired Army Green Beret master sergeant, who was on his way to Cody to hook up with a friend for a black bear hunt. And this gentleman, who looks like John Wayne, is a longtime hunting guide in these parts. His name is Pete Zouvas. They both offered to help," said Annie.

Before Brice or either of the men could say a word, Kathy and Lynne spoke up.

"Hey don't forget us, 'Bricie!'" said Lynne.

"We can shoot," added Kathy.

"'Bricie?'" repeated Brice, as he looked at the two women, barely able to contain his amusement at how Lynne had addressed him. Though they'd each showed surprising strength lifting and moving the heavy timbers for the last twenty minutes, the two of them looked like fragile, peaceful grandmothers whom one would find serving salads at a church picnic.

"Our eyesight, reflexes and stamina aren't what they use to be, but I guarantee you we could both handle those funny looking shotguns you have there," said Kathy pointing to the Benelli shot guns with the automatic feeders that were laying amidst the weaponry.

"These terrorists would have to climb over my dead body before they harmed a hair on the head of any of my school kids. Kathy and I might have trouble hitting a fast flying quail at thirty yards, but nailing a bad guy at thirty feet would be a piece of cake," said Lynne confidently.

"Lynne, those shotguns look like they have those new fangled, automatic feeders. We'd be unstoppable," said Kathy with a twinkle in her eye.

"OK, my two bird shooters, those shotguns are all yours," said Brice.

Brice was slowly realizing that the experience and background of Annie, Kathy and Lynne was far different than their female contemporaries who lived in the affluent coastal towns of Southern California, near Camp Pendleton. Annie was a full time teacher so he knew she didn't spend her weekdays cruising the malls in a huge SUV with a cell phone glued to her ear, sipping lattes at Starbucks with her girlfriends or racing to a yoga class in a two hundred dollar "Lululemon" outfit. Then, there were the two bus drivers, Kathy and Lynne. They probably grew up in the country on ranches or farms where killing predators was part of their everyday life. They were now facing two legged predators who could shoot back. He had a strong hunch, however, that these older ladies could more than hold their own against inexperienced terrorists.

2:08 PM MDT (4:08 PM EDT)

As Brice turned his attention to the two male volunteers, .30-caliber machine gunfire rattled from two separate locations. Everyone instinctively dropped to the road.

"Brice and Bobby, are you, OK?" asked Chet over his headset.

Before Brice responded, he removed his headset and turned up the volume so those around him could hear his radio communication. "We're good, Chet? Did you see what happened?"

"The terrorists just fired at a couple of park rangers and 'looky loos' that were moving towards the fallen trees at the head of the column. I think they scared off a similar group at the tail end of the buses as well. I hope to hell they don't have anything heavier than .30 caliber," said Chet over his headset.

"Roger that! Nor, more than those two machine guns. Have you heard from Adair?" asked Brice.

"Yes. He has me on hold. They're linking my call up with the commandant, Homeland Security and the FBI. I've taken a bunch of cell phone pictures of our position and the hillside and have sent them to Adair."

"Roger. We've got some civilian personnel who can handle weapons. I'll brief you on my defensive plan once I finish with them," said Brice as he replaced his headset and turned down the volume.

"Before Major Daniels flew into West Yellowstone, he checked on the availability of military support in the surrounding three state area.

There are several Air Force bases, but none of them are staffed with combat infantry nor set up with aircraft to provide close air ground support. There are also no nearby cities with large SWAT teams. And, as we just heard, that was .30-caliber machine gunfire from two separate guns that fired on park rangers and 'looky loos' at the front and rear of our column who attempted to come to our aid. The fact that nearly simultaneous .30 caliber fire occurred, at both ends of our column, tells me that this ambush was carefully planned, and that there is communication between their leader and, at the very least, their two machine gun nests. Lastly, we're hemmed in, according to Annie's report.

"What all this means is that we may have to defend ourselves for quite some time before the cavalry arrives.

"Our first goal is the kids' safety and well-being. Annie, I want you to instruct all the teachers and civilians to keep the kids as calm as possible. I don't want any distracting yelling, wandering off, laughing or rough housing. Have the teachers tell the kids that they must control their water consumption. They may be behind that retaining wall for quite some time. Also, I want them to keep their jackets close by. In the event a thunderstorm rolls in, I don't want three hundred kids developing hypothermia. If they make a quick retreat under the cover of a heavy downpour or darkness, they'll need those jackets," said Brice.

"I'll take care of all that," said Annie confidently.

Brice's next goal was to fortify the center of his defenses. In Iraq, when he and his men were hemmed in and close air support wasn't readily available, he knew the bad guys would oftentimes attempt to overrun the Marines with a suicidal frontal attack by waves of drugged up, inexperienced teenage recruits. He'd seen a number of just such teenage boys at the terrorist camp in Dennis. They could cause deadly confusion if his defenses weren't properly prepared for them.

He dropped to one knee and began to outline their position on the asphalt road with a piece of chalk… the orientation of the hillside above them, the road and retaining wall, his estimate of the location of the machine guns and the position of the fallen trees, buses and cars. While he was drawing, he spoke to the two male volunteers.

He learned that the first volunteer, Pete Zouvas, was a fifty-year-old, semi-retired rancher who worked as a hunting guide in the fall. He'd been driving his car to Cody to visit his brother. As a guide, he said his specialty was hunting elk, mule deer, bighorn sheep and black bear on horseback trips into the Frank Church Wilderness. The man was six foot, six inches tall and built like an oak tree.

"Do you shoot the bears or wrestle them?" asked Brice glibly.

"Just shoot now. When I was younger, I had one memorable tussle with a medium size black bear while hunting him with a bow and arrow. I escaped with my life because the bear left me for dead after he tossed me over a cliff. Fortunately, I landed in a stand of small trees and brush that cushioned my fall," said Pete matter of factly.

In stunned silence, Brice and the other civilians studied Pete's face as he described the incident. There wasn't the slightest hint of duplicity in his expression. The guy had actually wrestled a bear.

The second volunteer, Al Edwards, was a sixty-two-year old, retired U.S. Army Special Forces master sergeant. He was the one who had complemented Annie earlier on her assessment of their predicament. Though he'd retired fifteen years earlier, his strong, youthful face gave everyone the impression that he was far younger than his actual age. Whereas Pete was an oak tree, this African-American, master sergeant was a bull of a man.

"A 'snake eater!'" said Brice.

"If necessary. Do you jarheads always travel with a small armory in the back of your pickup trucks?" asked Al grinning.

"What good is a Marine, if he's unarmed?"

"Yeah, right! Somebody's foresight in the 'crotch' was perfect. I have the funny feeling I'm going to remember this adventure for quite some time," said Al with just the slightest trace of a southern accent.

Army Special Forces types, often referred to as "Green Berets," were highly trained, brutally efficient killing machines. Thank goodness Al Edwards is on our side. He probably has more combat experience than I do, thought Brice

Brice pointed to his chalk sketch as he began to describe his defenses, "At any moment, I expect the terrorists will probe the center of our defenses, which is right where we're gathered, behind this middle bus. They'll likely throw four or five teenage attackers at us in their first wave of attacks. Conserve your ammunition and only use single shots. Ladies, only use your shotguns if there are more than five attackers or they get within twenty feet of your position. I don't want them to know the full extent of our firepower. After their initial probe, we can expect full on charges. Between our light machine gun and the shotguns, they'll race into a wall of hot lead. Fortunately, our arsenal is such that we have enough weapons to provide each of you with at least two weapons apiece.

"Annie, you're going to be my center line rover. I'd like you to also help Bobby in our command center that will be under the engine block of this third bus. You and Bobby will share a satellite phone for outside communications and you'll both have headsets that will be on an open net with me, Chet, Pete and Al.

"I'd like you to be armed with a sniper rifle, without suppressor, and a M-16 automatic rifle. You will also oversee Kathy and Lynne's fire, and I'd like you to take sniper shots at every target of opportunity.

"Also, and this is important, I'd like you to instruct the civilians, your fellow teachers and a few of the larger 6th grade boys how to chuck smoke grenades. If we have to make a run to the tree line, the smoke could provide invaluable cover for everyone. Once I'm through with this brief, I'll show you how the smoke grenades work," concluded Brice.

"That's not necessary. I already know how to use them. On long-range competition shots, I'd trade off with my fellow competitors in chucking those things. We use them to indicate wind direction at the target site. And, the absence of a suppressor on my sniper rifle… that's so I won't lose any accuracy!" said Annie knowledgeably.

Brice looked at Annie and simply nodded his head.

Of course she knows how to throw smoke grenades. How stupid of me! She is also, in all likelihood, a better long range shot than me.

"Bobby, do you think you can manage the SAW, light machine gun? I'll make sure it's well balanced on a stable bipod. If not, I can… "

"I can handle it!" interrupted Bobby.

"Good! You'll also have a M-16 as well. Annie, you'll be responsible for keeping Bobby's light machine gun loaded with 200 round belts of ammunition. Kathy and Lynne, as I mentioned earlier, you'll each be armed with the shotguns. That means two automatic Benelli shotguns for each of you!" said Brice with emphasis.

"*Double, double toil and trouble,*" sang Lynne lyrically from Macbeth, as the two ladies high fived one another. The ladies' courage was infectious.

Turning to Al and Pete, Brice waved a hand at the weaponry lying on the road behind him and said, "Take your pick!"

"I used to instruct my men on the use of this baby," said Al as he picked up a multiple grenade launcher. "This is a newer model, but I guarantee you I can cause major pain and suffering with this weapon, especially with those high explosive Hellhound rounds you have."

"It's all yours, Al," said Brice.

"I like this rifle with the scope. It looks very much like my Remington 700. I could nail an elk at 500 yards with my Remington. I'm sure I could do the same this rifle. I don't need the suppressor though," said Pete.

"That rifle should look familiar, its design is based on the Remington 700. It's our 'go to' sniper rifle, a M-40A3. It's been fine tooled by the Marine Corps. You could take down your elk at 1,000 yards. However, take the rifle with the suppressor. I'll tell you why in a minute."

"In addition to your primary weapons, both of you should take a M-16 as well. No sense in leaving any of these weapons idle," said Brice.

"I'll take one of those two extra grenade launchers," interjected Bobby.

"Good idea. Annie can help you reload it. We'll keep the last grenade launcher in reserve. Lastly, if any of you have any questions or recommendations, please don't hesitate to speak up," said Brice.

2:12 PM MDT (4:12 PM EDT)

"Well I'll be! Up in the sky, on my right everyone. Would you look at this!" said Lynne excitedly.

All heads turned in that direction.

A huge bald eagle, with a seven-foot wingspan, was diving from the curling, cumulus clouds towards the center of the road. A moment before the eagle reached the road, he came out of his dive and rolled towards the school buses. His fierce, black eyes stared at Brice's team of defenders as he headed directly towards the timber bunker between the second and third buses. As he zoomed, a mere foot or two over the bunker, he dipped his wings and soared back into the clouds. A single feather fell from his tail and drifted, from side to side, towards the group of defenders. They all watched mesmerized as the feather floated gently onto Bobby's lap.

Annie's eyes were the size of saucers.

"That was cool," said Bobby lightly.

"Do you realize what just happened?" said Annie emotionally.

"Yeah, we were buzzed by an eagle."

Annie gave Bobby a sharp poke in his ribs with her elbow and said, "Dark Horse you are either an ignoramus or you have much to learn."

"Hey, that hurt!"

"It was supposed to. If one is given an Arapaho name, they must understand and respect Arapaho symbols. The eagle is a sacred bird to our tribe. As the eagle soars above us he can see the past, present and future. He connects us to our Creator. His feathers are especially important. Eagle feathers adorn our chief's headdresses, and oftentimes warrior lances. A warrior with an eagle feather on his lance indicates that he is a brave hunter with great skill, and one who fears no enemy. This is a wonderful omen," explained Annie.

"I remember that now. Your aunt explained all that to me years ago. It was the night I returned her horse and your uncle named me, Dark Horse." Bobby paused, and with great effort extended the feather towards Annie. "Pin this eagle feather to your jacket. It will remind all of us of the courage and great skill we'll need today," said Bobby sincerely.

While Annie was securing the feather in the lapel of her windbreaker, the barest of knowing smiles crossed Al Edwards face. The eagle feather reminded him of his time in the jungles of Vietnam, forty years earlier. He and his Green Berets had been involved with Hmong tribesmen from Laos on several joint missions against the North Vietnamese. Though the Hmong were culturally unique among other Asians, they proved to be damn fine soldiers. An aspect of their culture that always intrigued him was the many strange spiritual beliefs they practiced. Al had no clue as to the origin or meaning of their bizarre practices, other than whenever they went into battle together, they seemed to possess a sixth sense that allowed them to anticipate the enemy's every move. The Hmong also possessed the same fierce, black eyes as that eagle.

"OK, back to business. Our first offensive goal will be to take out the terrorists two .30-caliber machine guns," said Brice as he grabbed a foot long splinter that had fallen from one of the timbers. Using the splinter as a pointer, he began to point out and explain his surprise attack on the rough map he had chalked on the road.

"If we don't take out these machine guns, they will turn these thin skinned school buses into a smoking pile of rubble in minutes. We need the buses to hide our movements and defensive positions. Additionally, we can't have the bastards attack us from our flanks.

"Pete, you will be with me. First, we will perform a little reconnaissance to locate the .30 caliber machine gun that is covering the tail end of our line of buses. Once we locate that gun emplacement, I'll rely on your long-range shooting to cover me as I sneak up on that machine gun nest. The suppressor on your sniper rifle may compromise some of your accuracy, but I can live with that. What's critical is keeping your position concealed for as long as possible."

Pete nodded in assent as he considered the risky objective of the gutsy, young Marine sergeant.

This kid has a huge pair of brass balls. I think I'd rather take my chances wrestling another bear then trying to single handedly sneak up on a .30-caliber machine gun nest.

"Al, I'll introduce you to Chet. I have a pretty fair idea of the location of the terrorist's forward machine gun position. It's hidden on the hillside, amidst a couple of fallen, dead trees. They have an open field of fire which will prevent you from sneaking up on them so I'm hoping that a good old dose of 'shock and awe' from both your and Chet's grenade launchers will put them out of action."

"I use to specialize in 'shock and awe,' especially with high explosive Hellhound rounds," said Al simply and coldly.

"Before we saddle up, a quick review. Bobby will coordinate all our offensive movements and defensive positions from beneath this third bus. It's our command post. All of us will communicate our field intelligence to him.

"Annie will be stationed beside Bobby in the command post assisting him with communications, loading his light machine gun and grenade launcher, and keeping an eye on Kathy and Lynne.

"Kathy and Lynne will have the shotguns and secure the center of our line of buses from behind the timber bunker. They will also keep Bobby and Annie supplied with ammunition from our small ammo dump.

"Kathy, Lynne and Annie, when there is a break in the action, please brief the teachers on our defensive status. It's important that they know how we're holding up. In the event it looks like our command post is going to be overrun, I want every smoke grenade we have thrown over our buses on to the road. Hopefully, that will provide the kids and civilians a measure of cover while they make a run for the wooded area a half-mile behind us. I hope it doesn't come to that, but that is my standing order.

"Lastly, all of us will wear armored vests, starting now. Any questions?"

No questions.

Much like America's earliest citizen soldiers, the civilian volunteers coolly selected their weapons and began slipping their arms into armored vests. Though they were outnumbered by terrorists who held the high ground, there was not the slightest sign of fear amongst any of the defenders. Every one of them was prepared to fight to their death.

Al's pockets bulged with ammunition and fragmentary grenades hung from his Glock pistol belt. Brice lifted a box of Hellhound grenades and said to him, "Follow me. I'll introduce you to Chet Daniels. Pete, I'll be back in a minute."

Before Al left, he stepped towards Annie and reverently touched her eagle feather with his free hand.

"I believe in tribal powers. They have saved my life on more than one occasion. Take care Little Raven," he said smiling.

Annie returned his smile. Before she could say a word, Al turned to catch up with Brice.

"Take care, 'snake eater,'" whispered Annie to his back.

2:16 PM MDT (4:16 PM EDT)

Bobby lay in a prone position under the engine block of the third bus. Kathy and Lynne had placed two timbers along Bobby and Annie's front for defensive purposes. His binoculars rested comfortably on the top of one of the timbers. A few inches to his shooting side was the stock of his light machine gun, which was supported on a bipod. It was locked and loaded and aimed at the empty tour bus. Annie lay anxiously in a prone position on the opposite side of Bobby's light machine gun. She too had a pair of binoculars and a sniper rifle, with bipod, on which was mounted a sniper day scope (Schmidt & Bender 3–12× 50 Police Marksman II LP rifle scope with illuminated reticle). Two M-16's, the grenade launcher and several boxes of ammunition were within easy reach behind her. In front of them, propped against the timbers, were a dozen each of smoke and fragmentary grenades.

"Can you see the top of the hillside and the felled trees at each end of the road through your binoculars?" Annie asked.

With great effort, Bobby slowly raised his binoculars a few inches and bent his head forward until his eyes rested on the binoculars rubber eye rims. His range of motion had slightly improved in the last thirty minutes. He attributed the improvement to adrenaline, lots of it racing through every fiber of his body.

He studied the felled trees at both ends of the ambush site. He next turned his binoculars towards the top of the hillside. Two men were erecting what looked like a satellite dish. "Yeah, I can see fine. Take a look with your binoculars to the top of the hillside, about ten feet to the left of that large burned tree trunk. Is that a satellite dish those guys are erecting?" he asked.

Several moments later Annie responded, "Yes, that's what it looks like."

Bobby considered the timing of the terrorists' unusual effort. He posed a hypothetical question to Annie, "If you were in the midst of setting up your duck blind and a dozen fat ducks glided onto the water in front of you, would you: Ignore the ducks and continue building your duck blind, or start blasting away?"

"That's easy. You shoot the ducks and build the blind later."

"Right! So why are the terrorists screwing around with a satellite dish before they attack us. We were sitting ducks the moment those trees fell across the road."

"Good point!" After careful thought, Annie added, "I think I know what happened. Our school is locked up for the summer. When the buses returned from this field trip, the kids couldn't loiter inside the school, go to the bathrooms or call their parents for a pick up from the principal's office.

"Therefore, the school printed up several hundred 6th grade field trip flyers, with our departure and return times, which the teachers posted all over town. The terrorists knew our schedule.

"However, we left Yellowstone two hours early today because a couple of kids became sick after they drank water from a spring that they thought contained clean water. The bad guys weren't ready for us when we arrived.

I have a feeling they want to film or record this attack and send it over the airwaves. Thus, the erection of that satellite dish."

"Exactly!" said Bobby.

Without hesitation, Bobby immediately pushed the talk button on his headset and informed Brice and Chet of Annie's theory. Brice concurred with Annie's view and added that the tail pipe on the terrorist bus was still smoking when the tree explosions occurred.

"When that dish is up and running, they'll attack," concluded Bobby.

"Excellent field intelligence, Bobby. Give Annie a big 'attagirl' for us and keep us apprised of the progress of that dish. I can't see it from this angle," responded Chet tersely. A moment later, he added, "The bastards don't televise negotiations, only executions, massacres and bombings. When they attack, let's give them a major Marine Corps ass kicking."

"Roger that, Chet. 'Semper fi,'" said Bobby confidently.

The civilians heard Bobby and Chet's transmission. With grim determination written across their faces, Lynne and Kathy silently nodded at one another. Pete grunted in understanding and Al thought, *I will deliver a major Army ass kicking.*

"Bobby, let's get ready for a frontal attack. Let me see you maneuver the light machine gun. I want to see what your field of fire is," said Annie anxiously.

After a few grunts, Bobby was in position on the light machine gun. It's stock was set firmly against his shoulder and his shooting eye was perfectly aligned with the gun's sight. With the aid of the gun's bipod, he was able to incrementally swivel the barrel of the light machine gun from the rear and forward wall of fallen trees, about a 140-degree field of fire.

"Can you visually line up your targets?"

"No sweat!" answered Bobby.

"How about your trigger finger? Is that strong enough to pull the trigger?" asked Annie.

"Without firing, I'd say, no sweat again!"

"You have more range of motion than I originally thought. I didn't mean to disrespect you, Bobby. I just didn't... "

"Say no more! I'm a little surprised myself with my improved range of motion. This ambush has certainly got my heart and adrenalin levels pumping. Maybe that combination has jump-started some of my nerve endings," said Bobby as he reflected on his newfound mobility. "Very interesting! I'll remember this. Not that I would recommend a terrorist ambush as a source of therapy, but it has seemed to have helped me," said Bobby with a curious smile.

As the minutes slowly passed, Bobby and Annie chatted intermittently about a number of light subjects, all unrelated to their current situation. Bobby deliberately steered their conversation away from the deadly gravity of the moment. However, eventually their light banter ceased and each of them sank into the grim reflection of their present predicament.

Bobby ruminated on the horror and terror of his first firefight with the Marines in Fallujah. He and a buddy were standing guard behind the opening of a blown off front door in a partially destroyed building. It was dark and quiet, just a few hours before dawn. His platoon was bivouacked inside the building. Both Marines were each partially hidden behind a blown off doorframe and looking casually into the black emptiness of the street that fronted their building. In whispered speech, they were discussing the pros and cons of different motorcycles when all of a sudden Bobby heard a loud thwack, like the sound of a butcher slapping a piece of raw meat with the flat side of a meat cleaver. A warm jet of liquid sprayed across his face. The liquid was his friend's blood. A suppressed sniper shot had ripped through his buddy's neck. His friend was dead before he collapsed to the ground.

A moment later, automatic gunfire, from multiple locations, tore into the building's concrete walls and a horde of drugged up teenagers raced towards him firing indiscriminately with their automatic rifles and emitting ghoulish cries. He remembered adjusting his night vision goggles, dropping to one knee and calmly re-setting his M-16 fire selector switch from three-round burst fire to semi-automatic single shot. In slow motion, he shot one teenager after another. He didn't hear the sounds of gunfire nor his sergeant's order to hold fire until he felt the sergeant's friendly hand on his shoulder. Standing, he gaped in horror at the body of his dead friend. The crooked corpses of nine teenagers lay in a half circle, thirty feet from his post.

After viewing the carnage, he vaguely remembered vomiting and being led by a fellow Marine to a quiet corner of a dark room in the building's interior. Someone washed the blood off his face with a wet cloth and gave him a canteen from which he took several sips of sweet, cool water. His arms pulled his knees close against his chest, in an attempt to control his shaking. After several minutes, the shaking subsided, his head sank to his knees and he wept uncontrollably for his fallen friend.

Annie was not a hunter, just a target shooter. She had never shot and killed any living thing, not birds, not deer, not elk, nothing! She valued and respected all living creatures. She forced her thoughts away from the prospect of killing human beings and, instead, replayed the ambush in her mind. The events unfolded like scenes in a play. Firstly, she shepherded all the kids in her bus to safety behind the retaining wall. Secondly, per Gunnery Sergeant Brice Miller's instructions, she recruited several experienced men to help the Marines. Thirdly, after careful reconnaissance, she presented Miller with her clear and thorough opinion of their retreat options, which were not promising. Fourthly, she described her skill in target shooting. Lastly, she and Bobby set up the command center under the third bus, which is where they both currently lay.

Her thoughts raced, *How would this final scene play out? Would this real life play be a success story or a tragedy? Would good trump evil? Would she be remembered as a heroine or a casualty? Shooting clay pigeons or a paper target was one thing, shooting live people was another matter entirely. When the time came, could she pull the trigger and kill disillusioned teenagers?*

Bobby could smell Annie's perfume. He could also see out of the corner of his eye that her eyes were watering, and her lower lip was quivering.

In an effort to calm and distract her, he said, "You smell nice Little Raven. What's your perfume called?"

"Huh!" said Annie, caught off guard by his remark.

"Are you OK?" asked Bobby.

"Do I look OK, Bobby?" she barked. "Christ, I've never done anything like this before."

"Mind if I give you a little advice?"

"Please! I'm losing control. I'm sorry I snapped at you," she said as tears began to roll down her cheeks.

"Killing people or possibly getting killed effects people in different ways. Trained soldiers under fire for the first time can freeze, panic, cry, wet their pants, run. I've seen it all. When this firefight begins, my advice is not to think or dwell on the human side of your actions. React don't think. Hit the targets as if you were shooting skeet. Once the shooting is over and your adrenal stops pumping, your emotions will catch up with you. I'll be here to help you with that," said Bobby kindly.

"Skeet! That's the damn problem! These are human beings, not skeet!" cried Annie softly.

"Listen to me! Normal, compassionate human beings don't ambush innocent children and slaughter them. Though I hope I'm wrong, I've seen how the bastards act! Nothing is sacred to them. They kill mourners at a funeral; blow up schools and places of worship; and torture people of all ages and sex. Every fucking fiber of their being is evil!" said Bobby evenly.

Annie's head dropped to her forearms as she wept quietly for a minute. As her crying subsided, she inhaled deep gulps of fresh air and muttered, "Promise, you'll help me."

"I promise. My squad leader was there for me after my first firefight. I was a total mumbling, stumbling wreck with uncontrollable shakes," said Bobby with a sincere, compassionate smile.

After a few moments, he added kindly, "I'll give you instructions on what to do. Do what I say and you'll be all right."

Annie smiled weakly and asked, "What about Kathy and Lynne? How are they handling this?"

"Kathy and Lynne are armed with automatic shotguns. I showed them how the shotguns work before I crawled under the bus. Neither of them has a problem killing the bad guys. They are like enraged mother bears who will protect their young cubs with their dying breath. These terrorists will learn the hard way what it's like to face the wrath of a female, which is something they aren't used to in their own culture."

Bobby continued, "I also showed three 6th grade boys how to throw both smoke and 'frag' grenades. Their teachers said that each of the boys volunteered to chuck grenades. As it turns out, they each have an older brother in the military. Two of the brothers are in the Marines and one in the Army. They're big boys for their age. All three look like they could pitch bales of hay from dawn to dusk. Though they won't see their targets, I told them it would be just like throwing a football over the top of a school bus."

"So that's what that was about! I saw them climb over the retaining wall and speak with you. Frag grenades! I thought they were just going to throw smoke grenades. Will they be *safe* throwing frag grenades?" asked Annie.

"We're beyond *safe*. I think we'll need all the firepower we can muster to hold these bastards off! I'd like you to be in charge of the boy's grenade throwing, if it comes to that."

Annie nodded and, after a time, said quietly, "I'm wearing a perfume called 'Lovely.'"

"Lovely… the name suits you! Can I buy you dinner in a couple of days on my return trip from the VA clinic in Sheridan? Say, Friday at 7:00 PM at the Irma Hotel in Cody?"

Annie's faced brightened. A date, a social event, something to look forward to, this was a pleasant thought. "Did you know Buffalo Bill Cody built that hotel and named it after his daughter?"

"Yup! Let's not get sidetracked, Little Raven. How about dinner?" Bobby was keeping Annie engaged and distracted. He knew that a host of negative thoughts could paralyze a soldier.

After a long moment, Annie replied flirtatiously, "You're on, but on one condition *big boy*."

"What's that?"

"I'm buying. It'll be a make up dinner for slapping you twelve years ago."

"Regret that, do you?" said Bobby smiling.

"Maybe."

Without warning, the deafening sound of sustained .30 caliber machine gunfire, from both of the terrorists' machine guns, ripped through the school buses. Broken glass and pieces of ragged sheet metal rained down on the pavement in front of Bobby and Annie's position.

2:22 PM MDT (4:22 EDT) Bobby's command post beneath the third bus.

After the gunfire ceased, Bobby raised his head and turned towards Annie. Her eyes were the size of silver dollars and her face was white.

In a calm, even tone Bobby said, "They're softening us up. My guess is that their broadcast equipment is up and running." In comforting manner, he rested one of his hands on Annie's arm, "Follow my lead and you'll be OK. You can do this!"

Kathy interrupted them. "Excuse me, my cozy, little lovebirds. We have a visitor coming our way," said Kathy, leaning under the bus and pointing beyond the last bus in line.

Bobby and Annie looked to the rear. They watched a middle aged, overweight, white male who was wearing a crumpled, cheap suit struggle to climb over the felled trees behind the last bus. A medium sized suitcase that he griped tightly with his right hand slowed his progress.

*

While Bobby was prepping Annie for the upcoming shootout, Brice and Al found Chet listening intently to a conversation on his secure global satellite phone.

"Yes, sir. Yes, sir! General Shook, Gunnery Sergeant Miller and a civilian volunteer have just arrived. I'll activate the low volume speaker so they can hear what's being discussed," said Chet.

Brice turned to Chet and whispered into his ear, "Who's on the horn?"

Chet whispered back into Brice's ear that it was the commandant along with a number of other "heavies."

"Gunny, this is your commandant speaking. On the phone with me are the Deputy Director of the FBI, Rich Rose; the Secretary of Homeland Security, Lowell Preston III; and Col. O'Brien and Lt. Col. Adair from Camp Pendleton."

"Major Daniels has explained to us how you were ambushed. He has also sent us a number of photographs via his cell phone camera that are quite informative. We have a clear picture of the superior terrain that the enemy holds on the hillside above you. We can see the impassable mountain of felled trees that has trapped your vehicles. And, it appears that the open field to your rear is not a viable retreat option during daylight hours.

"Gunny, do you know how many civilians you are protecting and have you set your defenses?" said the commandant authoritatively.

"Good afternoon General Shook, Col. O'Brien, Lt. Col. Adair, gentlemen," began Brice before the commandant suddenly interrupted him.

"It's not a good afternoon, God damn it!" After taking a moment to regain his composure, Shook continued in a restrained, but forceful manner, "Report!"

"Yes, general. There are 305 6th graders, twenty-seven civilians and three Marines for a total of 335 individuals who are trapped in this ambush. Regarding our defenses, I've teamed Annie Youngblood with Bobby Ridger who was medically discharged from the Marines and who, as you may know, is somewhat immobile. Annie is a young teacher in her early twenties who is an expert rifle target shooter. She has recruited several competent and experienced civilians to assist us. Further, she has already provided excellent field intelligence with respect to our lack of safe retreat options.

"She and Bobby will coordinate all our onsite communications and field intelligence from our command post that is located beneath the engine block of the third bus of five. We've reinforced this position with roadbed timbers and I've ensured that they are adequately armed. We're all linked with secure radio headsets for local communications. This team will maintain contact with all outside agencies via the satellite phone."

"Define *adequately armed*?" commanded Shook.

"They are armed with a M-40A3 sniper rifle with telescopic lens, a M-16 automatic rifle, a M-32 multiple grenade launcher, a M-249 SAW light machine gun and lots of ammunition," responded Brice officiously.

"Jesus! That adds new meaning to *adequately armed*. We'll get back to this after your report," said Shook.

"With respect to our defenses, I've had all the school buses move together, bumper to bumper, with the exception of a small gap between the second and third buses that now holds a four-foot high timber bunker. The timbers are discarded roadbed timbers that are thicker than railroad ties. Having the buses move together doesn't provide any hard protection, but it does hide our activities and firing positions. I've stationed two older female bus drivers, who are experienced bird hunters, at the timber bunker that is just a few feet from Bobby's command post. Both women are each armed with two automatic Benelli shotguns and they enjoy an unobstructed field of fire along our front line.

"I don't know if you heard, but a few minutes ago two enemy .30-caliber machine guns, positioned fore and aft end of the column of buses, fired on 'looky loo' civilians and park rangers who were approaching the felled trees. Though I haven't discussed this with Major Daniels yet, I was going to recommend to him that he and I each attack a machine gun nest simultaneously with a civilian named Al Edwards supporting the major, and a hunting guide named Pete Zouvas supporting me.

"Al Edwards, who is next to me and is listening to this conversation, is a retired Army master sergeant who served in Vietnam as Green Beret," explained Brice.

The commandant interjected, "Excellent! You are heaven sent, master sergeant. You're a very welcome and timely addition to Major Daniel's team."

"Thank you general. I'll do all I can to help your Marines, sir," said Al formally.

"I know you will, master sergeant. Continue, Gunny."

"Bobby Ridger will provide each of us with 'eyes on' field intelligence as we approach our separate targets. We have to take out those machine gun nests before they reduce our buses to a pile of rubble," concluded Brice.

"I concur with Gunny's plan, general," interjected Chet.

"Very well then. I'm terribly concerned about protecting those kids. That shall be your number one priority. Is that clear men?" barked the commandant.

Brice and Chet responded together, "Yes, general."

"Getting back to the subject of arms. Major Daniels, I seem to remember suggesting to Col. O'Brien that you should be *appropriately armed* when you joined the gunny. Just how well armed are you?" asked the commandant.

O'Brien chimed in, "I'll answer that general. Per your suggestion, general, I flew Major Daniels to West Yellowstone airport this morning on a C-130 transport plane. The *appropriate arms* that accompanied him included... " O'Brien proceeded to rattle off the lengthy list of weapons and equipment with the ease and familiarity of a parent describing their loving children, which, in many ways, was how O'Brien viewed the weapons.

The commandant and O'Brien had, on multiple occasions, previously served together. During their tours together, they informally addressed one another using nicknames. O'Brien's nickname was "OB."

"'OB,' I would say we have a little different interpretation of the meaning of *appropriately armed*. I was thinking that Major Daniels might carry an individual side arm and, at most, a couple of automatic rifles. The level of weaponry you sent with Major Daniels may very well save the day. Excellent work, OB! I commend you on your prudence," said the general.

OB responded, "I learned that 'prudence' from you during Desert Storm in 1991. You were my battalion commander at that time. Your constant mantra was 'a lightly armed Marine risks death, whereas a heavily armed Marine simply risks fatigue.' That mantra was just as compelling then as it is today."

"Yes, that has been a life long refrain of mine. Thank God, you remembered it."

"Yes, general. And fortunately, we have young Marines, like the gunny, who have more common sense and savvy then all of the federal law enforcement agencies in Washington DC combined. Christ, he identified multiple terrorist threats in the national parks, told them where their training camp was and the idiots still dropped the ball."

"Whoa! Hold on! Hold on, colonel! Did you say training camp?" said Rich Rose, the deputy director of the FBI.

"Yes, sir. In case you hadn't heard or forgot, Gunny discovered a terrorist's training camp at a remote hunting lodge near Dennis, Montana four days ago while hunting for a wolf on horseback. He immediately called in his field intelligence by radio to Corporal Ridger's dad, Bill Ridger, who was also a Marine. Bill Ridger called in the information to Homeland Security's office in Fort Harrison, Montana.

"I, we, only learned of this field intelligence this morning when Major Daniels met with Gunny in person at the West Yellowstone Airport. Minutes after Gunny described his discovery of the terrorist camp to Major Daniels, the major called in the information to my regimental office at Camp Pendleton. The law enforcement 'powers that be' in Washington DC never thought it necessary to apprise us of this matter, as they did for their advance precautions at Zion, Bryce and the Grand Canyon."

O'Brien continued his diatribe, "Upon receiving the news this morning, I personally spoke with Bill Ridger over the telephone and he confirmed the accuracy of the gunny's report. His daughter was with Miller when he spotted the camp. According to Miller's report, many of the terrorists were extremely young. They were being trained to fire and field strip their weapons, which were primarily automatic rifles and light machine guns. If I had prior knowledge of a heavily armed terrorist training camp in the vicinity of Yellowstone National Park, I would have ordered a fully armed platoon of Marines to accompany Major Daniels on that C-130 transport this morning," said O'Brien, clearly agitated.

"Preston, were you aware of this?" demanded Deputy Director of the FBI, Rich Rose.

"I'll discuss that with you offline line later, Rich," said the Secretary of Homeland Security, Lowell Preston III sourly.

"Typical Washington 'BS.' I should have expected as much. Unfortunately, we have more pressing issues to address at this moment rather than 'he said, she said' crap. But, I'll tell you this much Preston, you better start praying that the United States doesn't suffer any casualties in this ambush or else I'll personally see that you become a casualty as well," sneered the commandant.

"Your empty threats don't intimidate me, general. I was hoping to avoid embarrassing you and the Marine Corps during this multi-party phone call, but we are clearly beyond that now," interjected Lowell Preston III arrogantly.

"Preston, I have the feeling that in the very near future you will learn, by my hand, that the United States Marine Corps has never, nor ever will make 'empty threats,'" roared the commandant.

Preston naïvely continued, "I personally looked into Gunnery Sergeant Miller's alleged terrorist training camp observation. His report was unfortunately another military exaggeration and falsehood. When Miller's report arrived on my desk, I too made a telephone call, rather calls, and was referred to the individual who manages this remote hunting lodge for an offshore holding company. The manager's name is Nick Leone and he just so happens to be the highly respected Majority Whip of the Montana Senate, and very much a rising star in my political party. His family has all but run the state of Montana for the past twenty years. Leone explained to me that the lodge was rented to a Saudi prince for a very benign religious retreat.

"Unfortunately, Leone couldn't disclose the name of the principal of the holding company for confidentiality reasons. However, I did speak, over the telephone, with the renter, Prince Abdul Mustafa. He's a wealthy prince from Saudi Arabia whose family is very pro-United States. His purpose in renting the lodge, located on the outskirts of Dennis, Montana, was to entertain and thank moderate, American based Muslim clerics for spreading the peaceful image of the Muslim faith throughout the United States. He specifically chose this *remote hunting lodge* for his retreat so as to avoid the growing and misguided perception held by most U.S. law enforcement agencies that all Muslims gatherings have terrorist or evil objectives. The rifles that Miller saw on site were those of the prince's security team. They apparently used them on occasion to shoot rabbits and birds.

"When I questioned Mustafa about the lodge being used as a terrorist training camp, he was so offended that he threatened to file a multi-million dollar defamation lawsuit against the United States with the World Court, at The Hague, Netherlands. He and I both agreed that this was another disgraceful example of the United States' ceaseless and unfounded vilification of Saudi Arabia and his Muslim religion. This is not an ambush! A couple of dead trees fall across the road and our trigger happy Marines start shooting benevolent Muslims."

"But… " interjected Brice.

"Shut your mouth, Miller. You insolent, impulsive dolt," screeched Preston. "I sent my assistant secretary, Tony Dirdle, out from Washington to meet with Mustafa at the hunting lodge to dissuade Mustafa from filing this humiliating lawsuit and, secondly, to confirm the use of the lodge. After two days of telephone calls back and forth between the prince, and myself, Mustafa finally agreed to meet with my assistant two days ago. Dirdle thoroughly inspected the grounds and found no indication whatsoever of terrorist training activities.

"Fortunately, Dirdle calmed Mustafa down and persuaded him to forsake his plans of filing his lawsuit in exchange for a one million dollar cash payment. The suggestion that this *remote hunting lodge* was used as a terrorist training camp is absolutely preposterous," concluded Preston vehemently.

"That was very considerate and thoughtful of you Preston, to request permission to meet with Mustafa before showing up. I can only imagine how embarrassed poor Mustafa would have been had Doodle arrived, unannounced, in the middle of his terrorists' .30-caliber machine gun practice. Apparently forty-eight hours advance notice was enough time for Mustafa to clean up the lodge and relocate his terrorists," said the commandant disingenuously.

A moment later the commandant continued, "I trust you haven't seen any of the current TV broadcasts that are televising photographs and a video taken by a college student moments after the ambush occurred. The photographs of Mustafa's benign Muslims pointing .30-caliber machine guns at the Cody school buses is quite convincing. By the way, has Doodle forked over the million bucks yet?"

"First, I don't trust the news media. They can alter photographs with 'rotoshop'," said Preston.

"It's called 'photoshop,' Preston, not 'rotoshop.' By the way, your agency has an entire photo intelligence department that can ascertain the veracity of those photographs. But, since you apparently don't use your own department's resources, I suggest you turn on a TV and take a look at what everyone else in the country is watching.

"Oh, and one other detail. If you pick up the phone on your desk and call your own internal corporate records department, they will give you the name of the principal behind this offshore holding company that owns this *remote hunting lodge* on U.S. soil. If you recall, your political party sponsored a bill last year, which was overwhelmingly approved, that requires the disclosure of all foreign individuals who acquire real estate in the U.S. through a blind offshore holding company or other similar entity. You, on behalf of Homeland Security, personally urged the passage of this bill," said the commandant derisively.

"I'll look into that," said Preston indifferently.

"The American people would appreciate that. I realize that this modest investigation may be a stretch for you, since it requires a modicum of common sense, which you apparently don't have," concluded the commandant.

None of the commandant's comments made any impression on Preston's insular thinking. He did, however, like the commandant's use of the "American people." It had a nice ring to it.

After several moments of silence, Preston continued unperturbed, "Firstly, this ambush is a hoax! Pure 'bunkum!' Someone in our government or military is perpetrating a terrible trick on the 'American people' and I don't like it one bit. Secondly, my assistant secretary's surname is Dirdle, not Doodle. And no, Dirdle hasn't delivered the cash to Mustafa yet. He picked up the money this morning from a bank in Bozeman and was flying to the hunting lodge in a helicopter when this current deception began to unfold. I redirected him to Yellowstone and the site of this monstrous embarrassment. Tony Dirdle is my assistant secretary and he has the full authority of my office. Furthermore, he will take command of the site when he arrives and handle all discussions, negotiations and reparations with our Muslim guests. Is that clear, general!" said Preston.

Before the commandant could respond, Rose shrieked "Negotiations! What are you talking about? This administration doesn't negotiate with terrorists!"

In the mysterious halls of Washington politics, Preston would have been Jed Adams' last choice for the post of Secretary of Homeland Security. But, to overcome the opposition party's resistance to his latest defense budget, the president agreed to the unusual compromise of appointing a member of the opposing party to his cabinet. As a consequence of this arrangement, Preston became the Secretary of Homeland Security.

Preston was a gadfly from Massachusetts who previously served in the prior administration as the Deputy Director of Housing and Urban Development. In that position, he established himself as an underachieving and meddlesome bureaucrat. There was categorically nothing remarkable about Preston's public service in Washington other than his huge contributions to his party's campaign coffers. The source of these contributions came solely from inherited millions.

Additionally, Preston never held nor was he ever offered a job in the private sector because he never lasted more than a few minutes in a preliminary job interview. Interviewers found his smug, self-important personality utterly detestable. His curriculum vita, which was always at the ready, described him as a Boston educated, expert on Middle East cultures. In truth, Preston knew very little about modern day Middle Eastern cultures, less about Muslim extremists and absolutely nothing about negotiating with Middle Eastern terrorists.

Two senior staff members at Homeland Security, who were loyal to Adams, assured him that they would keep close tabs on Preston. With that assurance in hand, Adams reluctantly appointed Preston to the post of Secretary of Homeland Security.

"Rose, Mustafa's guests aren't terrorists. And, the mood of our countrymen and the sentiment of our congress has changed. The most senior members of my party and I are of a like mind. We firmly believe that two sensible countries or factions, with disparate ideologies, can resolve their differences without bloodshed. Surely our U.S. dollars offer significant benefits, especially to poorer countries. It enables these countries to provide their people with basic human needs... nutrition, clothing, healthcare, shelter, etc. The list is endless!" sermonized Preston fervently.

Rose fought to retain his composure, "Preston, have you read a newspaper in the past twenty five years? Many, if not all, of these poorer countries that you refer to are governed by cruel, despotic dictators who use all manner of foreign aid to buy weapons and line their own pockets. The more their people suffer, the more these despots expand their repressive tactics with modern weaponry and increase their offshore savings accounts.

"And you're giving Mustafa a million United States dollars for some bullshit accusation." Rose's composure dissolved, "This is fucking incredible! I'd say you are one misinformed 'dolt' and you're trespassing on international policy that clearly isn't your bailiwick. You and whichever party members you're referring to do not have the authority to dictate United States policy," screamed Rose.

"Rose, I'm afraid you and the commandant are the one's who are misinformed. The FBI has a dismal record of interrogating suspected terrorists. And, the Marine Corps has a history of killing innocent civilians under the name of collateral damage. The times have changed. This is a humane administration that strongly believes that this country shall always take the high, moral road when dealing with peaceful Muslims. Further, I, as well as the president, firmly believe that we can negotiate with terrorists, should that occasion occur, without loss of life," said Preston with a confident air of superiority.

"I saw the assholes at the lodge. They were terrorists! You saw the bastard with the black mask take a shot at the old guy who got out of his car after the trees fell," whispered Brice to Chet.

Chet nodded in agreement and silenced Brice by putting a finger to his lips.

4:20 PM EDT (2:20 PM MDT)

"I heard that Gunny," squawked Preston. "Such appalling language for a man in uniform! He certainly doesn't reflect well on the Marine Corps, general. Now, let me be perfectly clear on your rules of engagement. None of the Marines, or anyone else is permitted to fire a weapon under any circumstance. Your men, general, circumvented and broke the law when they brought those weapons into a national park. You can rest assured I will bring charges against them for these deliberate violations of the law."

As the commandant was about to respond, the sound of .30-caliber machine gunfire was transmitted through Chet's satellite phone. The sustained gunfire lasted twenty seconds as it ripped through the thin skin of the school buses. The Marines on each end of the call were familiar with this ominous tactic. The enemy was softening up their target before they attacked. To the trapped kids, the thunderous pounding of the machine gunfire coupled with the sound of breaking glass and tearing metal was terrifying. Many of the kids began to cry uncontrollably.

When the firing ceased, Preston seethed, "Major Daniels and Sergeant Miller, I spoke with Tony Dirdle over the phone moments ago while you blatantly disregarded my 'no gunfire' order. He is nearly over the fallen trees at the rear of your column as we speak. He should be at your location in just a minute. When he arrives, he will arrest both of you and take you into custody."

The commandant, Rose and O'Brien replied to Preston's arrest pronouncement with a cacophony of curses, threats and insults. Their outburst reflected years of frustration with dull witted, naïve, spineless and grand standing politicians.

2:22 PM MDT (4:22 EDT)

Moments after the machine gunfire subsided, an overweight man, dressed in a baggy suit, fell over the last tree trunk that separated him from the line of school buses. As he fell onto the pavement, his medium sized suitcase slipped from his grip and sailed through the air. When the suitcase landed on the hard asphalt it opened and stacks of cash flew in every direction. Everyone on both sides of the road saw the cash fly. The man quickly scrambled to collect the cash, which he stuffed back into his case. He stood and unconsciously attempted to straighten his shapeless suit. When his composure returned, he began to strut down the middle of the road towards Brice and Chet's position as if he was taking a midday walk in a park.

Brice screamed, "Get behind a bus! Take Cover!" Brice took an involuntary step towards Dirdle, in an attempt to guide him to safety, but Chet grabbed Brice's forearm and held him firmly in place.

All those listening over the satellite conference call heard a new, far off voice, "I'm the Assistant Secretary of Homeland Security, Tony Dirdle. Major Daniels and Sergeant Miller please come forward, you are both under arrest."

Chet looked at Brice and slowly shook his head from side to side.

Don't move a fucking inch. We're staying put!

Suddenly, a small, dark man with a scruffy beard appeared near the front bumper of the white tour bus on the opposite side of the road. Dirdle recognized the man and smiled. He was Abdul Mustafa's assistant, Ajani, who toured him through and around the *remote hunting lodge* during his inspection several days earlier.

"Ajani, I am so sorry. Another regretful misunderstanding has, yet again, occurred. It appears that old, decaying trees have fallen and blocked the road. Our overzealous military misunderstood this act of nature and unfortunately fired their weapons. Please accept my apologies," said Dirdle as he bowed obsequiously.

In Dirdle's unseeing and unthinking belief that the Marines were the guilty antagonists, he hadn't bothered to check his surroundings. If he had, he would have realized that the smoke that was drifting over the road was coming from the school buses that had been riddled with machine gunfire and not from the white tour bus that Ajani was standing beside.

"What's in the bag?" said Ajani with his strong Middle Eastern accent.

"It contains the one million dollars in cash that the United States government promised to pay Prince Abdul Mustafa. I was flying by helicopter to your lodge this afternoon to deliver this money when this unfortunate incident occurred.

"My government rerouted me to this site about thirty minutes ago. I'm relieved to see that you are OK. The president of our country will punish those who are responsible for unfairly targeting you and your peaceful Muslim followers," said Dirdle submissively.

Ajani waved Dirdle to his side. Dirdle plodded towards Ajani and handed him the suitcase full of money.

"Go!" spat Ajani as he pointed towards the school buses.

It took Dirdle a moment to comprehend Ajani's heavily accented command. As he began to shuffle towards the school buses, he realized something was amiss. *Why were the school buses bullet ridden and smoking?* He glanced over his shoulder at Ajani's unscathed tour bus. He saw Ajani lift a radio to his mouth and say something like, "suit im'."

Unheard to all, but the smiling Ajani, was the response from the man he radioed, "Allah named you correctly, Ajani… 'he who wins the struggle.'"

In Dirdle's last second of life, he deciphered Ajani's strange, accented radio command, it was "shoot him," not "suit im'." A flash of fear filled his eyes an instant before his body was ripped apart by a burst of gunfire from one of the terrorist's .30-caliber machine guns.

"Sergeant Miller, I told you no gunfire. You apparently don't follow orders. I will personally see that you are court marshaled and sent to Leavenworth prison for a very long time," said Preston witheringly.

"Dirdle's dead!" said Brice softly, shocked by the senseless death.

"Totally unnecessary," was all that Chet could mumble.

Al Edwards spoke quietly to no one in particular, as he rolled his eyes skyward and shook his head in disbelief, "Incompetent and inexperienced politicians! Another uncalled-for death in a very fucking long line of uncalled-for deaths! I thought this shit ended with Vietnam." Seeing Dirdle die as he did and hearing Preston's comment regarding 'rules of engagement' also released another emotion in Edwards that he'd struggled to keep in check since his days in the jungles of Vietnam, forty years earlier. His sad words came from a place deep in his heart where he remembered friends lost in battle, "Senseless 'rules of engagement!' Those who make such rules should be required to spend one day, maybe even one minute, on the receiving end of a bullet or, in the case of those poor pilots, a surface to air (SAM) missile before they dictate such insanity."

Chet heard Al's mournful and cathartic words. He punched him lightly on the shoulder and said, "Amen, to that! Now, let's kick ass!"

"That shooting you heard Preston was .30-caliber machine gunfire. Our men aren't armed with .30-caliber weapons. Your peace loving Muslims just killed your assistant secretary in cold blood," said the commandant despondently.

4:26 PM EDT (2:26 PM MDT)

Suddenly, Chet's phone crackled and all those who were connected to the satellite call heard a computerized sound track.

"White House intercept! White House intercept! This is a secure transmission and this call is being recorded. The president of the United States is on the line," announced a mechanical voice.

"This is President Jed Adams. I have the Chairman of the Joint Chiefs of Staff, General Randy Rexman, USAF, with me in the Situation Room of the White House. We have been listening to this transmission since Major Daniels initiated this call to his commanding officers at Camp Pendleton. Can all of you hear me?" asked the president.

A roll call response proceeded. All the listeners stated their name and title and confirmed their clear reception of the president's phone call. A new listener spoke last. "This is John Migliori, Director of the FBI, I hear you clearly Mr. President."

"Lowell, you are relieved of your duties immediately for failure to perform your sworn duties and illegal actions that threaten the lives of U.S. citizens. John, please arrest Lowell and take him into custody. I don't want him giving one more order to anyone in the government. Additionally, I would like your Deputy Director, Rich Rose, to immediately assume the management of the Department of Homeland Security until I nominate a replacement secretary.

"But, Mr. President... we're not a police state, these Muslims in Yellowstone Park are law abiding citizens..."

"Shut up, Lowell. You swore an oath to protect and defend the people of our great country. In case you hadn't noticed, the terrorists are the one's who have ambushed five school buses and just shot and killed your deputy."

"The leaders of my party and I feel it's time to extend an 'olive branch' to the Muslim world. Peaceful negotiations are the key, not bombs and bullets."

With all the restraint the president could muster, he said evenly, "This is not the time nor place for a debate on Muslims, but let me say this… I believe that the majority of Muslims, throughout the world, lead peaceful and kindhearted lives. The problem that we, and other countries, face is the outright evil teachings of a small percent of Muslim clerics and their radical followers. These Muslim extremists believe that they can attain their misguided, self serving political and religious goals by virtue of their indiscriminate use of terror and intimidation. What we are currently facing is a terrorist act on U.S. soil that threatens the lives of 335 U.S. citizens.

"In closing Preston, I don't want to hear one more naïve, overly simplistic and asinine comment from you. Your independent and illegal actions have severely compromised the safety of 305 6th grade school children and thirty others. John Migliori, where are you men?"

"They're entering Lowell's office as we speak."

"Have one of your men activate Preston's office intercom speaker so his entire staff hears my forthcoming message," said the president forcefully.

"Yes, Mr. President."

A few seconds later, the Director of the FBI, John Migliori came back on the phone, "Mr. President, the intercom speaker is activated."

"This is the president of the United States, Jed Adams, I have just relieved Lowell Preston III of his duties as Secretary of the Department of Homeland Security because of his failure to defend the people of the United States from foreign enemies. The Deputy Director of the FBI, Rich Rose, will be taking over the interim management of Homeland Security until I nominate a permanent replacement for Preston. Any person who does not fully cooperate with the orders or instructions of Rich Rose shall be arrested. That is all. John, please disconnect the Homeland Security intercom portion of this call," ordered the president.

4:28 PM EDT (2:28 MDT)

The president then addressed those on his original conference call. "I have further instructions. Rich, I'd like you to get over to the offices of

Homeland Security as fast as you can. You are now my acting Secretary of Homeland Security."

"Yes, Mr. President," said Rich Rose crisply.

As everyone on the conference call knew, President Jed Adams was an extremely proactive, hands-on leader. He wasn't an advocate of meetings, committees or executive caucuses. He made decisions and his assistants and cabinet members followed them. The president's chief of staff, formerly recognized as the president's "gatekeeper," filled an entirely different role than that of his predecessors.

Jed Adams' chief of staff was Steve Rosetta. He had been Adams' second in command since his first days in office in Texas. With two exceptions, Rosetta was a clone of Adams. The first exception being that he was twenty years younger than the president. And, the second exception was that Rosetta could keep track of more data than a super computer. Proof of that were the three smart phones that Rosetta carried with him at all times, often using all three concurrently. Jed labeled him as his "implementer" rather than his "gatekeeper."

Past presidents would have also relied upon the country's domestic intelligence agencies to coordinate a response to this ambush, specifically the National Security Council. However, this situation was clearly unique. Homeland Security had failed and the FBI was tied up cleaning the prior day's aborted terrorist attacks. In light of the ambush defenders urgent need for support, the president recognized immediately that he would have to be involved. He also recognized that the only means of support for this remote ambush in Yellowstone was going to come from the military. Thus, there was no reason for him to involve the National Security Council who would simply forward his commands to other government agencies and likely cause a high degree of confusion at a time when immediate action was required.

With the Chairman of the Joint Chief's of Staff, Gen. Randy Rexman, USAF, sitting beside him in the situation room of the White House, the president was going to operate as a true commander-in-chief of his military.

"Gen. Shook your Marines and the U.S. civilians they are protecting are clearly under attack. Contrary to Preston's idiotic and improper instructions, your men and any civilian volunteers are authorized to use their weapons in any manner they chose to defend themselves. I've ordered Gen. Rexman to fully utilize every resource available to the federal government to assist your Marines on site. Further, I've ordered the Director of the FBI to request support for your men from every local law enforcement agency in the area," said the president.

"I appreciate that Mr. President. Do we have any additional intelligence on how many terrorists my men are facing?" asked the commandant.

"Hold on! I'm reading a note that was just handed to me." The president proceeded to summarize the note aloud, "After hearing my intercom message at Homeland Security, a field agent at Homeland Security called a friend of his at the FBI. The agent at Homeland Security is on the telephone, as we speak, relating field intelligence to the FBI that he gathered yesterday during the round up of terrorists at Zion National Park. Apparently, when Preston was told of his agent's field intelligence, he had the agent flown back to Washington, under guard, in an attempt to suppress his findings. I'm going to be patched into that call now. I'll be back in a minute. Gen. Rexman will remain on the line. Son of a bitch!" said the president angrily as he left the conference call.

"Daniels, do you have any idea of the number terrorists you are facing?" continued the commandant.

"We can't see their positions, general, because the hillside is heavily wooded but my best guess would be forty to fifty. I don't think they could fit more than that in their bus along with weapons and gear," said Chet.

"Damn! I don't like those odds, or their superior hillside position. I hope to hell those bastards didn't make more than one trip in that bus to this ambush site. Tell me more about your problems with a retreat?"

Chet nodded to Brice who answered, "General, this is Gunny Miller. The prospects for a retreat or escape are not good. There are ravines with sheer walls at both ends of our section of the road so a lateral escape is not possible. A retreat, perpendicular from the direction of the road, is over gently sloping grassy plains with no cover of consequence for about half a mile. There is also a narrow creek running through the plain that will slow the kids down as they attempt to cross it. That is, if it's even possible to cross. We don't know the depth or speed of the water, but we do know it's freezing cold. There is no moon tonight so we will experience full nighttime darkness, but that won't occur for another five to six hours. And, we have no idea if the terrorists have night scopes."

"Shit! General Rexman, what about nearby military support?" said the commandant with growing frustration.

"There are a few Air Force bases in the neighboring states, but their primary missions are strategic missile defense and the long range interdiction of incoming enemy aircraft," responded Rexman.

"Fuck! This is one heck of a well-planned ambush in a remote location. Daniels, we'll let you get back to organizing your defenses. We'll call you back once we learn more from the president. Everyone else, stay on the line," ordered the commandant gruffly.

"Yes sir, general," snapped Daniels.

4:32 PM EDT (2:32 PM MDT)

Minutes later, the president returned to the original conference call. "I'm back on the line," said the infuriated president.

"Mr. President, while you were offline, Lt. Col. Adair at Camp Pendleton has come up with an idea that might work. We took the liberty of patching into this call the commanding general of Nellis Air Force Base, Brigadier General Robert Watts. In a moment, you'll realize the importance of his input. Adair please outline your rescue plan to the president," said Rexman.

"Mr. President, last week we sent a platoon of Marines from Camp Pendleton to Nellis Air Force Base, Las Vegas, to participate with the Air Force on a joint desert operation near Elko, Nevada. The operation was completed earlier this morning and the platoon is staged and ready to return to Camp Pendleton in four Air Force HH-60 Pave Hawk helos," said Adair.

"What is the distance from their location to the ambush site, and do you know the range and speed of those helos?" interrupted the commandant tersely.

"Approximately 470 miles to the target, and all four helos have external tanks which give them a range of about 500 miles. The helos are fully fueled and fully armed with two 7.62 mm miniguns. The maximum speed of those helos is 220 MPH," said Adair, as he hastily read from his scribbled notes.

"Is the platoon armed?" asked the commandant.

"Yes, general. They were fully re-supplied this morning. They're ready to roll. They're also a very experienced rifle platoon that returned from Iraq a couple of months ago. They are attached to a rifle company in the 3/5," said Adair.

"General Rexman, what do you think?" asked the president.

"I'm going to defer to Gen. Watts, Mr. President," said Rexman.

"Mr. President, Adair's report is accurate. My best guess is that, at a flying speed of 180-200 MPH, it will be at least two and one half hours from now before our helos reach the ambush site. We can't fly those Pave Hawks at maximum speed or they'll run out of fuel before they reach their destination. As it is, they may be running on fumes by the time they offload the Marines.

"After the Marines are debarked, I can make arrangements for a HC-130 P/N Combat King tanker from the Mountain Home Air Force base to be in the vicinity to refuel all four helos in the air. Our Mountain Home base is located southeast of Boise, Idaho near Twin Falls. Once the Pave Hawks are refueled, they can provide close air ground support for your Marines with their 7.62 mm miniguns.

"I wish Mountain Home could provide more support for the Marines and civilians in Yellowstone, but that base is the home of a fighter wing, the 366th. Their aircraft are primarily long-range tactical fighters, F-15's, which are not designed for close air ground support in tight quarters" said Watts.

"Gen. Shook, do you concur with this plan?" asked Rexman.

"Absolutely. It sounds good to me," replied the commandant.

"That's it then. This is our best and, for now, only option. Generals Shook and Watts you have my permission to execute this plan immediately. Gen. Shook once you've given your orders to Col. O'Brien and Lt. Col. Adair, please return to this call. I will then apprise all of you of the updated field intelligence that I just received from the agent at Homeland Security and his FBI friend," said the president firmly.

"Yes, Mr. President. I shall direct my men and return to this call," said the commandant. The commandant hammered the 'hold' button on his conference call line and began giving simple, non-stop orders to O'Brien and Adair who he spoke to over a separate phone line. The clear and unqualified message that he imparted to both of them was that his Marines on site had complete freedom to do whatever they deemed necessary to protect the safety of the 6th grade children and the other civilians. In his own words, there were "no fucking rules of engagement!"

"I'm back on the line, Mr. President," boomed the commandant.

"That was fast work!" said the president.

"My Marines don't need much direction, especially when it comes to combat. Mr. President, can Homeland Security, the FBI or other local law enforcement support my men while the helos are in transit to the ambush site?" asked the commandant.

"I had my chief of staff check on that and, unfortunately, there is very little support any of them can provide within the next couple of hours. This ambush site is too darn isolated," said the angry president.

John Migliori, the Director of the FBI, added, "Gen. Shook, the FBI has only a handful of agents in that region. They are contacting the park rangers and local law enforcement in an attempt to coordinate support, but it may take longer than two and half hours to put any experienced response team together. A few park rangers would be ineffective against a large number of terrorists who are armed with automatic weapons. Plus, most of their experience involves dealing with unruly sightseers or campers."

"'Effectiveness!' Aside from my Marines, hundreds of young kids are relying on the 'effectiveness' of handful of civilians that include two sixty-year-old ladies with shotguns. God bless'em! Give us any help you can as soon as you can, John," begged the commandant.

"I understand. We'll do all we can, general," said the director of the FBI.

"What about Homeland Security?" asked the commandant?

"Unfortunately, no help from this department. I've learned that all the agents who intercepted yesterday's terrorist attacks at Zion, Bryce and Grand Canyon National Parks are still in those areas ensuring that they grabbed all of the terrorists," said the acting Secretary of Homeland Security, Rich Rose.

4:36 PM EDT (2:36 PM MDT)

"My boys will just have to hang on until those helos arrive," said the commandant who was dispirited by the absence of nearby support. "Mr.

President, what was the gist of the field intelligence that you received offline several minutes ago?"

"The Department of Homeland Security (DHS) agent, who I spoke to, was part of the DHS-FBI task force that captured the group of terrorists yesterday that was headed to Zion National Park. While he was cuffing one of the terrorists, the terrorist boasted of the success of their primary mission in Yellowstone National Park.

"When the DHS agent questioned the terrorist for further details, he told him he could watch the killing of over three hundred of the infidel's children by sixty to seventy of his brother Muslims on the Internet. He added that his fellow brothers had filmed the Yellowstone operation and sent it, via satellite, to a secret al-Qaeda television studio somewhere in Syria where it was likely being broadcast throughout the Middle East.

"As we now know, this terrorist's boasting was one day premature. What may have contributed to this misinformation was that there were two separate training camps. The FBI agent, who was also on the call, said that the FBI had just learned, thirty minutes earlier, that all of the terrorists captured yesterday at Zion, Bryce and the Grand Canyon all trained together at a camp in Northern Arizona, near Flagstaff," concluded the president.

"Therefore, none of the Northern Arizona terrorists were sent to Yellowstone National Park, which makes sense. Christ, Yellowstone has to be over eight hundred miles from Flagstaff. That's too damn far for a dilapidated, white tour bus to travel with all those terrorists on board. They would have to eat and relieve themselves, which would have surely attracted someone's attention," exclaimed the commandant. A moment later he added, "The later time zones in the Middle East may have also contributed to the screw up in the jump off day for these multiple attacks from two separate training camps. We've seen that happen before. The Yellowstone attackers thought they were to attack on Monday, rather than Sunday," said the commandant.

"Exactly," said the president. "So, when Preston got word of his agent's discovery, he elected to suppress the intelligence. He placed his agent under house arrest and transported him back to Washington. His actions totally compromised our ability to thwart this Yellowstone ambush. According to one of Preston's aides, who vehemently opposed Preston's actions, Preston felt that the FBI agents, who were jointly working with his agent during the terrorist arrests at Zion, had influenced his agent's understanding of what he heard.

"Preston, thereby, felt that his agent's discovery was just as false as Miller's training camp observation," said the president.

"That and the disloyal prick couldn't accept the possibility that his newfound buddy, Mustafa, had thoroughly deceived him," interjected the commandant.

" Exactly!" said the president.

"Preston's assistant, Dirdle, recognized the terrorist who took the bag of money from him at the ambush site. He had met with him and Mustafa several days earlier at the lodge in Dennis," said the commandant.

"That's right, general! This is the same bunch of thugs that Miller observed in Dennis," grumbled the president.

"I don't wish to make your day worse, Mr. President, but I've just read Preston's emails. He never elevated, nor sent your 'High Alert' threat order to any of the park rangers at our national parks. Additionally, he sent a puzzling email to the Attorney General in which he challenged your authority to elevate the domestic terrorist threat warning without his permission.

"In this email, he states… 'that without the actual occurrence of a terrorist act, it was discriminatory and unfair to investigate suspected terrorists simply because they possess explosive devices, weapons or communicated with one another about committing terrorist acts.' I've just sent a flash message to all national parks notifying them of your 'High Alert' threat order," said the acting Secretary of Homeland Security.

"Good work, Rich. Please forward a copy of that email to me. Using the words 'discriminatory and unfair' to describe our investigative efforts has a familiar ring to me. A small group of outspoken and misguided lawmakers from my opposing political party have recently used those specific adjectives," said the president resignedly.

"Will do, Mr. President," said Rose. A moment later, his self-control dissolved, "'Unfair,' fuck, that's insane! It's like saying we can't investigate or preempt the planned bombing of a crowded subway until the bomb is actually detonated and kills people."

Unstated, but evident to all of those on the conference call, was the realization that this ambush could have so easily been avoided had Preston simply performed his sworn duties and applied just the slightest element of common sense.

Moments later, Chet's satellite phone crackled. The commandant added Chet and Brice to the president's conference call.

"Daniels, your estimate of fifty terrorists is low, the president has informed us that the actual number is between sixty to seventy. Further, intelligence gathered from yesterday's captured terrorists also indicates that the bastards who are attacking you are filming their ambush for propaganda purposes," said the commandant.

"No need to say anymore, general. The gunny and I have been to this rodeo before. They think they are going to film a massacre! Well, screw them," growled Chet.

"Yes, Daniels, screw them! O'Brien and Adair are working on a rescue plan, but it may be close to three hours before help arrives. You must hold on," urged the commandant.

"Gunny has set up a good defensive position. All of the kids are hidden behind a retaining wall and are safe for now. We should be able to hold them off so long as there are no more surprises, like mortars or RPG's (rocket propelled grenades)," said Chet.

Multiple bursts of .30-caliber machine gunfire boomed over Chet's satellite phone.

"What's happening?" asked the commandant.

"Their .30 caliber machine guns are again raking the cars that are outside of our ambush perimeter. That will definitely discourage any local support from any onlookers. I also think they're preparing for an attack."

With a forceful note of encouragement in his voice, the commandant said, "You've been trained to respond to these types of situations, Daniels. Focus on your most immediate threats and protect your flanks. I know that you, Gunny Miller and Corporal Ridger will show these bastards how United States Marines fight!"

"Aye, aye, general. The gunny and I better take up our positions. I'll leave this channel open and give the phone to Bobby Ridger and Annie Youngblood," said Chet, as he and Brice started moving into position.

"Godspeed, men," said the commandant.

"Good luck, boys. Those children's lives are in your hands. I wish I could do more," said the president despondently.

The president's clenched fist punched closed the telephone speaker connection. A cloak of futility enveloped him as he closed his eyes and sank deeper into his plush leather chair. Sun blotches and deep, weather beaten creases crowded the face of the six-foot four inch angular Texan. His carefully trimmed short gray hair, bold nose and square jaw contrasted sharply with rest of his rough-hewn, uneven countenance. Shades of crimson were now beginning to spread across his rugged face.

After a long minute of contemplation, Jed's body slowly twitched to life and his eyes, which were partially hidden by a wild thicket of salt-and-pepper eyebrows, gradually opened and began to focus. His eye color that was normally a gentle green-gold was now an angry mixture of dark green and black.

Preston had steered him and the country into a situation from which there seemed no escape. He knew, with absolute certainty, the crisis that now confronted him would never have occurred were it not for the insufferable and mindless scorched-earth politics that influenced every congressional decision of import on Capitol Hill.

Jed absently kneaded his forehead with the fingers of his right hand. A moment later, both of his large calloused hands moved to the sides of his face to massage his temples. After a concerted, but vain, effort to relieve his growing anger and frustration, his hands dropped to the conference table and he sighed in resignation. He'd never felt so powerless and defenseless. The iniquitous, and age-old political maneuvering on Capitol Hill was draining his last ounce of self-control. He turned towards Rexman. His eyes pleaded for an idea, a possibility, anything.

Rexman silently lifted his palms upwards in a helpless gesture and shook his head despondently.

Suddenly, like a thunderhead that reached its flashpoint, he swore aloud, raised his right arm above his head and slammed the conference table with his large, open hand. The table shook as if struck by lightning. "If Preston were in front of me now I don't think I could stop myself from putting a bullet between his eyes," said the president heatedly.

Rexman nodded sadly in agreement and said, "I feel the same way."

"Thank God for the Marines!" growled the president with his

distinctive west Texas drawl as his hand pounded the conference table once again. As he did so, a bolt of pain coursed through his body. The source of his pain was the back injury he sustained when he was thrown from his horse at the age of fourteen. His hands shot to the elbow rests of his chair in an attempt to relieve the agony that rocketed from his lower back. The color in his face drained as he croaked, "Oh, God!" He felt like someone was jabbing his lower back with a pitchfork.

2:41 PM MDT (4:41 PM EDT)

Before Brice returned to Bobby's command post, he and Chet discussed a plan to take out the two machine guns.

"This is what I'm thinking," began Chet. "Surprise is the key. If any of their foot soldiers observe our movements and relay our location to their machine gunners, we won't stand a chance of getting close enough to take those guns out," said Chet.

Brice nodded, confirming Chet's analysis.

"The machine gun that Al and I will be attacking is perhaps eighty yards away from the first bus, but we can't get too close because of the absence of cover. My plan is to pound that general area with high explosive Hellhound rounds from our grenade launchers. If they move the gun or themselves we'll have a clear shot at them. I'll give you our attack countdown via my headset radio. When all hell breaks loose that will, hopefully, draw all the terrorist's attention to that area of the hillside. With any luck, that distraction will provide you and Pete an opportunity to sneak up on the rear machine gun position. Shoot the gunners and toss several grenades into their position. That should disable their gun. Get in and get out. We can't afford to lose any firepower. We're way under-manned as is," said Chet.

"Aye, aye, major," responded Brice unconsciously. "Once I'm in position, I'll call you on my headset. I better get back to Bobby," said Brice as he hurried off to Bobby's command center under the third bus.

No sooner had Brice returned to the timber bunker between the second and third bus when he heard Bobby loudly declare, "Here they come!"

In a low, but firm voice that all the defenders could clearly hear, Brice said, "Single shots only, no automatic fire. Kathy and Lynne hold your fire and keep your heads down. Bobby, Annie and I will handle this one."

Four wild eyed teenagers, all of whom looked and acted like they were stoned out of their minds, charged Bobby's position with their AK-47's on full automatic fire. The attack was a mirror image of what the three Marines had seen numerous times in Iraq. The al-Qaeda commanders used drugged and inexperienced teenagers as human cannon fodder to probe enemy defenses so they could assess the enemy's positions and level of firepower. In a matter of seconds, six well-aimed rifle shots dispatched all four terrorists before they reached the centerline of the two-lane road. Brice nailed two, Chet one and Annie the last.

Ajani radioed Abdul Mustafa, who was stationed adjacent to the satellite dish on the top of the hill, "Abdul, two, maybe three, shooters with hunting rifles. Their rifles probably have those small magazines that only hold four to six rounds. We can take them out anytime. Are you ready to film?"

"Just a few more minutes. The infidels arrived two hours early," replied the irritated, but excited Abdul Mustafa.

Annie's eyes were the size of silver dollars. She stared into space as her eyes filled with tears.

"Annie, their mission is to kill children. I know it's hard killing another human being. You're protecting your students. Innocent ten and eleven year old boys and girls," said Bobby softly. She was so vulnerable, so sad and so distraught. He wanted to hold her in his arms and comfort her.

"Shooting skeet! Shit! It sure didn't feel like it," she said, as she rested her head on her folded arms and began to cry.

Bobby inched his hand against hers and whispered tenderly, "We'll get through this together, Annie."

CHAPTER 20
THE MACHINE GUNS

2:53 PM MDT (4:53 PM EDT)

Brice whispered quietly into his headset radio, "Chet, Pete and I are well hidden in the jumble of trees in the rear. We have a clear view of the two men who are manning the machine gun that covers the last bus."

Chet replied, "Brice, Al and I are as close as we can get to the forward machine gun nest, which is partially hidden by trees. We can't see much of the two men in the machine gun nest. Al suggests we first target the tree trunks on each side of the nest with our grenade launchers. That way the back blast from the high explosive Hellhound rounds will either hit the men or, at the very least, encourage them to move away from the blast area and into our clear line of sight so we can shoot them. If that fails, we'll simply hit them with everything we've got. At worst, I think we'll destroy the gun. We'll be good to go in one minute. I'll give you a ten second standby and a final three second countdown."

"Chet, I'd like to suggest a modification to my plan of attack. Bobby, do you copy?" said Brice.

"Rodger, I copy, " replied Bobby.

"Chet and Bobby, this is what I'm thinking. Chet, while you and Al are hammering your target, Bobby provides supplemental firepower with his light machine gun. The sustained fire on that forward machine gun position should divert all of the terrorist's attention to that area. In the meantime, Pete and I will take out the two men manning the rear machine gun with suppressed sniper shots. Instead of trying to disable the machine gun with thrown grenades, I'll advance into their foxhole, if I can, and turn the machine gun on the bad guys. After that, I'll disable the machine gun. I'll remove the gun bolt, bend the spring rod and break the trigger. "

"That will certainly disable the gun, but keep it simple. Brice, don't risk your neck and get too ambitious. We need you. I just want these machine guns put out of action."

"I understand, Chet," said Brice.

"Good. Do it! Bobby, did you copy ?" asked Chet.

"Rodger, I copy. Out," said Bobby.

Brice turned to his partner, "Pete, we're taking headshots with our suppressed sniper rifles. You take the guy on the right, I'll get the one on the left."

"Gotcha! Geez this ain't at all like shooting elk. I feel a little queasy," said Pete.

"That's good. If you felt normal I'd be worried. If we nail both of our guys, I'm going to make a run for that gun. You'll cover me with your M-16, but don't fire any rounds unless you see I'm in danger or I point twice at a location. Once they hear you fire your M-16, our element of surprise is over," said Brice.

"Got it!" said Pete nervously. "Now, I know for certain I wasn't cutout to be a soldier. Killing folks isn't my cup of tea."

"Take deep breaths and relax. You'll be fine. Chet will give Bobby the command to fire, but hold your fire until I give you the command to shoot. We'll see if our targets make our shots a little easier."

"OK," gulped Pete.

Several moments later everyone heard Chet's preparatory command over their headsets, "Standby Bobby, fire on my count to three!"

Several seconds later, "One, two, three!"

Then, all hell broke loose. Though Chet and Al were approximately seventy yards away from Brice and Pete's position, and fifty yards away from Bobby's position, Pete thought the sounds of their exploding Hellhound rounds and the light machine gun was deafening.

The two terrorists manning the rear machine rose into a crouch, craning to see what was occurring forward of their machine gun position.

Brice whispered, "Fire!" They fired together. A cloud of red mist bloomed from the head of each target.

"Fuck!" groaned Pete, as he turned to his side and vomited into the trees.

"Cover me," said Brice as he bolted from their hidden position towards the rear machine gun nest.

Using his M-16 to clear his way through the smaller tree branches, Brice moved as quickly as he could over the thirty yards or so that separated him from the machine gun nest. He ran uphill over uneven undergrowth that was littered with dead trees and their limbs. It was slow going in his low cut running shoes. He tripped and fell several times before he jumped into the machine gun nest, landing next to one of the dead gunners who lay at the bottom of the foxhole in a puddle of thickening red blood. Blood splashed across his camouflage clothing. Though both gunners were dead, blood was still pouring from their shattered heads. The man on the gun had knocked the barrel of the machine gun skyward, at an awkward angle, as he slumped forward against the lip the foxhole. Brice rolled him next to his buddy as the pool of blood at the bottom of the foxhole began to spread. He then examined the layout of the machine gun nest. Beside the gun was a hard plastic box filled with belts of .30 caliber ammunition.

The slightest of smiles spread across Brice's face.

We'll see how these shitheads like being on the wrong end of a .30 caliber machine gun.

From his new vantage point, Brice turned his attention to the surrounding terrain. Below him, along the near side of the white tour bus, he recognized the small man that Dirdle greeted earlier as Ajani. The man appeared to be giving a pep talk to eight young terrorists. Brice raised himself ever so slightly from the machine gun nest to laterally reconnoiter across the slope towards the forward machine gun nest. He saw a scattered group of approximately ten men moving towards Chet's last known position. He could tell in an instant by their quiet, stealthy movements and hand signals that these were experienced fighters.

2:59 PM MDT (4:59 PM EDT)

He sank back to his knees and whispered over his radio, "Chet, I see approximately ten experienced hostiles moving towards your last known position. I've taken control of the rear machine gun, but cannot give you covering fire because there is a hillock with trees and boulders between you and me."

"We saw them coming and have moved uphill and forward of our original position. We took out the forward machine gun. We will attack the hostiles at our best opportunity," whispered Chet.

"Brice, Annie and I have visual contact on your position. There are eight to ten hostiles moving down hill in your general direction. They are difficult to see because of the trees. The nearest group of four hostiles is about fifty feet above you and headed directly towards you. I don't think they know you have possession of their machine gun. On your command, we can pin them down with Annie's sniper rifle and my light machine gun," said Bobby.

"Damn, three of them just popped up from the bushes ten feet behind you," blurted Pete through his headset. He immediately fired one well-aimed shot with his sniper rifle before dropping it and shouldering his M-16, which he fired on full automatic.

Annie simultaneously turned her sniper rifle towards the hostiles above Brice's position and snapped off several quick shots as well. In the meantime, Bobby began to pour hot lead into the same general area with his light machine gun. Annie's last shot hit one of the hostiles in the center of his forehead. Annie gasped as the man dropped like a stone.

The ground above Brice erupted with the impact of bullets. As he turned in the direction of the screams and shouts, a gangly young man dove through the heavy brush above him for the protection of the foxhole. The man's flying leap knocked Brice backwards, next to the two dead men who were lying in a pool of blood. The gangly man and Brice were sprawled face to face with Brice on the bottom. Brice blindly withdrew his Ka-bar knife from its sheath on his web belt and drove it through the man's throat. Warm blood and spittle from the dying man sprayed against

Brice's face with surprising force. It was like being sprayed with a garden hose at close range. He couldn't breathe. As he twisted the man's head to the side and gulped fresh air, he caught a glimpse of a second man sailing into the foxhole. He landed with a thud, a few feet away.

The second man may have seen Brice as he flew into the foxhole, but all that registered in the man's conscious mind was a pile of bleeding bodies, in a pool of blood, and an abandoned machine gun pointing awkwardly skyward. Hearing the distinctive death rattle of his teenage compatriot behind him, the second man assumed the young fighter had been shot in the throat. *No need to aid or comfort him,* thought the more experienced fighter, *the kid will be dead in seconds.* The experienced fighter wrapped both his hands around the machine gun's grip assembly and turned the gun's barrel towards the school buses.

With his Ka-bar knife still firmly gripped in one hand, Brice rolled the gangly man off his blood soaked body and slithered silently towards the back of the second man. With a lightning fast killing move, he grabbed the man's long hair with his free hand, violently jerked his head backwards and raked his Ka-bar across the man's exposed throat. More warm, sticky blood poured over him. Brice looked as if he'd been butchered.

Brice heard low voices of three to four more terrorists moving cautiously through the brush above him, just feet away. Rolling back into the tangle of bloody, dead or dying bodies that filled the bottom of the foxhole, he quickly pulled his last victim on top of him. With raised rifles, the terrorists crept to the side of the foxhole. The pile of bodies, the gurgling sound of Brice's last victim and the expanding pool of blood froze the group of inexperienced, teenage fighters in their tracks.

Eventually, the nearest teenager took one tentative step towards the foxhole and called kindly to his combat instructor, "Tariq, Tariq!"

The teenager moved closer to Tariq who lay face up, spread-eagled atop Brice. Tariq's eyes fluttered and his body convulsed involuntarily as a stream of hot thick, blood spat onto the chest of his curious student. The teenager jumped backwards and screamed. Tariq had expertly trained all of these teenagers during the past thirty days, but none of his training had prepared them for the bloody sight before them. Tariq's jerking body and his blood spurting throat wound unnerved all of them.

Brice lifted Tariq's arm, as if he were a puppeteer, and pointed it down the slope. He gurgled in his limited Arabic, "Gun jammed. Get him, the American. There is no power and no strength save in Allah."

The well-trained teenagers mechanically followed what they believed were Tariq's dying orders. When they began to race downhill, screaming for revenge against the American who was now behind them, Brice pushed Tariq to the side and knelt behind the machine gun. In two short machine gun bursts, he killed all four of Tariq's teenage students. Brice's element of surprise was over.

As Brice turned the machine gun towards the terrorist's white tour bus, he spoke over his headset, "Bobby, there are approximately eight hostiles behind the tour bus. I'm going to fire on them with the machine gun, which may drive them towards you. Get ready. After that I'm going to disable this gun and get the hell out of here. There is a lot of thick foliage around me. My visibility is really limited. Keep your eyes on my surroundings. I'll be the one who looks like he's wearing a red devil suit."

"I can cover you, Brice," said Annie. "Move directly west. Don't go up or down slope, you're surrounded. I can give you up slope cover."

"I can give you down slope cover though I think you just killed everyone down slope from you. I'll shoot at anything that moves," said Pete.

Chet chimed in, "Brice, we can't help you at all. We've got our hands full staying one step ahead of the bastards in our area."

The Marines and civilians would remember little of the next few minutes. Multiple firefights erupted simultaneously all over the hillside. Chet and Al sporadically engaged the ten hostiles that were after them. Bobby and the female bus drivers fired at the teenagers who were driven from behind the tour bus by Brice's final machine gun salvo. Seemingly out of thin air, one wave after another of wild-eyed teenagers charged their position. While this was occurring, Pete and Annie provided intermittent covering fire for Brice as he danced and darted away from several small groups of terrorists who were hot on his tail.

In the Situation Room, General Rexman had reestablished the conference call connection to Bobby's open satellite phone moments before the Marine's offensive jumped off. Annie's radio headset, which she removed before firing her sniper rifle, was also close enough to the satellite phone that all the conferees could hear the on-site communications and gunfire.

"Jesus H. Christ, it sounds like World War III," said the very worried president.

"I cannot believe what I'm hearing," said Rexman.

"Those are my 'kick ass' Marines," boasted the commandant. "Thank God you armed and trained them well OB."

"Yes, general. I don't know what to say. They're all doing a great job," said O'Brien, clearly shaken by the volume of gunfire.

Col. O'Brien, Lt. Col. Adair and Gunny Hammer Stephens were cloistered behind closed doors in the colonel's office at Camp Pendleton. None of them said a word as they sat, hunched over, in wooden chairs with their elbows pressed into their thighs and their hands holding their heads. The effect of the live satellite broadcast on these hard men was debilitating. Unconsciously, they each winced and groaned with the exchange of gunfire. During Brice's hand-to-hand combat in the machine gun nest, they alternately prayed and cheered aloud. They knew their brothers were outmanned and outgunned. If they could only hold a little longer until their Marine platoon from Elko, Nevada arrived. They'd done all they could. Now, it was simply a deadly waiting game.

3:27 PM MDT (5:27 PM EDT)

"Brice. Are you OK? Where are you?" asked Chet over his headset.

"I'm OK though I look like I've bled to death a couple of times over. I've almost returned to Pete's position," whispered Brice.

Pete heard Brice's quiet transmission as he turned and peered into the dark mass of trees behind him. He was used to hearing the careful footfalls of big game, but he hadn't heard a sound. A moment later, Brice emerged through the tangle of fallen trees and the color in Pete's faced drained. Though he had field dressed countless large game in his day, the bloodied sight of Brice caused him to recoil in horror.

"That bad!" said Brice.

Pete was lost for words. Finally, he spoke, "You add new meaning to blood bath. Geez! Every inch of you is covered in blood. You better clean your face and change those clothes before the kids see you or you'll scare them half to death."

"That's my plan. Thanks for your covering fire. On my way here, I spotted the terrorist's command post at that clearing near the top of the hillside. It's next to a portable satellite dish.

"By the way, you're completely hidden by this large mass of trees and limbs. These big tree trunks also give you some decent protection. I saw your crossfire down the centerline of the road. You nailed lots of terrorists. I'm going to link up with Chet and see about taking out that command post. Will you be OK holding this position by yourself?" asked Brice.

"Yeah! I'll be OK," said Pete stoically.

Brice emptied his pockets of M-16 magazine clips and placed them inside an open ammunition crate that Brice had initially lugged to their current position. The crate was now brimming with ammunition for both his rifles. Next, he unhooked the grenades that hung from his belt and placed them beside the crate.

"There is enough ammunition here to last me for a year. I'll bet there are 300-400 rounds in this crate," said Pete evenly.

"Nope! Closer to 1,000 rounds, but use your ammo judiciously. Keep your M-16 fire selector switch on semi-automatic that will give you three round bursts. Only go to full automatic if you're in extremis," said Brice matter of factly.

"I'll resupply myself on my way to Chet's position. Make every shot count. I don't know how long we'll have to hold out."

Pete nodded unconsciously and said solemnly, "You take care, Brice."

"You take care as well, buddy. You have to hold down this position or it will be the end of the line for all of us. Keep up the good work! You would have been a 'helluva' Marine," said Brice as he slapped Pete on the shoulder and headed towards the buses.

Thank goodness that kid is on our side, thought Pete as he watched the back of Brice's blood soaked shirt disappear into the fallen branches and tree trunks.

Alone and separated from the other defenders, Pete began to grasp the strategic implication of Brice's departing words, "end of the line for all of us." He felt like a lone defender, on an island, protecting over three hundred kids and thirty adults. *If I don't hold this position... oh, my God!* A tidal wave of fear washed over him and his body shook uncontrollably.

Pete battled his shakes for what seemed like ten minutes, but in reality was only a minute or two. Deep, slow breathing calmed his mind and eventually his shakes disappeared. He took stock of himself. He knew he was a damned good hunting guide who had survived a number of mishaps in the wilds of the Frank Church Wilderness, all of which could have become disastrous… running out of water, getting lost for a couple of days, breaking his arm and wrestling with a black bear. Further, in the last half hour, he had provided excellent cover for Brice during his attack and retreat from the machine gun nest.

His thoughts turned to the fighting spirit of the three Marines. There wasn't a smidgeon of fear amongst those boys. Even Bobby, who was nearly fully paralyzed, showed a lot of pluck. It was quite apparent that saving their own skin never crossed their minds. They did what was best for others, not what was best for them. His confidence in his abilities began to grow.

What would the terrorists try next? At least twenty of them lay dead, strewn across the road in front of him. Most of the dead hadn't gotten further than the road's white centerline. Their attempts to overrun the middle of the Marine's defenses had failed miserably. Suddenly, the past ravings of his revered high school football coach, David Harper, popped into his mind.

Pete had been a left tackle on the varsity team for three years. The coach loved him, partly because he was the biggest and strongest kid in the conference, but mainly because he dependably protected the blind side of the team's right handed, pass happy quarterback. Opposing teams spent hours designing all manner of stunts and blitzes to circumvent Pete's 'All State' blocking skills. If they succeeded in eluding him during the game and got their hands on his quarterback, they had a chance of winning.

I'm a left tackle again in a game of life or death. These bastards want to get their hands on over three hundred people.

Pete's understanding of his situation became crystal clear. The terrorists would next attempt to either circle around him or blitz his position. Circling wasn't an option because of the sheer vertical walls and the piles of trees. Thus, it would be a blitz. And, it wouldn't be just one or two terrorists, it would be their entire fucking outfit! It was the reason Brice suggested he switch his fire selector on his M-16 to full automatic if he were in "extremis." He also realized that there was no exit strategy and no lesser of two evil alternatives. Simply put, his only option was to hold his position until he ran out of ammo or died.

He took a deep breath and reached for one of the grenades that Brice had left behind. He moved it closer to his throwing arm. A moment later, he reached for another grenade.

I can do this. I'm part of a team. I will follow the Marine's example and will hold my position. Semper fidelis!

Once Brice reached the last school bus, he stripped down to his skivvies. A river of blood streamed from his pile of clothes. *Yup! That would have scared the kids.* He grabbed his blood stained boots, cell phone and sprinted to Bobby's command post.

Five minutes later, he was dressed in a clean set of camouflage clothes and sitting on the roadbed retying his boots.

3:42 PM MDT (5:42 PM EDT)

Kathy rested her shotgun against the timber bunker and spoke to her shooting partner, "Lynne, let me know if the bad guys start stirring. I've got to clean up our fearless leader."

Lynne turned to Brice and said wryly, "Whooee! He needs a cleaning."

With a bottle of water, Kathy wetted a cloth and approached Brice.

"If I had a mirror, Honey, the reflection of your mug would break it. You are a sight!" said Kathy as she began to wipe blood from Brice's face and hair with the wet cloth. The more she scrubbed, the more caked blood she found. "I'm getting the 'heebie-jeebies ' just cleaning you up." After a final swipe of her wash cloth across Brice's face, she pinched his cheek with motherly affection and said, "Keep that sweet face of yours clean, young man."

"Yes ma'am," answered Brice respectfully, as he shook his head in amazement.

Two amazing ladies! Both calm and collected. Not an ounce of fear in either of them. We're in the middle of a "do or die" shoot out and they find time to clean me up and give me a pinch on the cheek. What a pair! thought Brice.

Brice low crawled under the third school bus until he was next to Bobby. "Are you and Annie holding up OK?"

"We're OK! How about you? You gave us quite a scare in that machine gun nest!" said Bobby.

"I'm good. Thank God, I remembered my Arabic. That hillside is crawling with terrorists. There are clearly more than sixty to seventy! I think that white tour bus delivered more than one busload of terrorists to this location. We've got to destroy their command and control or we're going to lose a war of attrition.

"I think I've seen their leader in that small clearing at the top of the hill, next to those two fallen trees," continued Brice as he pointed to the hilltop. "I've caught a glimpse of several antennas and a portable satellite dish up there as well. My guess is that is their command post. I'm going to get together with Chet to discuss a plan of attack. I think our best line of attack will be around their eastern flank and up that hillside to their command post," said Brice.

"Good idea! We'll keep a sharp eye out for hostiles in your general area," said Bobby.

Brice turned on his side and called quietly to the two ladies, "Kathy and Lynne, I'd like you to hear my revised standing orders."

Both women kneeled into a crouched position behind the bus.

Brice addressed Bobby and the three civilians, "Because our defenses are spread thin and it looks like there are more terrorists than we originally estimated, I've decided to slightly modify my plans for a retreat. I hope it doesn't come to this, but if it does, there can't be any doubt in anyone's mind on how I want a retreat to occur.

"If it looks like the terrorists are going to overrun this center position, I'd like all four of you to withdraw below the retaining wall and chuck as many frag and smoke grenades as possible at the terrorists. Meanwhile, explain to the teachers that you'll provide suppressing fire as they help the school kids make a run for the tree line a half-mile to our rear. Instruct the kids to spread out as much as possible and to run in zig-zag patterns. Emphasize that under no circumstance are they to bunch up into groups. The terrorists .30 caliber machine guns are out of action so our chances of making it to the woods are better than they were an hour ago. Is everyone clear on this?"

"What about Bobby? He can't run," said Annie grimly.

"I'll carry Bobby," said Brice.

"And… if you're not present?" pressed Annie.

Brice looked into his best friends eyes. An unspoken form of understanding passed between them as they each nodded in agreement.

The kids' safety is our highest priority.

After several long moments, Bobby casually said, "No sweat! I'll have Pete or Al help me."

Bobby's lighthearted response didn't fool Kathy, Lynne or Annie. They each fought back their tears.

"God bless all of you," said Brice as he low crawled out from underneath the bus and for the second time that afternoon crammed extra ammunition into every available pocket and hung hand grenades from every existing opening on his pistol belt.

After Brice left, Bobby added a few more instructions to his team.

"Kathy and Lynne, the terrorist's charges in small groups aren't working. It's just a matter of time before we face larger groups. Once the fighting gets hot and heavy, you won't have time to reload. I recommend you recruit someone to assist you in reloading your shotguns. Also, change your firing positions once in awhile. If you feel like the terrorists are zeroing in on your stationary position… move! Moving around behind the buses also gives the terrorists the impression that there are more than four of us. Annie, that goes for you as well.

"If it looks like the terrorists are getting close to a breakthrough, Annie you must order those farm boys to start chucking frag grenades. Just before the kids make a run for the woods, have them switch to the smoke grenades. They should throw or roll them over, under or around the buses. Hopefully, that will provide some screening cover during the retreat.

"Lastly, each of you should take a rifle and ammo with you when you follow the kids. Your suppressing fire will help protect the kids and also discourage the bastards from chasing them down.

"It's been my privilege fighting beside all of you," said Bobby sincerely.

3:52 PM MDT (5:52 PM EDT)

Kathy and Lynne acknowledged Bobby's instructions somberly and returned to their post between the second and third buses. They briefly discussed and agreed upon the recruitment of two middle-aged female teachers as helpers to reload their automatic shotguns. Both helpers were occasional duck hunters.

Annie dropped down to the base of the retaining wall and waved the teachers to her side. She passed on to them Brice and Bobby's instructions for a prospective retreat.

When she returned to Bobby's side, her head fell atop her folded arms and she began to weep.

"You've been a tigress, Annie. I don't think a breakthrough will occur, but we should have a plan in place in case it does," said Bobby soothingly.

Bobby's satellite phone pinged.

"Gunny Miller, Major Daniels, this is Lt. Col. Adair at Camp Pendleton. Do you copy?"

"Yes, Colonel. I hear you loud and clear. This is Corporal Bobby Ridger. The gunny and Major Daniels are away from the phone. They are working on a plan to take out the terrorist leader and destroy his command post."

"That's a good idea. Now, pass this word at your discretion. We have a platoon of Marines from the 3/5 at Camp Pendleton that is airborne and inbound to your location on four Air Force Pave Hawk helicopters. The platoon is fully armed and the Pave Hawks have mini guns," said Adair.

"Camp Pendleton? They'll never get here in time!" said Bobby abruptly.

"They are coming from Elko, Nevada. They were involved in a joint, simulated desert exercise with the Air Force. Their estimated time of arrival is at best ninety minutes from now. All the helos are flying at top speed. How do you recommend we insert the Marines when they arrive? There are approximately ten men in each helo?"

Bobby thought for several moments. Could they hold on for ninety more minutes? It seemed like they were facing over one hundred terrorists. They'd been attacked by wave after wave of drugged up teenagers. If they could hold on, it would be a miracle.

"Land all the helos on the friendly sides of the fallen tree barrier, two fore and two aft of our buses. But, make sure the helos land at least 100 yards away from the barriers. I don't want them inserting our boys into a hot landing zone. I will direct them from there, if I can.

"However, if the helos see red smoke around the buses or in our path of our retreat, which is a gently sloping, clear plain behind us, land two helos in an open area between the kids and the buses and one each on the friendly side of the pile of trees," said Bobby.

"I copy corporal," said Adair.

"Also, ensure that the arriving Marines have the capability to direct close air ground support with the helo's in case my communications are down."

Bobby heard a background thump over the phone. It was Hammer putting his fist through the plasterboard wall in O'Brien's office.

Adair turned to Hammer and silenced him by placing his index finger to his lips. Hammer swore silently as he massaged his bloody fist. O'Brien sadly shook his head from side to side. They all knew it wouldn't be Bobby's communications that went down.

"Will do corporal? Anything else?" asked Adair.

"Yes, sir. What company is this 3/5 platoon from?"

"They are the 2nd platoon of Lima Company," responded the major.

"You're kidding, right?"

"Absolutely not. Why do you ask?"

"You don't know?"

"Know what?"

"That's Major Daniels former rifle company and Miller was their gunnery sergeant up until a couple of weeks ago. I was in that platoon when I was injured in Fallujah!"

"Christ! I never stopped to think about that. You're right."

"Well, send those Darkhorse boys our best wishes. We can hardly wait to see their smiling faces. I'll keep this line open," said Bobby.

"Good luck, corporal!"

CHAPTER 21
KIDNAPPED

Molly and Penny casually window-shopped as they strolled, arm in arm, along Main Street in Dennis. Both girls wore tight jeans and colorful tank tops. The late afternoon sunshine warmed Molly's exposed arms and shoulders. Her red hair fell loosely on her shoulders. Penny's curly brown hair framed her beautiful doll-like face.

While the two girls were gazing through the window of a boutique, Molly noticed longtime family friends and neighbors approach. They owned a ranch several miles south of the Ridger's. The slightly hunched husband, who was spare in build and in his late eighties, pulled his wife to his side as he slowed to a stop beside Molly and Penny.

He tipped his Stetson hat, smiled and gave a slight bow to the two girls as he said, with a touch of Western charm in his eye, "Good afternoon, Molly. You and your friend have certainly brightened the street of our fine town this afternoon. I hope you beautiful ladies are enjoying the sunshine and a little shopping."

"We are Mr. and Mrs. Cartwright. You both look very well. Are you doing a little shopping as well?" said Molly as she returned his smile.

Mrs. Cartwright interjected sourly, "Herman's eyes and hands aren't what they used to be. He can't tie flies anymore so we had to buy several salmon flies at Joe's fly shop. The salmon fly hatch has arrived. We're on our way to the Madison River for some long overdue fly fishing." Thrift and fly fishing were clearly important to Mrs. Cartwright.

"I was fly fishing at dusk last night and lost a twenty inch brown. He slipped off my barbless hook as I tried to net him. The salmon flies are everywhere and the trout are really feasting on them. You should have good fishing," said Molly.

"Thanks Molly. Have either of you comely lasses visited the new ladies shop… " began Mr. Cartwright, when his wife took his elbow and began to pull him towards their pickup that was parked a few cars away.

"Come on, Herman. That's enough of your 'comely' lines. I don't want to fish in the dark. Sorry, Molly," said Mrs. Cartwright, as she waved goodbye over her shoulder.

"Good luck!" said Molly as she waved back. Turning to Penny, she added, "'Comely lasses!' I think Mr. Cartwright was quite the ladies man in his day."

"Possibly, but it's obvious who rules that roost now. I like the way Mrs. Cartwright's steered Herman around. I'll remember that the next time I'm on a date," said Penny roguishly.

Molly bumped Penny with her hip and said, "You already steer them around. I think you could probably teach her a few new tricks. You're always thinking about boys!"

"Men! Boys are in high school, men are in college. And, what else is there to think about? We're on summer break!"

Molly smiled at Penny, took a deep breath of the clean Montana air and exhaled slowly. She was thoroughly enjoying this rare opportunity to leisurely pass the time away with her best friend. Her brother was being driven to Sheridan with his Marine Corps buddy, Brice Miller, and her dad was enjoying his favorite pastime, a solo horseback ride around the outer reaches of their ranch.

"How does a cup of tea sound before this lovely day ends?" asked Molly, as she pointed to a coffee shop across the street with several vacant sidewalk tables.

"Perfect!" answered Penny.

A half block behind them a Dennis police cruiser was parked in a red "No Parking" zone. Skip Dower was watching both girls intently. He was relishing a very short and temporary reprieve. His official suspension from the police force wouldn't take effect until a formal hearing occurred. In the meantime, the bitches had gotten word to the mayor that he was hassling them after school. And, he'd received further bad news from his contact in the State Highway Patrol. One of the girls had provided the state with information regarding his alleged rape of a waitress from West Yellowstone. The State Highway Patrol was looking into the matter and had begun a formal investigation. His blood began to boil when he thought of that expensive affair. $5,000 of his hard earned money was supposed to make that matter disappear. *How the hell did those bitches know about that?*

His loins throbbed in anticipation of the rough, physical questioning he had in store for them later that day. He'd get answers and more.

The ring of his cell phone interrupted his lewd and sadistic feelings. The screen on his cell phone indicated the caller was his father. The old man was following up on his inspection of the Leone lodge. He'd get to the lodge, but not without the bitches. He pushed a button on the side of cell phone and sent his father's call to voicemail.

Molly and Penny sat leisurely at an outdoor table, in the sunshine, as they sipped tea and shared a pastry. After twenty minutes or so of idle chitchat, they both enjoyed a second cup of tea and reclined in their chairs so they could sun themselves in the last of the afternoon's sunshine. Both girls appeared to be napping comfortably when a young family interrupted their peaceful reverie. A screaming baby and chair legs scraping over the sidewalk convinced both girls that it was time to leave. They calmly gathered their purses and jackets, paid their bill and slowly strolled back to Penny's pickup.

It seemed to Skip that the girls spent an eternity at that damn coffee shop. While they unhurriedly enjoyed themselves, Skip Dower's inner demons were screaming. By the time the girls settled themselves in Penny's pickup, his pent up rage was such that he thought his head would explode.

Less than a minute after Penny cautiously drove her pickup over the Madison River, heading south out of town, Skip raced his police cruiser to within a foot of her rear bumper. He turned on both his claxon horn and flashing bright lights. A moment later, over his bullhorn, he ordered

Penny to turn off the road into the Madison River drift boat launch area 100 yards ahead. His predatory rage was bursting at the seams.

"Vehicle inspection!" he blared over the bullhorn.

"Is that Skip Dower?" said Penny anxiously.

Molly turned in her seat and looked intently at the driver of the cruiser, "Yes, it is though I think he's trying to disguise himself. He's pulled a baseball hat down to his eyes and is sitting low in the drivers seat."

"That's not good. I thought he was suspended," said Penny uneasily.

"So did I. I don't like the idea of pulling into this launch area. You can't see it from the road and all the drift boat fishermen are still on the river. Why don't you pull over on the shoulder of the road," suggested Molly nervously.

As Penny pulled onto the shoulder of the road and began to slow, the cruiser's reinforced front bumper slammed into her rear bumper.

"Asshole," screamed Penny.

"This is a vehicle inspection. Pull into the launch area or you will be arrested for a safety violation," barked Skip over his bullhorn.

"Shit! I don't like this. I'm calling my dad," said Molly.

Molly hit the speed dial number for her dad's cell phone. There was no answer and she was directed into his voicemail.

"Damn, he's probably still out riding on the ranch. There is no cell phone reception on the remote parts of the property," said Molly.

When she heard the beep on her dad's voice mailbox, Molly began speaking quickly, "Dad it's 4:30 PM. Skip Dower is behind Penny's truck in his police cruiser. His lights are flashing and he just rammed her pickup. He's yelling at us with his bullhorn. He ordered Penny to turn into the Barney boat launch area for a vehicle inspection. I'm going to leave this call open so you can hear what he says."

"Good idea, Molly," said Penny.

Molly leaned towards the truck's dashboard and slid out the empty ashtray. She carefully placed the open cell phone in the ashtray and hid it with a crumpled Kleenex from her pocket.

A minute later, Penny rolled her truck to a stop close to the river. It was the most visible portion of the gravel parking lot.

"Don't put the truck in 'Park.' Simply come to a stop with your foot on the brake," suggested Molly.

Skip brought his police cruiser to a fast, skidding stop beside them. He quickly exited his cruiser, slammed his door shut and marched towards Penny's open drivers window. His handed rested menacingly on his holstered revolver.

His usual dull, pasty face was red and warped with rage. "Turn off the engine and exit your vehicle," he barked.

"What's this about Skip Dower?" said Molly loudly.

"Vehicle inspection. Turn off the engine," he ordered again.

"I just had this truck car serviced last week. All my lights and brakes are working fine," said Penny firmly.

Penny's confident reply fueled Skip's fury.

Damn bitches are always disrespectful.

"I saw Molly give a plastic bag of white powder to a husband and wife on Main Street about an hour and half ago. Turn off the engine and get out of the car. I have probable cause to search this vehicle."

"That couple was the Cartwrights. They're eighty years old and I didn't slip them anything. We're leaving Skip. You can get a search warrant if you like, but we're going back to my ranch. You're harassing us again. I'm sure my dad would like to hear the details of this phony baloney stop. Anyways, you've been suspended. We're leaving," said Molly resolutely.

Penny was unsure of what to do next and turned towards Molly. In her moment of indecision, Skip lunged through Penny's open window and reached for her ignition key. Penny was knocked to the side and her foot slipped off the brake pedal. Her truck began to roll forward as it dragged Skip, who was half in and half out of her pickup, across the parking lot. In Skip's attempt to turn off Penny's truck, he grabbed the automatic gearshift in the center console to keep from being thrown from the truck. As he pushed the gearshift into 'Park,' the truck jerked to a stop and Molly's hidden cell phone popped out of the ashtray onto the console.

Skip stared at the face of the cell phone in disbelief. The contacts name on the face of the cell phone read 'Dad' and the damn digital time reader was still advancing. It was an ongoing, open call.

"Bitches," he hollered as he clutched the phone and pulled his upper torso out of the cab of the truck. He closed the phone's clamshell face and dropped the phone to the gravel parking lot. An instant later, the heel of his black leather boot smashed the phone to pieces.

Skip's shouts, the grinding of gears and the skidding stop of the truck over the gravel parking lot caught the attention of a hidden, nearby fly fishermen. The fisherman, who had been lost in thought as he patiently stalked a large rainbow trout, peaked through the thick river brush to view the commotion in the parking lot behind him.

The fisherman watched incredulously as an overweight policeman drew his revolver and, at gunpoint, ordered two teenage girls out of a pickup truck.

"Go to hell, Skip Dower," screamed Molly as he snapped handcuffs onto her wrists.

Dower cuffed Penny and slapped duct tape over both girls' mouths. He roughly shoved both of them onto the back seat floor of his cruiser. From the trunk of his cruiser, he withdrew a blue plastic tarp that he draped over them.

Once behind the wheel of his cruiser, the highly agitated and soon to be "ex-cop" stomped his gas pedal to the floor. His churning, burning tires threw gravel twenty-five yards into the river and the brush that hid the fisherman.

"Son of a bitch! That wasn't an arrest. That was a fucking kidnapping at gunpoint by Skip Dower," said the fisherman to himself. He opened his cell phone and speed dialed the phone number of the town's judge and his longtime fishing buddy, Bill Bramley.

Twenty minutes later Skip parked his cruiser near the front door of Nick Leone's remote lodge. There was no sign of the Muslims. He briskly skipped up the front steps of the broad, covered porch and unlocked the front door. His cell phone's camera clicked steadily as he went from room to room taking digital pictures of the interior of the five-bedroom lodge. The lodge was spotless. Exiting through the kitchen's back door, he walked fifty yards to the large outbuilding.

The outbuilding was basically a modern conference center. Numerous pairs of exterior French double doors surrounded an approximately 3,000 square foot open floor plan. The eight-foot tall windows, high ceiling supported with rough-hewn wooden beams and a distressed hardwood floor gave the space a woodsy, natural feel. In one corner of the building were bathrooms and showers suitable for a professional sports team. The opposite ng corner of the building was built out with an industrial sized kitchen. The delivery door for the kitchen was a 12'X12' warehouse door on rollers that could be raised and lowered electronically.

Behind the outbuilding, the Muslims had set up their shooting range. No one, other than Brice and Molly during their wolf hunt, had heard any of the thousands of shots fired at the range. The prevailing westerly winds dispersed the majority of the gunfire noise up the narrow valley eastward towards the rugged backcountry and the Gallatin River twenty miles away. Four miles west of the lodge was the busy U.S. Route 287 that ran in a north-south direction. The outbuilding, lodge, heavily wooded terrain and two high hills, which caused the deeply rutted dirt access road to switchback on itself, blocked all gunfire noise to those who were traveling on U.S. Route 287.

The last time Skip was here there were shell casings everywhere and numerous crates filled with M-16's and AK-47's. He carefully walked the improvised shooting range and found just a couple of discarded shell casings. From his limited police experience, he knew that only those with bad intentions would wipe down and clean a place so thoroughly. He didn't know what the Muslims were up to, nor did he care. He sent the digital pictures to the Dandy along with a brief note that confirmed that the lodge and grounds had been completely cleaned and that the Muslims had left the site.

He returned his father's earlier cell phone call and explained that the lodge was clean. And, that he'd sent the digital pictures of the cleanup to the Dandy. In closing, he told his dad that there was plenty of leftover booze as well as two young women available for his pleasure.

Skip knew he needn't say more. Free booze and sex with young girls would motivate the old man. Fred told his son he'd get to the lodge in record time, twenty-minutes at most. Had Fred been more in control of his cravings and desires, he would have queried his son further about the girls. But, such questions never entered his mind.

Skip slipped his cellphone into his pocket and headed back to his police cruiser. A chilling, grisly smile crossed his face as he visualized the pleasures he would soon enjoy with the two defenseless girls.

CHAPTER 22
THE RETREAT

During the last ninety minutes, the three Marines and five civilians bravely held their fragile, but fading, school bus stronghold. All three Marines knew they were fighting more than the intelligence estimate of seventy terrorists. Twenty-five terrorists lay dead on the road and Brice and Chet's teams had killed or wounded at least that many during their hillside battles. Despite those body counts, the incoming volume of gunfire they were receiving was increasing. And, it was inexorably taking its toll on the defenders. *Shit, that white tour bus must have delivered two busloads of terrorists. We're fighting at least one hundred dickheads,* thought Chet during a break in the action.

Kathy and Lynne borrowed Bobby's and Annie's M-16's when the barrel of their shotguns became overheated. During one skirmish, both women began trading shots with three separate terrorist sharpshooters spread across the hillside.

"Darn Kathy, we've got to organize ourselves. We're just taking pot shots at those guys as they scamper around that hillside. How about we focus on one at a time?" asked Lynne.

"I like that. Let's get that skinny one on our far right. His shots are becoming a bother," said Kathy.

"Yup, he's a pest. He's been moving from tree to tree, all to his left. I'll pepper the tree he's behind and you nail him when he moves to that next tree."

"I like it, Lynnie. On my count to three, you fire at that tree and I'll bag the devil when he makes his move."

The plan worked perfectly and the ladies fists were coming together for a celebratory fist bump when a distant shot rang out and Kathy was flung backwards off her feet.

Lynne dropped her M-16 and rushed to her side. From the amount of blood that was gushing out of the hole in her left breast, she knew the terrorist's shot had likely ripped through or near her heart. Lynne had shot enough deer and elk to recognize the sight of a killing heart shot. Waves of grief and sadness overwhelmed her. Her best friend had only seconds of life remaining.

Kathy feebly raised her right hand and said, "Take my hand. I'm cold." A moment later, she uttered her last words, "I'll miss you, Lynnie."

Lynne held her head in her hands and cried like a baby. After a time, Annie knelt beside Lynne and wrapped her in her arms.

"She was a warrior. I know she was your best friend. Can you carry on?" asked Annie gently.

Taking several deep breaths before she responded, Lynne finally said sniffling, "Yes, I can. Kathy wouldn't expect anything less from me."

Before Annie returned to Bobby's position, she reverently placed a spare camouflage jacket over Kathy's body.

From Pete and Al's hidden positions in the felled trees, their accurate crossfire had been instrumental in thwarting one terrorist frontal attack after another. But, Bobby knew, from their last radio report, twenty minutes earlier, that they were each running low on ammunition. Compounding his concerns was the fact that the terrorist's had pinpointed their hidden firing positions. A firestorm of relentless terrorist gunfire was pounding their positions and literally turning their protective tree trunks into match sticks. Now, neither of them were returning any of the enemy gunfire or updating Bobby with their status. As a consequence, Bobby rightly feared the worse. If his flanks were compromised, Bobby knew they couldn't protect the kids.

Low levels of ammunition were also a problem for Annie, Lynne and him. His grenade launcher was completely out of ammunition and Lynne's shotgun was down to its last fifty rounds. The other issue that greatly concerned him was the breakdown in communications. Annie's headset simply stopped working and his headset had just experienced a crucial malfunction. His transmit function died. He could hear Brice and Chet, but they couldn't hear him.

When Annie returned to Bobby's side, after comforting Lynne, he turned his head towards her and began, "We better get the kids ready for a run to the woods. You know what to... "

Before he could complete his sentence, a terrorist grenade blew away a portion of the rear end of the bus that they were hiding under. A razor sharp piece of shrapnel ripped open a six-inch gash across his scalp. Bobby collapsed unconscious as blood poured from his head wound. Fortunately for Bobby, Annie had been trained by the Cody school district in first aid. She quickly grabbed one of the first aid kits and snapped open the plastic box. Grabbing the first aid items she would need, she expertly swabbed his gash clean and sprinkled "QuickClot" over his wound. Next, she applied several layers of sterile medical gauze atop the "QuickClot" which she held in place with several head wraps of medical tape. As Annie tore the last wrap of medical tape from it's roll, Bobby groaned as he began to regain consciousness. After a minute or so, his eyes became clearer and he mumbled a few words, but he was still woozy and not completely coherent. At the very least, she knew he had suffered a concussion and perhaps even a skull fracture. His ability to provide sound military advice for the time being was over.

"I'm going to get the kids ready for a retreat? Are you OK?" asked Annie anxiously.

"Retreat, huh! Retreat. Yes. Let me know when you go!" said Bobby weakly as smoke from the burning bus caused him to cough.

5:33 PM MDT (7:33 PM EDT)

Before Annie crawled out for under the burning bus, she slid the timbers that protected her firing position to Bobby's front. Once they were in place, she scrambled to the teachers who were gathered together below the retaining wall.

"Get the kids ready for a run to the woods and remind them not to bunch up. It won't be long before I give you the word to retreat," said Annie.

She turned her attention to the three boys who were standing beside an open crate of grenades thirty feet away. They stood stock still with their arms glued to their sides. She'd forgotten how large the boys were. The shortest boy was at least two inches taller than her and they all easily outweighed her by twenty to thirty pounds. It was apparent that they were terrified.

She hurried to their side, grabbed a fragmentary grenade, pulled out the pin and held her hand firmly against the grenade's spoon.

"Boys, I know Bobby showed you before how these grenades work, but let's review. This is what is commonly called a frag grenade. You have to pull the thin pin all the way out, like I just did. After that you must... I repeat *must*... hold this lever on the side of the grenade *down*... it's called the 'spoon.' When you throw the grenade the spoon pops open and the grenade is activated. It will blow up four to five seconds later."

Annie barked, "Everyone!" Lynne, the teachers and all the kids looked in her direction. With both hands, she signaled that she was going to throw the grenade and they should take cover. When they were all safely sheltered, she hurled the grenade over the nearest bus. She crouched below the retaining wall and a few seconds later a deafening explosion sent shrapnel tearing into the sides of the terrorist's white bus and their own school buses.

Straightening herself, she said, "Got it!"

The boys inched out of their crouched positions and stood stiffly, still frozen with fear. One boy had tears streaming down his cheeks. Annie knew there wasn't time for "hand-holding." She had to eliminate their paralysis. *Something forceful and electrifying*, she thought. She wound up like a baseball pitcher and slapped the crying boy as hard as she could. He nearly fell over. His wide-eyed friends were stunned.

Holy shit! Miss Youngblood has gone nuts, thought his two friends?

Annie moved to the crying boy and hugged him. Whispering into his ear, she said, "You can do this. You're strong." Turning to the other two boys, she pulled them to her side. With a hand on each of their shoulders, she gave them an encouraging squeeze and said, "Men. I know you're scared. I'm scared too, but we've got a job to do. We have to protect your classmates and teachers. You have brothers who are in the military. They'll be proud of you and they'll tell their friends how brave you were today." Her pep talk and the physical act of touching them helped the boys relax. Gradually, their racing hearts calmed and a sense of commitment replaced their paralyzing fear.

When that familiar look of Wyoming grit returned to their faces, Annie continued, "Very soon, I'll tell you to throw the 'frags.' Throw every one until the box is empty. After that, start chucking those smoke grenades. They're in the shape of a Coca Cola can," said Annie, as she pointed to an open wooden crate a few feet away. "Don't throw or roll them where Bobby Ridger is hiding, which is below the engine block of the third bus. Lastly, take one red smoke grenade from that furthest small box when you run for the woods. The red smoke grenade has a red lid. When the helicopters arrive to rescue us, throw the grenade into a clearing near you. That will indicate to the helicopter pilot where you are. Any questions?"

"Rescue? No one told us about that!"

"Yes, a platoon of Marines is on their way. They should arrive by helicopter any minute," lied Annie. She hoped that would reassure her young fighters. "Any questions?" she asked.

The boys answered in unison, "No, Miss Youngblood."

"Men, I know we can all count on you."

Annie knew when and how to emotionally connect with 6th graders. Her continued reference to the boys as men was inexplicably building their growing level of confidence.

Returning to the timber bunker, Annie dropped into a crouch beside Lynne. Dried tears streaked Lynne's grief-stricken face and her hair looked as if it had never been combed.

"How is your shoulder feeling?" asked Annie.

"I can't feel either one. There numb," said Lynne.

"Are you OK covering the kids during a retreat?"

"Yup. I'll use the M-16 for that."

"I'm going to give the signal to retreat shortly. I'm sorry about Kathy. I know the two of you were close," said Annie.

"Thanks. I really can't think about her now. I have work to do," said Lynne wearily. Several moments later she continued, "I've gone to church every Sunday of my life. I've prayed and promised never to take another person's life. Yet, at this time, my entire being is focused on killing these animals that are trying to kill my kids. I just never thought... this blood-lust... this hatred, could possess me like this."

"You're doing a great job," said Annie simply, as she gave Lynne a comforting hug.

She noticed that one of Kathy's fully loaded shotguns lay a few feet away. She grabbed it and said to Lynne, "I'm going to leave this shotgun with Bobby."

Lynne nodded with pained understanding.

5:38 PM MDT (7:38 PM EDT)

After crawling to Bobby's side, she set the shotgun on "Full Automatic'" and placed it within his easy reach. She gingerly replaced his headset over his bandaged head and kissed him sweetly on his cheek.

"Lynne and I are going to cover the kids' retreat. We've got a date next week. Don't stand me up."

His eyes fluttered as he gave her a weak smile and mumbled incoherently.

She dragged her sniper rifle with her as she crawled out from under the smoking bus for the last time. Standing, she gazed indifferently at the depleted pile of weapons and ammunition that lay on the tarp. Her eyes came to rest on the last remaining Glock pistol, holstered in a green nylon cartridge belt. Without a second thought, she strapped the belt around her waist and checked the Glock. The magazine was full and she chambered a round.

Moving back to the timber bunker, Annie carefully searched the hillside with her binoculars for Brice and Chet. There was no sign of them. Neither one had called in their status in the last hour. She and Lynne were the only defenders standing.

Better to retreat now, with a lull in the action, decided Annie.

She was about to tell Lynne that it was time to retreat when she heard a soft voice. *Was that Bobby speaking? Had he regained consciousness or was she hearing the semi-conscious ramblings of a concussed Marine?* She strained to hear him. He was speaking coherently to someone over the satellite phone.

"Wait! Wait! Yes sir, I see them. They're by the stone ledge, near the top of the hill. There are lots of trees and bushes, but I can see Chet clearly, he's in the open. Brice is behind him partially hidden by some trees. They're approaching a man lying against a log with a white flag fluttering near him. That's their command post. That's their leader. He's been directing their attack. Where's Annie?" muttered Bobby.

He paused, apparently listening to a question from the other party on the call.

A moment later, he replied, "Sir. I can hear them on my headset, but they can't hear me. My transmit function is busted. All I hear is them moving through the brush."

Bobby's voice had strengthened and Annie could now hear him clearly. She shifted her binoculars to the location he'd described. She first acquired Chet, then Brice, who was ten yards behind him and off to the side. Next, she swept her binoculars to the treetops nearest them. The leaves on the trees were stirring slightly in an eastward direction. The wind was at most 3-4 MPH. She set her binoculars on the timbers and shaded her eyes as she focused on the target with her naked eye. She estimated the range to be around 300 yards, perhaps a little more. She snatched her sniper rifle sniper rifle, pulled down the rifle's bipod and set it on the top timber. As she centered her scope's mil dots on the head of the man lying against the log, her range finder indicated a range to the target of 325 yards. Her naked eye range estimate was off by approximately 8%. *Not bad, especially for a steep, uphill target like this*, she thought.

Her gloating lasted only an instant, before she made a few minor adjustments to her scope for the uphill ordnance drop of her 200-grain bullets and the light wind. As she steadied her aim on the man's head, she suddenly realized her target was lifeless. The man was dead. "Son of a bitch," she whispered to herself.

Peering through her scope, she searched for the terrorist leader. There was no sign of him until he suddenly stepped out from behind several large bushes, which were directly in front of Chet. Chet raised his rifle towards the terrorist, but not fast enough. From twenty feet away, the terrorist fired a shot from his pistol into Chet's lower body. She watched in horror as Chet slowly sank to the ground. Before he reached the ground, the terrorist raced to his side and aimed his pistol at his head. The terrorist barked an order of some kind to Brice that caused him to reluctantly lower his rifle. The terrorist tossed Chet's rifle aside and ominously advanced towards Brice with his pistol aimed, at arms length, towards Brice's chest.

Bobby's nearby comments into the satellite phone compounded her dread, "The man on the ground was a decoy. He was dead. Their leader came out of the bushes in front of Chet and got the drop on them. Major Daniels tried to shoot him, but the bastard shot him. The major is down!" cried Bobby.

Annie forced all her senses to focus on the terrorist. She acquired him in her scope for an instant before he passed behind heavy brush and turned to the side to avoid a dead tree trunk. When the terrorist stopped, five feet from Brice, an intervening tree limb with a thick canopy of leaves obscured much of his body. Brice, however, was clearly visible. His face was red with anger.

With the tree limb in Annie's line of fire, there was no way she could take a kill shot at the terrorist's head. At best, she would wound him, leaving him alive to shoot Brice. Without conscious thought, Annie swiftly lifted her sniper rifle off the timber bunker, collapsed the rifle's bipod and raced up the nearby steps of the third school bus. All the windows in the bus had been shot out. She immediately kneeled behind the drivers seat and rested her rifle atop the driver's seatback. She prayed that she would have a clear view of the terrorist's head from her new firing position.

As Annie was searching for her target with her scope, she again became conscious of Bobby's live phone reports, just feet below her.

"Yes, general! Let's see. Their leader is yelling at Brice. I can hear him over Brice's headset. He's demanding that the kids surrender and come out from behind the buses," said Bobby.

In the meantime, Annie had acquired Brice in her scope and could lip-read his response to the terrorist's demand, "Never asshole!"

Shifting her aim a fraction to the side, her prayers were answered when the terrorist's body came into full view. As she carefully adjusted the scope's magnification so the terrorist's head was perfectly centered between the cross hairs of her scope, the bastard began to raise his pistol towards Brice's head. *Easy, easy, breathe deeply!* Calmly, she exhaled her breath and squeezed the trigger of her rifle. A millisecond after her rifle fired, she heard a distant, second shot.

The kick from Annie's rifle shot knocked her rifle to the side of the curved seatback. Her visual lock on her target was momentarily lost. Though she quickly re-sighted her rifle, there was no sign of her target. The bastard was in her sights one second and gone the next!

"Damn trees, damn bushes," she said aloud as she swung her rifle from side to side searching for her target through her riflescope. Neither the terrorist nor Brice was visible. Finally, she acquired Brice and her stomach heaved. He was on his knees swaying drunkenly, trying to keep his balance. A moment later, his arms flopped loosely in the air and he crashed to the ground. Her shot had missed and the terrorist had shot Brice at point-blank range.

Oh, God no! I missed and that bastard shot Brice. Brice and the major are dead. It's all my fault!

In a state of shock, Annie dropped her rifle to the glass littered deck of the school bus and slumped against the edge of the drivers seat. With her elbows braced against the seat, she held her head in her hands and began rocking back and forth. Her botched shot had resulted in Brice's death. Shame and blame overwhelmed her as she began to moan.

Lynne turned towards Annie when she heard her moaning. Though she understood Annie's reaction, she knew this was not the time for grieving.

"God damn it, Annie! Suck it up! Not every shot hits the mark. You're in charge! We've got 305 school kids to protect," barked Lynne.

Lynne's sharp rebuke had the same effect on her as the slap she had delivered to the crying boy minutes earlier. As she collected herself, the vague image of her uncle, Tom Youngblood, sitting cross-legged in front of a campfire flashed upon her minds eye. He was reciting a warrior story in his distinctive, chant like verse. Damn! She knew his message was important, but it was just beyond her conscious reach. Suddenly, the movie camera of her mind mysteriously adjusted. Her uncle's image came into focus and he spoke to her.

Clarity in battle only occurs in a state of calmness.

Annie slowed her breathing and squeezed her eyes shut. She pushed aside the image of Brice collapsing to the ground and her minds eye began to picture her ancestors in the midst of battle. Seconds later, she calmly stepped out of the bus and walked purposefully to Lynne's side.

She put her arm around Lynne's shoulder and said evenly, "I don't think we'll have the benefit of Pete and Al's crossfire to help us repel the next attack and Bobby is drifting in and out of consciousness. We'll hold this position until I tap you on the shoulder and I give the boys the order to throw grenades. We'll retreat together and provide suppressing fire with our M-16's while the kids run to the woods,"

"Right on! Glad you recovered from your funk," responded Lynne.

Dropping into a crouch, Annie retreated to a group of teachers who had gathered behind her, below the roadbed, "Get the kids ready. On my command, they run for the woods."

Turning to the three grenade throwing teenagers, who were anxiously standing thirty feet away, she said steadily, "Men, when I give you the order start throwing those frag grenades."

Men! That single word sent a charge through each of the boys. They now felt as if they too were Marines.

In just a few short hours, Annie Youngblood had been transformed from a target-shooter to a battle-hardened warrior.

Bobby heard every word of Annie's battle orders. As he painfully twisted towards Annie, from beneath the bus, he said, "Good luck, Annie. You know what to do. I'll cover your retreat as best as I can from this position." During his awkward turn, he accidently and unknowingly activated the mute button on his satellite phone.

5:45 PM MDT (7:45 PM EDT)

"Oh, Bobby!" whimpered Annie.

"I'll be fine. Don't forget our date," he said boldly.

Frenzied shouts from behind the white tour bus warned them of an impending attack. To Bobby's ear, the shouting sounded like it came from a force of fifty men. Whoever told them they were facing a force of seventy men was way off the mark. *Oh, well,* he thought resignedly, *Marines love long odds.* "Bring it on motherfuckers," he whispered.

Eight to ten teenagers rushed their position. Bobby, Annie and Lynne mowed them down in seconds. Bobby noticed that there was no supporting crossfire from either Pete or Al. That was not a good sign, but he couldn't think about them now. Thinking was a chore. As the cobwebs in his mind began to clear, he sensed that there was something familiar about this last terrorist charge. The memory slowly trickled into his mind. In Fallujah, his platoon had been trapped, much like their present situation. A suicidal frontal attack, exactly like the one they had just encountered, had diverted everyone's attention to their front. The platoon's fire teams protecting their flanks had been distracted by the frontal attack and caught off guard. It was one of the few times his platoon had been tricked by the enemy.

"Annie clear out. I believe they're coming around our flanks. That frontal attack was a diversion," yelled Bobby.

Annie stepped back from the timbers and looked towards the last bus. Sure enough, three terrorists were sneaking along the side of the bus. She raised her M-16 to her hip and fired a burst on full automatic. Two of the terrorists dropped in their tracks, the third collapsed behind the fourth bus.

Swiveling towards the front of the bus column, she chased two terrorists between the first two buses with a hail of bullets. She screamed to the teachers, "Send the kids to the woods."

"Men, throw three frag grenades each, then run for the woods. Each of you take one red smoke grenade so incoming helos can pinpoint your position." She prayed that there would be incoming helos, otherwise they'd all be dead within the next fifteen minutes. With her M-16 in one hand, Annie tapped Lynne on the shoulder and said, "Let's go!" She turned and hopped off the roadbed to the base of the retaining wall.

Annie turned back to Lynne to repeat her order when all hell broke loose. A large group of screaming terrorists, firing wildly with their automatic rifles, bolted from behind the white tour bus. One half raced towards the rear bus while the other half darted towards the first bus. Lynne and Bobby were firing at them, but their field of fire was limited. Amazingly, the three teenage boys had seen the terrorist's assault on their flanks. Coolly they lobbed one well-aimed grenade after another into their midst. It gave the retreating teachers and kids precious moments to disperse as they raced towards the woods.

"Lynne, come with me," shouted Annie over the din of gunfire.

A moment later Lynne's shotgun was empty. She dropped her empty shotgun and quickly grabbed her back-up that was partially loaded.

"Leave it! Come with me," pleaded Annie.

Lynne's head shook from side to side. She wasn't coming. Her best friend lay dead behind her, covered by a camouflage jacket.

Wait for me, Kathy, by those "pearly gates." It won't be long now! thought Lynne as she calmly set her back-up shotgun on full automatic fire and aimed at a horde of terrorists who were racing towards her.

Bobby spoke dispassionately into the satellite phone, "We're being overrun. We're being overrun."

There was no acknowledgement, other than "Bobby Ridger, come in. This is General Rexman."

Puzzled, Bobby looked at his phone and realized that his mute button was on. He fumbled with the key at first, but eventually managed to disable it. He was about to speak when a dozen feet appeared on the terrorist's side of their timber bunker.

5:46 MDT (7:46 PM EDT)

Suddenly, four rapid-fire blasts from a shotgun and the screams from dying men burst from the speakerphone in the Situation Room. The president and general bolted upright from their hunched positions.

"Empty!" said a woman's voice angrily. Her voice was as clear as if she were sitting at the end of the table.

"You die, infidel whore!" wheezed a man out of breath from running, his accent distinctly Arabic.

They heard a sharp thwack, a woman's muffled cry and the sound of a body being dragged over wooden timbers.

"Shit, that was one of the female bus drivers with a shotgun. She and her friend were posted next to Bobby between the second and third buses, behind the timber bunker. They were the last line of defense for the children hiding below the retaining wall," said the general despondently.

Bobby whispered quietly into the satellite phone.

Radio static. "...on us." More garbled radio static.

"Was that Bobby?" asked the president.

"Couldn't tell. It was garbled," responded the general.

The sound of more footsteps and the shouts of al-Qaeda terrorists streamed from the speakerphone. Next, they heard the distinctive, evil voice of the man who had struck the female bus driver. He spoke to his men in Arabic. Neither the president, nor the general understood a word he said, but from the reaction of his men they understood his meaning. The killing was about to begin and his men were stomping their feet and slapping their sides in excited anticipation of the bloodletting.

For what seemed like minutes, but was only seconds, the unnerving fog of imminent disaster lay heavy in the room. Both men's heads were bowed as if in prayer.

A young Marine corporal quietly slipped into the room and handed General Rexman a message. The general quickly scanned the message and pushed it across the conference table to the president. The president read it in a glance and sighed.

TOP SECRET

Flash Z Message

162346Z JUN 08

FM: NSA

TO: POTUS

CC: CJCS, CNO, CMC, SDHS, DFBI

SUBJ: Yellowstone Defense-Marines, civilians and 305- 6th graders.

Weak transmission analysis; Cpl. Bobby Ridger reports... "They are on us. We've been overrun!"

A moment later, the president and general's worst fears were realized when they heard the evil voice proclaim loudly, "Children of the infidel, you die," accompanied by the distant screams of children. Then, the horrific sound of patient gunshots... *crack... crack... crack.*

The president's fist crashed into the speakerphone sending plastics phone parts flying in every direction.

"God damn motherfuckers will pay for this," swore the president.

5:48 MDT (7:48 EDT) Three concurrent events...

... Under the bus

Bobby could only see the back of the mullah as he stood atop the retaining wall. An AK-47 was slung over his shoulder and he was wearing a traditional black turban. Except for the turban, his attire was clearly Western... hiking boots, jeans and a lightweight hunting jacket.

He turned to his side and spoke in Arabic to the five men who were with him. Bobby saw his roughly, bearded face and fiery eyes. His men began to stomp their feet and slap their sides.

Bobby had seen that death dance before. The bastards think this is going to be a turkey shoot. Slowly, he inched his body around until he was facing the retaining wall. He placed the stock of his shotgun against his shoulder and aimed. The mullah spread his arms towards the retreating children, "Children of the infidel, you die!"

As the mullah began to unsling his AK-47 from his shoulder, three gunshots rang out in unhurried, measured succession and he fell to the road. His dead, lifeless eyes stared at Bobby as blood began to pour from two rib cage shots and one small hole in the center of his forehead. There was no doubt in Bobby's mind that the three perfectly placed shots were the handiwork of the sharpshooting Annie.

Unfortunately, the mullah's death inspired his followers to faster action. A disassembled .30-caliber machine gun was dropped to the roadbed where the mullah had stood just moments before. Two men kneeled beside the pieces, unfolded the tripod and mounted the machine gun atop its base. Next Bobby heard the all too familiar, and sickening, sound of a .30-caliber ammunition belt being slapped into the gun's breech, the cover closing and the gun being cocked.

Bobby's mind raced. *Fuck, where the hell did this machine gun come from?* But, there was no time to dwell on that. It was time for action, fast action. His shooting angle was restricted because of the undercarriage of the bus and the buses right, front wheel. He could cause some serious mayhem at this range with the shotgun, but destroying the machine gun was unlikely.

Without a second thought, he slowly rolled onto his back and flopped an arm behind him. His fingertips brushed against one of the frag grenades that he had placed atop the protective timbers ages ago. Straining, he finally succeeded in wrapping his hand around a grenade. Next, he propped a knee against the bus's transmission case, which was inches above him, and used his leg to turn himself back onto his stomach. He inched the grenade to his free hand, pulled the pin, quietly released the spoon and silently counted three seconds... one, two, three! He rolled the grenade backhanded between the two men at the machine gun. He heard the briefest of roars and saw a flash of white light before he lost consciousness.

... The run for the woods

Annie wasn't more than fifty feet from the retaining wall when she slowed to help a teacher assist a small handicapped child who was retreating slowly. Ahead of her, she could see that most of the children were nearing the stream bank where they, contrary to their teacher's instructions, began to congregate into groups as they searched for a way across the narrow stream. The section of stream where the kids were gathering was a dark green color and it was moving fast. Dark green meant deep water. She knew the water was also ice cold. A strong adult swimmer could drown in that cold, fast moving water.

A moment later, she heard from behind her a mullah's chilling declaration, "Children of the infidel, you die!" Annie turned and studied the mullah who was standing atop the retaining wall with his arms spread. Until that moment, she hadn't known that she could recognize evil spirits. She thought that gift was only bestowed upon Arapaho chiefs, like her uncle, Tom Youngblood. But, there was no doubt in her mind that the beast who stood before her was evil incarnate.

He returned her stare and grinned menacingly, as he thought, *Another weak, pampered, female devil worshipper and such an easy target.*

Annie straightened and calmly marched towards the mullah as she withdrew her Glock.

His eyes grew wider. *The impertinent devil worshipper!*

She raised her pistol and held it steady in both hands as he fumbled for his AK-47.

Crack… 1st shot. A well aimed glancing shot off his rib cage, right side. Painful, but, not killing. "That's for Kathy!" said Annie evenly.

Crack… 2nd shot. Same shot as the first, except this one glanced off his left rib cage. The mullah groaned as struggled to stand. He used his AK-47 as a crutch to keep from falling. "That's for Lynne!"

Crack… 3rd shot. A perfectly centered forehead shot.

"That's for the children, you bastard!"

In slow motion, the mullah tumbled to the road.

Annie ran to the teacher and small child. She slipped her hand into one of the child's armpits and the teacher, without any prompting, did the same to the child's other armpit. The two of them lifted the child off the ground as they raced towards the stream.

Seconds later, an explosion shook the ground. Annie looked over her shoulder and saw bodies and a machine gun flying through the air. Bobby's work, she knew, as tears began to trickle down her cheeks.

… The lead Pave Hawk helicopter

1st Lieutenant, Bronson Jacoway, USMC, crouched between the pilot and co-pilot of the lead Pave Hawk helicopter. He was in command of the Marine rifle platoon sent to rescue the 6th grade children. Head winds had delayed their arrival to the ambush site and the pilot's fuel gauge indicator was touching the "empty" mark.

When Jacoway's helo was three miles south of the site, he saw the line of five yellow school buses. He raised his binoculars to his eyes and was shocked at the scene that he saw unfolding. Between the school buses and his helo, hundreds of young children were wildly running and falling along the far bank of a narrow stream that bisected a gently sloping, but rocky, open field. Thirty to forty children had forded the stream and were now frantically clawing their way up a slippery, steep stream bank. Jacoway was an experienced hiker and recognized instantly what was occurring on the far bank. Children who couldn't swim or were poor swimmers were beginning to panic. The frightened faces and screams of their classmates who were being swept down river in the deep, fast moving water added to their terror.

Moments later, he saw the flash of a grenade explode near the front of the third bus. Two men and a machine gun flew through the air.

Jacoway's radio headset, with a mounted camera, was tied into a satellite communication net that could provide both audio and visual information to a central command center at the Marine Corps headquarters and the White House. The four helo pilots were only audio linked to Jacoway.

Jacoway's radio headset crackled, followed by an incoming command, "Lieutenant, this is the commandant, report your observations and commence your live video feed."

5:50 PM MDT (7:50 PM EDT)

"Aye, aye, general. The video feed is now live. We're about one mile out now and approaching the site at approximately 100 MPH. The pilot is slowing so I can better see what's occurring. It appears that the terrorists have overrun the school buses and the defensive position below the roadbed's retaining wall. The children are running away from the buses and across a half-mile wide-open field that has no cover whatsoever. They're headed towards a wooded area that looks like it will provide decent cover. However, they have to cross a narrow, but fast moving stream that parallels the column of school buses. The few kids that have crossed the stream are freezing and they look exhausted. Some have collapsed and their friends are helping them move. Geez, they're all easy targets for the terrorists!

"Oh, no. We're closer and I can see several groups of teachers and children. There are approximately thirty individuals in each group. The adults are helping kids who can't run. They're moving slowly and haven't even reached the stream. Two red smoke grenades just went off. I can now pinpoint the front and rear sections of the retreating friendlies.

"We will commence a low, slow run over the field and hover over the rear section of the retreating friendlies. Our helo doors are open and I'll have my men provide the kids with covering fire."

For the next twenty seconds, the din from automatic rifle fire through the helo's open door drowned out all communications from Jacoway.

Suddenly, Jacoway gave his men the hand signal to halt their fire. Abruptly the gunfire stopped and everyone heard over the radio net Jacoway's urgent verbal command to his pilot, "Put your mini guns on those hostiles."

Pointing to the open stretch of road between the terrorist's white bus and the yellow school buses, Jacoway directed the pilot's attention to a group of about twenty heavily armed terrorists who were streaming across the road towards the center school bus. The pilot maneuvered the helo's cyclic and foot pedals. The helo slowly turned until his mini guns were aimed directly at the oncoming terrorists. To the children below him, the helicopter looked like a flying dragon. The pilot hit his gunfire button and a stream of gunfire laced with green tracers spewed from the sides of the menacing dragon. The terrorists returned fire with their AK-47's.

At three hundred yards, the AK-47's accuracy wasn't much of a concern. However, the helo pilot decided to abandon his hovering position and close on the hostiles. The air force pilot must have a 6th grade son or daughter, thought Jacoway, because he was closing on the hostiles like a man possessed. At first, there was an occasional pinging sound in the cockpit of a bullet hitting the helo's fuselage, but as Jacoway's helo rapidly closed on the hostile's position, the sound became more like hail beating on a tin roof.

Suddenly, several red lights on the pilot's instrument panel started blinking and the claxon horn in the cockpit began wailing. The pilot raised a free hand and signaled Jacoway to a drop down seat slightly behind him. He flipped a communication switch on his instrument panel and coolly broadcast a message, via his headset microphone, to everyone in the helo, "We're out of fuel and I'm losing oil and hydraulic fuel pressure fast. Everyone tighten your seat belts and prepare for a hard landing near the school buses."

His next message was to the helo behind him, "Schoolhouse 2, this is Schoolhouse 1, I've been hit and am going to make an emergency landing on the road. There are two women carrying a small child to the stream. They are at the tail end of the retreating friendlies. They are under small arms fire. Cover them. You are now in command of the mission. Over."

All the men in the lead helicopter, Schoolhouse 1, would forever remember their landing, which was more like a crash than a landing. It was sudden and violent. Several safety belts were pulled away from the bulkheads, but amazingly no one was injured. Jacoway's men piled out of the helo and ran towards the center school bus. They were greeted by a dozen or so terrorists who were expecting a dazed air force pilot to raise his hands in surrender. In a matter of seconds, ten Marines banished the prospective child killers to a nether world of eternal damnation.

Rot in hell, you bastards! thought Jacoway.

6:00 PM MDT (7:00 PM EDT)

The pilot remained behind in the downed helo, Schoolhouse 1. From the cockpit, he was shutting down all his engines and turning on fire suppression devices. At this stage, he thought, it would be a shame to have the helo blow up and injure nearby airmen or Marines. He was a considerate and fastidious man. As he flipped the last toggle switch for the helo's shutdown, a bullet shattered the large window beside him. A dark haired teenager stood no more than twenty feet from him. The teenager casually ejected the spent bullet cartridge from an old, bolt-action sniper rifle and flashed the pilot an intimidating smile as he chambered another round. All the Marines were on the opposite side of the helo, focused on hunting down terrorists amidst the school buses. He knew he would be dead in seconds if he didn't act fast.

Without any conscious thought, years of military training automatically took control of his response. He would never recall reaching for his side arm, a M9 Beretta pistol, or chambering a round, or pulling the trigger. His first memories of his deadly duel were of the thunderous explosion of his single shot, the physical kick of the pistol in his hand and the sight of a small dark hole that emerged from the teenager's sternum. His next set of memories was clearly etched in his mind and would stay with him forever. The teenager spun around violently with the impact of his bullet and he heard him scream in pain as he fell to the road. The boy's body collapsed against the hard pavement with a sickening thud. A pool of dark, red blood began to spread across the road from the teenager's pumping chest wound. His single shot had apparently severed a major artery to the teenager's heart. The boy was dead within thirty seconds.

Though the pilot had, minutes earlier, fired his mini-guns into the advancing terrorists from the distant, detached security of his cockpit, this killing was different. Like Dodge City gunslingers of yesteryear, he and the enemy had looked one another in the eye before their shootout. This was not a faceless enemy. It was a young teenager, close in age to his oldest son. But, unlike his son, this teenager was hell-bent on killing him and innocent school children. *Good versus evil*, he told himself repeatedly, but to no avail. His heavy heart grew heavier. Suddenly, his body shuddered and a primal cry of sadness rose from his chest. He pitched towards the helo's shattered side window an instant before he retched.

During the next hour, the Marine platoon quickly and efficiently mopped up what little terrorist resistance remained. As originally suggested by Bobby Ridger, two helos landed on the road; one forward of the column of buses and the other at the tail end, each two hundred yards beyond the fallen trees. Each helo rapidly inserted their contingent of approximately ten Marines and promptly lifted off to be refueled by the overhead tanker. The two groups of Marines converged on the last of the terrorists who still occupied the hillside. Fifteen terrorists had consolidated together in the center of the hillside for their final stand. Once the Marines engaged them, utilizing a classic pincer formation, their accurate and overwhelming gunfire annihilated them in minutes. Only four terrorists survived the Marine's murderous crossfire.

7:15 PM MDT (9:15 PM EDT)

Twenty minutes after the terrorists ill-fated hillside stand, Jacoway apprised all Marine units over his headset that the school buses and hillside were secure. He cautioned his men, however, to be on the lookout for any stray terrorists who may have slipped away. The last thing he wanted to risk, at this stage of the rescue, was a stray terrorist shooting one of the civilians or school children. In this regard, he ordered half of the Marines from Schoolhouse 2 helo to set up a defensive perimeter around those who had made it to the woods. The remaining Marines from Schoolhouse 2 helo, which landed between the stream and the buses, were to set up a defensive perimeter as well around those who hadn't crossed the stream.

After repeated calls from the commandant for an after action report, Jacoway called the commandant on a secure satellite telephone. The commandant immediately patched in the president and his men at Camp Pendleton.

"Report!" barked the commandant.

"Aye, aye general. We still have some daylight, though probably not more than another hour or so. I have two squads combing the hillside for escaped terrorists and searching for Major Daniels and Gunnery

Sergeant Miller. Both squads have corpsmen with them. Two of the helos, Schoolhouse 3 and 4, are refueling overhead, and once, refueled will join the search for escaped terrorists. All of the children are safe. For now, we have only discovered two KIA (killed in action) civilians.

"I have secured the site. Half of the civilians and children are hidden in the wooded area a half-mile from the buses, and the other half is protected behind Schoolhouse 2 near the stream. My Marines have set up a defensive perimeter around both groups. Doctors and nurses from local hospitals are moving towards them on foot with first aid kits, though I understand the only injuries are twisted ankles and a few scrapes and bruises.

"The following report covers the immediate vicinity of the buses only. I have two of my men checking on friendly MIA's (missing in action) in the large pile of felled trees that blocked the buses.

"Friendlies- Causalities- Two civilians killed in action. Dirdle from Homeland Security and one of the female bus drivers named Kathy Wardein. The other female bus driver, Lynne, was unconscious when we arrived. She has since come to and an attending doctor thinks she incurred a Grade II concussion. With rest, he thinks she'll fully recover.

"Missing in action (MIA)- All three Marines plus two armed male civilians.

"Hostiles- Killed in Action- Eighty-four in total. Sixty-one of the dead are scattered on the road in and around the yellow school buses. The rest were found on the hillside. 75% of the deceased are young men, 18-22 years of age.

"Hostiles captured- Twelve men. Of these, five are wounded and should survive.

"Jesus, that's ninety-six terrorists!" said the commandant who was momentarily at a loss for words. The odds of three Marines and a handful of civilians holding off that number of heavily armed terrorists was mind-boggling to the hard-nosed leader of the United States Marine Corps.

"Good work, Jacoway. Your men saved the day," interjected the president.

"With all due respect, Mr. President, I'd have to say the defensive stand the Marines and civilians made here was nothing less than a miracle. The carnage is indescribable. Dead terrorist bodies are everywhere, AK-47's and M-16's lie all around us, a .30 caliber machine gun was destroyed adjacent to the Marine's command post, and the buses are smoking hulks. Words can't describe the battle that must have occurred here."

"Amen to that," said the commandant solemnly. "Keep looking for our boys and the civilians."

"Aye, aye general," said Jacoway as he paused. "I'll get back to you in a few minutes, general. A young woman is running towards me from the river, waving her arms and shouting. I remember seeing her helping a child retreat when we flew in." He didn't mention that one of his squad leaders was chasing her and clearly losing the foot race.

A moment after Jacoway terminated his report, Hammer Stephens punched a second hole in O'Brien's office wall. O'Brien, Adair and Hammer began to anxiously pace the small office as they prayed for good news on the three missing Marines.

Annie Youngblood was breathing hard as she completed her sprint to the retaining wall. A couple of Marines knelt on the road and easily lifted her to the top of the wall. Jacoway smiled as he greeted her and handed her a plastic water bottle. The lieutenant's out of breath squad leader arrived seconds later and began to explain how she had escaped his defensive perimeter. With a subtle shake of his head, the lieutenant silenced him.

Annie took two deep gulps of water, then slipped the water bottle into a hip pocket. Before the lieutenant could introduce himself, Annie stepped closer to him until they were face to face, "One of your men wouldn't let me go. He ordered me to stay behind your helicopter at the river. Finally, I told him I was leaving and if he didn't like it he would have to shoot me."

Without waiting for a reply, she turned and hurried to the right front wheel of the third bus where she dropped to her knees. The bus was riddled with hundreds of bullets holes from the helo's mini guns and still smoking from Bobby's grenade explosion. Peering under the engine block of the bus, Annie saw Bobby's limp body.

"Ma'am it was for your safety. I ordered him to... "

"Shut up and give me a hand. Bobby Ridger is underneath this bus and he's badly injured," screamed Annie.

Jacoway and two nearby Marines scrambled to her side and saw the body. One of the Marines, low crawled under the bus and checked Bobby's vital signs.

"He's alive, but his breathing is shallow and he's unconscious," he said.

"I need a corpsman or civilian doctor with an IV here at the center school bus immediately. Schoolhouse 3 you are going to Medevac a Marine to the closest hospital. Land as close to the center school bus as possible," commanded Jacoway over his headset.

The pilot of Schoolhouse 3 was in the midst of a slow pass over the hillside when he heard the Medevac request.

"This is Schoolhouse 3. I have eyes on your location. I will land next to the last school bus. Over," said the pilot as turned his helo and dived towards his intended landing area.

As two Marines began to gingerly drag Bobby out from under the bus, Jacoway spoke to a nearby corporal, "There is a stretcher in Schoolhouse 1. Once we get him clear of the bus, we'll secure him on that."

"Aye, aye sir. I'll get it," said the corporal smartly.

Turning to Annie, Jacoway finally introduced himself, "I'm 1st Lt. Bronson Jacoway. Do you know where the closest hospital is?"

Annie replied, "Yes sir, I do. It's in Cody, which is directly east of here. Probably a ten to fifteen minute flight by helo. I apologize... ."

Jacoway's headset crackled, interrupting Annie's response, "Sir, this is Corporal Jones. I heard your request for medical personnel. I'm checking on civilian casualties in the backed up traffic, forward of the school buses. There are no casualties here so I'm directing a civilian doctor and nurse who are with me to your location. They have an IV and first aid kits."

"Good work Jones," said the Jacoway.

A whirlwind of activity surrounded Bobby during the next few minutes. The doctor and nurse arrived and checked his pulse, blood pressure and wounds. While the nurse hooked him up to an IV, the doctor examined Bobby's head wound that Annie previously treated with "QuickClot." He liked what he saw. Annie's application of the "QuickClot" staunched the bleeding of an angry looking gash across his forehead. Wordlessly, he swabbed several new wounds with an antiseptic cream and bandaged them. With the help of two Marines, they carefully lifted Bobby onto the stretcher and strapped him on to it. The four of them smartly lifted the stretcher and hustled Bobby to Schoolhouse 3, which had just landed on the road two hundred feet away. A minute later, Bobby's stretcher was firmly secured in the bay of the helo with the doctor and nurse beside him, tending to his wounds. The helo slowly rose, and sped towards the Cody hospital.

No sooner had the dust from Schoolhouse 3's rotor wash settled when Annie half turned to Jacoway and excitedly said, "I'm Annie Youngblood. How are Pete and Al doing?"

"Who are Pete and Al? And what did you say your name was?" asked Jacoway.

"Damn, you haven't checked on them either," said Annie as she bolted towards Pete's nearby hideout in the fallen trees.

"Uh, what did you say your name was? Hey, where are you going?" said Jacoway to Annie's sprinting backside.

Like his squad leader, who earlier couldn't keep up with Annie, Jacoway too was no match for the speedy Annie. In moments, she had reached the tall jumble of felled trees. Like a cat, she leaped onto one of the larger tree limbs and, balancing herself, scampered forty feet along the split, crooked limb until she reached a large tree trunk. She scrambled over the tree trunk and dropped out of sight into a pile of splintered tree limbs and trunks. Jacoway stopped once he had climbed atop the first limb. The young woman had disappeared.

Not fully recalling the young woman's name after her brief introduction and her abrupt dash to the fallen trees, Jacoway embarrassingly began to call out, "Hey, what's your name? Where are you?"

Now that the shooting was over, a number of first responders, including an ambulance with a doctor and nurse from the West Yellowstone Medical Center had converged on the friendly side of the felled trees, nearest the last bus and Pete's hideout. They too saw the running woman race along the felled trees and drop out of sight. The doctor, the nurse and a park ranger quickly joined Jacoway in search of her.

"Hello, hello! Where are you?" repeated the frustrated Jacoway.

Moments later, Jacoway and the other searchers heard a muffled reply, "Here! Here! Pete's badly wounded. He needs first aid."

Jacoway quickly found Annie's general location as she continued her cries for help. She was deeply immersed in a thick tangle of trees. Innumerable limbs, branches, twigs and leaves made it impossible for them to see into the darkness of the hidden warren. Without hesitation, the park ranger plunged into the thicket. As he descended, his gloved hands snapped branches and moved limbs to the side so as to create a rescue opening. When he finally reached Annie's location, his headlamp illuminated the scene. Annie was holding Pete's head in her lap and offering him small sips of water from her water bottle. She had ripped the one sleeve of her blouse off and wrapped it around his bleeding head.

Moments later, the doctor with his first aid kit descended to a tree limb perched above Pete's position.

"It's a little crowded in here," said the ranger kindly to Annie. "We can take it from here."

Wide eyed, she nodded in agreement and whispered appreciatively in Pete's ear, "You and Al saved the children. They wouldn't have made it without you."

Pete's eyes were clouded, but he was able to force a weak smile as he croaked, "Are the kids OK?"

With tears trickling down her cheeks, she kissed Pete tenderly on the forehead and said, "Every last one of them!"

Annie wiped tears off her cheeks with the back of her hand before she began to climb upwards out of the tangle of trees. As she neared the top of her ascent, Jacoway offered her a helping hand. She grabbed it with both hands and was quickly vaulted to his perch atop the uppermost tree trunk.

Jacoway gently held her elbow for balance as he said, "You did great finding him. We've got three more missing men. Let's discuss this further once we're on solid ground. But, no running off!"

Annie nodded.

When they reached the road, Jacoway asked, "By the way, what's your name again?"

"Annie Youngblood. I'm one of the 6th grade teachers from Cody."

Was this some kind of undercover ruse?

Jacoway's eyebrows arched in disbelief. He knew the FBI had been involved in interdicting the earlier national parks threats, so he naturally presumed she was an FBI agent. With gunshot residue smeared on her face and her holstered Glock hanging menacingly from her hip, she looked like a modern day Annie Oakley.

"I helped the Marines. I fought next to Bobby under that bus until we had to retreat," she said.

He nodded, unconvinced, "Unhuh! How so?"

"I'm an expert shot. Brice and Bobby gave me a M-40A3, sniper rifle, and a M-16A4, automatic rifle."

What female 6th grade teacher knows how to use the Marine's sniper rifle and assault rifle?

Jacoway's head unconsciously shook from side to side, as his skepticism peaked. He'd heard that FBI agents could be a little devious. But, why would this petit, young female agent want to mislead him?

Was she part of some government cover-up?

"I, we, ran out of ammunition. We were overrun. I ordered the retreat," she said, as tears poured across her cheeks. "I shot boys, not the bull's-eye of paper targets. I'm a teacher, not a warrior like Bobby, Brice and the major. I don't like killing people. Lynne and Kathy were killed. It was my fault," bawled Annie as she fell against Jacoway's chest and cried uncontrollably.

Jacoway was taken aback by Annie's crying. Her emotional outpouring wasn't that of a trained FBI agent.

Damn, I can't believe this. Could she really be a teacher?

Jacoway had been in combat in Iraq and was familiar with the visible signs of mental stress and anguish, especially amongst young Marines who'd seen the faces and heard the dying screams of those that they'd shot and killed in their first firefight. As he held Annie in his arms and comforted her with friendly pats on her back, he attempted to console her, "It's OK. It's OK. Take it easy. The shooting is over. You're safe and the kids are safe!"

As he spoke, he stared at the sixty-one terrorists, who were strewn across the road in macabre jumble of death. He could hardly believe his eyes.

This was not your run of the mill, brief encounter with an enemy shooting long range, harassment fire. This was a fucking three hour shit storm, at spitting distance, against nearly 100 trained and heavily armed terrorists.

After a minute, Annie regained her composure and Jacoway spoke to her gently at arms length, "You were very, very brave! You only did what you had to do to protect the children. By the way, Lynne isn't dead. She suffered a concussion and she'll be fine."

Annie's hands grasped her head as she wailed, "She's safe! Thank God! Thank God!"

Jacoway continued his gentle speech as he began to question Annie. "You're safe! Everything's OK! Can you tell me where you last saw Brice and the major?"

Annie turned and pointed to the top of the hillside. "See that clearing at the top of the hill. There are two fallen trees and a couple of antennas extending above them. I tried to shoot the terrorist leader with my sniper rifle, but I missed and he shot Brice," stuttered Annie as she cried and gulped for air.

Squinting, Jacoway could barely see a single antenna.

Geez, she also has amazing eyesight.

"Brice and the major were next to those trees."

Jacoway observed one of his squads laterally sweeping the hillside a couple of hundred feet below the clearing. He spoke over his headset, "1st squad. Proceed 90 degrees uphill from your present course. That is the last known location of Major Daniels and Gunnery Sergeant Miller."

"Aye, aye sir," came the instant reply from the squad leader.

"OK! We'll check on them. What about this guy named Al? Where is he?"

"Follow me," she said as she began another sprint towards the first bus in line.

"Not so fast. Slow down," gasped Jacoway, as he vainly attempted to keep pace with the young teacher.

While running, Jacoway re-called Corporal Jones on his headset. Jones was still patrolling the area ahead of the forward jumble of felled trees.

"Jones, this is Jacoway. Are there any additional medical personnel or policemen near you?"

"Yes, sir. The place is crawling with them."

"Good. In a couple of seconds, you'll see a young female teacher jump atop the felled trees nearest you. Gather rescue and medical personnel and follow her. She's headed to the last known position of one of the civilian defenders. He may be badly wounded."

"Aye, aye sir." Seconds later, he added. "I see her, Christ, she must be a sprinter! Damn, will you look at her race along those fallen trees. It's like her feet are floating over those tree trunks and limbs, man!"

"Don't lose track of her. She'll disappear in a moment. Mark her location," barked Jacoway.

"Woops! She vanished! How the heck did she do that? " replied the surprised corporal. "But, I marked her last location. I've got a team with me and we're moving towards her."

8:33 PM MDT (10:33 PM EDT)

Forty-five minutes later, Jacoway re-called the commandant on his secure satellite phone.

"I have good news, general. We've recovered the missing persons… all three Marines and both of the male civilian defenders. They're all alive and are at or in transit to hospitals."

"Wonderful! Fucking, wonderful! Hold one moment while I patch in the president and Camp Pendleton," said the commandant.

Seconds later the telephone crackled and the president and O'Brien confirmed their connection to the call.

"Report, Jacoway," said the commandant cheerfully.

"Aye, aye general. All three Marines and both of the male civilian defenders are alive and at, or in transit to hospitals. Bobby Ridger is in critical condition. His heart apparently went into cardiac arrest while he was being wheeled into the emergency room at the hospital in Cody, Wyoming. Fortunately, they had those defibrillator paddles handy and they were able to re-start it. I'll keep you apprised of his condition as I receive more updates.

"Major Daniels suffered a gunshot wound to his leg and lost quite a bit of blood. However, the doctors have given him several pints of plasma, which has stabilized his condition. Gunnery Sergeant Miller was shot at close range with a heavy caliber pistol, but his armored vest saved him. The blast, however, violently threw him backwards into a tree trunk. Landing head first against the tree, he incurred a concussion that has caused him to drift in and out of consciousness. During a moment of consciousness, he had enough presence of mind to apply a tourniquet to Major Daniels leg, which probably saved his life. Miller's chest and ribs ache, but he'll be OK in a day or so. Both of them are being flown to a hospital in Bozeman.

"Pete and Al, the male defenders are pretty badly banged up. They each incurred multiple, grazing gunshot wounds and quite a few splinter wounds from the trees. Both men were buried under twelve feet of tree trunks and limbs. One of the rescue doctors told me that both men should fully recover," concluded Jacoway.

"Fine work, fine work," repeated the commandant.

"Thank you, general. I've a clearer picture of what occurred minutes before my helos arrived. Would you like a verbal brief now? I'll include all the details in my after action written report."

"I'd like to hear your brief now," interjected the president with his folksy Texas drawl. "General Rexman and I have been confined in the Situation Room for hours keeping tabs on this damn ambush."

"Very well, Mr. President," began Jacoway. "First, let me describe the hero or rather heroine of the hour. When I terminated my previous call, it was because a twenty three year old, 6th grade teacher named Annie Youngblood was shouting and running towards me. In short, she is a champion marksman and was very much a key player in supporting the Marines and defending the children.

"I don't quite have all the details, but what I have pieced together is this. She killed the terrorist leader who shot Major Daniels in the leg and Gunny Miller in the chest. Her perfect headshot with our M-40A3, sniper rifle, was an uphill, single shot of approximately three-hundred and twenty-five yards. Further, from what Gunny Miller told me during one of his brief periods of lucidity, her shot was perfectly aimed between several tree limbs and hit the terrorist leader a moment before his intended execution of Miller with his pistol. The terrorist's aim fell, as he was hit, and he shot into Miller's armored vest.

"One of the teachers also told me that she assisted Bobby Ridger, while positioned beneath one of the buses, with sustained, deadly gunfire during each and every terrorist frontal attack.

"Lastly, she was the lone defender standing when she ordered the children's retreat. Ridger had previously announced to Annie and the other civilians that he would stay behind to provide rear-covering fire while the kids and civilians made a run for the woods. As you probably know, he's virtually a quadriplegic and there was no way he could retreat with the kids. He was going to fight to the bitter end!" said Jacoway, in speech choked with emotion.

After a few moments, he collected himself, "She was the last to leave the buses and was no more than 100 feet away when the terrorists overran her former bus defenses. She and another teacher were helping a handicapped student retreat. A mullah stood atop the retaining wall and shouted that he and his men were going to shoot and kill all the children. A nearby, retreating teacher heard his threat and looked over her shoulder to see what was happening.

"This teacher told me that she saw Annie calmly unholster her Glock and walk directly towards the mullah. The mullah was apparently surprised by her aggressive action and struggled to unsling his AK-47. When she was within twenty feet of the bastard, she raised her pistol with both hands and shot him three times."

"Those were the three shots that we heard over the speakerphone," exclaimed the excited president.

"Yes sir, Mr. President. Annie Youngblood's shots. After that, the other terrorists began to set up their .30 caliber machine gun. Fortunately, Ridger had enough strength and mobility, from beneath the closest bus, to roll a frag grenade into the machine gun and the gunners, which bought the teachers and children vital time to further their escape. The front wheel of the school bus protected Bobby from most of the blowback blast of the grenade.

"I was about one mile out when I saw the machine gun blow up. Moments after the explosion, another wave of terrorists moved into firing positions between the school buses. They were short work for our helo's mini guns."

"Just a matter of seconds," sighed O'Brien.

"That Annie Youngblood sounds like my kind of warrior. I wonder if she'd have interest in applying to our Platoon Leaders Class. She sounds like the perfect candidate for our first female Marine Corps infantry officer. I'd like to meet her," said the commandant sincerely.

"Me too!" added the president.

CHAPTER 23
A SLIGHT DETOUR

Brice didn't remember tying the life saving tourniquet on Chet Daniels leg, or being rescued by his former platoon buddies, or speaking briefly with 1st Lt. Bronson Jacoway before he was lifted onto the deck of the Pave Hawk helo for medical evacuation to the Bozeman Deaconess Hospital.

As he lay half conscious on the deck of the noisy helicopter, a familiar ringing sound penetrated his dulled senses. Gradually, his mind crept to life and his eyes blinked open. At first, the deafening sound of thumping helicopter rotors and the vibration of the cargo deck overwhelmed him. However, once he regained an awareness of his surroundings, he realized that there was a corpsmen, dressed in battle fatigues, crouched beside him. The corpsman was applying bandages to someone a couple of feet away on a stretcher. Opposite the corpsman was a man dressed in civilian clothes with a stethoscope hanging from his neck. Gingerly raising himself unto his elbows, he saw that they were both attending to Chet who was strapped to the stretcher. He winced in pain as he inched to a sitting position. His chest and ribs felt like a truck had hit him.

Am I being Medevac'd out of Fallujah?

"Water! Where am I?" he said feebly.

"You and Major Daniels are being evacuated to a hospital in Bozeman," said a familiar face who handed him an open bottle of water.

He drank greedily from the bottle. "Is Chet OK?"

"He's lost a lot of blood, but you saved his life by applying a tourniquet to his wounded leg. We have him hooked up to an IV and are monitoring his vital signs, which are good."

Brice's eyes focused on the man. "Bozeman? Where's that? You gave me sleeping pills at Camp Pendleton, Doc. What are you doing here?"

"Yes, I gave you sleeping pills. I'm 2nd class Petty Officer Red Ramos, assigned to your former 3/5 platoon at Camp Pendleton. Our platoon just rescued you, Major Daniels and the school children from the terrorist ambush in Yellowstone National Park. We're flying you to the Bozeman Deaconess Hospital in Montana," said the Navy corpsman evenly.

"Is this a dream?" rasped Brice.

"No. You've been drifting in and out of consciousness. You received a concussion when you were knocked into a tree. It's a good thing your head is harder than that tree trunk. You should be fine in a few days."

Yellowstone National Park... school children... terrorist ambush... 3/5 rescue. Bits of images danced through his mind.

"The 3/5! Are you kidding? How... "

Red Ramos interrupted him as he lightly put his hand on Brice's sore chest, "Lie back down. Take it easy. We should be at the hospital in twenty minutes."

Minutes later, Brice again heard the familiar ringing. It was his cell phone that he had left in the chest pocket of his armored vest. He never carried a cell phone during a combat mission. Men had been killed because of such stupid mistakes. He fumbled for the flap opening of his chest pocket, but he couldn't locate it. Red leaned over Brice, unbuttoned his pocket, withdrew the cell phone and handed it to Brice.

"Hello!" said Brice groggily.

"Brice, this is Bill Ridger. Are you OK? Is Bobby with you?"

"No, no! I don't know! Where is he? Where's, Bobby?" shouted Brice as he tried to raise himself. .

Red placed his hand on Brice's chest again as he gently pressed him back to a prone position. "Easy now!" he said as he reached for Brice's phone.

"He's Bobby Ridger's dad and he's a sheriff in Dennis, Montana," rasped Brice.

A loud backfire from one of the helo's engines drowned out the first half of Brice's comment. All Red heard was that the man on the phone was a sheriff from Dennis. He gave the sheriff a brief overview of the ambush and a summary of the casualties. With respect to casualties, he explained that all the civilian defenders and the Marines experienced multiple injuries with the exception of two civilians who were killed in action. Lastly, he said that a young teacher named Annie Youngblood was the hero of the hour.

Bill Ridger's heart stopped. *Oh, God no! My only son, Bobby!* "Who were the two civilians?" asked Bill nervously.

"One of the civilians was a female bus driver named Kathy Wardein. The other civilian was a male… shot and killed… " The helo's engine backfired again.

"Say again after 'civilian male,'" asked Bill.

"The other individual was a male, Tony Dirdle, who worked for Homeland Security."

"What about my son, Bobby Ridger? How is he doing?" implored Bill.

"Oh! I didn't hear that you were Bobby's dad. It's noisy. Our pilot just received a radio report on your son. It was touch and go for a while, but the West Park Hospital in Cody has just upgraded your son's condition to stable. I have to get back to my patient. Here's the gunny," said Red as he handed the cell phone back to Brice.

"This is Brice."

"Thanks, Brice, for taking care of Bobby. The corpsman mentioned Annie Youngblood. Do you know if she's any relation to Tom Youngblood?"

"She's Tom's niece. Bobby said he'd met her before at a picnic when they were kids. Annie and Bobby manned our command post in the center of our defensive line of buses. They and two female bus drivers repulsed non-stop terrorist frontal attacks for hours. They were magnificent. When Bobby lost consciousness, Annie took control. Annie saved all of us."

"If she's a Youngblood, it doesn't surprise me one bit. They're great people and great friends. I'll pass this news on to Tom," said Bill. "Listen, I have bad news. Late this afternoon, the sheriff's son, Skip Dower, kidnapped Molly and her friend, Penny. Fortunately, a fly fisherman saw Skip grab the girls and he called the mayor. The mayor contacted the State Highway Patrol who were able to pin down Skip's location through his cell phone GPS. He's at the remote hunting lodge that you and Molly discovered several days ago. His father, Fred, is there as well. The head of the highway patrol, Alan Fischer, believes that the Dower's have been aiding the terrorists.

"I was glued to my TV set watching the news of the ambush and didn't realize that I had left my cell phone in my truck. The mayor called Jan Dank when I couldn't be reached. Jan arrived at my front door ten minutes ago and explained to me what happened. We're just leaving my ranch now to rescue the girls. I thought you should know," said Bill.

When Brice heard the news of Molly's kidnapping, he bolted upright. In the process, a stab of pain caused him to whimper. His mind churned as he recalled the topography and wooded areas that surrounded the lodge. The owner had cleared the land around the lodge for firebreak purposes. There was only one line of approach to the lodge that offered any concealment.

"Hold on Bill. I have an idea. I'm going to mute this call for a minute."

Brice touched Red's arm and leaned towards his ear so that he could be heard over the sound of the thumping rotors, "Get the co-pilot and bring him to me."

Red's eyes questioned Brice's order for an instant. He had served with the 3/5 in Iraq at the same time as Brice and had heard numerous stories about his courage and judgment. He turned to get the co-pilot.

The co-pilot was a young Air Force 2nd lieutenant who looked to Brice as if he were a freshman in high school. Brice spoke into his ear for a minute.

The 2nd lieutenant turned to Red and repeated the gist of Brice's request into his ear, "What are the medical risks to Gunny Miller if we make an intermediate drop off and leave him in the care of two sheriffs for a couple of hours? The sheriffs are in pursuit of two terrorists who have kidnapped two girls. Apparently, he is the only one who is knowledgeable about the terrorist's destination. He will be directing the sheriffs and not participating in any armed confrontation. We can return to the drop off point and pick him up after we deliver Major Daniels to the hospital in Bozeman."

Red, who was several years older than the co-pilot, nearly laughed aloud when the lieutenant naïvely declared that the gunny would not participate in any armed confrontation. The man had obviously never spent any time around Marines in combat. Only death or unconsciousness could keep a Marine from using his rifle.

Red thought for a moment before he turned to the gunny and said, with a resolute look, "He'll be OK, but only under my direct care. I go with him. I won't be missed. A civilian doctor is attending to Major Daniels."

The co-pilot returned to the cockpit and put on his helmet and headset. After discussing the gunny's request with the pilot, he turned in his seat and gave the corpsman and the gunny the thumbs up, "OK."

Brice released the mute function on the cell phone and explained to Bill Ridger that he and a Navy corpsman were going to be dropped off on U.S. Route 287, next to the dirt access road that led to the lodge.

"Bill, I'm going to give the cell phone to the co-pilot. Please give him directions to the drop off point. We just flew over West Yellowstone, so I think we're only minutes away. I'll lead you and Jan to the lodge so they don't hear or see us coming," said Brice.

"Good, that will be helpful. Are you well enough to do this?"

Brice spoke loud enough so that Red could hear, "With a pain killer or two and perhaps a stimulant, the corpsman tells me I'll be good as new "

Red rolled his eyes. *Typical Marine!*

Fifteen minutes later, the sound of the helicopter's rotors disappeared into the night sky as it continued its flight to Bozeman. Brice, Bill, Jan and Red stood by the open tailgate of Jan's pickup. Total nighttime darkness had arrived. A length of canvas lay open in the bed of the pickup. Lying atop the canvas was Bill's bolt action 308 Remington rifle with a telescopic lens; Jan's well-oiled 1903 Springfield .30-06 rifle with a snipers lens; and Brice's M-16 and side arm, a Glock pistol.

Before Brice was evacuated from the ambush site, one of the Marines had tossed his weapons into the helo beside him. That act wasn't happenstance. All Marines knew that a Marine without his rifle was useless. It was part of their rifleman's creed that had been pounded into each and every Marine during boot camp.

Brice's armored vest, which he was still wearing at Red's insistence, also held two full M-16 ammunition clips, extra ammunition for his Glock, a smoke grenade and a small flashlight equipped with a red light. Red was armed with a holstered Glock, and he carried a first aid fanny pack.

Brice introduced himself and Red to Jan Dank. Brice hadn't met Jan before, but he'd heard from Bill how he and Jan had become secret deputies for the State Highway Patrol. He next introduced Red to Bill Ridger. After the introductions, Jan spread out on the truck's tailgate a "Google Earth," large-scale aerial photo of the area that he had printed at a local copy store. His headlamp clearly illuminated the photo that depicted the woodlands, vegetation, open fields, creeks, trails, lodge and the existing dirt road to the lodge. Beside the printout, lay an aged topographical map that Jan used for hunting.

"I estimate the lodge is about three miles back up this draw," said Jan pointing to the map.

"We can drive in about two miles using the truck's headlights, but after that we'll be on foot. Let's talk tactics and strategy in the cab. Red do you mind riding in the back?" asked Brice.

"That's fine with me. However, one note before we shove off. Gunny Miller is on painkillers because he has injured ribs and he incurred a concussion several hours ago. I have also given him a stimulant. So, don't let him drive and please keep an eye on him."

The other three looked at the corpsman as if he were from another planet. They each shared the same thought, *'No stinking' bump on the head can slow a Marine!*

Jan's truck rambled along the unkempt and deeply rutted dirt road, bouncing violently every time the truck bottomed out in a pothole or vaulted over a rock. When Jan stopped briefly to remove an "elk call" bugle that popped free from beneath his front seat and lodged near his brake pedal, it gave Brice an idea that he discussed with the others. Ten minutes later, they slowed to a stop beneath a solid canopy of tall Douglas fir trees.

"Brice, I like your suggested plan. Let's go over it on the map," said Jan Dank.

With his red flashlight illuminating the maps that lay on the tailgate, Brice began to describe his rescue plan. Much of it for the benefit of Red who hadn't heard it while riding in the bed of the truck.

"First, a quick overview. Skip Dower is twenty-four years old and ex-military by way of a bad conduct discharge. His father, Fred, is fifty years old. Both Dower's are bad news, crooked cops who are holding two twenty-year-old girls against their will at this lodge," began Brice.

"What?" cried Red. "You told me and the helo pilots that these were terrorists."

Brice slowly turned towards the corpsman, his hard eyes bored into him. "Let's not split hairs, Red. These are bad cops who collaborated with the terrorists that executed the Yellowstone ambush," said Brice firmly.

Red nodded reluctantly.

Brice continued, "Earlier this afternoon, according to Bill, Skip abducted both girls at gunpoint. The girls are Bill's daughter, Molly, and her friend, Penny. The State Highway Patrol has confirmed their presence here by tracking their cell phone's GPS. Both men are armed, experienced with weapons and may be preparing to flee in light of today's failed ambush.

"Several days ago, Molly and I discovered the terrorist's training activity at this lodge. We observed them from this ridge. There is also a conference center of some sort east of the lodge," said Brice as he pointed to the locations on the topographical map. "The terrorists were firing their weapons when I observed them, and there were automatic weapons everywhere. My guess is that they took all their weapons with them to Yellowstone when they moved out, but we should be mindful that there might be a few extra M-16's or AK-47's laying about that the Dowers could utilize.

"The front windows of the lodge overlook this open field. I suspect that the Dowers and the girls will be in the main lodge. We will split up into two teams. Jan and Bill in one, me and Red in the other. Jan and Bill will advance to the rear of the lodge through the trees. One of you will use Jan's 'elk call' bugle and the other will rattle the lodge's large metal trash bin that is behind the lodge. Hopefully, that will attract one or both of the Dowers. If neither comes out the back, the team will set off a smoke grenade. Hopefully, at least one of them will investigate the possibility of a fire.

"Red, you will be stationed to the side of the lodge, in this general area. There are plenty of trees for you to hide behind, but you must be visible to all of us when you use your red light. I won't approach the front door of the lodge until you shine your red light on a thumbs up hand signal, which will indicate that one or more of the Dowers has exited the rear of the lodge to investigate the noise or the smoke," said Brice.

Jan interjected, "One other matter, Brice. When the head of the State

Highway Patrol, Alan Fischer, gave me the GPS location of Skip, I asked him about what level of force we were allowed to use. He said, 'If they don't surrender, we are authorized to use deadly force.' The state has classified this crime as a double kidnapping!"

In total darkness, all four of them walked in a line through the brush and tall trees. Brice led the group with his red flashlight, his hand cupped over the lens to eliminate detection. No loose gear jangled from their clothing and their careful footfalls were noiseless. Once they were thirty yards from the rear of the lodge, they kneeled together in a circle. It appeared as though every light in the lodge was on and they could hear the loud, drunken voices of the Dowers through several open windows on the main floor of the lodge. The lodge and its immediate surroundings were clearly visible through the trees.

Because of Bill's proximity to his kidnapped daughter, Brice sensed his heightened level of anxiety. He put a hand on Bill's shoulder and whispered, "Just a few more minutes and we'll have the Dowers in cuffs. I'm sure Molly hasn't been touched. Heavy drinking usually precedes sex in these situations." He had no idea if his *heavy drinking* comment was true or not, but he wanted to calm Bill. What he was certain of was that calm and composed thinking always trumped excited, overzealous behavior when a gunfight developed.

"Safeties off your weapons. There is enough light for all of us to see Red behind that tree," whispered Brice as he pointed to a large Douglas fir. "When I'm in position at the side of the lodge, I'll give Red my thumbs up that he'll in turn give to you. That will be your signal to commence your diversion. When Red observes one or both of the Dower's moving to the rear of the lodge, he'll give me a second thumbs up that will be my signal to approach the front of the lodge. My plan is to come through the front door and get the drop on whoever is guarding the girls. Let's move out," said Brice.

Bill and Jan crept closer to the rear of the lodge. Brice left Red posted behind the large tree and, in low profile, raced to the side of the lodge. He slithered quietly amidst the shadows of the lodge's sidewall to where it met the elevated front porch. He rested his M-16 noiselessly against the porch and withdrew a mirror from his vest pocket that he'd earlier swiped from the civilian doctor on the helicopter. The instrument had a six-inch handle and an adjustable mirror. It was perfect for peeking, undetected, around the corners of rooms and through windows.

He slowly raised the one square inch mirror into the corner of a screen less, open window. Molly and Penny were sitting next to one another on a large living room couch. Their hands were bound in front of them with plastic ties, as were their feet. The residue of mascara streaked their faces, purple bruises covered their wrists and their hair was tussled. Both of their blouses were still primly buttoned and the laces on their hiking shoes were carefully tied. It appeared that the girls had resisted capture, but had not yet been molested.

Fred and Skip sat on stools at a fancy mahogany bar that was fifteen feet behind the couch. They were taking long pulls of whiskey from an open bottle. A dozen or so empty beer cans littered the bar top. Amidst the empty cans lay two pistols. Both kidnappers were already quite inebriated. Brice reconsidered his "elk call" ploy. He turned to Red and gave him a "thumbs down" signal and waved him to his side.

Several moments later, Red arrived at his side. He whispered quietly into his ear, "Do you have a cell phone with you that can take videos?"

Red whispered back, "Yes and yes! My Nokia cell phone takes good videos."

"Good, this is the new plan. Both Dowers are 'shitfaced' at the bar in the living room. The bar is approximately forty feet from the front door. Their pistols are laying on the bar top. Off to the side are the two girls on a couch. Both are bound and appear to be unmolested. I'm going through the front door at full speed towards the Dowers with my pistol raised. I'll shout 'U.S. government, raise your hands, you're under arrest!' It's important that your cell phone camera record my entry statement and what occurs after that. If a shoot out occurs, I don't want any of Dower's white supremacist buddies or 'anti law and order' types bitching that I used excessive force."

Red's eyes widened, "Ah, you think this is the best way to do this?"

"Absolutely. The front door is open and I'll surprise them. It'll be over in seconds."

"Uh, huh, do you think they'll surrender peacefully?" probed Red.

"Of course not. That's why I want you to witness and videotape this confrontation," said Brice matter-of- factly.

"I see. What about Jan and Bill for back-up?"

"You've got a side arm. Use it if need be. There isn't time to get them."

Man, the stories about Brice were true. He does have a large pair of brass balls, thought Red.

A moment later, Red's Nokia cell phone was ready to shoot the video and he gave Brice the thumbs up, good to go signal.

Brice silently crawled on all fours towards the front door. The solid front door swung inwards and was wide open. An exterior screen door was closed, but slightly ajar. He checked the safety on his Glock, the pistol was ready to fire. Ever so carefully, he silently pulled the screen door towards him and duck walked into the living room. The girl's eyes bulged when he appeared, but they remained quiet. A coffee table with a large lamp and a tall potted plant provided just enough cover for him to sneak undetected to within twenty feet of the bar.

In one swift motion, he stood, aimed his pistol, with both hands, at the Dowers and said in a loud voice, "U.S. government, raise your hands, you are under arrest."

Skip Dower moved quicker than Brice expected. In a blur, he grabbed his pistol off the bar and aimed it at Brice, as he barked, "You! You're a dead man!"

Two shots rang out nearly simultaneously. Skip's shot whizzed by Brice's left ear. Brice's shot hit Skip in the center of his forehead and threw him backward against a wall. He slipped slowly off his bar stool onto the floor. A few involuntary muscle spasms later and he was dead.

"You bastard, you god damn bastard," slurred his drunken father, as he sloppily reached for his for his pistol.

"Arms up Dower! Do as I say!" shouted Brice.

"You killed my son. I'm going to kill you!"

"Leave the gun alone. Arms up. Last warning!"

Fred ignored the warnings and picked up his pistol, and like his son began to turn towards Brice. Brice tried to discourage him with a shot near his feet, but it didn't slow him in the least. Rage and drunkenness fueled his madness. He continued moving his pistol towards Brice. Brice's next shot grazed Fred's arm, it had less effect than his first shot. Fred took a wobbly, awkward step towards Brice and began to take aim, in slow motion, at Brice's head. Brice's last shot of the day thundered through Fred's forehead.

His legs buckled as he dropped his pistol and collapsed to the floor, only feet from his dead son.

A moment later, Jan and Bill came running into the living room from the rear of lodge, their rifles at the ready. Brice stood standing over Skip and Fred with his lowered pistol hanging by his side.

Molly and Penny, overwhelmed by the shooting and rescue, began crying uncontrollably. Bill went to both girls and quickly cut them free of their restraints with a penknife.

Molly jumped to her feet, hugged her father and buried her head into his shoulder. Her chest heaved with sobbing. Jan sat beside Penny on the couch and held her hands in his. A moment later, she buried her head into Jan's shoulder as she too began to cry uncontrollably.

The slap of a screen door closing caused everyone to look towards the front door. Red took several unsteady steps into the room and lurched to a stop. His gray face reflected utter disbelief. Gun smoke from the pistol shots drifted lazily around him. He looked like he'd seen a ghost.

"You OK, Red?" asked Brice.

"Me! Huh! What about you?" stuttered Red.

"I'm good. Why don't you sit down for a moment? Catch your breath," said Brice.

Holding up his cell phone, Red said, "I captured everything on video like you asked. Your killing shots occurred at the last possible millisecond. You either have a death wish or the fastest trigger finger known to man. I do not believe what I just saw. I need a drink," croaked Red as he side-stepped the two dead men and moved to the bar.

Brice smiled at the shaking corpsman and turned towards the two girls, "Molly and Penny, are you OK? Did they harm you in any way?"

"We're OK. They didn't touch us. The Dower's were too busy drinking to pay us much interest," said Molly bravely.

"Yeah! Well, I could tell that Skip wasn't too far from wanting something more than booze. You arrived just in time Brice if you ask me," said Penny.

CHAPTER 24

HONEY BEAR

The next evening, Tuesday, June 17, 2008, Chet was awakened by the intermittent sound of soft chimes and a woman's voice. He was lying on his back on a hospital bed. His left leg was heavily bandaged and elevated by a pulley system. A nurse stood beside him and appeared to be speaking to him, but he didn't understand what she was saying.

"Medicine, it's time for your medicine," she repeated patiently.

"Unhuh! Where am I?" he croaked.

"The Deaconess Hospital in Bozeman, Montana."

"What happened?"

"First, the medicine and then I'll explain."

After swallowing a handful of pills and taking a sip of water, he repeated one word, "What… ?" Then, fell sound asleep.

He awoke ten hours later. It was early, Wednesday morning and the sun was just beginning to stream through his hospital room window. *How long have I been here?* he wondered. His whole body ached and his left leg itched. As he reached involuntarily to scratch his leg, a bolt of pain shot stopped him and he groaned.

A man was sitting in a chair beside his bed. He stood and moved towards him. He was dressed in a hospital gown and his face looked familiar. It was hard to focus and harder still to concentrate.

The man softly touched his shoulder and whispered in his ear, "It's Brice Miller, Chet. You are at the Deaconess Hospital in Bozeman, Montana. You were shot in the leg during the ambush in Yellowstone National Park, and are expected to make a full recovery. The children and civilians are all safe," lied Brice. Kathy Wardein hadn't made it, but he'd explain that later. "My former platoon came to our rescue. Hard to believe, isn't it? 2nd platoon, Lima Company from the 3/5. Great karma with that platoon!"

"Lima Company? I was their company commander in Iraq. Where am I?"

He fell back to sleep. An hour later, he awoke, rested and more conscious of his surroundings. His eyes were clear, the memory of being shot by the terrorist quite vivid and the pain in his leg unmistakable. To his left, Gunny was slumped crookedly in a chair snoring aloud. On the other side of the curtain, in his semi-private room, he heard the sound of another man snoring.

"Gunny, Gunny wake up!" he whispered.

Brice's body jerked to life. He studied Chet. He was no longer disoriented and his eyes were clear and focused.

"How are you feeling, Chet?"

"Sore, thirsty, and my damn leg is throbbing."

Brice smiled knowingly at his friend's grumbling. Those in the Corps firmly believed that a complaining Marine was a healthy Marine. Chet was on the mend. Brice picked up a cup of water off the nearby rolling meal cart and steered the bent straw to Chet's lips. Chet greedily sucked the cup dry. Brice refilled the cup and that was quickly emptied.

"Tell me what happened after I was shot. I must have passed out," said Chet as his head fell back against his pillow.

It took Brice an hour to explain the final minutes of the ambush and his unplanned detour to the Leone lodge.

"As usual, my brave gunny was busy. How is the recovery going for the others?"

"Kathy was killed in action. Shot through the heart, she died in seconds. Lynne suffered a concussion, but she'll be OK." Brice paused and took a deep breath. "Both Kathy and Lynne fought like lionesses protecting their cubs. I'll never forget the courage of those ladies," said Brice sadly. With the back of his hand, he brushed a tear off his cheek and took a moment to collect himself.

Chet closed his eyes and said a silent prayer for Kathy. "Tell me about the others," said Chet somberly.

"Pete and Al were pretty badly banged up; multiple grazing bullet wounds and lots of large, nasty splinters from the trees. However, Bobby got the worst of it. He suffered concussions from multiple explosions, including a frag grenade that he rolled into the terrorists, fifteen feet from his position. It provided the kids vital time to further their retreat. The bastards were setting up another .30 caliber machine gone atop the retaining wall when he took them out. The buses right front wheel protected him from being blown to bits.

"They're all expected to recover though in Bobby's case it may take a little longer. Bobby and the civilians were originally sent to a hospital in Cody, but it was felt they should be moved here. This is a larger hospital with more facilities. Everyone is on this floor. And, the White House wanted all the patients in one location for patient privacy and security purposes. The government is still searching for stray terrorists and following up on suspicious activity in and around national parks throughout the country. Something they should have done in the first place."

"What about Annie?" asked Chet.

"She saved the day, if you ask me." But, before Brice could elaborate, a gruff voice rose from the opposite side of the curtain in the semi-private room.

"Hey, pull that curtain aside. I 'wanna' see who's there!"

Brice drew the curtain back.

Al Edwards lay in his hospital bed with medical gauze wrapped around much of his body.

"It's Al," said Chet cheerfully. "How are you doing old buddy?"

"How the heck do you think? Look at me. I've got bandages everywhere."

"You look like a mummy. Why all the Band-Aids, big guy?" asked Chet lightheartedly.

"Splinters! Big, fucking splinters! Remember those felled trees you told me to *stay in* for cover. Well, those 'friggin' trees are now part of me. I feel like a human pin cushion."

Al's cranky protest persuaded Chet to hold off on further banter. Instead, he offered a compliment, "You sure handled that M-32 grenade launcher like a 'pro!'"

"Like a 'pro?' I am a 'pro' with that baby!" Al rolled to his side so he could see Brice and Chet more clearly. As he did so, he groaned, "Damn them trees."

Brice knew that splinter wounds, left untreated, could lead to serious infections. In Al's case, however, he was now under the watchful care of a number of doctors.

"Splinters, huh! That's a damn sight better than being buried in a solid wooden box," snickered Brice unsympathetically.

Al glowered at Brice through swollen red eyes. Brice's silly grin was infectious. A second later, Al chuckled. Then, all three laughed aloud.

Their laughing was interrupted when Al's cell phone rang.

"Would you get that for me, Brice. I'm guessing that's my fiancé. The nurse said she's already called a couple of times," said Al.

Brice answered the phone, and explained to the female caller that he'd check on Al's condition. Brice turned the cell phone to Al so he could see the caller's name identified.

"I'll take it!" whispered Al as he reached for the phone with his bandaged hand.

Al cleared his throat and began to speak with his usual strong voice, "Hi sweetie."

He patiently listened to the caller for several moments before he spoke, "Good morning to you as well, 'Sugar'... Yes, I've seen some of the news accounts on TV... I'm OK! Just a few scratches, but I'll fully recover... Unhuh, my plumbing is fine. A couple of Marines helped out during the ambush... Right, of course, your grandson is a Marine. From what I saw they're decent fighters... Yeah, I agree he should return your phone calls... Unhuh, he sounds forgetful to me as well. Yes, the nurses are nice and I've got company in my semi-private room. His name is 'Jet' and he's one of the Marines. No, I wouldn't say he's real friendly. He's actually kind of bossy. He ordered me to stay in a pile of fallen trees... I've got huge Goddamn splinters everywhere! Yes, yes, you're right... I shouldn't use God's name in vain... I'm sorry, Sugar... Yes, I promise.

Well, a nurse just arrived and she seems anxious to give me some medication. I think it's time for your 'honey bear' to sign off."

"'Honey bear!'" shrieked Chet. "You're 'honey bear?' You're my grandmother's fiancé. Get me that phone Gunny. And, my name is Chet, not 'Jet,' Edwards!" barked Chet.

As Brice began laughing, he said, "Here's the phone. I'm going to check on Bobby. I'll leave you girls alone with Sugar."

Several rooms down the hall from Chet and Al's shared hospital room was Bobby's private room. Because Bobby was a quadriplegic, unconscious and badly wounded when he was transferred to the hospital the day before, the medical staff felt a private room would be more appropriate for his medical needs. When Brice walked into his room, it was as if he had just entered his favorite tavern during happy hour on a Friday afternoon. The room was packed with people and all were in a very festive mood.

He recognized Bill and Molly Ridger, Tom and Annie Youngblood, and Col. O'Brien from Camp Pendleton. There were also two men in white coats that he didn't know.

As he extended his hand to the nearest stranger in a white coat, he said, "Hi! I'm Gunny Miller."

"Dr. John Matthews. I've been overseeing Bobby's recovery for the past six months."

"Dr. Bill Stark. I'm the Chief Medical Officer of the hospital," said the other man as he too greeted Brice with a handshake.

Brice was showered with hugs, kisses and further handshakes from everyone, except O'Brien.

Lastly, O'Brien stepped up to Brice until he was inches from his face, "Great job Marine! You, Chet and Bobby are a great credit to the Corps. I thank you as does the Commandant of the Marine Corps, for a job well done." He took Brice's hand and delivered a vice like handshake.

"Thank you, Col. O'Brien. However, I think that Bobby and Annie deserve much of the credit... "

O'Brien interrupted, "We can get into individual accolades later. You arrived just as both doctor's were about to brief us on Bobby's current condition."

"You OK, Bobby?" said Brice worriedly as he quickly turned towards his best friend.

Bobby was sitting upright, atop his bed covers. His head and arms were bandaged and tubes of all shapes and sizes were connected to his body.

"A few aches and pains, but I couldn't be better," said Bobby as he lifted his right arm off the bed a couple of feet and gave Brice a goofy thumbs up waggle with his right hand. A moment later, he did the same thing with his left arm.

Brice's eyebrows arched uneasily.

The bastards have loaded him up with morphine. He doesn't know where he is.

Bobby leaned back into a pile of pillows and drew his knees towards his chest.

Damn, what have they got him on!

Slowly, his mind realized what his eyes were seeing. Bobby was moving his legs and arms.

"What the fuck!" blurted Brice.

Everyone, with the exception of O'Brien, smiled. "Gunny! Ladies are present. Mind your Marine Corps bearing!" growled the colonel.

"Yes, sir!" said Brice as he brushed past the colonel and rushed to Bobby's side.

The two best friends hugged, laughed and cried together. After a few moments, O'Brien interrupted their celebration, "Marines, Dr. Matthews will now report."

Matthews gave a brief history of Bobby's injury before getting to the details that interested Bobby and his visitors the most, his analysis and opinion of Bobby's miraculous recovery.

"In closing, we doctors like to think that modern medicine is an exact science, but it isn't. Prayers, persistence, hard work, luck and the all-important support of family and friends, all play a big part in a patient's recovery. Many of these factors have and still are contributing to Bobby's recovery. However, Dr. Stark and I also feel that the science of physics may have contributed to Bobby's recovery. Farfetched as it may sound, we think that it's possible that the concussive force of the grenade that Bobby rolled into the terrorists, a mere fifteen feet from himself, could have 'unkinked' the blood vessel supply to his spinal nerve endings, and allowed the improvement you see," said Matthews.

"Will he continue to improve, John?" asked Bill Ridger tentatively.

"It is a little early to say. However, in light of the rapid improvement of his range of motion in just the last few days, Dr. Stark and I believe that his blood supply has returned to his spinal nerve endings. Going forward, we feel that it will simply take time for all of his muscles to come to life. They've been dormant for quite some time."

The room erupted in cheers. Bobby raised both fists together with the thumbs up signal and hollered, "Oorah!" It was his beginning of a new life.

The cheers halted just as quickly as they had started when a stranger entered the room. The man wore an aged, corduroy sport coat with scuffed, leather patches on the elbows; a light blue dress shirt, open at the collar; tight chinos; and Rockport walking shoes. He looked to be in his late 50s with long, gray hair pulled into a ponytail. The ponytail hung a good six inches beyond the collar of his jacket.

O'Brien unconsciously sneered at the man.

"Can I help you?" asked Dr. Stark.

"Perhaps, my good friend," said the stranger disingenuously. "I was told that Gunnery Sergeant Brice Miller has taken up residence here in this fine establishment." His poor attempt at humor, or whatever it was, fell flat on those in the room.

"This is a hospital, not a cocktail lounge!" snapped Dr. Stark.

"And who may I ask are you, my 'good friend?'" interjected O'Brien frostily.

"I am Theodore R. Radcliff II... doctor of psychology at the Veterans Administration here in Bozeman... at your service," said the man with a slight, haughty bow and a snapping of his heels.

"And what is your business with Gunnery Sergeant Miller, Theodore?" asked O'Brien, who was now clearly riled.

Radcliff smiled patronizingly at the colonel whose face was taut with annoyance.

"My dear fellow, I have been directed by his regimental commander to provide him with psychological counseling for PTSD. Let me enlighten you, PTSD stands for... "

O'Brien took two, quick giant steps towards the man until his face was inches from the psychologist's. "First, I damn well know what PTSD stands for, as does every Marine in the Corps. Further, when something involves the Corps, I deliver the 'enlightening,' I don't receive it. Second, in case you hadn't noticed, I am in uniform and am a colonel in the United States Marine Corps. I am not your 'dear fellow.' Hold on for a moment, Theodore!"

Turning his head to Brice, O'Brien barked, "Gunny, how do you feel?"

"Other than a few aches and bruises from the impact of that gunshot into my armored vest a couple of days ago, I feel fine. The extended leave I took in Texas helped me clear my head. I've had no headaches or nightmares in weeks, colonel" answered Brice.

O'Brien returned his hard stare to Theodore, "Third, I am Gunnery Sergeant Miller's regimental commander, and you are informed that he is cured. Last, you have five seconds to get out of this room and leave the hospital's grounds or you will find yourself as a patient in this 'fine establishment.' Do I make myself clear, Theodore?" thundered O'Brien.

Theodore R. Radcliff II got the message. With his ponytail bobbing, his corduroy sport coat flapping and his spindly legs flailing, he looked like an excited ostrich as he raced out of Bobby's hospital room and sped towards the elevator.

When the laughter subsided, Brice spoke to the colonel "I'm sorry colonel. I completely forgot about the counseling. I was busy… "

O'Brien held up his hand, "Say no more Gunny. It's my fault as well. Ladies, if my interaction with Theodore offended you, please accept my apologies. His deportment wasn't quite up to Marine Corps standards."

Fueled by Theodore's entertaining interruption, Bobby's celebration increased in intensity until his eyes grew heavy and he began to doze off. The nurses recognized his fatigue and politely suggested to his family and friends that they return later that evening after he'd caught up on his much needed rest.

As his visitors stood to leave, Bobby asked Annie to hold his hand. She smiled brightly as she walked to his bedside, firmly took his hand and tenderly kissed his cheek. Before he closed his eyes, Bobby turned his gaze towards Tom Youngblood who was standing nearby. He muttered an enigmatic phrase that no one in the room understood, but Tom.

Healing my torn body and discovering contentment is within me.

Tom tipped his head towards Bobby in acknowledgment.

Bobby's heavy eyelids began to close as he continued to mumble. Annie put her ear to his lips and listened.

"You promise," she said softly.

"Yes and yes, Little Raven," he responded emphatically. Everyone in the room heard his reply. Tears began to stream down Annie's cheeks.

A moment later Bobby was softly snoring.

"What did he whisper into you ear?" asked Brice for the benefit of those present.

"Dark Horse said two things," said Annie.

"Darkhorse! That's the nickname of our 3/5 battalion," said O'Brien stiffly.

"I know that. Bobby explained that to me earlier today. However, Dark Horse is also Bobby's Arapaho name. My uncle, Tom Youngblood, who is an Arapaho chief, bestowed that name upon him many years ago," said Annie patiently.

They all turned towards Tom Youngblood who simply said, "I did."

"OK! But, what did he say?" asked Brice rather impatiently.

Annie straightened, somewhat taken aback by Brice's abrupt manner.

"I'm sorry, Annie. I didn't mean to question you like that. I'm tired and not my usual self."

Annie smiled, "I understand. The last few days have been trying for all of us. Bobby rescheduled a dinner date we have at the Irma Hotel in Cody, Wyoming. He also told me to tell you and Col. O'Brien that he's not going to 're-up' with the Marines. I don't know what that means, but he emphasized that his fighting days were over. Referring to the Yellowstone ambush, he said that for him it was…

… the last stand of Dark Horse !"

Brice and the colonel nodded.

"We get it!" said O'Brien kindly as he ushered Brice out of Bobby's hospital room.

CHAPTER 25

THE ARRESTS

On Monday, June 23, 2008, one week after the Yellowstone ambush, the governor of Montana, Aidan Barrett, placed a scheduled phone call to the Honorable Bill Bramley in Dennis, Montana.

"Good afternoon, governor," replied two voices in unison into a speakerphone. "I've got the mayor of Dennis, Murph Hayes, sitting with me as you requested," said the judge.

"Thanks, Bill. Murph, we've met a few times in the past. I think the last time was on the golf course a year or so ago. You won our one dollar bet if I recall."

"You remember correctly, Aidan. I look forward to another round of golf with you once our lives return to normal," said the mayor.

"You got that right! Helena and Dennis are making headlines for all the wrong reasons. Let me update you on events in Helena and ask a favor," said the governor.

"Let's hear the latest," said the judge.

"First off, our U.S. Attorney in Helena has just been relieved of his duties and the Justice Department has replaced him with one of their own attorneys from Washington on an interim basis. He's a holdover from the Clinton administration and highly regarded by both parties for his fair, but tough approach to government corruption. He's going to investigate influence pedaling by Richie Smith with our former U.S. Attorney. Not surprising is the recent revelation that Smith was a former bagman for Jack Abramoff.

"Pinning any kind of criminal activity on our former U.S. Attorney may be difficult because Smith is dead. Allegedly murdered by a disgruntled colleague of his, Rod Turdlow." The governor paused before continuing, "You won't believe this. The FBI was lead to Turdlow's doorstep by a Twinkie wrapper they found in Smith's pocket. It had Turdlow's DNA all over it."

"Good detective work," interjected the judge.

"The FBI has Turdlow in custody and he's telling them all he knows in exchange for a favorable plea agreement. His revelations also extend from Washington to Los Angeles. He's spilling the beans on a couple of crooked federal magistrates in the Los Angeles area, his former home 'turf,' who received kickbacks for their excessive damage awards on many of the ADA (Americans with Disabilities Act) lawsuits that came before them.

"Next, the federal government, led by President Adams, is hell bent on nailing anyone and everyone from Montana to Washington who may have played the slightest role in the ambush in Yellowstone National Park. The FBI has learned that the 'whip' of our state senate, Nick Leone, owned the hunting lodge that the terrorists used for training purposes. The rental deposit and cleanup fee he required of them was so exorbitant that it made it possible for him to buy and finance the lodge without investing any of his own money. Nice trick if you ask me! It's also an indication that he knew the bastards were up to no good. He's facing multiple federal indictments that could result in his incarceration for twenty-five years or more of hard time in prison.

"Once the feds get into hot and heavy questioning with Nick Leone I bet he will *tell all* in exchange for a favorable plea agreement. He may even disclose enough dirt on his uncle that we'll finally be able to indict him on corruption charges. Rumor has it that he was also involved with Abramoff as well as crooked tribal leaders holding positions with the Bureau of Indian Affairs.

"Unbelievable," sighed the judge over the phone.

"Kudos to President Adams for being tough on anyone involved with that terrorist ambush. I hope that fucking weasel, Preston, at Homeland Security gets the needle," said the mayor.

"He may get the hangman's noose from what I hear," said the governor.

"Hangman's noose! That sounds like good old Texas justice to me. I trust that those 'dipshit' politicos in Washington who influenced or conspired with Preston on his naïve and incredibly stupid undertaking will learn the hard way the error of their ways," said the mayor.

"I agree, I don't think this president is going to let any of those 'dipshits' slip off the hook! Moving on, there is one last matter regarding the Leone lodge that has been kept secret. The morning after the two kidnapped girls were rescued from the Dowers, the FBI and Homeland Security descended upon the Leone lodge to investigate the goings on there. While they were taking pictures and brushing for fingerprints, a chemist drove up to the front door of the lodge with a van loaded with meth lab equipment and the necessary ingredients."

"Your kidding," blurted the mayor.

"No! You can't make this stuff up. I couldn't believe it myself. The chemist was arrested on multiple drug offenses and has implicated Dick Dandor and Rod Turdlow. Dandor, called Dandy by his co-workers, was an administrative manager at the State Highway Patrol's headquarters in Helena. He was also Nick Leone's secret mole in the State Highway Patrol who kept Leone and his accomplice's one step ahead of our top cop, Alan Fischer. It's too early to say who was directing the setup of the meth lab because, as you would expect, Dandor and Turdlow have conflicting stories. However, my best guess is that Dandor, as Leone's rental agent, was responsible for setting up the meth lab location at Leone's lodge. All behind Leone's back. Your classic double cross! I think Turdlow was the one who engaged the chemist.

"It's also become clear that Dandor was more interested in future meth lab revenues than a modest fee to manage Leone's lodge. Dandor funded the Dower's never ending series of transgressions from a 'Leone lodge' slush fund. His goal was a twofold layer of security for his planned meth sales. He had the local police protect his illegal business and, with the Dower's help, he could rest assured that he wouldn't have any meth competitors enter his market."

"Unfucking believable," said the judge.

"You got that right, Bill," said the governor.

"How can we help you in Dennis?" asked the mayor.

"I have one favor to ask. As you know, the image and reputation of our great state and the town of Dennis have been tarnished by all these recent events. Now that the Dower's are *fortunately* no longer with us, I know that you need to replace your sheriffs. Fischer would very much like the two men he temporarily deputized to the State Highway Patrol, Jan Dank and Bill Ridger, to fill those positions. He's in dire need of trusted local help. His office is being deluged with inquiries from both the FBI and Homeland Security regarding both past and prospective terrorist activity in the Dennis area. Those government agencies are also taking a long overdue look at white supremacist activities in our state as well," said the governor.

The mayor responded immediately, "Great minds thinks alike. We have already asked Jan Dank to fill the vacant position of chief of police, to which he has agreed. Bill Ridger has also accepted our offer to be his assistant. However, both of them requested that their positions be temporary in nature until younger and more experienced officers can be found to fill these positions on a permanent basis.

"That's perfect! I know Fischer will be relieved to hear that. Listen, I've got to run, but I before I do I want to thank you for all your help. A few bad apples have tainted Dennis' image, but I know, as do you, that that is an aberration. Dennis is a great town with damn fine people."

CHAPTER 26

INDUCTION DAY

July 2, 2008

United States Naval Academy

Office of the Superintendent

Vice Admiral John Mulderig shook hands with the president as he entered the superintendent's office. The admiral admired the president's smart looking Texas attire. He wore a tan, summer weight Western suit. The chest pockets on his linen suit were curved, Western style and highlighted with stylish embroidery. Highly polished, ornate cowboy boots, a white Western shirt and a Texas Ranger bolo tie completed his outfit. *Damn, he looks sharp*, thought the superintendent. As a courtesy to the United States Navy and the admiral, the president removed his white, summer Stetson hat when he entered the superintendent's office.

Mulderig offered the president a seat in his commemorative wooden Navy chair as he moved into his chair behind his desk. They chatted briefly about mundane matters, the president's trip to Annapolis and the weather. During these few moments, Mulderig studied the president. He'd never seen him before in person. His short cropped silver hair needed trimming. *Not quite to Navy regulations*, he thought. However, what intrigued him most was the president's face. His bold nose, wrinkled skin and one slightly, droopy eyelid reminded him of someone. Finally, it came to him. During his last command at sea, as the skipper of the aircraft carrier U.S.S. Abraham Lincoln (CVN 72), he had hung a small portrait of President Abraham Lincoln beside his bunk in his "at sea cabin." Except for Lincoln's beard, protruding ears and black hair, Adams had a strong resemblance to the sixteenth president.

Perhaps he'll deliver a "Lincolnesque" address today, mused Mulderig.

"Say, where are you from?" asked the president easily.

"Born and raised in Oklahoma, just outside of Oklahoma City on a dry, hot and dusty ranch. Same as you, but a different state."

"Why the career in the U.S. Navy?" asked the president.

"Because by the time I had finished high school, I'd had enough of dry, hot and dusty climates to last ten lifetimes. Anyone who could stick it out for a lifetime in that kind of environment, like yourself, is a tougher and more resilient man than I," said the admiral.

"I see! Some might say 'simpler and more stubborn' rather than 'tougher and more resilient'," added the president lightly.

Mulderig smiled, "I think 'tougher and more resilient' is more accurate."

"Did I read in your military biography that you are due to retire from the Navy in the near future?"

"Yes, Mr. President. I'll miss the Navy," said Mulderig as he took a quick glance at his watch. This conversation could continue later. In the meantime, he realized that they better start moving towards the steps of Bancroft Hall where he would deliver the oath of office to the incoming class of 2012.

"Mr. President, we've got a tight schedule. Let's head out to the induction ceremony," said Mulderig.

"I understand. I'm looking forward to this ceremony. It's one of our countries great traditions."

"I couldn't agree more. I was inducted here in the class of 1978," said Mulderig.

As they walked, side-by-side, to the steps of Bancroft Hall, the president asked, "Admiral, does my short speech precede your swearing in the class of 2012."

"Yes, Mr. President. That's right."

"Before I make my speech, I'd like to present awards to eight individuals. Is that OK with you?"

"Absolutely! May I ask who they are and what it's for?" queried Mulderig.

"Of course. Three are Marines and five are civilians. One of the civilian awards will be presented posthumously. They're being decorated for their valor at Yellowstone National Park in saving the lives of 305 6th grade children. Col. O'Brien will be joining me at the podium and help me conduct the ceremony," said the president.

Mulderig turned towards the president and lightly held the president's elbow as they came to a stop. The admiral extended his hand for a handshake and looked the president square in the eye, "Mr. President, those Marines and civilians made one hell of a stand. They're all heroes in my book. On behalf of the Naval Academy and myself, we're deeply honored that you've elected to make this presentation of awards at this time and place." After a moment of thought, Mulderig offered his view on the president's disgraced, ex-cabinet member, "I trust that Preston will cool his heels in a jail cell for many years while he contemplates his unbelievably stupid and reckless actions."

"We're on the same page there, admiral. But, I've got more than a 'comfy' jail cell in mind for that SOB," said the president vehemently. "Further, had any of those kids been harmed, you can rest assured that I would have personally seen to it that every ally, accomplice or sponsor of those terrorists, whether foreign or domestic, met an early and painful death," growled the president emotionally.

"I'm pleased to hear you say that Mr. President. All of my Navy and Marine Corps buddies feel the same way."

"Hear, hear! Say, why don't we use first names? Sooners and Texans are cut from the same cloth. Please call me Jed," said the president smiling.

"Will do, Jed. And, please call me, John," said the admiral.

As the two continued their walk, the president said, "One of the award recipients is a fellow Texan who I, and my wife, have become quite close to in the past week, Brice Miller. My wife and I don't have any children. We invited Brice and his adopted parents, Jack and Judith Powell to have dinner with us in the White House a week ago. The dinner was so enjoyable that we asked them to stay on with us for a few more days. Jack and Judith are 'salt of the earth' Texans. And, Brice! Christ, I could go on for hours about that young man. In short, we had a wonderful time together. For want of a better word, we all bonded.

"During Brice's stay, we also had the opportunity of meeting Brice's girlfriend, Molly Ridger, her dad, Bill Ridger, and her brother, Bobby. Bobby Ridger was the paralyzed Marine who helped defend the children at Yellowstone. His paralysis is rapidly receding and he's one of the eight I'll be decorating today." The president's eyes watered as he recalled their miraculous stand at Yellowstone. A moment later, he added, "You do know that Brice Miller is an inductee in this Annapolis class of 2012?"

"Yes, Jed. I know. His regimental commander at Camp Pendleton, Col. John O'Brien, USMC, was my roommate here at Annapolis. He was the one who encouraged him to apply. I understand that he's a wonderful young man. I've heard a lot about him, but I have not yet met him," said Mulderig.

"You'll like him. He's a real hero who this country owes a high level of gratitude too. Though I'm not a blood relative, my wife and I feel pretty darn close to that boy," said the president earnestly, as he recalled his wife's comments, at breakfast, a day earlier.

Brice Miller deserves another medal for agreeing to the United States Naval Academy's strict visitation policy. How could the poor boy stay away from his lovely girlfriend, Molly Ridger, for such a long period, bemoaned the president's wife?

Such is life for those who elect to enter our service academies. Fortunately for us, I went to Texas Tech, responded the president mischievously.

His wife returned his smile and said with a wink, *you're lucky you were a Red Raider. I don't think I'd be as understanding and patient as Molly Ridger.*

After her remark, he'd leaned awkwardly over the coffee table, kissed her and waved his hand with the Texas Tech "guns up" hand sign. In the process, he inadvertently dragged his tie through his oatmeal, which caused both of them to giggle like young teenagers.

Returning to the moment, the president continued, "I don't expect Brice to get any special treatment at Annapolis, but on the other hand I wouldn't want to hear that any overzealous, mean spirited, 'dickhead' upperclassman made his life miserable, all of the time. He has already paid his dues to the military many times over."

"We have no... ."

The president raised a hand, "John, save your breath. There are dickheads everywhere. I had one in my cabinet up until a couple of weeks ago. I'm sure you have fewer here than in most colleges since this is an elite service academy, but please keep an eye on him for me. Neither of us rose to our current positions by being naïve."

Mulderig sighed, "Jed, you're right. Nearly all of the disciplinarian problems I deal with here are caused by just a few intractable dickheads. I won't name names, but you probably know some of their fathers in Washington. Their fathers call me regularly when they think I'm dealing unfairly with their screwed up son or daughter. 'The apple hasn't fallen far from the tree' in some of those instances, if you get my drift."

"Yes, I get your drift. If any of those 'rotten apples' from Washington give you a hard time, please let me know. Some of our wayward public servants require a little guidance counseling from time to time. Now, let's dwell on the positives and make this a memorable day, shall we 'pardner?'" asked the president, as they neared the steps of Bancroft Hall.

"Thanks, Jed, for your offer. I hope it never comes to that, pardner."

Once they exited Bancroft Hall, both men came to a stop several steps above the official podium.

The podium was located on a viewing area below them, between two tiers of marble steps approximately forty feet wide. In the center of the podium was a lectern with a row of seats on each side. Behind the seats, prominently placed, were the flag of the United States, the flag of the United States Navy and the flag of the United States Marine Corps. An ornate building façade, supported by six large Doric columns, spanned three stories above them. Set back from the majestic entrance, rose the four story high, gray limestone walls of Bancroft Hall. The largest single dormitory building in the world, with multiple wings, and home to approximately 4,000 midshipmen.

Dormitory wings to the right and left of the podium surrounded the courtyard, known as Tecumseh Court. The bronze statue of Tecumseh sat on a pedestal, on the far side of the courtyard, facing Bancroft Hall.

Numerous Naval Academy traditions and stories surrounded the great chief who silently watched over the midshipmen.

Two brass cannons, eighteen-pound long guns, were mounted on each side of the buildings entry steps. The cannons were taken from a British frigate, the HMS Macedonian, by the USS United States during the War of 1812. Below the cannons, at ground level, were two ceremonial bells. To the president's and the superintendent's right was the Gokokuji Bell, which is rung after each of Navy's football victories over Army. On their left was the U.S.S. Enterprise Bell, which is the original ship's bell from the U.S.S. Enterprise (CV-6) and is rung for Morning Colors and Navy's team victories over Army. The U.S.S. Enterprise (CV-6) was the most highly decorated United States ship during World War II. Highlighting Bancroft Hall's entrance were sweeping, semi-circular walkways that arched around each side of the lower tier staircase and lead to the building's viewing area.

It was a picture perfect, sunny summer day with not a cloud in the azure blue skies. Though the temperature had crept into the high 80s, the humidity level held steady at a reasonably comfortable 35%. The Navy band was boldly playing "Anchors Aweigh" as 1,261 incoming inductees to the class of 2012, their company officers and a number of upper class midshipman stood before them in Tecumseh Court. Behind the sea of white uniforms were thousands of cheering friends and family members. They were very much a proud and vocal group.

Mulderig discreetly signaled his aide to his side and whispered, "We have a change in the program. The president and Col. O'Brien are going to decorate eight individuals for their actions at Yellowstone. The president has their names. Let's add eight chairs, for the award recipients, behind the special guests on the podium. I'd like our four active duty Marine Corps inductees to come to the podium as well to witness the presentation of awards. Coordinate that with O'Brien and the brigade commander."

"Aye, aye, admiral, but there are five active duty Marine Corps inductees!" whispered the aide.

"I know. But, one of them, Brice Miller, is an award recipient. He'll already be on the podium."

"Yes, admiral. I understand. I'll take care of this," said the aide, as he quickly turned away from the admiral and spoke into a radio.

Turning back to the president. Mulderig said passionately, "What a sight, Jed! Makes one proud to be an American."

"Damn proud, John," responded the president, over the soulful, background music of beating drums and brass instruments.

Mulderig and the president stepped down to the podium.

The inductees were standing upright at attention, dressed in their summer white uniforms and wearing their distinctive Dixie cup, blue ringed, white sailors cap. Behind the podium was a colorful array of service flags with the United States flag standing tall in the middle. On each side of the podium, were five Navy chairs. To the president's left, also standing at attention, were the Chairman of the Joint Chiefs of Staff, Chief of Naval Operations, the Commandant of the Marines Corps and Col. John O'Brien from Camp Pendleton. The fifth chair on that side of the podium was reserved for Vice Admiral John Mulderig. Standing to the right of the president was the interim Secretary of Homeland Security, one U.S. Senator from Maryland, the Governor of Maryland and the U.S. congressman from the local district. The vacant chair nearest the podium was reserved for the president

When they reached the podium, Mulderig sharply saluted the president and said officiously, "Welcome, Mr. President." Turning towards all those in Tecumseh Court, he said firmly into the microphone, "Seats!"

In unison, all the inductees and those standing on the podium sat. The admiral first recognized the president of the United States, followed by all those seated beside him on the podium, the incoming class of 2012 and lastly all those friends and family members of the inductees. Many of the inductee's parents had travelled great distances to support their son or daughter on this special day. He next gave a brief overview of the oath of office and its required sworn affirmation by all incoming inductees to the United States Naval Academy.

Mulderig further added, "We have one addition to todays program. Prior to my administration of the oath of office, the president will make a special presentation of awards to those civilians and servicemen who gallantly defended the school children during the Yellowstone National Park ambush several weeks ago. So, without further ado, special guests, ladies and gentlemen and the incoming class of 2012, the President of the United States," announced Mulderig.

As the president stepped to the microphone, the brigade commander of the midshipman, Rocky Anderson, barked for all to hear, "Attention on deck!"

All those seated, immediately stood and came to attention.

Vice Admiral Mulderig raised his right arm in salute to the president as he approached. With his Stetson hat firmly in place, Jed Adams smartly returned the admiral's salute. When Mulderig moved to the side, the president stepped to the microphone and pulled the wireless microphone from its holder. He turned up the volume dial on the microphone so all those present could hear his personal greetings to those on the podium. He'd long since abandoned the usual practice of mumbling unheard greetings to special guests.

The president greeted each of the civilian guests with a handshake and a few cordial words. Moving to the senior military leaders on his left, he returned each of their salutes correctly, shook their hands firmly and personalized his thanks to each of them for their service to the country. Not a trace of mundane formality emerged during any of his face-to-face greetings. Everyone in Tecumseh Court was impressed with the president's unassuming sincerity.

He turned to the standing inductees and said, "Ladies and gentlemen, please take your seats."

Once seated, the Chief of Naval Operations, Admiral Joe Brantuas, leaned towards the commandant and longtime friend, Gen. Shook, and whispered, "It's nice to feel appreciated."

"Dang, you got that right. This boy is a man of action. I like him. He's completely different than them other 'fellers.' And, he even knows how to give a proper salute."

Brantuas grinned at his friend's folksy observation.

As the president moved behind the podium's lectern, he stood ramrod straight and gazed at the sea of inductees. For what seemed like minutes, he smiled broadly and nodded occasionally as his eyes slowly swept over every inductee seated before him. At first, Mulderig wondered if the president had taken ill, but then he, as well as well everyone else, realized what he was doing.

He's making eye contact with every one of the 1,261 inductees.

Finally, the president cleared his throat and began to speak, "Inductees! It is my proud honor to stand before you today.

"Earlier this morning, I was given a personal tour of Memorial Hall located just off the rotunda behind me. On those granite walls, I viewed the Medal of Honor panel, numerous individual plaques and the names of hundreds of Annapolis alumni who have been killed in action. I was truly humbled as I read those names. Their sacrifices inspire me, as I know it does you. It also reminded me of how very thankful I am to those men and women who are currently serving and to those veterans who have served in our armed forces. We would not be the great country we are today without their service and sacrifice.

"In a few minutes, your class of 2012 will be sworn in to the oath of office. Though my presidential oath of office is slightly different than yours, I decided as I walked by Memorial Hall with your superintendent, Vice Admiral John Mulderig, to these steps a few minutes ago that I too will raise my right hand with you as you affirm, and I reaffirm, our promise to every American to support and defend the constitution of the United States against enemies both foreign and domestic, so help me God!" said the president resolutely with his recognizable West Texas drawl.

The crowd cheered, the inductees whooped and the guests on the podium clapped. The ovation surprised the president. He lowered his head for just a moment to gather his emotions. Later, Gen. Shook would swear he saw a tear trickle down the president's cheek.

Once the cheering quieted, the president continued.

"Several weeks ago this country was attacked by terrorists. We were able to preempt their attacks in all of our national parks, save for one. Today's special presentation recognizes eight individuals who bravely risked their lives, and in one case gave it, several weeks ago in Yellowstone National Park. Col. John O'Brien, USMC, 5th Regimental Commander, 1st Marine Division, U.S. Marine Corps base Camp Pendleton, California, and United States Naval Academy class of 1983, will you join me and call forward those to receive awards."

"Aye, aye, Mr. President," boomed Col. O'Brien as he bounced out of his seat and strode purposefully to the president's side.

Coming to ramrod straight attention, he crisply saluted the president who returned his salute and handed him the microphone along with a 3"x5" card with the names of the eight award recipients. O'Brien slipped the card into his pocket without bothering to read it. The names of the recipients were as familiar to him as his own name.

"Will the following three Marines, one retired Army master sergeant, three civilians and the daughter of a civilian killed in action, please come front and center when called for the receipt and decoration of awards: Major Chester P. Daniel, USMC; Gunnery Sergeant, Brice Miller, USMC; Corporal Robert T. Ridger, USMC (medically discharged); Master Sergeant Alvin Edwards, US Army (retired); civilians, Miss Anne R. Youngblood, Mrs. Lynne R. VanderMeid, Mr. Peter Zouvas and Miss Erin Kelly Wardein, for the posthumous receipt of award by the daughter of Mrs. Kathy Wardein who was killed in action. Further, will the midshipman brigade commander call four active duty Marine inductees of the class of 2012 to the podium to witness the presentation of awards," said O'Brien.

The president raised an eyebrow.

Four active duty Marine inductee witnesses! What was this about?

After Brigade Commander Rocky Anderson called the names of the four inductees, he stated that these four men were active duty Marines who previously served in missions in Iraq or Afghanistan. He further explained that these four Marines and Gunnery Sergeant, Brice Miller, USMC represented the entire contingent of active duty Marines that were going to be inducted into the class of 2012.

The president realized that this last minute inclusion of these active duty Marines on the podium must have occurred when Mulderig whispered to his aide as they walked to the steps of Bancroft Hall.

Very nice touch! He's my kind of man.

Four of the award recipients required a little extra time to make their way to the podium. Major Daniels, Peter Zouvas and Master Sergeant Alvin Edwards, U.S. Army (retired) were still recovering from their Yellowstone injuries and required the use of crutches. They were assisted to the podium by three of the four 2012 Marine inductee witnesses. Annie Youngblood assisted the fourth award recipient, Corporal Bobby Ridger, USMC (medically discharged), who inched forward with a walker.

Beads of perspiration lined Chet's forehead as he struggled towards the podium. His doctors in Bozeman were against his attending the induction ceremony, but the major told them to save their breath. He was attending even if he had to be pushed to the podium on a gurney. Brice, Bobby, Annie and the others were heroes. He would damn well pay them his respects.

"I thought you were invincible, major! Hot lead didn't seem to faze you at all in Fallujah."

Chet turned his head to the side to take a closer look at the young pup inductee who was helping him up the steps and made the wisecrack. "Charlie! What are you doing here?" said the major.

"Same, same as my former squad leader, Brice," said Staff Sergeant Charlie Linville, USMC.

"I'll be damned. Brice and Bobby! Look who's helping me!" said Chet in an uncharacteristic lapse of military bearing.

Brice and Bobby looked towards the major and greeted the sergeant in unison, "Hey, Charlie!"

The president grinned, as did all those on the podium with the exception of O'Brien. He loudly cleared his throat as his laser-like stare bored into the four talkative Marines. His unspoken command immediately quieted them.

On the podium, the president and O'Brien greeted the eight receiving awards and the four Marine witnesses from the class of 2012 with crisp salutes and firm handshakes.

O'Brien began, "These eight Yellowstone defenders will be decorated today for risking their lives, and in one case giving it, to save the lives of 305 school children and twenty seven civilians. Without their intrepid bravery and courage, against a much larger terrorist force, our Marine and Air Force personnel would not have arrived in time to assist in the rescue of these innocent children and civilians."

Pausing for a moment, O'Brien collected his memory of the president's earlier sentiment. "The president of the United States felt that it would be appropriate to honor these defenders in the shadow of other heroes who are commemorated for eternity on the walls of Memorial Hall behind me."

Brantuas elbowed Mulderig, who was sitting next to him, and said quietly, "I'd say Memorial Hall impressed the president. This is an outstanding way to honor these individuals. Did you have anything to do with this?"

"Memorial Hall should impress everyone. Though you'd be surprised at the number of 'big wigs' who visit me from Washington, especially those who oversee our purse strings, that don't have the slightest interest in visiting Memorial Hall," blurted Mulderig derisively. After a moment, he added, "But to answer your question, no. I didn't have anything to do with the awards ceremony other than adding the four Marine inductee witnesses. I knew at least one of them had previously served in the 3/5. I am pleased to see that he knew the 3/5 Marines being decorated."

"I'll tell you, there is not an ounce of political bullshit or equivocation in this president. All of my top admirals feel the same way. He's one 'helluva' Commander in Chief," whispered Brantuas.

Cameras flashed and the crowd cheered during the next twenty minutes as O'Brien called each of the defenders forward and recited their acts of valor. He pinned decorations onto the left breast of those former and current servicemen and presented the civilians with a velvet-covered box that contained their award. Further, he offered each of the defenders an opportunity to share their personal views of the ambush. It was impossible to say who received the loudest or longest applause because the crowd was so moved by each of the defenders recollections.

The surviving sixty year old, female bus driver, Lynne VanderMeid, moved the crowd to tears when she emotionally spoke of the loss of her best friend, Kathy Wardein, who was killed in action by a sniper round moments after she had killed a terrorist with a long range shot.

Master Sergeant Al Edwards compared the Yellowstone ambush to a firefight he experienced in Vietnam, against an elite company of Viet Cong. "In both of these 'do or die' fights, my side was outnumbered twenty to one. However, in that tussle with the Viet Cong, I had artillery and air support and I was fighting with experienced and heavily armed Green Berets. Yellowstone! Yellowstone!" repeated Edwards dramatically. The back of his hand wiped tears off his cheek as he continued, "I can't say enough about the heart and courage of those I fought beside. Other than two healthy Marines, there were two sixty-year-old female bus drivers, a twenty three year old female schoolteacher, a quadriplegic Marine and a fifty-year-old part time hunting guide. What they accomplished against a superior enemy force that held the high ground and who were armed with automatic weapons, including three .30 caliber machine guns was nothing short of a damn miracle," said Edwards as his voice cracked and he staggered back to his chair. Holding his head in both hands, the huge man began to cry uncontrollably. Annie Youngblood hurried to his side, put her arm around his heaving shoulders and whispered to him privately as she attempted to comfort him. The crowd jumped to their feet and gave him a standing ovation that lasted over a minute.

When the award ceremony ended, O'Brien said, "Ladies and gentlemen, the president of the United States."

As the president looked over his audience, he studied the faces of those not in uniform. Moments earlier, they had all been standing and cheering the heroics of the Yellowstone defenders. But now, they looked emotionally drained and somewhat disinterested in another Yellowstone account. He knew the news media had bombarded them over the past few weeks with insights, opinions and pictures of the ambush. *Perhaps the curtain has fallen and it's time to move on to the induction ceremony,* thought the president.

The president nonchalantly crumpled his prepared notes and stuffed them into the side pocket of his jacket. *I'll give them a preview of coming events. Perhaps that will rouse their interest,* thought the president. Some of the details, he knew were still classified, but, what the hell! He knew it was just a matter of time before someone in government leaked the classified details to the press.

"To the majority of you, the events of '9/11' are a distant memory. To those among us who were sadly touched by that event, it is an everyday nightmare. Though the terrorist ambush that occurred in Yellowstone National Park on June 16, 2008, endangered fewer individuals than 9/11, it avoided being another national nightmare by the narrowest of margins. That is, except for the family members and friends of Kathy Wardein, for them their nightmare will last forever. This terrible incident should remind and warn all of us that this country is vulnerable to terrorist attacks no matter how many billions of dollars we pour into domestic security and law enforcement services."

"Four chance events occurred at Yellowstone that saved the lives of three hundred and five children, twenty seven civilians and three Marines.

Had any one of these four events not occurred… " the president paused, as he was overcome with emotion, "…well, I'll let you be the judge.

While on leave, Gunnery Sergeant Brice Miller observed suspicious activity in the Grand Canyon and Zion National Park so he alerted his commanding officer, Major Chet Daniels, at Camp Pendleton of his observations. Gunnery Sergeant Miller's valid concerns were passed up the Marine Corps chain of command to the Commandant of the Marine Corps. In the Marine Corps, when a Marine Corps gunnery sergeant suspects something is amiss, it gets the attention it deserves. This was not the case with my ex-secretary of Homeland Security, Lowell Preston III, who elected to manipulate his field intelligence for his misguided, personal purposes.

While the president began to describe this first chance occurrence the audience's interest level began to build. They were hearing, heretofore, classified details.

While the FBI and my department of Homeland Security were investigating this suspicious activity, the Commandant of the Marine Corps made a critical, precautionary decision and ordered another experienced Marine to join Brice Miller and Bobby Ridger during their trip to the Veteran Administration hospital in Sheridan, Wyoming. He also suggested to the Commanding General of the 1st Marine Division, stationed at Camp Pendleton, that this accompanying Marine be *appropriately armed*. When this order filtered down to Col. O'Brien, he selected Major Chet Daniels to accompany the two Marines and he ordered the major to take with him a truckload of weapons that he personally selected. Without the crucial weapons, those who were ambushed would not have survived.

Five of the civilians who were surrounded by the terrorists happened to be quite handy with a rifle. A hunting guide; a retired Army Green Beret master sergeant; two senior, but experienced female bird shooters; and one young female teacher who happened to be a champion target shooter.

By pure coincidence, three Air Force Pave Hawk helicopters and a Marine Corps rifle platoon were conducting a joint desert training exercise in Elko, Nevada that occurred once every five years. Those Marines were rushed to the Yellowstone ambush site by the three Air Force Pave

Hawk helicopters and arrived just as the terrorists overran the Yellowstone defender's positions.

"In short, no one in Washington DC, except for the Commandant of the Marine Corps, made any meaningful contribution whatsoever to the Yellowstone rescue effort. Not the National Security Council, Homeland Security, the NSA, the FBI or the CIA. And, as all of you know, my ex-Secretary of Homeland Security supported and enabled the terrorist ambush.

"Were it not for the vigilant actions of the Commandant of the Marine Corps, Gen. Chip Shook, USMC and Col. John O'Brien, USMC, this country would be in a state of mourning. Our military, who is not normally involved with domestic terrorist activities, saved the day! At this time, I would like to publicly thank and commend Gen. Shook and Col. O'Brien for their astute, life saving actions. General and colonel would you please stand."

As they both stood, the sharp eyed president observed that everyone in the audience, except the Washington DC press corps, stood and gave the two Marines a standing ovation. As the president made a mental note of the press corps' indifference, he recognized one member of the press corps who was off to the side. Chris Beirn with CBS was standing and vigorously clapping. The rest of his colleagues simply scribbled brief notes in their notepads and rolled their eyes. To them, the president's recognition of the commandant and Col. O'Brien was noteworthy, but barely so. They viewed this moment as nothing more than more grandstanding by a conservative president.

"Lastly, I'd like to conclude my discussion of the Yellowstone ambush by revealing one detail of the ambush, which up until now, I have elected to keep confidential.

"The Yellowstone attack was to be the cornerstone of a major al-Qaeda propaganda campaign. The terrorists had assembled high quality television cameras on their hillside position and were filming *live* their entire attack. Their video was to be sent, via satellite, to a secret al-Qaeda television studio somewhere in Syria where it was to be edited and broadcast throughout the Middle East. The title of this propaganda piece, 'Children of the Infidel Die!'"

An audible gasp rolled through the crowd at the president's reference to the propaganda's title. None of the prior news reports mentioned anything about the terrorist filming and broadcast of the attack, much less the title of the piece. Members in the news media raced for their news vans as they speed dialed the editors of their home office news desks. This was breaking news. Within the next hour, every television channel throughout the United States was interrupting their regularly scheduled programs to broadcast the video clip of the president's Yellowstone revelation.

"The Yellowstone attack was an unadulterated form of evil. Evil that doesn't negotiate. Evil that revels in the killing of children. I hope all of you present and all those who watch my speech on the evening news tonight remember that!"

The president gave the audience several long moments for his message to sink in, before he continued, "Now, to a better world with our future officers and leaders. Will those on the podium please stand with me. We will first listen to the upper class midshipmen, affirm their oath of leadership to the class of 2012 after which I will reaffirm my oath of office, along with the inductees," said the president enthusiastically.

Once the superintendent, Vice Admiral John Mulderig, administered the oath of office to the incoming plebes, the president moved to his side and spoke into the microphone, "Plebes, it was my honor to recite that oath of office with you. Good luck and Godspeed to all of you!"

Mulderig stood beaming beside the man who resembled and acted like Abraham Lincoln.

The crowd erupted in applause and, in an unexpected departure from all prior induction ceremonies, the plebes tossed their Dixie cup hats into the air as they would upon their graduation and commissioning four years hence. Jack and Judith Powell who, along with Molly Ridger, were seated with the president's wife in the nearby VIP section jumped to their feet and joined in the cheering. Bill Ridger, Col. Jan Dank USMC (retired), the Hon. Bill Bramley and Mayor Murph Hayes who were seated in the front row of the guest section stood and whooped as they pumped their fists in the air. Alice Daniels who was seated between them wiped tears from her eyes with a Kleenex and looked towards the podium. Her fiancé, Al Edwards, who had balanced himself on his crutches, had his free arm around the shoulders of his son-in-law to be Major Daniels. The two were smiling and laughing together as they held Alice's eyes.

Just as the excited applause began to quiet, Molly Ridger's emotional reserves collapsed. She cried aloud and buried her head into the shoulder of the president's wife who was seated next to her.

The president's wife comforted her and said, "Let's see Brice!" With that, the president's wife helped Molly to her feet and led her to the podium. Plebe Brice Miller opened his arms as Molly fell into him and wept uncontrollably against his shoulder.

The applause gained further momentum when Annie Youngblood took Bobby Ridger's hand in hers and kissed him on the cheek. The crowd's applause reached a thunderous crescendo when Alice Daniels darted wobbly up the sloping walkway to the podium to hug and kiss her son and fiancé.

The president clapped and waved his Stetson as secret service agents scurried about and O'Brien looked totally flummoxed. Tears of laughter rolled off Mulderig's face as he watched his former roommate's eyes bulge and his face turn red. Mulderig could read his friend's thoughts,

This is not prescribed induction behavior. Women rushing to the podium and plebes tossing their Dixie cup hats into the air. Very irregular and quite unsatisfactory!

EPILOGUE

President Jed Adams finished reading the Harvard Law Review article, "A Bad Man is Hard to Find," and dropped it on his desk. Leaning back in his chair, he closed his eyes, rested his chin on his steepled hands and thought.

Annie Youngblood was of Arapahoe descent. She was attacked and threatened with murder by terrorists with whom my cabinet member collaborated. All events occurred in Yellowstone National Park, the former ancestral lands of the Arapahoe's and twenty-five other Native American tribes. Land which they continue to lay claim to and which they still view as sacred.

He opened his eyes and sat upright. He picked up the article again and re-read the first page...

A BAD MAN IS HARD TO FIND

In January 2003, a young woman named Lavetta Elk got into a car with an Army recruiter whom she had known since she was sixteen. She believed that she had been accepted as an enlistee — her dream was to work eventually as an Army nurse — and that he was taking her for a medical evaluation. Instead, Staff Sergeant Joseph Kopf drove down a deserted road and, once they were miles away from the nearest building, sexually assaulted Elk. Kopf was never prosecuted for his crime in civilian court; his Army court-martial resulted in no prison time. However, because Elk was a member of the Oglala Sioux Tribe and the assault occurred on a Sioux reservation, she had access to an unusual cause of action.

Nine treaties concluded between the United States and various Indian tribes in 1867 and 1868 each contain what is known as a "bad men" provision. Within each of these provisions is a clause in which the United States promises to reimburse Indians for injuries sustained as a result of wrongs committed by "bad men among the whites, or among other people subject to the authority of the United States."

Although these "bad men among the whites" clauses have rarely been used in the last century and a half, they remain the source of a viable cause of action for Indians belonging to those tribes that signed the nine treaties of 1867 and 1868. In 2009, Lavetta Elk won her action for damages under the Fort Laramie Treaty of 1868, recovering a judgment in the Court of Federal Claims of almost $600,000 from the United States government.

Interesting case, but not relevant to Lowell Preston III's principle offense, he decided.

He would continue to pursue his current course of action against the former cabinet member. An action that he'd be damn sure was bullet proof. However, there was one point in the article that did apply to Preston. He was a "bad man!"

He swiveled his chair to the side and stared glumly at the pile of white papers, briefs, letters and executive orders which had accumulated in his "In Basket" during his brief trip to Annapolis the day before.

The intercom on the president's desk buzzed and he heard his secretary announce that his *urgent* 10:00 AM meeting had arrived. "Send him in," he said lightly, somewhat relieved that he could avoid his stack of paperwork for a few minutes.

A moment later, she opened the door to his office and directed the man to the president. He was a young congressman from the opposition party. Surprisingly, the senior congressman who had requested this *urgent* meeting was conspicuously absent.

The president vaguely recalled meeting the congressman once before. If he remembered correctly, the young man was a freshman congressman from a district in the Los Angeles area. The president stood, walked around his desk, shook the man's hand and offered him a seat opposite his desk.

Once he returned to his desk chair, the president took a moment to study his visitor. Mid-thirties, nice tan, spiked hair, black blazer with narrow lapels, a wrinkled white shirt and a bright, multicolored tie which the man wore loosely at the neck. Except for the blazer, he could have easily passed for a waiter at a hip Southern California restaurant. *How the formalities and the behavior of the lawmakers on the Hill have changed,* thought the president.

Looking down at the notes his secretary had given him, the president was reminded that this *urgent* meeting had something to do with a cabinet replacement for Preston's position at Homeland Security. That was all he knew. *What was his opposition party up to now,* he wondered?

He didn't have long to wonder.

The young man didn't bother with idle chitchat, nor try to warm the president to his purpose. "Now that Lowell Preston III has resigned his cabinet position as Secretary of Homeland Security, my party has a new nominee to fill that position. All of this, of course, is in keeping with your promise to appoint a member of my party to your cabinet."

"I see... of course!" said the president evenly. His famous temper held in check by the slimmest of margins. He drummed his fingers tips on his desk while he thought. Part of him was sorely tempted to correct the young man, but why chastise the messenger. Lowell Preston III had been relieved of his duties. He hadn't resigned. Furthermore, his Attorney General was preparing formal charges against Preston.

After more finger drumming, the president reached a conclusion. He calmly touched the intercom and spoke to his secretary, "I'd like you to set up a conference call now with the following parties. Let's see, the Attorney General, the Director of the FBI, the senior congressman who arranged this morning's *urgent* meeting, the House Minority Whip, the House Majority Whip and the Chairman of the Joint Chiefs of Staff. Also ask Chris Beirn from CBS to come to my office as well, so he can participate in this conference call. Chris was in the pressroom earlier this morning. I think that should do it. If any of the parties ask what the call is about, tell them you don't know."

"I understand, Mr. President," replied his secretary, then added, "CBS? Will this be a secure call?"

"No, it will not be a secure call. Also, invite Steve Rosetta, my chief of staff, and Mark McLaren, our press secretary. Apprise each of them that Chris Beirn of CBS will be joining us as well," instructed the president.

"Yes, Mr. President. It could take fifteen minutes or more to organize this."

"That's fine. Let's also add the drinking buddy of the senior congressman who requested this *urgent* meeting. I can't think of his name offhand."

"I know who you mean, Mr. President. I'll take care of it."

The president turned his attention to his "In Basket" completely ignoring his visitor. He signed letters, speed read briefs and made notations on reports requesting action by others.

Eighteen minutes later, his secretary called on the intercom, "Your conference call is ready Mr. President. All parties are on the line. They all know that the call is not secure and that Steve Rosetta, Mark McLaren, Chris Beirn of CBS and the young congressman will be with you in the oval office during the call. Should I send Steve, Mark and Chris into your office now, Mr. President?"

"Just Steve and Mark for now. I'll let you know when I'm ready for Chris."

"Yes, Mr. President."

After greeting Steve and Mark, the president introduced them to the freshman congressman who didn't bother to stand.

"You both have a list of those who will be on this conference call?" asked the president.

They replied affirmatively.

"What's this about?" asked Rosetta.

"Preston's replacement," said the president, as he stepped closer to both men and put an arm around each of their shoulders. He spoke quietly, so the nearby apathetic congressman couldn't hear, "In the past, I've discussed with both of you the idea of inviting an outside news media reporter into our midst to witness how I lead."

"Yes, Mr. President. I remember our conversations on this matter," said McLaren.

"Me too," said Rosetta.

"Well, the time has come. Let's strap on our seat belts and see how this goes!"

Both men smiled at the president's ingenuity. There wasn't an ounce of deception in the man. His candor was his club.

A moment later Chris Beirn walked into the oval office and was formally introduced, by the president, to Steve, Mark and the freshman congressman who was still glued to his chair. Though Chris knew both Steve and Mark, he thought the president's introduction was a gracious gesture.

"Chris, you will be the first national television correspondent to be present during one of my live conference call conversations with key members of my administration and several congressional leaders. This call will be recorded and Mark will ensure that before you leave the White House you are provided a 'White House certified' audio and transcript copy of the call and a list of all those who were privy to the call. Mark will release additional transcript copies of the call to the rest of the White House press corps tomorrow morning. Is that clear?"

"Yes, Mr. President."

"Chris, I'm providing you a well deserved 'scoop.' I appreciated your support yesterday at the United States Naval Academy. Your network may use as much or as little of this recording as you like. There will be no restrictions or editing from my office whatsoever. Is that also clear?"

"Yes, Mr. President, but if you don't mind my asking. What is this about?"

"You'll know in a minute. Please take your seats and let's get started," said the president in a manner that neither Mark nor Steve had heard before.

When everyone was seated in front of his desk, the president leaned forward in his chair and touched his intercom. He asked his secretary to forward the conference call. As he leaned forward, he unconsciously massaged his lower back. It was beginning to tighten. The injury he'd incurred as a young boy when he was thrown from his horse still plagued him. He had ignored his dad's warning of rattlesnakes on that fateful day and it would pain him for the rest of his life. Some of the misguided legislators on Capitol Hill would soon learn, as he had, that were consequences for their actions. They would also learn that there were varying degrees of consequences based on the depth of their transgressions. Up till now, many of them viewed themselves as above the law and immune from prosecution.

The president pressed the flashing button on his speakerphone and began the call. After an introductory greeting, he thanked all those on the call for interrupting their busy day and stated that the call was being recorded for the benefit of his office and the CBS viewing public. He further explained that his current visitor from the Hill, a freshman congressman, had been sent by a senior member of his party to deliver the name of a new nominee to the position of Secretary of Homeland Security. The appointment, he added, was in keeping with his original promise to the opposition party to appoint a member of their party to his cabinet.

"Before we get to the opposition party's nominee, I would like my Attorney General, Tim McCracken, to bring us all up to speed on the sentencing guidelines for the surviving Yellowstone terrorists," began the president. "Tim, when we last spoke, a day or so before I left for Annapolis, I asked you to look into the punishment possibility of lining these surviving terrorists up against a wall and having them shot to death by a firing squad. My feeling then and now is that this might discourage further attacks of this nature. What did you learn?"

"I have researched 'death by a firing squad,' as you requested, Mr. President. My short answer, at this time, is 'no.' But, life in prison, at a maximum-security prison, 'yes.' My short explanation, much of it based on fairly recent Guantanamo Bay detention camp rulings, is as follows: First, per international law, suspects have to be tried, even though they are from countries who are not parties to Common Article 3 of the Geneva Conventions. Two, if suspects are convicted, the current federal sentencing guidelines are unclear because the Guantanamo Bay detention camp rulings only cover suspected terrorist activity. In this case, however, we have captured video, filmed by the terrorists themselves, of their actions and we have a number of reliable, American eyewitness accounts. This is definitive terrorist activity, not suspected," said Tim McCracken.

"Mr. President," began the House Minority Whip, who was a member of the president's opposing political party, "You can't be serious about shooting these suspects. That's barbaric! Capital punishment is cruel and unusual punishment in and of itself! What would the civilized world think if we shot and killed these suspects?"

"Suspects? That doesn't really describe these terrorists, does it?" declared the president.

"They are undeniably suspects and are presumed innocent until… "

The president cut off the Minority Whip, "We have the terrorists on film, their film! What would the civilized world have thought if these terrorists had slaughtered 305 innocent sixth graders? Is that not barbaric?"

"That film may not be admissible in court, Mr. President!" continued the Minority Whip.

"Oh, I forgot probable cause! You mean the Marines may have acquired that film without probable cause," said the president sarcastically.

"Exactly, Mr. President. The federal government could also be liable for tens of millions of dollars of monetary damages for false imprisonment and defamatory comments. This is 'discriminatory and unfair' treatment of Muslims. We should be offering an 'olive branch,' not punishing these suspects," added the Minority Whip.

False imprisonment and defamatory comments, 'discriminatory and unfair' treatment of Muslims, 'olive branch'… Preston's exact words! Bingo! The president suspected the Minority Whip was behind Preston's actions, now he was certain. "Are you suggesting that we should release these suspects on their personal recognizance until a judge rules on these matters?" said the president disingenuously.

"It's the law of the land, Mr. President. You've sworn an oath to uphold the U.S. constitution. You can't break that oath," said the Minority Whip.

The president knew that the Minority Whip, who was still a named partner in one of the country's largest tort law firms, had likely said enough to certainly end his political career.

"Let's leave this terrorist sentencing matter for the time being and return to the issue of your nominee to my cabinet," said the president evenly.

The president looked at the freshman congressman and asked him to repeat his request.

"Certainly, Mr. President. My party and I appreciate the opportunity of discussing this matter openly. Providing CBS copies of this conversation for public dissemination is also in line with my parties long standing desire for full government disclosure," said the brownnosing freshman congressman.

The president nodded his head slightly. The congressman mistakenly presumed that the president had accepted his bullshit hyperbole.

"My party's request is as follows, now that Lowell Preston III has resigned his cabinet position as Secretary of Homeland Security, my party has a new nominee to fill that position. All of this, of course, is in keeping with your original promise to appoint a member of my party to your cabinet when you took office three years ago."

"Did everyone hear that request clearly?" asked the president.

A series of affirmative replies followed.

"OK, good. Tim would you kindly explain to all the listeners the definition of treason as it applies to the charges we will be filing shortly against Lowell Preston III," said the president.

"Treason! Preposterous!" screamed the Minority Whip.

"Congressman, save the bullshit bluster. As you will hear, Preston very clearly committed acts of treason. Explain Tim," said the president calmly.

"There are two primary charges. One, he used the power of his position to jeopardize the safety of U.S. citizens. Two, contrary to your written and public mandate, he independently refused to provide protection for said U.S. citizens."

More protests erupted over the speakerphone from the two other opposition party members. Their voices were clearly recognizable. The president ignored their cries. *Let them dig their own grave,* he thought. The details of this call will be aired on CBS's evening news tonight.

"And the punishment for treason, Tim?" asked the president.

"Minimum of five years in jail or death per the U.S. Constitution."

"Death!" screamed multiple voices over the phone. The Minority Whip's being the loudest and clearest.

The president neglected the protests and calmly continued, "As you all know, one female bus driver was killed and several Marines were injured while protecting 305 sixth grade school children during the terrorist ambush at Yellowstone National Park. You have all heard as well, during the nightly news, the audio recording we released to the press in which the Homeland Security agent stated that Preston specifically ordered him and several other agents, not to share his ambush intelligence with other U.S. intelligence and law enforcement agencies.

"By the way, we have four other signed affidavits from Homeland Security agents who have confirmed Preston's orders," said the president.

The president waited a few moments for this new revelation to register with his adversaries. "Tim, can we hang Preston?" asked the president.

Tim McCracken had to practically shout his response over the protests and profanities that erupted from the speakerphone, "I don't know, Mr. President."

"Really, Mr. President. This is ridiculous. Hanging!" screamed the spineless, senior congressman who had sent, in his place, the freshman congressman to the oval office.

"Congressman, are you hard of hearing? Death is the maximum penalty. It's clearly spelled out in the U.S. Constitution. Tim, please look into the permissible forms of punishment."

"Yes, Mr. President."

"Lastly, what are the chargeable crimes committed by those who aided or abetted Preston?"

"That's treason as well," said Tim.

Only a single, barely perceptible sound was heard over the speakerphone and it was the audible gasp of cold fear.

"Minority Whip, are you aware of anyone in your party who aided or abetted Lowell Preston III in the execution of his treasonous acts?" asked the president firmly.

"Ah, well, ah! I'd like legal counsel before I respond to that question, Mr. President. Your question covers a broad range of activities and over-lapping policies. Further, this is a totally inappropriate forum to discuss such matters," said the Minority Whip.

"How would you feel if I held public hearings on this matter, say at the elementary school in Cody, Wyoming? Would that forum be more to your liking?"

Silence.

"Minority Whip, are you still there? I should remind you that by the time the hearings are held in Cody, there may still be a few, very pissed off parents of sixth graders or friends of the deceased Kathy Wardein who would love nothing more than to put the head of Preston or any of his collaborators in the cross hairs of their riflescope. I could ask CBS to film the hearings. Perhaps CBS could name the hearings something like 'Life on the Hill for a Traitor.' If CBS is lucky, perhaps they'll capture on film these traitors revealing the same cold fear all the sixth graders experienced when they were in the cross hairs of the terrorists' rifles.

"Further, once you leave the insular refuge of the capitol, you will also learn that my view of child killers is shared by everyone else in the United States. They are the lowest of the low! There won't be an iota of national sympathy for anyone who supported these terrorists."

Silence.

Though the president was pleased with what CBS was learning during the conference call, it didn't diminish his outrage with those who collaborated with Preston.

"Gents, in case you're missing my point, let me be crystal clear. We're not horse trading in a congressional cloakroom, or bickering over the wording of a legislative bill. What occurred in Yellowstone National Park was an overt act of terrorism on U.S. soil and Preston's treasonous actions would have surely cost the lives of 305 innocent children, twenty-seven civilians and three Marines had not a miracle occurred. Those who were responsible for this attack and those who jeopardized the safety of U.S. citizens will be held accountable for their heinous actions.

"With specific respect to Preston, and any of his collaborators, nei-ther the country nor I will agree to any form of immunity for their acts of treason. If there were any members of your party who couldn't quite distinguish the difference between scorched earth politics and treasonous acts, you can rest assured that I will personally see that those guilty parties are punished to the fullest extent of the law, which may include swinging from a hangman's noose. I trust that you get my message.

"Now, I'll ask you one last time, Minority Whip, are you aware of anyone in your party who aided or abetted Lowell Preston III in his treasonous acts?" asked the president.

Silence.

The president and others on the line could hear muffled background whispers over the speakerphone. No doubt the Minority Whip, the senior congressman and other leaders of the opposition party were conducting an offline conversation over cell phones.

After several minutes, the Minority Whip spoke, "We withdraw our request to nominate a replacement cabinet member." He and his fellow party members then terminated their connection to the conference call.

"Mr. President, CBS will air the details of this call during tonight's national TV news. The Minority Whip's silence was sickening. It was tantamount to an admission of complicity by he and other members of his party in Preston's actions. I think the country will be outraged," said the veteran correspondent for CBS news, Chris Beirn, as he stood to leave the oval office.

"As they should be, Chris. By the way, I will be nominating Vice Admiral John Mulderig to the cabinet vacancy of Secretary of Homeland Security. He is the current superintendent of the United States Naval Academy. He retires in a couple of months from the Navy and has agreed to accept this position upon his retirement. You can air that exclusive news item as well if you like," said the president as he stood. The tightness in his back was gone.

"Thank you gentlemen for your time," said the president evenly as he firmly shook everyone's hand.

Steve, Mark and Chris stared curiously at the freshman congressman as they left the oval office. He was still glued to his chair, though he now looked more frozen to it than glued. His gray face was as pale as a lifeless cadaver's.

"I didn't have anything to do with Preston. I swear," stuttered the congressman with his hands raised above his head as if surrendering to a policeman at a crime scene.

Wordlessly, the president pointed to the exit door of his office.

As the congressman shuffled towards the door, he heard the president utter an unusual phrase under his breath... "I shall deliverth the rod and sendth their souls to hell." It was mangled verse from Proverbs that the president reserved for those who weren't worthy of salvation.

What idiot would mess with that Texan? wondered the congressman, as his step lengthened and he scurried out of the oval office.

Book 2 in the Brice Miller and Annie Youngblood series, *The Last Days for Bad Men,* will be available at Amazon on August 2017.

Made in United States
North Haven, CT
03 June 2023